A WHOLE BRASS BAND

A WHOLE BRASS BAND

a novel by
Anne Cameron

HARBOUR PUBLISHING

HARBOUR PUBLISHING
P.O. Box 219, Madeira Park, BC Canada V0N 2H0

Cover illustration and design by Kelly Brooks
Typeset in Baskerville II
Printed and bound in Canada

The assistance of the Canada Council and the Cultural Services Branch, Ministry of Municipal Affairs, Recreation and Culture, Government of British Columbia are gratefully acknowledged.

Canadian Cataloguing in Publication Data

Cameron, Anne, 1938–
  A whole brass band

  ISBN 1-55017-075-9

  I. Title.
PS8555.A53W5 1992   C813'.54   C92-091514-0
PR9199.3.C35W5 1992

For my kids
Alex
Erin
Pierre
Marianne
Tara

my grandchildren
Sarah
David
Daniel
Terry
Sheldon
Jenelle
and "AndyPandy"

and for Thora and Jerry Howell who run the best damn
cultural centre-boardinghouse in the country and are
the lifeblood of THE WEST COAST KNITTING,
QUILTING, COOKING, EATING AND
ANARCHY SOCIETY

and most especially, for Eleanor, who not only
recognizes but understands Great Notions... and has a
few of her own!

sometimes I live in the country,
sometimes I live in the town,
sometimes I take a great notion
to jump into the river and drown

Completion of this novel was facilitated by a grant from
the BC Cultural Fund. My sincere thanks to the
taxpayers who picked up the tab and the government
department which administers it.

When Jean Pritchard left her house the cat was eating a chickadee on the porch. "Get that mess out of here," she snapped, giving the bundle of fluff, feathers and gore a nudge with her foot. It fell to the top step, she gave it another shove and sent it off the edge into the straggly mess that tried to disguise itself as a rose bush. The cat glared with slit-green eyes, jumped down to reclaim its prize, and gave Jean another "one of these days, you bitch" look before continuing to crunch the small bones. "Yeah," Jean told the cat, "and your mother was another!"

It wasn't Jean's cat. God alone knows what kind of cat it would have been if it were hers, although probably it would have been dead long ago because Jean had little use for cats and no use at all for the kind of cats which never stayed home and insisted on scratching up other people's door frames and other people's banister posts. "Go find your people," she suggested bitterly. The cat ignored her totally.

Nobody on the block would admit to owning the cat or even harbouring it. At least twice a week it showed up on the porch, crouched and glowering. Not even the kids felt a nurturing urge to put out food for the striped horror which spat, hissed and showed its claws if you so much as looked at it. Every now and again, just to keep them on their toes, the cat crapped, right in front of the door, where the unwary were almost guaranteed to step.

The gate didn't open all the way, but that was only fair because it didn't close all the way, either. Jean turned sideways, edged her way through the rusted permanent space and hurried to the left, toward the bus stop. The autumn monsoons had hit. The sidewalks, streets and buildings were glistening wet, the puddles collected where the fallen leaves, trash and general mess clogged the storm drains.

The morning wasn't all bad news, however. Someone next door had taken Brucie into the house. His rusty chain lay on the porch, slack and silent. Those mornings when Brucie was still outside were guaranteed to jump-start the day and get the adrenalin pumping. There's something just a tad jarring about opening your door and having the early morning quiet exploded by the roars of a neurotic Rottweiler. Bruce just couldn't seem to get it through his skull that Jean lived in the house next to his, the entire concept of 'neighbour' was foreign to him, all anyone had to do was step out into what he considered to be *his* world and all two hundred overfed pounds of hysteria were lunging madly.

Maybe if she got one of her own it would at least keep the cat out from underfoot.

Jean had to wait five minutes at the bus stop, shivering slightly, standing under the faded canvas canopy over the front window and doorway of the corner grocery. Inside the store the proprietor and her husband sold cigarettes and bags of potato chips, cans of pop and chocolate bars, loaves of bread and cans of mystery meat you could only open with the little key provided — the key that invariably snapped off, leaving you with a half-open can of something you wound up digging out with a fork and then chopping into sandwich spread when you had originally intended to slice the stuff. They chatted to each other in a language nobody waiting for the bus would have understood.

Inside the plexiglass box that was supposed to be the weatherproof bus stop, three drunks were sprawled, sleeping. One of them had barfed and the people for whom the kiosk was intended stood in the drizzle, glaring angrily. Jean supposed someone ought to feel compassion but the acrid stench and the sodden helplessness aborted any kind emotion in her own soul and she supposed other people felt the same mixture of fascination and disgust. It wasn't the sleeping in the bus booth, it wasn't the homelessness, it wasn't even the inability to stay clean. It was the stink. You'd think if people could find the wherewithal to buy enough rotgut to knock themselves out they could find...what? A bar of soap, some decent clothes, a razor blade, an education, a job, an apartment, an income tax refund and some good person to fall in love with them, cook their meals, do their laundry and keep them on the straight and narrow?

Everyone stepped back when the bus arrived. Water sprayed, then settled, and they all surged forward, cramming themselves into the aisle. "Move to the back, now," the bus driver called, "Give everyone a chance, move to the back."

Jean tried. There were already so many people jammed to the back that the best efforts she made only pressed her face deeper into the wet woollen jacket of a very bored-looking young man. "I'm sorry," she blurted, "I'm being shoved."

"Yeah," he blinked, but did not focus his eyes on her.

She stood as steadily as she could, clinging to the shiny overhead bar, and the bus pulled away with a jerk almost guaranteed to send the aged and infirm flat on their asses. "Cowboy," she muttered.

"You gotta pass a test," the young man said suddenly. "They measure your asshole. If it's as tall as you are, you're a bus driver."

"Move to the back!" the driver called, although Jean was certain he had not been able to hear the comment, not over the uproar coming from someone's blaster. "Turn off the radio," the driver yelled. A few voices catcalled protest from the back of the bus, other voices yelled "turn it off, Chrissake." Jean stared past the heads of those lucky enough to have found seats, watching the traffic, the street signs, anything at all rather than stand jammed and unaware; a person could fall asleep that way. Then you missed your damn stop and had to either catch another bus back or walk.

The neon signs reflected back at themselves from the wet pavement, the cars all drove with their headlights on, but in spite of all the electricity being used, the gloom was winning. The concrete was light grey, almost white in the summertime. As soon as the rains set in, it turned dark. Concrete or brick buildings went gloomy when wet, the patches in the road turned black, clouds sat on top of the taller buildings and after a while your eyes got so used to dingy colours you stopped being able to see the lights, or the colours of the imported flowers in the gift shops.

Many of the people out there carried umbrellas. Almost all of the ones with the bumbershoots were dressed in business suits, while the workie population leaned toward plastic slickers, stiff rubberized jackets, sodden denim or Cowichan or Arran sweaters, still lanolin-rich and water resistant. A few upwardly mobile types sported Gore-Tex rain suits, expensive maroon, purple or burgundy coloured backpacks and hi-tech hiking boots. It was like a uniform, you saw it and knew these people had given five dollars to Greenpeace.

When they got back to their parked cars, they would climb into Volvo station wagons with rainbows on the back window and a Save the Whales sticker on the bumper.

She recognized the car lot, the double string of bulbs, the flapping orange plastic pennants. She managed to reach over and pull the cord, and started immediately trying to shove her way to a door.

"Out the back, please," the driver yelled.

"I can't!" Jean shouted.

"Enter at the front, exit at the rear," the driver insisted.

"I CAN'T!" Jean repeated. The driver sighed, the bus stopped, the door opened, and Jean had to shove against the tide of humanity fighting to get into the bus at the same time she was fighting to get out of it.

"Thank you," she managed.

"Any time," the driver answered. "Move to the back! Make room for the people, move to the back."

The teenagers were out in full force listening to walkmans or gathered around ghetto blasters. They leaned toward wet denim, plaid bush jackets and soaking wet ninety-dollar designer sneakers that looked as if they had been intended for jungle warfare or moon exploration. A few hardy or foolhardy souls were skateboarding across the supermarket parking lot. Where the supermarket lot abutted the car lot, salesmen prowled nervously, watching eagle-eyed in case one of the kids left a handprint on a car with a new wax job.

At the liquor store in the small shopping centre, people were inning and outing with cases of beer and tall thin brown bags containing bottles of wine, none of it cheap, not much of it very good. Some came out carrying plastic-and-cardboard containers of cheap plonk, the kind with names like Berryvat and Strawberry Sundae, the kind that would be syrup or jam except it had been fermented and would get you drunk enough to climb porches and bay at the moon. Teenagers lurked around the liquor outlet doors trying to con adults into buying an extra case of beer or a jug of wine for the under-age crowd. Incredibly, a large number of adults, mostly male, were willing to take the kids' money and get booze for them.

Jean wove her way across the parking lot, avoiding people with shopping carts who seemed determined to get into accidents with cars, which glided back and forth, into and out of parking spaces with little regard for life and limb. Incredibly nobody got crushed or flattened. A driver honked indignantly at a little old lady in ankle-high duck-foot rubber boots. The white-haired pensioner didn't even look up, she just flashed an upraised finger and continued trundling her cart. Jean thought of her own Aunt Alice. A stranger seeing Alice might smile and think of gingerbread hot from the oven, with homemade applesauce and fresh-whipped-in-the-kitchen cream. And Alice had, for at least all the years of Jean's life, entered and won not only the nail driving competition, but the Ladies' Axe Throw at the Powell River Logger's Sports during Sea Fair. Uncle Bill, married to Aunt Alice for almost forty-five years, insisted if they were ever anywhere near someplace which held Highland Games, he was entering Alice in the caber throw.

Jean pushed her way into the supermarket and hesitated briefly, adjusting her eyes to the glare of fluorescent lights and her ears to the din of voices. Kids wailed, babies howled, adults smiled determinedly, carts slammed into other carts and two turbaned men seemed to be having one helluvan argument in front of the Produce section. A very large man with a midsection like a potbellied Vietnamese pig left his shopping cart in the middle of the aisle and, totally oblivious to the bottleneck he caused, waddled over to look at the various kinds of cookies on the middle shelf. A little old woman who could have been a cousin of the one who had fired the bird at the driver on the parking lot, very casually grabbed the heavily loaded cart by the handle and shoved it out of her way, down an intersecting aisle where it glided slowly until it came to a stop against a pyramid of Cheez Whiz. The pyramid collapsed, the bottles crashed to the floor, the orange ooze spread, the little old woman smiled, and the man with the belly whirled, realized his cart was gone, and lumbered off in search of it. Two floor creepers raced for the mess. Cheez Whiz, for the love of Jesus. And the floor creepers had to clean it up. They glared at the Michelin Tire Man who had made the tactical error of grabbing his cart by the handle, thus claiming it and the blame for the sticky mess. He began babbling, trying to convince the world at large that he, himself, so help him God, had no part in the accident. The little old lady moved on, smiling, smug, and totally above suspicion.

Jean shook her head and moved toward the back where the employees' room was squashed in between the loading bay and the storage area. Time to take off the coat, take off the rubber boots, put on the nicely shined shoes, make sure the slacks and white blouse hadn't picked up lint, mud or dog hair on the trip in. Time to get herself tickety-boo and ready for her stint at Checkout Number Three.

The customers were all insane. On any given shift you expected a good ten percent of them to be a bit odd, but every now and again, particularly when it had been raining for over a week, the entire lot of them went from odd to right off the fuckin' walls, and today seemed to be the day. Jean kept her smile fixed in place and passed what seemed like an endless jumble of mostly unnecessary shit over the electronic scanner. She had heard it beep so often she no longer paid any attention unless it made no sound at all, then she heard the silence and instead of pushing the item in her right hand all the way to the left, to be packed, she pushed it again over the scanner. Every now and again nothing you did would make the bugger work and you had to punch in the code.

She barely noticed the group of late-teens early-adult punkers who came into the store looking like alien invaders from a distant galaxy. Part of her mind registered the oddness of carrot-red tips on bile-green spikes of hair, but it takes, as someone said, all kinds to make a world. The punkers spread out casually, sauntering boldly, enjoying the looks of disbelief and disapproval they got from the other customers.

A loud crash from behind an aisle display jerked Jean's attention from the scanner. A pyramid of oranges in the produce section rolled from the bin, fell to the floor and turned the aisle into an obstacle course. The floor staff moved quickly to clean up the mess, their mops and heavy pails at the ready. From the other side of the store a louder crash echoed and this time it was a display of sweet pickles smashed on the linoleum, spreading vinegar and gherkins underfoot.

And suddenly a punker in an expensive studded leather jacket raced across the store, a large butterball turkey under each arm, dodging and evading as well as any professional football player. Before anybody could do anything except gape, the punker was gone, taking the turkeys with him. The floor staff moved to chase the turkey snatcher and a female punker, the one with the carrot-red tips on her puke-green spikes, ran as if hysterical, right into the floor staff. She straight-armed the assistant manager and sent him into the produce display. Lettuce and avocados tumbled and rolled underfoot. "What's goin' on, man, what's goin' on?" she screeched.

She made it through and past the floor staff and raced for the door at the opposite end of the store from the one through which the turkey snatcher had gone. As she approached the doorway, a kid with a skateboard came in from the parking lot, holding the door open politely. The female punker yelled "HUT!" and a large beef roast flew through the air. Carrot-tips reached up, grabbed the roast, tucked it under her arm and went out the open door. The kid with the skateboard stood shaking his head in fake disbelief.

Jean watched in genuine disbelief. This was so obviously prac-tised, so totally choreographed. Now a fully loaded shopping cart careened down the aisle unaided. Just before it slammed into a glass door, Skateboard made his move, the glass door was shoved open, the loaded shopping cart sped outside. While Skateboard stood innocently, a girl dressed in rags and tatters over a layer of expensive and trendy black skin-tight exercise togs raced full-tilt boogie toward the open door. In front of her she pushed a shopping cart full of cartons of cigarettes. Other punkers in outrageous gear raced away with canned hams, trays of chicken legs, frozen whole salmon and, in one case, two live lobsters held by their tails, their pincers waving frantically.

The assistant manager sped after the thieves. Jean turned, watch-ing. Through the glass doors she saw a pickup truck race for the exit, people with purloined groceries leaping into the back of it. Someone ripped open a carton of cigarettes and threw packages to the pave-ment. The lounging kids ripped forward, snatching for the smokes the way they dodged and darted after candies thrown from the floats in a parade. The pickup truck slowed, found a space in the traffic and deked into it as the cars behind slammed on their brakes, drivers screamed insults and the assistant manager ran straight into a knot of kids still scrabbling to pick up packages of cigarettes. He was dumped on his ass in a puddle, and the kids raced off with their loot. In all the fuss and confusion the kid with the skateboard, the one who had opened the getaway exit door, slipped off, unnoticed.

The clean-up took hours. If the television crews had been given their way the clean-up would have taken weeks. Some enterprising shopper, realizing early on what the punkers were up to, had found a working pay phone — no small miracle in itself — and dialled the CBC front desk. No sooner had the CBC truck and news crew headed out the basement garage than all the other stations caught wind of a story.

They weren't exactly like locusts descending on a barley field. Locusts don't ask the same questions repeatedly or shove foam-covered metallic tubes in your face, nor do locusts trail cables and electrical cords or shine blinding lights in your eyes. Jean would have preferred locusts, they would at least have eaten most of the mess dumped on the floor. The television crews wanted to ask everyone questions: what happened, can you describe any of these raiders, what is your own personal reaction to what happened, how does this affect your opinion of city life, is the youth of today going to the dogs, and what about law and order.

The shift supervisor wouldn't let the TV crew bother the checkout women as they tried to move the customers out of the store and clear a space for the clean-up crews, so the intrepid media found out where the employees' room was and went there. That meant when you finally did get your coffee-and-smoke break, you had to deal with the buttinskis on your own time. Jean wanted to tell them all to go fuffle up a gum tree but she knew that was exactly the clip they would choose to show on TV, in extreme close-up so the pores in her face looked like potholes and her nose hairs looked like those mooring ropes they use to tie deep-sea freighters to the dock. Anyway, she didn't want to make her debut to the folks back home with a snarl on her face. God knows their opinion of her had never been exactly lofty, why finish off the few shreds. When the reporter asked her to please put out her cigarette because it made editing more difficult, Jean just shook her head. "This is my break," she said gently, smiling her best smile, "and I don't care about your editing, I have to calm my nerves or I will not survive the next part of my shift." She knew they wouldn't use that. They were so disappointed about the cigarette smoke and how much of a problem it would be for their continuity that she actually answered their stupid questions as lucidly as she could.

"How does this affect my opinion of city life?" she repeated, choosing her answer carefully. "I guess it doesn't affect it at all. Things happen. Wherever you live, things happen. And none of these kids had weapons, nobody got hurt, and what they took was food. That probably means they're hungry. And I think it's awful that kids are hungry. After all, they're maybe only weird-looking freaks to most people, but each one of them is somebody's daughter or son."

"So you don't think today's youth is going to the dogs?"

"I thought we were the youth that went to the dogs," she answered. "Wasn't it us who were going to cause the decline of western civilization? You mean we really left something for our kids to do?" and she laughed. "I've got kids," she added, "and I don't think they're going to the dogs. The dogs probably wouldn't have them."

As with most of the things Jean Pritchard said, it caused The Look. The reporter just stared, unable to decide if Jean was joking or absolutely serious but very badly bent. Most of Jean's life people had wondered about the things that came out when she opened her mouth. For years she had revised her sentences as soon as they got said. "That's a joke," she would add, or "and you know I'm kidding when I say that, right...." Lately she hadn't bothered, they could figure it out for themselves. And fuck 'em if they can't identify a joke.

By the time her shift was finished the media had gone, thank God, and she didn't have to push her way through a gauntlet of people desperate to have something — probably anything — for the local late news. They had hours of tape to edit. Jean wondered what they did with all the stuff they didn't use. If everyone they had stopped had been asked the same questions and the tape had rolled for every syllable of every answer, probably miles of stuff had been exposed. All for a thirty-second clip. Where did all those other answers go? Did they have a huge bin into which they plopped the stuff they didn't show? And then what with the bin? Was it emptied into an incinerator? Did they haul it off to a landfill site? Would future archaeologists unearth a roll of crap and play it back, and would Jean herself be seen by her great-great-great-grandchildren, and what would they think of what she had said? Maybe her words wouldn't be unearthed, maybe she would stay in the landfill, trapped forever on plastic videotape which will probably never, in the future of the galaxy, rot or disintegrate, which would hold up the corner of an enormous building, a loony bin maybe, they'd be sure to have loony bins in the future, Christ the world was getting crazier by the minute, of course they'd have loony bins. By then there would probably be more loonies than non-loonies and only the supposedly sane would be locked away — for their own protection, of course.

The liquor outlet was still doing a booming business, but the car lot was secured for the night. The 24-hour convenience store was selling submarine sandwiches and cardboard cups of hot brown drink they insisted on calling coffee. The neon and fluorescent fought against the dark of night, and the rain continued to drizzle sulkily.

She caught the bus home and actually found a seat for the last three blocks of the ride. The bus stank of wet wool and feet too hot in artificial-fleece-lined rubber boots. A collection of umbrellas stood near the driver, people take them out of the house and forget them. She wondered if once you had lost an umbrella you felt free to just grab another one when you needed it. She didn't use the damn things. They were always getting hooked on something, and too often that something was someone else's face.

She got off the bus and headed down the sidewalk, her hands stuffed in her pockets. Bruce came hurrying down the steps, his lips twisted in his usual snarl. "It's okay, Bruce," she called, "it's just me, calm down, there's a good boy." But Bruce wouldn't calm down. He growled, he barked, he lunged against his chain, attached to a giant rusted ring-and-bolt riggings set into the support beam of the porch roof. "One of these nights you're going to haul that beam off," she told him, "and the whole friggin' porch roof is going to come down on top of you. Hope when it does it snaps your spine, you stupid bastard." He hit the fence with his front paws, the pickets shuddered, the gate rattled. "Go lie down, Bruce," she repeated. "There's a good boy, good Bruce."

Bruce was the same kind of snarling Rottweiler the Roman army had used as war dogs. He had a head as big as most cows' heads, and teeth the size of the ones witch doctors wore on thongs around their necks. The fools who owned him insisted Bruce wouldn't bite but Jean didn't believe that of any dog, especially not of Bruce. Sometimes she fantasized she would get rid of Brucie once and for all. She figured an entire roast turkey carcass ought to just about do it, especially if she put the bones back in a hot oven for an hour or two to make them supremely brittle. Then maybe dipped them in ground glass. Maybe you could take a half pound of stew meat, soak it in malathion or something and then toss it over the fence. With her luck all it would do would be kill off Brucie's fleas.

Well, maybe if she had a wide, thick, metal-studded collar fastened around her neck, and was kept chained to a twelve-by-twelve porch support, left on her own for ten or twelve hours a day, minimum, only occasionally brought into the house, seldom taken for a walk and never for a good run, she'd be more than moderately off the wall and inclined to bounce at the end of her tether and slam against the pickets of the fence.

The For Sale sign was getting frapped. It looked as if each kid who went down the street reached out and gave a good solid tug. The edges were ripped and the corners missing, someone had obviously given it a good solid kick and split the plastic, but you could still tell it was a For Sale sign. She'd had so many landlords in the past five years she could hardly remember what they looked like. Each one had showed up once, usually to change the locks on the doors, hand her a key and charge her five dollars for it, then warn her if she lost it she'd have to pay another five dollars for a replacement. With two kids still at home, either or both apt to lose a key a day, two or three of them on a bad day, Jean had learned to wait no longer than it took for the new landlord to eff off, then she went to the corner store and got the Chinese proprietor to run off a half dozen copies. Five dollars my foot!

Each landlord upped the rent, each tried to weasel or screw a few more concessions from the tenants, each promised to fix the front steps, repair the roof, do something about the bricks falling out of the chimney, send a plumber to find and fix the leak in the basement, fart wonders and shit miracles. None of them did any of it. Before you had time to memorize their names the house was back on the market, price increased, and one day you answered the ringing doorbell to find another smiling man with a paper informing you the house had been sold and Smiley was your new landlord.

She was hungry. Damn hungry. She thought of her favourite recipe for pasta. You melt butter, then stir into it three tablespoons of flour. Stir and let cook a bit, then slowly, stirring all the time, add a cup and a half of milk. Cook, stirring constantly, until the mixture begins to thicken. When thick and smooth add a cup of grated cheese, a pinch of cayenne, a half-teaspoon of paprika, and dry mustard — "to taste" said the recipe in the book but experimentation had taught Jean that meant a teaspoon, for bite. Serve over noodles of some kind, especially spinach fettuccine.

She wanted mustard-cheese sauce on fettuccine. She settled for Krap Dinner. It was quicker, and she was too hungry to fritz. She might have taken the time to do herself a favour but the house was a mess and she supposed if she didn't clean it up, nobody else would, either. While her flour-paste macaroni boiled she collected the milk-stained glasses, the jam-smeared plates, the dirty knives, the eggshells someone had left on the table. She wiped peanut butter off the counter and table top, she wiped mayonnaise off the fridge door, and she fumed. What she really ought to do was just leave the mess, wait for the little christers to get home, then jump them and make them clean up after themselves or else. But it was easier to do it. She couldn't stand a messy kitchen. Damn kids. Walk through life with that look in their eyes, the look you only expect to see in the eyes of the retarded, that bland unseeing look, as if you're transparent so there's no use even trying to focus on what isn't there. Maybe that's where all the lost marbles go; for years, spring couldn't happen without marbles, she herself had probably invested a hundred dollars in marbles, most of them coming in red plastic bags which lasted no time at all. Win or lose, good player or hopeless dud, there were never any marbles the following year, and it was out to the store to buy more. Not all the marbles went up the hose of the vacuum cleaner. Maybe they went somewhere in the ozone and were used in the heads of any kid over the age of eight. They go to bed one night and they are your darlings, warm and snuggly, sweet-smelling and to die for. Some horrible transition happens, and in the morning what comes down the stairs is intolerable. It whines, it bitches, it argues, it doesn't smell the same and the soft eyes full of laughter and love have been replaced with vacant, shiny orbs. Maybe all those old myths about changelings and how the fairy folk would put their babes in the place of human ones were true. If you could get a government grant and hire an academic you could probably prove statistically that custody cases involving children under a particular age are fights over who will get the kids and custody cases over a certain age are fights over who *won't* have to put up with them any longer. Some days she knew if Attila the Hun came looking for recruits she'd gladly hand over her own little darlings. But Attila would probably bring them home before bedtime.

The young couple downstairs were playing their music too loud again. Jean would have liked to take the broomstick and pound on the radiator but there weren't any radiators in the place, just air vents that carried sound a lot better than they conducted any heat. Oh well, the poor kids were in a real bind at the best of times. She was pregnant again, and the baby not even fully toilet-trained yet. They were so young! Jesus, had she ever been that young? Yes, she'd been that young, just about the time she'd been pregnant with Sally. Sometimes Jean couldn't remember a thing about that time of her life, other times she remembered it all too well. Maybe that's why she never hollered down the air vent. The poor kids, if they didn't have their music what would they have? He worked, and he worked damn hard, she'd seen him coming home looking as if he could hardly put one foot in front of the other, and he worked steady, but he didn't get paid a lot and they'd had nothing when they got married, had everything to try to buy. It was a lot when you thought about it: beds, dressers, some chairs to sit on, a table, and even if you got it secondhand, it was a bite out of each paycheque. Let them play their music for God's sake.

There didn't seem to be any in-laws or grandparents in the picture. Nobody who looked to be in either category had ever come to visit, or been mentioned in the few conversations Jean had passed with them. There was no new stroller for the toddler, no expensive high chair, nothing that spoke Grandma Grandma Grandma. Maybe that was part of what turned the eyes to glass marbles. Maybe with more Grandmas and Grandpas there would be fewer neon-red and puke-green hairdos, fewer navel-gazing pushing-thirties still behaving like children. Late blooming is one thing but that other thing is a waste of time and the world's dwindling resources.

The assholes upstairs were another story, though. Out every night, then back again just about an hour after you got to sleep. Clatter clatter clatter up the stairs, jarring you awake, then stomp stomp stomp across your ceiling. Toilet flushing, shower running, God, couldn't they just come home and go to bed and fuck quietly until their eyes bled? How did they manage to time it so they woke you up only after you'd had just enough sleep to keep you from falling back into dreamland immediately? Just enough to keep you groggy and aching and so angry you could feel your pulse, hear it beating in your left ear, wanting to drift off and unable to until the footsteps and the trips back and forth from living room to kitchen, from kitchen to bathroom, from bathroom to living room, stopped. What kind of line of work were they in that they could bash around like hippos in heat half the night? The mind rebelled. Some nights they even managed to waken the kids. Well, that wasn't bad, maybe she should arrange to have the kids wakened every night. Sally had just up and out of bed, marched down the hall like Alexander the Great heading for Carthage with news of another victory. Out into the hallway, up the stairs and bang bang bang on the door. Then her voice, clear as a bell, "what the fuckin' bloody hell are you doing and is there any reason in the world you can't do it quietly, I mean fuck around, man, there's this thing called consideration and it would be nice if you managed to find some because if you don't you're gonna have more goddamn trouble than you can deal with, I might seem like a nice kid but when I get mad I'm a fuckin' monster, okay!"

A good parent would discipline a kid who spoke like that to the neighbours. A good parent would discipline a kid who spoke like that to anybody. But Jean had just sighed deeply and rolled onto her left ear because that was the only way she could stop the sound of her own pulse, and once she was sure Sally was back in her bedroom, safe, Jean had relaxed. Maybe not enough to get to sleep in a hurry but little increments are better than none at all. God, you had to admire a kid who would stand there, five foot two and a half inches tall, and scream up into the face of some six-foot asshole who still wore sideburns.

She took her Krap Dinner into the living room, dropped herself into the sagging recliner, turned on the television and stared without really seeing while spooning mouthfuls of pap into herself. The macaroni bits were so small the only way to eat them with a fork was to spear them, and it was to drive you insane spear spear spear and the fork tap tap tapping on the bowl, easier to just use a spoon and get the glup into you.

The program was about working women. The women didn't look like the women Jean worked with. The TV working women all had jobs in advertising and were married to neurotic professors or to stress-harried middle management executives. The TV working women dressed for work in clothes too expensive for Jean to buy for special occasions and they were still, for Pete's sake, walking around in those rape-shoes, teetering on spikes, unable to tuck their heels under them and run if the occasion warranted. Oh well, when had women ever been realistically presented? It wasn't just TV. Movies, novels, everything. Unless Jean had just happened, all her life, to meet up with and become part of the exceptions which we are told prove the rule.

She could, of course, switch it off and read the paper. Except the publishers had decided to change from an evening rag to a morning one. That meant either you set the clock and got up earlier, to give yourself time to find out what had been printed, or you came home from work and sat down to read stuff already a day out of date. The advertisements showed happy well-dressed people sitting on a comfortable, warm, brightly lit and only half-full bus, cheerily getting the news on their way to work, starting off each day well informed and up to date. Obviously none of them lived in her neighbourhood and had to catch the same bus she took to work. When the kids were small and she was at home full time she'd taken both newspapers and read them front to back including the Hatched, Latched, and Dispatched.

Besides, the horde-of-two had already got at the damn thing and it was scattered all over the floor. The thought of trying to get it back together in some kind of order was too much. Easier to just watch this glowing tube and try to unwind a bit.

She pushed the remote and switched the channel to the early late news. The announcer talked on gravely about the Asian youth gangs, the special task force, the rivalry between the El Diablos and the Red Dragons. Jean shook her head in disbelief. My God, is this still going on? Did they mean to tell her that cops, with cars, guns, communication, dogs, and two-thousand-dollar-a-month salaries couldn't get on top of a few teenagers? Maybe the question wasn't Which teenagers are doing this but Why are they doing it. Someone with a fleshy and very well-shaved face was talking about how much time and manpower the police and governments were expending (expending?) on the fight against drugs. But, he said, it isn't easy to find the drugs or the drug importers and pushers. A cop on a huge salary, with the technology of the western world at his command can't find drugs and a fourteen-year-old kid on a skateboard can? Maybe she should write them a note and drop them the hint that anytime you saw a Mercedes Benz parked in front of a building slated for demolition, something was happening that was a bit out of the ordinary. Or maybe it wasn't out of the ordinary, maybe that was part of the problem. Maybe three fifteen-year-olds in a rented limo might be a hint, guys.

Yet another ongoing standoff on the Mohawk reserves. The Prime Minister, his chin in Thursday while the rest of him was still in Monday, was talking about how proud he was of the Canadian Army which had managed, against all odds one would presume, to surround fifty people. Pray they never come up against the Asian youth gangs. If people who have been patient for three hundred years can bring the whole thing to a grinding halt, what will happen if the army tries to do something with the El Diablos or the Red Dragons?

The Prime Minister did not want to deal with the question of the land claims issue or the three hundred years of broken promises. He kept talking about how anybody with illegal arms was breaking the law of the land and that as long as the law of the land was in jeopardy, the army would move, the police would move, the full might of the nation would be called on to move. One week ago, maybe two weeks ago the KKK had a picnic and invited the Aryan Youth, the white supremacists and the skinheads, many of whom were walking around with masks over their faces and automatic weapons dangling like ancillary penises. A woman reporter had been repeatedly raped, journalists of both sexes had been beaten up, illegal weapons were in plain view and no sign of the army or the police. It's easier to show force to pacifists than to those who are apt to take your weapon and ram it up your ass sideways. And why was there so much bumf about the illegal activities of the warriors and you heard virtually nothing about the Sûeté Quebec attacking a group of peaceful demonstrators and democracy being ensured for all time when one of the fat slobs beat the shit out of, kicked repeatedly, and put in intensive care a three-year-old boy?

Then the Pee Ehm, in a different expensive suit and shiny shoes, was being interviewed in a different hallway. His chin was probably still in the first one. He looked uncomfortably sober as he droned on with practised sincerity about the eighty-seven million dollars the government had decided to hand over to some unidentified experts to study the problem of global warming.

Now why in hell would they hand over a wad of dough like that when there were published studies up the ying-yang clearly deline-ating the problem already? Why not put the money into cleaning up the mess causing the problem?

Well, what else could you expect. Not long ago the same bunch in the brain trust had decided to cut funding to the transition houses which sheltered battered women. Then the intellects announced they were giving fifty million to do yet another study on spousal assault. Of course the people doing the study wouldn't be the people who had spent two decades working with the survivors and getting the gov-ernment to pay attention to the statistics. Oh no, we need to bring in the guys in suits for this one.

Down below the border the political merry-go-round was twirling again. Jesus, didn't they just finish electing the head of the CIA to the position of president? Don't we get a rest? Already into the endless primaries. Pray to God that nation never gets any bigger, by the time every state has had their turn at the rah rah rah we'll be going into the Impeachment proceedings.

One of the candidates had been named in a sex scandal. Someone was bleating that anyone who would deceive his wife with another woman would deceive the public as well. Harumph harumph. What about Ollie North, Iran–Contra, Ronnie RayGun, etc. ad nauseum. What about the hostage deal? What about George and the rumours of the affairs, what about JFK and his prick-mastering, what about Bobby and Marilyn, what about Olive Oyl–Popeye–Bluto and *who* was Swee'Pea's dad, anyway? And did the kid have feet or was his nightie bunched at the hem to hide his deformity? Wasn't it just last week Public Access had the hour and a half documentary on how Sun Myung Moon and his Centre for the Defence of Free Enterprise and his American Freedom Coalition were linked with Japanese and Korean big business and political interests? Who is deceiving whom about what and why are the cameras turned to tacky motel encounters instead of what is really going on in the world?

If we have to discuss morality why not look at the Rev and his cronies? And the funding he gets from the billionaire who controls the gambling on the motorboat races, that same friend of the world who was implicated in the torture and murder of the Canadians captured when Hong Kong fell, that same genial gent who was put in Sugamo prison where he formed a close alliance with two other suspected Class A war criminals. One became the head of the underworld, the other went into politics and became the Prime Minister. So we have the Rev, the thug, the politician and the billionaire closely entangled and nobody questioning the morality of that or asking why it is so many presidents of the US have glad-handed any or all three.

And who would know if not for public TV?

Jean's link to the world was her television. She watched as much of it as she could. Her kids called her a news junkie and complained all she watched were documentaries about the World Bank or exposés on the abuses of Foreign Aid. Never anything interesting like cops'n'robbers'n'car chases. Just stuff about how the seed companies are part of the fertilizer-pesticide companies who are part of the drug companies. So what. It was that or stare at the wall. Or listen to the radio, which was nothing much more than TV without any pictures. When had people stopped playing music and why? What was this noise that poured from the radio? The kids bopped around with headphones permanently attached to their ears, wiggling and bouncing to what happened when balding, pot-bellied, varicose-veined bums stood up and hammered out the three chords they had managed to learn to play and some weirdo shouted lyrics no better than the insults you could get for nothing by just walking into a bar and drinking the beer for which someone else had paid. Bad as it might be, TV beat the alternatives. Of course there were art galleries, museums, and such better-class things. Who could afford to go? Who could even get up the energy to head out and challenge the transit system again?

It was TV and the Conspiracy Theory or go bark back at Bruce!

A starling with nothing better to do than fly above the city at night would have seen Granville Street swarming with kids, thrill-seekers, law-dodgers and hustlers moving and cruising in the rain. The Arcade, brightly lit and giving at least the illusion of inviting warmth, drew kids the way shit draws flies. They stood inside, dumping money into machines, pushing bright red or yellow buttons, trying to annihilate entire fantasy galaxies, genocide taken to some technological low point, beta waves altered by the display, hand-eye co-ordination honed to a new kind of instant twitch reflex. You pays your money and you takes your choice but no matter how well you do, this is a game where you can't win anything, there are no prizes. But then there weren't any for pinball, either. Or pool. And they are all, somehow, the same thing.

The starling might have heard police sirens, might even have cared more about the noise than the rounders on Granville did. The bird, bored, might have perched herself on the wires and watched the winos, addicts and homeless in Pigeon Park, the ones with nothing much to care about, or for, the ones clustered in sodden groups under bits of plastic sheeting, keeping themselves unaware of their misery by a constant sip sip sip at jugs, bottles, jars or cans of one kind of numbing poison or another.

The sirens screeched toward the park, the blue-and-whites pulled up, spotlights trained on the helpless. The shabby eyesores realized they were the ones about to be rousted, and a few tried to shamble away, their last shreds of self-protective instinct roused, briefly. But the boys in blue were not to be denied, they poured out of the vans, cars and cruisers, their billy sticks at the ready, prepared to serve and defend. The weary, with the experience of too many years of the same shit coming down, the harmless but hopeless, trudged to the riot vans and climbed in voluntarily, hoping for a few nights in cells where it is at least dry, and food comes to you without any need for you to beg or grovel or plead. The police, bored past any kind of rational response, roughed up the co-operating bums. They wanted the human refuse stored away as fast as possible and were not interested in spending one minute more than they had to in this damn eternal rain.

Any self-respecting starling would have shit on the whole lot and flown away to find a cozy spot under the overhang of one of the public buildings.

The populace of the city, those not sent by the unseen lottery to a lifetime of plastic-sheeting-and-lath shelters and jail cells hardly noticed what was happening.

There were no television news crews, no city newspaper reporters, no crusaders about to take sides with the innocent, it all happened quick and slick and no sooner had the vans driven off than the pigeons returned to their ledges and set about their eternal task of redecorating the brickwork.

Jean Pritchard neither knew nor cared about the rousting of the bums. She was busy in the kitchen, finishing the sinkload of dishes. Her Krap Dinner sat like a cozy warm lump in her belly and already she felt the yawns building. If the kids would just show up so she knew they were home, and safe, she could go to bed.

The doorbell rang insistently. She sighed, pulled the plug, wiped her hands on the dish towel and went to let in whichever of the two had, again, forgotten to take her or his key.

It wasn't the kids. It was Tommy, her ex, standing in the porch light with a case of beer under his arm, grinning as if all those things hadn't been said, and felt, and meant.

"Hi doll." He obviously expected to be asked inside. Did she want a scene here on the porch for the neighbours to see and hear?

"The kids aren't home," she said carefully.

"I didn't come to see the kids, I came to see you." He moved forward and it was either step aside and let him in or get into physical confrontation. Jean stepped aside. She wanted to tell him to go away, buzz off, go fuck himself, but she didn't want a scene, and anyway, old habits die slowly or not at all.

He moved to the sofa, sat down, shrugged off his jacket and dropped it on the cushion beside him. He put the beer case on the floor by his feet, pulled the cardboard top open, hauled out a big can, and pulled the tab. She sat in her chair and looked across the faded carpet at the man who had once been a gorgeous hunk and the pivot of her life. But you can't fake 'er forever, the mortar was coming loose, the brick shithouse starting to sag, the world-famous boyish charm seems more than a bit stupid when the face is lined and sagging, the hair thinning and greying and fifty looms with forty already fading.

"Hey doll," he grinned, "you want one?"

"No thank you," she managed to be at least polite. After all, you'd speak politely to the bus driver if the bus driver ever bothered to speak to you.

"Not even one?"

"No thanks."

"You gotta learn to have fun, Jeannie. You never did know how to have fun."

"No, I guess I never did." Not if fun was what was going down all those years of never enough money and too many harsh words.

Tommy lifted his can of beer in something that might have been intended as a toast or a salute, then drank thirstily. When he lowered the can he was smiling. "Funny thing, though, I always had fun when you were around. Hard to figure, eh?"

"No, not hard to figure," she said gently. "You were the little boy who refused to grow up and life was a party. I never knew if I was supposed to be your big sister or your momma but I knew I had to make sure you didn't get into trouble...and that made me the spoilsport."

"Oh, hey, lighten up, Babe, we're here for a good time, not for a long time! Plenty of time to be stiff-necked when we're both dead, eh?"

"Why did you come, Tom?"

That stopped him. Anything direct always had the effect of bringing Tom Pritchard to a halt. It was foreign territory to have it put out plain and simple, minus the heifer dust, right in front of his face.

"Well, what it is, is this." He dug in his jacket pocket and she knew before he brought it out what it would be. He held it out to her but she shook her head, not interested in taking the paper. "What is this?" The smile was gone. "Is someone tryin' to make me lose my job, or what?"

Jean didn't answer. Tommy waited. Then he waggled the paper as if it was supposed to say something. "Listen, Babe, jobs are not easy to come by, okay? What good will it do you or the kids if I lose my job?"

"What harm will it do us?" she countered. "You haven't paid child support for four and a half years so we won't be out one thin dime."

He leaned forward, no longer relaxed, his beer can clutched in his hands. "Listen, Jeannie, they're talking 'legal action'. They're using words like 'possible incarceration'. You wanna see me in *jail?*" and he eyed her like a wounded spaniel. "You didn't use to be so hard-nosed, Babe."

"I didn't use to feel I had to be, I guess."

"Two hundred fifty a month for thirty months...where am I supposed to come up with that kind of money?"

"Sell your car," she suggested.

He grinned and the malice he was working overtime to not show surfaced and glittered like the point of an ice pick. "I don't have a car," he smirked. "What I drive is registered in Cheryl's name."

"I know," Jean made herself smile, "and the apartment lease is in her name, the new furniture is in her name, everything is in her name. That's why we garnisheed your wages. They aren't in her name."

Tommy sighed angrily, twisted his body, flopped on the sofa, his feet up on the worn arm. He lifted his can, drained it, reached down, took another from the case, then dropped his empty can into the space in the box. "Jesus, Jeannie, this has got to stop."

"Oh, I agree completely."

"Listen, she's got two little kids, okay? There's no way Cheryl can go out to work, she's home with the kids. If she did get a job every penny she made would have to go into kid care. So why bother? That means I've got four people to support. Give me a fuckin' break here, okay?"

"Why?" she smiled, wishing she could reach out and rip his nose off his face. "When did I get a fuckin' break? When my kids were small I had to get up, get them ready, get myself ready, race them to the babysitter, race myself to work, put in my eight hours, go get the kids, get them home, make supper and pay the babysitter out of what I made. Where were you while I was doing all that? And how much of what I made did I wind up with in my hand? And how much of *your* pay did you bring home? And how much did you leave in the bar or in a poker game or in the hands of someone who just sold you yet another goddamn car? Why should I give you a fuckin' break, Tom? You've had a lifetime of fuckin' breaks, and the easy ride is over."

"Oh, don't give me that tired old horseshit."

"Right! If you say it, it's gospel; if someone else says it and it isn't what you want to hear, it's horseshit."

They might have got into it thick and fast right about then, but the front door opened and Mark came in, his denim jacket soaked through, his jeans dripping, his sneakers squishing. Obviously the kid hadn't been able, yet, to decide if he was going to be a rocker or a biker, although most of the choice had already been made for him because it's damn hard to be a biker without a bike.

Mark looked into the living room, saw his father and took off his jacket. Under it he wore an old red and black checked bush shirt, similarly soaked. He took it off, too, and hung it on the hook in the hallway. The sneakers were kicked off and shoved onto the hot air vent, hopefully to dry one of these days. Mark walked into the living room and moved to his mother, to uncharacteristically kiss her cheek gently. "Hi," he smiled and patted her shoulder.

"So, you can't speak to me or something?" Tom growled.

"Yeah. I can speak. Happy Birthday to me," Mark answered easily.

"That's why I'm here, guy," Tommy lied, sitting up and grinning widely. He reached for his wallet and Jean felt as if her heart was cracking again because Mark wanted so badly to believe this. "I looked around, but I figured better you pick what you want than wind up getting what I think you might like."

Mark looked over at Jean who made sure she did not meet his eyes. Tom was spreading it around with an overly generous hand and the kid was smart enough to recognize the smell. Mark got up, his eyes no longer shining hopefully, and moved two steps to lean over and take the money. "Thanks," he nodded. "I'll get some sneaks with it or something."

"You see your sister tonight?" Jean tried to deflect whatever was growing between these two.

"No. You okay?" Mark turned, and Jean wanted to stand up, gather him in her arms, hold him, pat his back and say It's all right little boy, it's okay, Mommy's here. But you can't do that when they're taller than you. "Well. . ." He forced a sickly smile. "I think I'll go to bed or somethin'."

"You have a good sleep, sweetheart." Jean made herself stay in her chair, made herself just wiggle her fingers in a goodnight wave. He nodded, and she knew he knew she wanted to scoop him up and run with him to safety. She just sat, watching as Mark left the room and hurried down the hall.

"Surly little shit," Tom grumbled.

"His birthday was three weeks ago," Jean reminded him. "He has reason to be surly."

"I'm out of town a lot!" Tom's voice was raised, his guilt showing itself as anger.

"You didn't leave until three days after his birthday," she countered. "He phoned you twice, left messages on your machine, and you didn't even phone back. He saved you a huge piece of birthday cake, then got angry and threw it in the garbage. He's still just a kid, Tom, and birthdays are important."

"Someone should smarten him up," Tom snapped, "teach him some manners. Little punk's got no respect."

"Respect isn't something you get handed on a platter! You work for respect, you earn it."

"Oh spare me the lecture."

She knew it would do no good to tell him to leave. He wanted a fight. He wanted to feel the adrenalin flow, hear his words coming fast and cutting deep. That's why he'd brought his case of beer. Maybe Cheryl wouldn't fight with him. Maybe he was just too conditioned to finding Jean when he wanted to spew out some of his own frustration and anger. Well, she would go to hell in a shopping cart but she would not give him the goddamn satisfaction of once again working her into an absolute fit.

How do we walk into it? Why do we either marry the duplicate of our own father or try so hard to swing to the other extreme we marry the mirror image? Tom hadn't seemed to be any of that twenty-odd years ago. And everything everyone had said to warn her had seemed like petty meanness. But now, looking at it all from the other side of the fence, she knew if any bozo sailing past twenty-five and heading toward thirty came sniffing around after her teen-aged daughter she would find the money to go to the nearest Satan's Choice biker house and have the lothario taken out at the knees. Or higher.

God he'd been gorgeous. Thick dark curly hair hanging halfway down his back, muscles rippling, and she hadn't known what all those tattoos really said about him. He'd stopped his gleaming fancier-than-new twenty-year-old pickup truck and leaned out the rolled-down window, his grin an invitation to everything she hadn't even started to wonder about. She could remember the first words he ever spoke to her, "Hey, Babe, want a ride?" She'd said no, and then he winked at her and said "Well, then, little girl, would you like some candy?" and he had laughed softly. It was so exactly what Nana had warned her against, it was so hokey and corny and silly she had laughed, and moved to the pickup truck, her hand reaching to open the door.

Oh, they'd all warned her and had she listened? Had anybody ever listened? Somewhere deep inside herself she had been afraid they had all been right. But maybe they would be wrong. Maybe ten or twelve years wouldn't make a huge difference. Maybe the warnings were ridiculous. And even if they weren't, didn't she have a right to find out for herself? Well, she'd found out right enough. And then they could all sit back and wait for her to do what her mother had done. And Jean herself could make damn good and sure whatever else she did she didn't do what her mother had done.

So, instead of pulling out as soon as she knew the pot of gold was just another sack of shit, she had hung in there, telling herself she was hanging in because of Patsy, because she, Jean, knew herself how miserable it was for a kid to be left behind in the care of a grandmother and a father who never got over what he saw as the ultimate betrayal. And then, of course, there was not only Patsy to hang in for, but Sally and Mark. And hanging in had been something Jean had learned how to do well, so she did it long after it made any sense at all. Did it long after the touch of him, the smell of him, the taste of him was her reward, meagre as it might be. Done it until she just flat out could not be bothered doing it any more.

"Why?" he had asked.

"Because I'm tired of moving," she had said.

They had moved. Lord God in heaven, but they had moved. From Galley Bay to Sechelt, from Sechelt to Gibsons, from Gibsons to Nanaimo, from Nanaimo to Cowichan, from Cowichan to Burns Lake, from Burns Lake back down to Gibsons, from Gibsons up to Pouce Coupe and from there to Prince George. Then to Quesnel, then to New Westminster, then to Cloverdale, one after the other until they all seemed the same, big old houses that smelled of other people's cooking, yards tangled with weeds, fences falling down and septic tanks that didn't work properly, kitchens where you couldn't plug in more than one thing at a time or every light in the house would go out, drain fields that plugged and mildew growing like a pale blue fuzz in the corners of the rooms or in a red glup along the aluminum stripping around the draughty windows. They were in Vancouver when Tom announced he had a line on a job in Houston. "No," she had said. "I'm not moving again."

But of course she had to move again. The house they were renting was too expensive for her to carry herself on what she brought home. And that time she had to move with only the kids to help. And move down the scale, to a place worse than anything she'd lived in with Tom. He'd pointed that out to her. "Might as well have moved to fuckin' Houston, Jeannie, at least you wouldn't have rug riders for landlords."

She lucked out, though. Moved in, unpacked, and two months later started at the supermarket. Not exactly one of those high profile jobs in an ad agency, like on the TV, but it paid better than any job she'd had and she knew she was good at it. Knew, too, that no matter how good at it she was she would never be one of those management trainees. You needed outdoor plumbing to qualify for one of those jobs. Women ran the check-out stands. God had decided that and written it in flaming letters across the western sky. Probably had something to do with the masculine hand being unable to come up with the dexterity to punch cash register keys. Too much power and strength in the muscles, probably.

Tom was passed out on the couch when Sally came home. She walked into the kitchen and glared at her mother, sitting at the table doing the crossword puzzle. "When did he arrive?" she snapped.

"A couple of hours ago," Jean yawned. "You're late."

"Not very. He's sound asleep!"

"Don't blame me." Jean pushed her chair back and stood up. "I didn't pour the beer down his throat."

"So he stays the night again, I suppose?"

"On the couch, sweetheart, on the couch, don't make it sound like what it isn't."

"Don't you ever stand up for yourself? Don't you ever just say Go back to your new family? Don't you ever wonder if maybe it isn't your spine keeps your shoulders higher than your hips? Mom, really!"

"Stand up for myself?" Jean made herself laugh. "Oh, come on, if I was going to do that I'd have to start with you and if I started with you the first thing I'd do is ground you for coming home late."

"Mom, don't *do* that!"

"What, ground you?"

"No. Evade, and avoid."

"Go to bed, Sally, it's only important if you decide in your head that it's important."

What had her own mother decided was important enough that she packed almost nothing at all and headed out of town with a second-loader? Einarr had never talked about it. Nana had made only oblique references. The neighbours had never shut up about it, but said nothing to Jean's face. And after the second-loader there was the chokerman and after him the rigging slinger. It all blurred from then on. Truck drivers, millworkers, even a hard rock miner for a while. Postcards from here, there and everywhere, and names changing all the time. Evelyn Crawford, Evelyn Dyson, Evelyn Sandland, Evelyn Campbell, Evelyn Romaniuk, Eve Dillman, Eve Martin, Evie Lewis, two months, six months, the guy who hung around for a year and a half must have been a saint, Layard, his name was. And the jobs! Who in hell else do you know had a job working in a factory where they processed kelp? And into what, pray tell? But Eve had worked at the kelp factory doing whatever it was kelp processors did. That one, she had said, drank too much. How much could too much be to a woman who might never be drunk but was seldom sober?

Bunkhouse Bertha, Float Camp Floozie, Fire Season Sweetheart, the names just went on and on. Loggers' whore was what they meant. And Eve was. That's why once Jean had watched Tom drive off to Shoelace or Mosquito Knee or wherever in hell it was he was going for a while, there hadn't been any other men in her life. It was not true "like mother like daughter"! Damn if she would. Which Tom took to mean she missed him and wanted him back. So damn if she didn't, too, because she wouldn't, not in a million years.

She wakened to the sound of voices, to a clinking and clattering, a rattle and some soft laughter. Sunlight poured into the room from outside and the crystals hanging in the window grabbed it and broke it into little bits of rainbow that danced on the white-painted gyproc.

Her dresser was pushed against her bedroom door, no midnight rambler could have stumbled into her bedroom and flopped onto the bed, just for a few minutes, Babe, lemme get some sleep, okay.

She got up and pulled on her clothes, went to the kitchen and started water for coffee before she even dared look out the back door. The garage was unpainted wood, still black from the rain, and the alley little more than a place for garbage once it had escaped from the can. A rust-laced early-sixties Pontiac, hood open, was parked next to the garage, a number of late-teens early-twenties males clustered around it in black tee shirts and tired, saggy-kneed jeans. Two of them were hanging casually onto the legs of someone who seemed to be half swallowed by the engine of the car.

"Would someone mind awfully telling me what in hell is going on?" Jean called.

From the space where the car engine is supposed to be rose the torso and upper body of her son and heir. The ones holding his legs let go and he slid upright, grinning happily, his face and arms smeared with something very thick and very black. "Hi," he said proudly.

"I bet you think you've all been really considerate, right? Kept the music turned down low, kept the noise down to a dull roar, let the maternal parent get some sleep, right?"

The bad lads of the neighbourhood grinned and nodded, and Jean wondered why black tee shirts have to mean a misspent life.

"If we chip in and buy a can of coffee, would you make it for us?" Mark asked.

"Sure," she agreed, "coffee. Which you will drink sitting on the steps so I don't have to wash car grease off the kitchen walls, right?" They grinned at her again, nodding obediently. Well, why not? They were, after all, someone else's kids. Better they fix a car in her back yard than go out and steal one from someone else's.

The apparition who brought the coffee to the back door also brought a full pint of cream, a couple of packages of bacon, three dozen eggs and two loaves of bread. Jean stared at the broad hint spread out on the counter.

"Cat got your tongue?" she asked tiredly.

"M'name's Kevin," he confessed.

"Hell, son, everyone your age is named Kevin. Except for the ones named Shawn." He grinned and nodded, waiting hopefully. Jean poured him a cup of her own dripped coffee and pushed the sugar bowl where he could reach it. "Just let me finish my coffee before the starving lineup for breakfast, okay?"

By the time Tom got himself off the sofa the bacon, eggs, toast and coffee were near history. Half a dozen rockers were sitting on the back porch eating with surprisingly good manners, calling compliments designed to twist Jean's rubber arm and get her busy making seconds. She resisted nobly, and let the hopeful hints fall to the floor to wither and die. Sally was out there with the fugitives from the local tar pit, but not one of them tried to suggest she ought to get busy at the stove. They knew her, knew she'd die a slow death by torture before she would be Suzy Homemaker. If the feminist movement hadn't already started before Sally was born she'd probably have kicked it off herself about the time she started kindergarten. Ask her to make toast and she'd tell them oink oink you bloody male supremacist dork.

"What's that smells so good it woke me up?" Tom hinted, padding into the kitchen in his sock feet and smiling ingratiatingly.

"Too late. The locusts descended."

"Well for god's sake," he sagged. "Some how-dya do!"

"There's coffee." She sipped her own, not getting up to pour it for him. "And then I think maybe you should do something about getting yourself home to your new family. Something more than the linoleum is wearing thin around here, if you know what I mean."

Tom poured himself a coffee, then sat across the table from her, stirring sugar, adding cream, stirring, stirring, stirring, clinking his spoon against the side of the cup, sighing deeply. Did he know which buttons to push or was he just stumbling around, accidentally bashing into them? It was hard to tell with Tom, he could be the most vengeful bastard this side of Ottawa or he could be the least tactful, and just when you were ready to twist his ears for being deliberately spiteful you'd find out he had no such intention and was just being a bumbling puppy.

"I promise you, Babe . . . word of honour . . ." he began.

"No."

"Just sign a cease action so they don't garnishee and then every month, so help me God," he smiled, as charming as a snake oil salesman.

"No."

"I'll have it sent from the payroll office, direct to your bank."

"Go into family court, see the legal worker in charge of it all, and sign their papers."

"Fuck them!" he shouted. Silence slammed down on the steps outside. Tom didn't notice, he was getting ready to go into one of his patented tantrums. His charm didn't fail him very often, and the few times it had he'd been unable to deal with it. "What in *hell* is wrong with you anyway? You didn't use to be such a goddamn pain in the ass!"

"We've been this route before, Tommy." Her voice was so soft, so gentle, so much the tone you'd use with a three-month-old baby or a congenital retard that its very softness fed his anger. "Word of honour, right hand to God, cross my heart and hope to die . . . that's what you said last time and you still haven't . . ."

"I'm warnin' you, lady," he leaned forward, pointing his finger, "If I have any trouble at work you're going to be one sorry bitch because . . ."

"Don't point your finger at me, Tom; it has a nail in it!" she laughed. The door behind her slammed open and Sally came down on the kitchen like a bitch wolf in heat.

"You don't even *live* here!" she shouted for openers. "What gives you the right to holler and stomp? You've *got* a place, with new furniture, a new woman and a couple of new kids . . . and maybe they aren't *yours* but what-the-hey, eh, that's an excuse to ignore them the way you ignored us!"

"You watch your mouth young lady or . . ."

"Or what!" She stood, hands clenched into fists, daring him to do his worst. Tom shoved his chair back, it fell over and clattered on the floor, and then Mark was between Sally and his father, the grease-balls in the doorway silently promising to back up any move he made. Kevin moved protectively near Jean's chair, and she wondered if he'd parked his white horse next to the rust bucket near the garage.

"Keep the Sabbath as a day of rest," she sighed, "for indeed it is a holy day."

"Jeannie, I'm warnin' you . . ."

"Go home, Tom," she suggested, "this can only get worse."

"Why did you even let him *in*?" Sally shrilled. "Don't you ever stand up for yourself? Are you going to let him walk all over you for the rest of your life?"

"No." Jean stood, so angry with Tom she was ready to hit Sally. "No, his turn for walking all over me is finished. Now I let *you* walk all over me!" She grabbed her coffee mug, stalked to the sink and dropped it, hoping it would break. It didn't.

Tom grabbed his jacket and stomped for the front door, the greaseball brigade following to be sure he really did leave. Mark's lips were pale, his eyes glittered with tears of rage, and Sally was still holding forth on the gutlessness of people in general, her mother in particular. Jean decided it was as good a time as any to do the laundry. At least she'd get out of the house, even if it was just to go to the corner and sit dropping quarters into machines.

The young couple who rented the bomb shelter in the basement were still standing in their doorway, staring after Tom's tire-screeching car. The black tee-shirted hit squad was moving around the side of the house, back to where the rust-laced bucket of bolts waited for more tender loving care. Jean pushed the ancient baby buggy down the steps carefully, her black garbage bags stuffed upright in the bed. Ignoring everyone else in the world, she pushed the wonky-wheeled relic ahead of her, through the stupid gate and to the right, along the cracked sidewalk. The young couple watched her, then looked at each other. Twenty years ago they might have been Tom and Jean; they still might if they stayed too long in the dungeon.

The Laundr-Oh was on the corner, with the cappuccino bar right beside it. The coffee place was deserted, the Laundr-Oh almost as empty. Jean had no trouble finding empty washers, and she used them all, dumping in presorted laundry, feeding precious quarters to the insatiable machines, forcing herself into the routine, letting the familiar motions calm the anger and fear inside her. When the garbage bags were empty and the washers full she stuffed the bags back in the baby buggy and walked through the swinging half-doors from the laundromat to the coffee house.

She sat on a high stool at a small table sipping café latté and reading yesterday's evening newspaper. Some day off. Off what? Off your rocker, maybe? But it was quiet, the sounds of the washing machines muted and the music not intrusive. The dark-skinned man behind the counter yawned and went back to reading his little book, reassured by the knowledge that he wasn't making much money yet, but he would as soon as the late-risers got themselves out of bed.

Jean had finished the first section of the paper and was starting in on the Leisure section when the ruler of the coffee machine looked up briefly. "Machines are done," he told her.

She ordered another coffee and went back to the other half of the building. She took her wet laundry out of the washers, stuffed it in dryers, fed the beast a shitload of quarters and returned to read about the latest theatrical miracles, tickets only fifty dollars each. Maybe the people who went to those theatres didn't have to spend their money on laundromats. Maybe they wore paper clothes.

She was so disinterested in the idea of going back home for another round of Why Don't You with Sally that she took the time to neatly fold every piece of laundry including the dish cloths and dust rags. When she couldn't pretend even to herself that there was anything other than cowardice to keep her from home, she reloaded the baby buggy and headed back.

A big car was parked in front of the place, the front yard was jammed with people and the downstairs neighbours were protesting vehemently, the young woman weeping, the infant howling. Sally was in it, and Mark, backed up by the black tee shirt gang. Brucie, in the yard beyond the sideshow, was lunging at the end of his chain, long strings of drool hanging from his jowls and splattering on his chest. The landlord was just about hysterical and three men in bright-coloured turbans were discussing the whole sideshow in their own language.

"Oh God." Jean almost caved in, faced with what looked like the start of a local rerun of Beirut, and then it all hit her as hilarious. She was laughing when she got to the wonky gate.

The For Sale sign had a huge bright red SOLD sticker across it.

"He says we have to move!" Sally screeched.

"He sold the place and the new guys want it for themselves," Mark offered.

"Can't expect people to find another place to live with only three months' notice!" the downstairs neighbour raged.

"Anyways, you can't evict people in the wintertime! It's against the law!"

"Whose goddamn house is it, anyway?" the landlord defended.

"Nice attitude, fella," Mark sneered.

"What a bummer," Kevin commiserated, picking up the baby buggy and walking up the front steps with it as if it didn't weigh a half pound.

"Thank you," Jean smiled, deciding to ignore the entire comedy being played out on the front lawn. When the landlord, now the former landlord, tried to appeal to her, she just smiled vacantly and followed Kevin. Her refusal to be sucked into the go-round encouraged one faction and seemed to signal start to the other faction, who stopped talking to each other and started arguing with the already enraged. They were still yammering at each other and trying to drag Jean into it when she went through the front door, then closed it behind her. Kevin put the baby buggy in the hallway, smiled shyly and went back outside to get in on round three or four or whatever. Jean wanted to lock the door behind him but decided that would only complicate matters.

She put the laundry bag with Mark's clothing in it just inside the door of his room, left Sally's two bags just inside the door of her room, and took her own bag into her bedroom with her. Then closed her bedroom door and leaned against it.

She looked at her bed and yearned to crawl into it, pull the covers over her head and let the whole world go to hell in a handcart. But faint in the distance the bugle of Duty sounded and she responded; there was housework to do, a meal to cook, a semblance of normalcy to be found and claimed, at least temporarily.

She ignored the furor outside and eventually it drove away in the big gleaming car. The resurrection of the rust bucket continued, but when the hints began coming about how welcome a plate of sandwiches would be, Jean ignored them. They didn't go away. Instead, Kevin and another giant came to the back door with a bag of groceries and asked permission to use the counter and a slicing knife. They made enough sandwiches to feed everybody at the Harbour Lights Mission, but they cleaned up their mess, so Jean didn't feel too imposed upon until she found out they had forgotten to buy mayonnaise, used hers, and emptied the jar. At least they washed it out.

She wasn't sure it was quite right, somehow, for Sally to be in up to her elbows in grease, oil, transmission fluid and whatever else flowed sluggishly through the veins of the old bazoo out back. Liberation, equality, consciousness-raising and all that good stuff was one thing but black fingernails were something else all together. Still, she was at home, and not in an opium den in Surrey, or held captive by a white slave market in Langley and for these small mercies to our Lord make praise.

Near four-thirty there was a roar and a rumble, then the mind-destroying sound of an engine being revved, followed by cheers and loud *Aaaahhlllriiight!*'s. More people than you could believe would fit climbed inside the car and it headed off down the alley. From what it left behind a body would be within her rights to suppose the vehicle burned soft coal. Jean hoped it had valid plates, she hoped someone had a driver's licence and she prayed they didn't prang it in a left-hand turn.

How long since they had been able to afford roast beast? How many dead chickens had they consumed instead? Why did farm fish look and taste like blotting paper dipped in cod liver oil? And why, dear God, are there flies?

She basted the chicken, put the potatoes on to boil, and started in on the salad. By the time the gravy was made, the potatoes mashed, the table set and the salad sitting in the middle of the table, the kids were back and had even taken a layer or two of grime off their hands. They sat down, loaded their plates and started in. She watched them and wondered how it was they could eat, talk, breathe, chew, swallow and grin at the same time. Maybe they vacuumed in the food. Maybe they could breathe through their ears. That could come in handy some day, if they didn't forget how they did it.

"Did you put your clothes away?" she asked.

They nodded.

"Did you iron my pink shirt?" Sally asked.

"I ironed my stuff," Jean corrected. "Yours is in your laundry bag. Which tells me you haven't put your clothes away or you'd have seen the pink shirt."

"Well, gee whiz, Mom, for all the time it would have taken you to . . ."

"Well, gee whiz, Sally, for all the time it would take *you* . . ."

"Yeah," Mark agreed, grinning happily, "and it's your turn for dishes, too."

"It is *not!*"

"Sure it is. I did them yesterday."

"In a pig's eye you did," Jean snapped. "They were waiting for *me* when I got home from work! So Mark can wash, Sally can dry and put away, and Mark can tidy the counters and wipe the table."

"What a ripoff!"

"Yeah!"

"And if you don't there's no allowance."

"Doesn't matter," Mark teased, "I've got the money Dad gave me, anyway."

"Gave *you*? He gave you *money*?"

"For his birthday." Jean felt the sinking sensation that warned her she was on thin ice here, another balloon could go up at any minute.

"You got a *present*," Mark accused, "a real *present*. I got a gee-I-for-got-here's-some-cash."

"*He* didn't get the present, what's-her-name got it. Great stuff if you happen to be nine years old."

"She probably thought you were, after hearing you talk."

"Oh fuck off and die, Mark."

"That's enough of that. He is, after all, your brother."

"And I'm to be held responsible for *that*?"

"Shut up Sally. Shut up Mark."

"Democracy, I love it."

The balloon settled back down to earth again, and they even managed to speak nicely to each other. The Sunday Family Dinner could be marked in the book as a success, and neither of them slit the throat of the other during the minor firefight that was called Doing The Dishes. Jean left them to it and sat in front of the TV. It was like watching TV during the Viet Nam war only now the Amerikan Empire was turned loose in the Middle East. What was it about them that made her immediately distrust every move they made? Why did they seem to think they had the moral edge on everyone else? Hadn't they learned anything? Didn't they remember they had been lied to for years by their own government? Didn't that make them wonder if they weren't being lied to again? How come nobody seemed to want to remember they had not only sold weapons to the people they were now trying to annihilate, they had given them weapons? And at the time they were arming the people they were now killing, they had praised the leader they now called an insane terrorist, and they bragged to the rest of the world that he was the only leader in the Arab world who had a policy of equal rights for women! Or had Jean imagined all that?

She closed her eyes and fell asleep in the recliner. Sally and Mark finished the dishes and tiptoed quietly from the house. The TV played on, unwatched.

3

The street was quiet, the sidewalks deserted. Lights shone behind drapes in the big picture windows of the living rooms of the pleasant houses flanking the pavement, and the rain fell steadily on the well-tended lawns.

A large black van turned the corner, moved slowly down the street, then stopped in front of a white-painted stucco house. Light came from basement windows, too, sure sign of a probably illegal rented suite. The van sat, motor running, the driver leaning his forearms on the steering wheel, a cigarette in his fingers.

The side door of the van slid open, a dozen youths jumped out and moved quickly, silently, toward the house. And suddenly, shockingly, they were swinging baseball bats and lengths of chain, throwing bits of brick and fist-sized stones, two of them lunged against the wooden door, lunged again, and again, cracking the door, fracturing the frame.

From inside the suite came the sounds of girls screaming, furniture falling, then from a second door, around the back, seven or eight youths came racing, shouting angrily, some with Ninja sticks, some with punji sticks, the cargo hooks on the ends glittering viciously.

The fight spread across the lawn, the picket fence between the two yards went down with a splintering crash. A gunshot echoed hollowly, then another and someone was screaming, screaming, screaming. The two gangs broke, one gang racing for the van, the other gang racing to where a form lay on the ground, a girl standing over it, mouth open, screaming. One of the youths raced into the basement suite.

The fleeing youths leaped into the van, someone shouted, the van moved away, the side door sliding shut. In the brightly lit doorway the youth who had run into the suite appeared, a shotgun in his hands. He raised it and fired, pumped, and fired again.

The slugs hit the van, punching marble-sized holes in the metal. Someone in the van gasped, then screamed. The driver floored the gas pedal, turned the corner on two wheels, the third blast sounded, the slugs missed the van and ripped through the window of a house, sending glass throughout the living room where a family had been watching TV until the noise of the fight sent them all to the floor, hopefully safe and out of the line of fire. Several people were badly cut by flying glass and all of them were tipped into hysterics.

Four blocks away Jean was awake, watching a cop show, the living room filled with the recorded sounds of gunshots, police sirens and yells. It took her a minute or two to realize not all the sounds of warfare were coming from the tube. Like a total fool she moved to her living room window, slid open the drapes and peered outside, holding her hand to her face to hide herself from the reflected light.

She didn't see anything so left the window and moved to the front door. She was out of the living room and just one step into the hall when the front window through which she had just been peering, disintegrated. Jean fell to the floor, not because she was hit but because every cop show she had ever watched had people falling to the floor when gunshots sounded. Ah, television, mass educational communication media.

She crawled down the hallway to the kitchen, rolled in front of the electric stove and lay there, trembling with terror. Above the uproar she could hear old Brucie pitching a hairy, his barks becoming something close to a constant insane howl of mindless fury.

The van left the street, bounced over the curb, smashed into a tree on the boulevard and stopped, radiator pluming steam. The side door opened and the youths inside leaped out, two of them supporting a third who tried to move his legs and couldn't. He said something, one of the boys supporting him shouted a denial, and they moved away, dragging him between them.

Police cars came down the street in both directions, lights flashing, sirens blaring. They squealed to a halt, the doors opened, and police dogs were turned loose. Bruce just about had a heart attack when he saw strange dogs on his street. He catapulted himself from the top step, his long-suffering leather collar split, and the massive Rottweiler was over the fence and on the move.

One of the fleeing youths turned in time to see a German shepherd leaping for his shoulder. He fired his gun, the police dog fell, yelping feebly. A second police dog attacked and again the gun spat, the second dog fell dead, head destroyed. And then Bruce arrived on the scene, his adrenalin pumping, years of frustration boiling.

The police spread out, guns in their hands. Slender bodies scattered in all directions, two of them vaulted Jean's fence, raced down the side yard and into the back alley, Bruce right behind them. One youth headed left, the other headed right, and Bruce went right, his head down, his enormous body moving with the speed of fury. In no time flat Bruce was heading left, and the youth who had gone to the right was sitting against a blood-smeared garbage can, trying to stop his blood from pumping out of what was left of his calf.

Some of them got away, most didn't. The three Bruce mauled were loaded into ambulances and sent off to hospital. Bruce himself was loaded into a black plastic bag to be taken to the incinerator. He had two bullets in his body, put there by gang members, and one in what was left of his huge head, put there by a cop. You do not bite a cop, but how was Bruce to know the difference, how was Brucie to know which guns and bullets were bought by the gang members and which supplied by the taxpayers?

When the shooting stopped and the ambulances arrived, Jean got up off her kitchen floor and moved to her front porch. A young cop approached, a notebook in his hand, to ask questions. "I didn't see anything," Jean blurted. "My window blew up and I dropped to the floor and that's all I know except for the noise . . ." The cop wasn't sure if he should believe her or not. How in hell could all this come down and not one of the neighbours see anything? Hadn't anybody been the least bit interested? "I was terrified," she said repeatedly, "I just dropped to the floor and prayed."

One of the German shepherds went to the incinerator with Bruce; the other, so badly wounded the vet worked all night keeping it alive, got the credit for stopping three of the gang members.

Jean went back into the house long enough to get a jacket and come back to watch the mop-up. The police photographer was busy taking pictures of everything, the television news crews were setting up their lights and cameras, the young couple downstairs stood in their doorway, watching, as terrified as Jean herself, and down the sidewalk, sauntering too casually to be believed, Sally Pritchard made her way home, a smile on her face, a glaze in her eyes.

Jean ran down the stairs, grabbed her daughter by the wrist and dragged her to the safety of their home. Sally smiled with a calmness that was terrifying.

"Where's your brother?" Jean gasped.

"Gee Mom, I don't know, he's not in my pocket," Sally answered easily.

"You could have been killed!"

"What do you mean? I wasn't even *here* when it happened. You were closer to killed than I was."

"It's just not safe out on the streets." Jean hugged Sally tight, almost weeping with relief.

Sally looked in the living room and laughed. "It doesn't look too safe here, either!"

Jean looked, too. What had been the huge picture window was dust and shards all over the sofa, glittering in the rug, embedded in the plaster of the walls. "Oh, shit," she mourned.

"Yeah," Sally agreed. "Guess we better staple a blanket over the hole, or something. The new landlords are going to *shit*!"

Sally was just too laid back, too casual about the uproar and mess to be believed. But Jean couldn't smell liquor or the heavy after-scent of pot so she couldn't accuse the kid of being on something, because Sally's first response would be "oh yeah, what?" and Jean had no idea. But people can't just bop around the house to music only they can hear and expect other people not to suspect something.

Mark cleared it up when he got home. "Gravol," he laughed.

"Snitch," Sally smiled pleasantly.

"Gravol? You mean . . . for travel sickness?"

"Sure. A lot of bubblegummers use it if they can't get good stuff." Sally smiled gently. "I'm older than you are, little bro."

"Good stuff?" Jean snapped. "There's nothing *good* about any of it!"

"Hey, Mom, don't whiz out on *me*, eh? Okay, I can see you've had a rough night, but *I'm* not the one shot out the window and *I'm* not the one ripped on Gravol."

"I'm sorry." Jean looked over at Sally, sprawled in the big chair, still smiling. "What do I do about Gravol?"

"Nothing. She'll just go to sleep after a while. She'll be fine."

Sally didn't go to sleep right away, though. She sat staring at the window, where the blanket fluttered and waved gently in the breeze. Every now and again she shook her head wonderingly. "Ever wonder," she asked, "what makes some people tick?"

"Often," Jean agreed.

Seeing yourself on TV is a humbling experience. Mercifully, some editor had decided nothing Jean had to say about the punker raid at the store was worth putting on air, so all she had to endure was the sight of herself sitting in the coffee room talking to the interviewer, while the voice over gave a rundown on what had happened and how shocked everyone was.

"How come you didn't say anything?" Mark accused.

"I did. It just wasn't what they wanted to hear, I guess."

"What a ripoff. How you ever going to be discovered for a movie star and become rich and famous if they don't give you lines? Hey!" he pointed, excitedly, "that's our street!"

"Jesus, it's cold in here," Sally decided.

"Put on a sweater."

"Wow, some goings-on, and I missed the whole thing." Mark leaned forward eagerly, trying to piece together the events that had led up to his street becoming the OK Corral. "Did you see any of it?" he asked.

"I saw the floor," Jean said drily. "And all I heard was a sound that told me Bruce got loose."

"Bruce-loose," Sally giggled. "Bruce got loose and cooked the goose."

"Shut up," Mark suggested. "I want to hear this."

"Where would we be without the tube?" Jean sighed. "It comes down practically in our living room and we don't have a clue what it's all about until the eleven o'clock news tells us how close the call was. I wonder if it's like that for people in a war zone, too? Do you have to wait until it's all over to find out which side killed off most of your family? Would 'side' matter by then?"

"Is that ALL?" Mark sat back, shaking his head. "Boy, they spent more time on some stupid thing about a guy who grows fish in a ditch than they did on our house being wrecked."

"The house wasn't wrecked. A window was broken is all."

"There, see, I told you she'd fall asleep," he pointed.

"Sally, come on, it's time to go to bed."

Sally wakened, smiled, and with Mark on one arm and Jean on the other, she drifted off to bed, smiling gently. They just gave her a little push and let her flop on her covers. Jean dropped the quilt over her and left her, clothes and all.

"I'll have a thing or two to say to her in the morning, believe me," she warned.

"Won't do any good," Mark told her, "she'll be real detached from everything for a couple of days. No matter what you say it'll be water off the duck's back." He stood in front of Jean, his face on a level with hers, his expression serious. "Why don't you back off on *what* she did and try to find out *why*?" he suggested.

"What?"

"Is it such a crime? A few Gravol is all. I mean, if she'd been one of those nuts who blew out the window maybe you'd have a real reason for coming down like the hounds of hell, but . . . you don't even need a prescription for Gravol!"

Jean couldn't think of anything to say that wouldn't either make her sound stupid or kick off an argument she didn't want to have in case she lost it. She went to bed. She thought she'd lie awake worrying about burglars coming in through the blanketed window, or worrying Sally would quit breathing or Mark would decide Gravol wasn't strong enough and start mainlining Drano or something, but her head no sooner snugged into the pillow than Jean was asleep. She didn't waken until morning, and then it was the pounding on the front door that pulled her unwillingly up out of slumber.

It was the new landlords, who pitched fits all over the living room because of the broken window. Three quarters of what they said came out in a language only they understood, but the tone of voice said it all.

"Hey!" Jean snapped. "Grab a Gravol and chill out, okay? *We* didn't do that. *We* cleaned up the mess! *We* covered the hole so the rain wouldn't wipe out your entire living room!" She might have said a lot more, but the film crew arrived with thousands of questions and a camera. The landlords stopped accusing and arguing and pointed dramatically to the mess, Sally and Mark both confessed to not being home at the time of the uproar and Jean repeated for all the world to hear that she hadn't seen anything except the floor.

"How do you feel about this type of thing?" the reporter asked.

"Overjoyed," Jean answered drily. "It saves money on aerobics class. Something like this happens and you get all the cardio-vascular workout you would ever want."

The glazier arrived to replace the window, and the film crew got shots of that. Neighbours stood around gawking as the tow truck hitched up the van and dragged it off, but already the whole thing was becoming old news, and the street was returning to normal. Or what passed for normal in the neighbourhood.

One of the wounded gang members, questioned by police when he wakened from the anaesthetic, let the ghost of Brucie out of the bag. Credit for the capture of the slashed-to-ribbons thugs was grudgingly removed from the police dogs and given to the dead Rottweiler, along with a lecture to the public on the dangers of owning a poorly trained dog of a breed known to be dangerous. Jean figured two hundred or more urban residents immediately reached for the Yellow Pages to try to find kennels which sold pit bulls, Japanese akitas, and Mongol war dogs.

Everybody at work wanted to know what had happened. Jean got tired of saying all she saw was the floor. Nobody believed she hadn't been witness to every move, every twitch. They looked at her with open disbelief, and she supposed they thought she was protecting her own back, not wanting to make any kind of public statement for fear the survivors of the gang came back and did their karate practice on her face.

"How could you not *see* it?" Rita asked.

"It was easy to not see it," Jean answered testily, "all I had to do was fall on the floor and shove my nose into the carpet! They were *shooting* for God's sake, Rita! People who open doors to peer out into a war zone are apt to wind up part of the casualty count."

"If it had been *me*," Rita said staunchly, "I would have seen something!"

"Yeah? If it had been you I suppose you'd have opened the door and invited them all in to fight it out in your kitchen."

"I'd have seen *something*."

Jean shrugged. Rita couldn't even see the nose on her own face. She still wanted to believe all the things they had taught her to believe, she still wanted to live in the happily-ever-after, still thought if she just managed to find the right eye shadow she'd bring herself to life, somehow, be promoted from out behind a till, get to be middle management or better, and get it all together before it was time to move into the Happy Acres Retirement Complex.

And who should be waiting at home but Patsy, Jean's eldest. Every time Patsy opened her mouth, Evie leaped out and confronted Jean, and that was almost more than a person could be expected to bear, especially since Patsy had seldom even set eyes on Evie. "Well, it just goes to *show* you," Patsy machine-gunned, "this neighbourhood is on the way *down*. Not that it's ever been *up*. You've *got* to *move*, Mom, it isn't *safe* here."

"Sure, Patsy, and where are we going to move that will be safe?"

"Put your *mind* to it, Mom, don't just *accept* things. The time you spend *denying* is time and energy you could spend *fixing* your *life*."

"If it ain't broke don't fix it, remember?"

"But it *is*, Mom, you just won't *admit* it. *Nothing* has been the same since you told Dad to take a *hike*. You *know* he wants to get back together, you *know* he'd do *anything* to heal the wounds. Just stop being so *stubborn* about it and give the man a *chance*."

"Give your head a shake," Sally snapped. "Can you hear yourself? Do you spend your life talking in *italics*? Do you *think* like that, Patsy? Does it all *stand out* in your *mind* that way?"

"I don't know *what* you're *talking* about."

"Shut up," Jean begged, "both of you, please, just shut up and give me a rest, okay?"

"Well, he *phoned* me and he's *upset*. He thinks you're trying to send him to *jail*."

"I'd send him to the moon if it was me," Sally offered.

"Devil's Island will do," Jean agreed.

"I think it's *awful*. All this *fuss* over some *money*."

"Easy for you to say!" Sally leaped in again, fangs exposed, claws bared. "I notice *you* don't help out."

"*Me*? I've got *all* I can *do* just to . . ."

"Oh, right! Of course! You're the one just *says* and never *does*. Fuck, Patsy, reach out and grab some of the real world, will you? Talk about fuckin' denial! You been livin' in la-la land all your life!"

"Shut up, both of you, please," Jean snapped, but neither of them paid any attention. And why should they start now after a lifetime of doing it all their own way?

Jean left them to it in the living room and went to the kitchen. She heard the knock on the front door and ignored it. Let the combatants call it a draw long enough to answer it, whoever it was hammering to be let in probably wanted to talk to the younger crowd anyway. It seemed as if everyone in the world, except possibly the religious fanatics who went around handing out pamphlets containing information about salvation and damnation, wanted the younger crowd. She wondered if people who no longer had kids living at home went days, possibly weeks, without someone pounding on the door? Didn't anyone knock politely any more?

She was sipping tea with honey when Eve walked into the kitchen, Patsy smiling widely behind her, Sally bringing up the cow's tail with a look of wonder on her face. Jean just stared, all words gone from her mind.

"I recognized you on TV," Eve blurted. "I wanted to see you. You could have been *killed* and we'd never have had a chance to talk, and that scared me so . . ."

"Have some tea?" Jean managed, knowing it was not the thing to say to your long lost mother, but unable to come up with anything else. Her mother smiled and took the chair Sally nearly herniated herself getting for her. Eve looked like the woman in the pictures which had been taken from the albums and stored in a shoebox in the basement, except she looked like that woman after the picture has been folded, crumpled, dropped to the floor and jumped on several times. Her hands were thin, corded and ropey, with long, claw-like nails thick with shiny red lacquer. Her face was made up and then the make-up was made up, she must lay it on with a trowel left over from plastering the roof of the museum of unnatural curiosities. Her mouth was a cupid's bow of lipstick, her false eyelashes made Tammy Faye's look conservative, her eyebrows were all pencil, no brow, and her hair, my God, not even the *National Enquirer* would have run an ad for that wig. It was so totally, blatantly, stick-it-in-your-ear a wig. Not just the intricacies of the set, not just the high and wide of it, the colour screamed wig-wig-wig-wig-wig like a bright red neon sign. It had to be an outfit, a costume. Nobody with enough sense to find her way inside that riggins would have been stupid enough to wear it unless it was another way to tell the world to go eat beetles. And it has to be my mother. It couldn't be someone else's mother. It couldn't be someone who was never mother to any helpless soul. No, it has to be my long lost rejoice for she who was lost has been found, she who was gone has returned, kill the fatted calf and welcome the prodigal mother.

It was to make your mind pack its karazinka and leave home. She couldn't think of five times the square root of sweet bugger nothing to say so she just sat and watched as first two, then all three of her children met their maternal grandmother and threw all sense and reason out the window. And Eve–Evie–Evelyn–Whoever not only knew it was happening, she let it happen, she encouraged it to happen, she joined in the happening and turned loose every bit of charm she possessed, could borrow or invent. There's something to be said for the skills and slicks a person can develop sitting in one bar after another, meeting strangers by the tens, twenties, fifties, hundreds, working overtime at being fun, being acceptable, being sociable. Give the woman two dapple grey mares, a wagon with fold-up sides and a washtub in which to mix her magic potion and she could travel the country making a fortune selling cure-all to people who had nothing wrong with them to start with. Maybe, Jean thought, I could open a used car lot and put the old bitch to work selling heaps to people who don't need them, we'd all get rich, maybe even rich enough I could buy myself a one-way ticket to someplace she isn't and can never find. She was afraid to ask Why Me, Dear Lord in case the clouds parted and a huge forefinger poked through at her and the thunderous voice roared Because you piss me off, bitch.

Bunkhouse Bertha's Travellin' Road Show, come one, come all, only a dollar a bottle and your troubles are gone. Just step right up ladies and gentlemen, for one golden-tinted loonie you, too, can be the first on your block to have this patented medicinal cure-all, removes warts and shrinks haemmorhoids, reduces inflammation and erases those ugly varicose veins. Just one loonie, worth only seventy cents yew-ess, hardly to be noticed, not worth carrying in your pocket, and in return, you get faith, hope and fifty percent alcohol by volume. . .

And Jean overloaded, short-circuited and retreated to someplace where all she had to do was breathe in, breathe out, observe and nod. Every now and again she would get up, put the kettle on, rinse the teapot, get tea bags, put them in the pot, add boiling water and take the pot back to the table. She was so dumbfounded she didn't even think of supper and when Mark started to complain, Evie moved faster than a salamander. "There's gotta be delivery pizza," she beamed, reaching for her purse. "Figure out how to use the dial on the phone, and tell 'em to send two of their biggest and best," and she cavalierly handed Mark a mittful of money. "Right on, Gran," he crowed. Gran? *Gran?* The woman hadn't impinged on his life for most of the duration and she was Gran six minutes after he came drifting in from wherever he'd been.

Jean pulled her act together enough to throw salad stuff in a bowl and whip up her half-a-minute-and-no-more-than-that salad dressing. Two crushed cloves of garlic, an ounce of olive oil, let it sit fifteen minutes to half an hour, add the juice of a lemon and call it Done.

"This is delicious," Evie complimented. "Is it Italian or something? Real flavourful." She smiled, then shrugged. "I always figured anyone who knew how to cook had it made. I'm a good cook," she added, "it's how a person shows love, you know," and she was off on a philosophical exercise the kids swallowed as eagerly as they swallowed their food. Jean bit her tongue rather than say Well, if that's how you show love I guess you didn't have much to show because Nana did the cooking. Why kick a dead cat?

They were still clustered around the table yammering away, picking at the last of the pizza, when Jean begged off on the grounds she'd had a very hard day and took herself to bed. She just about staggered down the hallway, not noticing the luggage neatly stacked just inside the front door, and she couldn't have told anybody which came first, the washed face or the brushed teeth, she only knew she got the necessaries done and hit the pillow.

When she wakened in the morning Sally was sawing logs in a sleeping bag on the floor. Jean nearly stepped on her head.

"Easy," Sally warned, "I've got a face attached to that."

"How did you get here?"

"Quietly."

"Why are you here?"

"Patsy's got the couch."

"So did someone hijack your bed?"

"Gran's sleeping in my room."

"*What?*"

"Well, we couldn't just open the door and shove the poor old thing out into the rain, could we? I mean, after all these years? Suitcases and all?"

"Suitcases? Oh my aching ass."

"Is that any way to be? She's your *mother*, Mother."

"Is that an echo echo? What's Patsy doing here?"

"*Oh*, you know *Patsy*." Sally rolled over, glaring. "If something is *happening* she just *has* to be *part* of it. Picks my ass."

"She's your sister, Sister."

"Get ready for work Mom, please, I don't know how much of this I can cope with before coffee."

"Right. But it might be too much to ask you to make the coffee, huh?"

"I'm the kid. You're the mom. Role model patterning and all that stuff."

"Up yours, kiddo."

"Up my what? Up my role model patterning?"

"That, too."

Jean made coffee, and had a cup of it before she hit the bathroom. Damn shift work. You never got your body clock adjusted properly. So many days of this shift, so many days of that, go in three hours earlier, go in four hours later, stagger it around so there are always fresh people showing up at the cash registers, and never mind what it does to their personal lives. Nobody pays you for your personal life, the one who pays the piper decides when and where the piping will be played. Ya ta ta tat!

Work was work. That's why they call it work, if it was anything else they'd have another word for it. Coffee break was one of those awful sessions where someone has heard something from someone else and is passing it on to everyone. All of whom are suitably shocked and threatened, and bursting with questions nobody can answer. "How can they get away with that?" "What about the union?" "What about the labour laws?" "Well, how *come* they can do that?" "Is it legal to close a store, say you've sold it, then just change the name and hire nonunion people?" "Are they allowed to put them on roller skates so they can get around faster?" "What about the government?" "You think maybe the guys doing this have friends in high places?" "What's the country coming to, anyway?"

At least when you go in for early shift, you get home before night is falling all over your life. Jean came in with a bag of groceries under each arm, and nearly stopped dead. The place was clean, the place was tidy, and good smells came from the kitchen.

"Hi," Patsy smiled happily.

"I thought you had a job to go to," Jean managed.

"I phoned in sick." Patsy's smile didn't waver even half an inch. "I've got some accumulated sick leave and decided since I can take up to three days without having to have a paper from my doctor I'd justify this by calling it mental health." All that and not one italic.

"Sit down and take a load off your mind." Evie acted as if it was her own kitchen. She put a cup, sugar and cream on the table, poured the tea into the cup, pulled out the chair, practically pushed Jean into it, then turned her attention to the grocery bags. "I'm not sure where everything goes," she chattered, "but we'll muddle through. How was your day? Patsy says you're a cashier, that must be real hard work, on your feet a lot I suppose and having to deal with all those people all the time, I'm not sure I could do that, I take off my hat to you, believe me. Did you have to take a course? How do you remember all those prices? Of course you always were bright, there's no getting away from that," on and on like water flowing from a spigot. Jean just smiled and sipped her tea. "Hope you like pot roast. It's kind of by way of being my own personal speciality so since I'm tryin' to make a good impression here, I thought I'd pull out all the stops. What it is, see," she looked right at Jean, and the sirens went off inside, "I figure if I get the kids on my side I've got 'er aced around here."

"Oh, *Gran*," Patsy crooned, "you've already *got* us on *your* side. I've been waiting all my *life* for a chance to get to *know* you."

Today's wig wasn't neon red, it was glossy black, not like the hide of a well-fed labrador retriever, not even like the fur of a ready-for-hibernation bear, but the black of plastic garbage bags. And it didn't pile up on her head in swirls and loops, it hung to her shoulders, waved just exactly so, as if Cleopatra had discovered home permanent.

It got worse. The others came home from school and sang the Hallelujah Chorus over the pot roast. "Mom hardly ever gets around to really cooking," Sally blurted.

"Oh, cut me a bit of slack," Jean groaned. "You could maybe tell me what it was we ate on my day off?"

"That's what I mean, we have to wait for your day off before we have a real meal."

"Fifteen million kids your age die of hunger every year on this globe," Jean snapped, "and you're going to bitch about having nothing but pork chops and mashed potatoes?"

"Now, now," Evie smiled, "it's not easy when you're a kid to realize just how hard it is to be a working mom. Listen, take it from one who knows, until you've been on your feet for eight hours steady with everyone else's wants and wishes getting put ahead of your own, you don't *know* what the word tired means. And," she reached out, rumpled Mark's hair, "don't give me that stuff about how Everybody Else's Mom Can...because you know life isn't the Waltons on summer reruns, okay? Now give your mother a break for a while here and let's get on with making supper. I need someone to show me where the flour, salt and pepper are, and let's find out what else you've got for spice or seasoning around here. Markie... have those rolls risen yet?"

Rolls. My God in heaven, rolls. The woman has been Polly Homemaker here since ten this morning! Maybe I should do to her what she did to Nana: just up and fade and leave her here with the whole shootin' match. I could get up from this chair, go to the hallway, pull on my damp jacket, open the front door and ride off into the soggy sunset because a woman's gotta do what a woman's gotta do. Cash my paycheque, go into Chinatown, find a Fan Tan or Pan Gini game, neither of which I know how to play but pick us not nits at this point, sit in, win, and with that minor fortune, hie myself off to some place like, oh, Saskatoon or WinterFridge or maybe Hen's Asshole Alberta, open a den of total iniquity and sit back and laugh laugh laugh.

But she didn't. She went to her bedroom, stripped off her work clothes, pulled on her robe, went to the bathroom and filled the tub with hot water, then sat in it trying to baste the pieces of her mind back together again.

Of course, Einarr had seen the TV news, too. He didn't know what shift Jean was on but knew there would be someone there to answer the phone around six. They were well into the pot roast when he called, and the only piece of luck Jean had was that she answered before anyone else could. "No, Poppa, I wasn't hurt. Yes, Poppa, I'm sure. At least we're getting a new window out of it, the one they shot out was so old it rattled in its frame and we had to put plastic over it in the wintertime to stop the wind from blowing us off our chairs while we watched TV."

"Well, I never could figure out why you stayed there in the city anyway. You coulda come home any time. But to each her own, I guess. How are the kids?"

"Fine, Poppa, they're having supper. Patsy's here," she bribed him. He would walk on water for Patsy. "Want to talk to them?"

"You just betcha!"

When Jean answered the phone she could say what needed to be said and then let the kids carry the burden. If they answered the phone they filled Einarr with so many different versions of the same events it took Jean five times as long to unscramble him and let him know he had no reason to worry. She wasn't sure she'd have been off the blower before midnight if Patsy and her italics had been the first one to describe the van wreck.

"All over the *floor*," Patsy thrilled, as if it hadn't been cleaned up before she arrived, "and bullets everywhere! The neighbour's *dog* got killed and Mom was still so *upset* when I got here! It's just *awful*, Gramps, I mean it's *awful*, and I guess you *heard* about the raid on the store where she *works*. It's as if she's a *lightning rod* and it's all just coming *down* all over *her*."

"Christ, a couple of turkeys get stolen and Patsy's ready to call it a mob hit."

"Well, dear, some people live their lives in technicolour." Eve bustled to the stove and pulled Jean's half-finished supper out of the oven where she'd put it to keep it warm. "Here, you finish up your nice pot roast."

She knew the precise moment it started. She had been waiting for it to start. The pot roast and gravy was halfway to her mouth when she saw Patsy set her shoulders a bit straighter and walk, smiling, right into the buzz saw. If the cat was going to come out of the bag, anyway, Patsy's method had always been to yard it out by the scruff of its neck, display it proudly, wave it around a bit and demand some respect for it, however ratty it might appear to be. And Patsy knew, had always known, the best way to work the family politics. Why shouldn't she? There had hardly been any family politics before Patsy. She had not so much started them as been the reason they had started; from her first hour of birth there had been a shift in the way Einarr treated people. He judged everyone, living or dead, by the way they treated his Patsy. If you wanted to be on the good side of Einarr, you were nice to Patsy, italics and all. Conversely, if you wanted more trouble than you could handle, look sideways at Patsy and have Einarr all over you like ants over a honey sandwich.

"Oh, *Gramps*," Patsy teased, "now why would I care about *that*? It was *old news* before I was even a gleam in my father's eye!" Eve became very still, and very quiet. So still and so quiet Jean almost felt sorry for her. "No, of *course* not!" Patsy laughed easily, "and you just *stop* it, Gramps."

Jean concentrated on the pot roast, barely tasting it. They'd all taken over. She was just along for the ride. People were bringing luggage into her house, people were moving out of their bedroom and into hers, sleeping bags lay where small rugs ought to be, pot roast was cooked on her stove and rolls baked in her oven, all with no help from her. Let them handle phone calls the same way. Let she who thinks herself head of the UN negotiation committee, she who thinks she is the one could, given half a chance, get the Arabs and Israelis to sit down and eat bacon and eggs together, slide it to Einarr that his ex-wife, who had walked out on him leaving him holding the bag and the baby, was sitting with his grandchildren, having a Family Dinner the same as if past history didn't exist and everything was what the world at large still insisted on calling normal.

The store manager dumped it on them without warning. None at all. He just handed out envelopes as the staff arrived for their shift.

"Layoff?" Jean gaped. "What do you mean layoff? For how long?"

"I'm sorry." The manager didn't look the least little bit sorry. "They're talking of . . . closing the store."

"Closing? The store?" she looked around as if she had never before seen the place. Huge clusters of balloons hung from the ceiling, streamers stretched from walls to ceiling, tinsel hung glittering. Every aisle was decorated. SHOPPERS CELEBRATION WEEK the banners bragged, IT'S YOUR PARTY!

"Some party!" she blurted.

"They'll try to transfer as many top seniority people to other branches as possible, but . . ."

"Oh, bull." Jean felt rage rising to replace disbelief. "If you'd been going to do anything like that you'd have told the union about this three months ago. What you're going to do is close this store, which puts us all on unemployment enjoyment, and effectively ends this union local! And then they'll change the name of the store or something and hire nonunion people and that is what it is all about."

"The store was barely breaking even before we had that dreadful raid."

"Dreadful raid? Wasn't five hundred dollars went out of here."

"There was breakage, too."

"And insurance, let's not forget the insurance. But you'll blame the punkers just to cover up what's really going on! I mean don't, please, mess with my head. I saw the financial section of the paper. I saw the shareholder's stock report. You're doing FINE. You just want to do better, is all, and dumping the union is a good way to do better."

He ignored her, of course. Why not, she was who she was, nobody, and he was who he was, and it was a case of mind over matter; he didn't mind what she said because in his eyes she didn't matter. The decision had been made. Jean didn't have enough seniority to hope for what little protection the union would be able to squeeze, she had less than six years while others had more than a dozen in this store alone. All she could do was work her till for the time left, then hit the road.

"We'll put a picket line up around this place," the union rep vowed. Jean nodded, but she didn't believe it would happen. The union was going to have to make its deals, and finding placements for as many as possible was the most it could hope to do. There wouldn't be a picket line, and if there was it wouldn't make any difference. Jean had a couple of weeks' work left and then it was unemployment enjoyment, S.O.L., shit outta luck.

She was so angry, so frustrated and so aware of how economically vulnerable she was that she didn't notice at first how often she was sneezing. When her head began to plug up and her nose began to drain she bought a big bottle of 1000-mg vitamin C and started to pop, but to no avail. It was as if at three in the afternoon she was fine and at three-thirty she had a full-blown nose whopper.

She rode home on the bus with tissues held to her face and Niagara Falls draining from her head. She thought of what Patsy had said about accumulated sick time. If the bastards had no more consideration for her than to lay her off because they wanted to dump the union and bring in nineteen-year-olds on roller skates, fine, that could work both ways, by God. She hadn't taken a sick day the whole time she'd worked there but she'd take each and every damn one of them before she had to go on pogey.

She passed on supper, made herself a double Neo Citran, took it with her and crawled into bed to sip lemon drink, sniffle into toilet paper and try to focus her swollen eyes on her battered copy of *Lonesome Dove*. Life was simpler in those days. You didn't have to put up with it so long. Just dive into a river and get bit to death by snakes instead of having to work with them for six years. She blew her nose and immediately the inside of her face began to squeak, then to ping. Hot blood-tinged water dripped, she wiped at it, heard herself squeak again and moaned. Not just a nose whopper, a goddamn sinus killer. Her cheekbones must be like Swiss cheese, with each hole inflamed, and draining. She dragged herself out of bed and went for the vitamin C and the vitamin B, as well. If she didn't start popping the B's she'd have a top lip covered with cold sores. Even if she did pop the B's she'd get cold sores but at least this way she could console herself she'd done everything she could to stop them. The sinus fluid must be swarming with virus. God damn. Life has come to a morbid pass, she decided, when you spend time explaining to yourself what is going on in the war zone your sinuses have become.

"Drink lots of juice," Eve ordered.

"You taking your C's?" Sally demanded.

"Boy, you look rotten," Mark said cheerily.

"*Why* are you out of *bed*?" Patsy italicized. "All you had to *do* was *yell* and I'd have been *glad* to get it *for* you."

"Me? Yell?" Jean wheezed.

They brought her supper in bed and then were disappointed because she couldn't eat much.

"You can't expect to get *better* if you don't *feed* yourself," Patsy warned.

"Come *on*, now sweetheart," Eve picked up the slack, "give her the good old *try*, just a *bit* more." The wig tonight was an ash-blond bordering on grey, short and sleek to her head like the fur over the arse end of a fat pet rat. It would have looked almost acceptable on a twenty-six-year-old, but almost only counts in horseshoe.

It almost made work at the supermarket seem attractive. But the Neo Citran did whatever it was the advertising claimed it would do, and she slept. When she crawled out of bed in the morning she was so obviously sick nobody even suggested she try to eat. She drank juice, she drank tea, she drank anything anybody thought to bring to her room, but mostly she slept.

"Anytime you get a cold," Sally lectured, bringing in more hot lemon, "it's absolute proof positive you've been doing too much. This is your body's way of telling you to slow down because you're overdoing it."

"Who told you that?"

"Everybody knows that."

"You get a cold because of a virus."

"If you weren't worn down your immune system could handle the virus. The air we breathe is swarming with viruses. Our water is full of viruses. If just having viruses in your system meant you were going to be sick you'd never have a healthy day in your whole life."

"Why is it one day they're gnawing at your ankles and you no sooner turn around than they're taller than you and talking like Linus Pauling?" Jean popped a C and took a couple of aspirin. "You make it sound as if my life is just one big round of party-party-party, burn the candle at both ends, dance away the night."

"Well, there are other ways of overdoing it. Getting an ulcer over things you can't do anything about and didn't cause, for example."

"Don't lecture me, Sal, please, I'm apt to burst into tears."

"Might do you good. I don't know that I've ever seen you cry. Might do us both good."

"What? And undo all those years of proving to you that I really was Wonder Woman?"

"You aren't, though." Sally leaned over and kissed Jean's cheek. "I never really believed you were. I just thought you did a damn fine imitation."

Eve got the bright idea Jean shouldn't stay in bed all the time. "Come on, sweetie," she beamed, "up and *at* 'em . . . down the hall to the kitchen, there's a nice bowl of soup got your name on it."

"I don't really feel very . . ."

"Come *on*. You're so sick you don't know what's *good* for you." So Jean got up, snorfing and snuffing, and made her way to the kitchen. The soup might have been delicious, but Jean's head was so stuffed she could neither smell nor taste. And her nose kept dripping. She wiped, she wiped, finally she excused herself, left the table and *blew*.

"My *God*, what's *that?*" Eve pointed accusingly at the toilet paper.

"It's just sinus fluid. I'm draining," Jean sighed.

"Sinus fluid my ass, that's *blood*."

"Yeah, well that happens sometimes."

"That means *infection*. You need antibiotics!"

"Listen, nobody does house calls. And I'm not even going to think about trying to make my way to the clinic to . . . never mind, I'm going to bed."

"*I'll* get you antibiotics!" Eve vowed. And somehow, she did. No doctor came to the house but when Mark got home from school he was sent to the pharmacy six blocks away and there was a prescription ready, with Jean's name on it.

"Now *take* it."

"Thank you."

She didn't tell them the antibiotics just made her feel as if she wasn't sure where she was or what she was doing. She didn't bother telling them about how if you do bugger nothing about a cold it will last a full week and a half but if you baby yourself you can get over it in ten days, she didn't bother with anything at all, she just let herself enjoy all those hours in bed. Regularly, the pings and zings in her head would start, she would roll to the side of the bed, let her head hang over the edge, and drip what looked for all the world like carrot juice onto a huge wad of toilet paper. When the torrent stopped, she wiped what was left of the middle of her face and put her head back on the pillow. Often she slept. Until the pinging and dinging started and it was time to lower and drain again. "Carrot juice," she whispered harshly, "Jesus God can't I ever get anything that doesn't turn out to be so disgusting it nauseates me just to think about it? What illnesses do they get in movies, the ones where the heroine lies around looking pale, wan and totally gorgeous while wealthy young playboys and suave men-about-town shower them with imported orchids and bottles of expensive champagne? Why do I get something *septic*? Isn't there some infection that produces *pretty* drainage? Does it all have to be such vile colours?"

It lasted ten days. The inside of her nose felt raw, her top lip was still patched with cold sores, the vitamin C had her peeing all sorts of strange shades and by the time she was able to get out of bed and move around with any degree of assurance or credibility, Eve was so firmly installed in Sally's bedroom it would have taken dynamite to get her out.

But at least Patsy had moved back to her own apartment. Thank you God for that much.

Sally Pritchard enjoyed having her grandmother staying with them. It took some getting used to, but it was nice to come home from school and know before you opened the door the house wasn't empty. She was used to being a latchkey kid, and didn't mind, not really, she understood all too well how few the options were and had always been. But it was nice to unlock the door, step into the house and know the kettle was hot, know by the time she had taken off her boots and jacket, put them in their places and made her way to the kitchen, someone would be fixing a pot of tea, putting peanut butter cookies on a plate and smiling welcome.

What she didn't enjoy was the safari to get where she had to be in the morning. It was as if day after day a person had to hack and claw her way through a jungle, practically fending enraged natives off with a machete, like in *King Solomon's Mines* or some other awful old racist movie.

By the time the bus got to her stop it was jammed. No use trying to catch an earlier one, they were all jammed, too. No use trying to catch a later one, either. So when the doors opened you flew up the stairs and launched yourself, like bodychecking someone into the boards at a hockey game. If you were good enough at it, you managed to get yourself wedged in with the crowd.

Then, just to make you wonder if you were going to die on your feet, smothered because the press of other bodies made it impossible to take a deep breath, one of the electric busses had to go and drop its damn hook off the overhead line. Traffic ground to a halt. Drivers, already frustrated by gridlock and probably half drunk on exhaust fumes, leaned on their horns, as if the noise alone would accomplish what needed to be done.

By the time everything was untangled and traffic moving, Sally was already almost late for school.

When the bus stopped across the street she popped out of the press like a champagne cork, and raced across the intersection, setting off another chorus of horns and another fit of temper from enraged drivers. Then wouldn't you know it, her combination lock had to jam, her locker door stick, one thing after another, and by the time she got everything sorted out and made her way to socials class the hall bell was ringing shrilly. But it *was* still ringing. And class didn't officially start until the bell stopped. Everyone knew that.

Everyone except Festerface, the socials teacher. Mr. Jonas spent most of his time so lubricated with Canadian Club he didn't know if he'd been punched, bored or stapled, but he wasn't what anyone would call a jolly drunk.

"You're late," he accused.

"Not yet." She tried her smile on him, the one that worked just often enough to keep you thinking there was justice and mercy in the world. She closed the door and took a step, and the bell stopped its damn din. "See?" She gave him more of the smile.

"You're late," he repeated coldly.

"A trolley came off the overhead and. . ."

"Take your excuse to the office. You can't get into class until I've seen your excuse slip."

"Ah, come on, Mr. Jonas, I was in the room before the bell quit!"

"The office," he repeated, and turned away from her, ignoring her totally. She whirled, yarded the door open, went out of the room and slammed the door.

Down in the office they were going berserk, phones ringing, a dozen kids waiting for late slips, the staff overworked at the best of times, and none of them in any better a mood than Sally herself.

"I need a late slip," she announced.

"Wait your turn," the secretary snapped.

"All's I need is a late slip!"

"I said wait your turn!"

So Sally waited her turn. She leaned against the wall, her face telling the world her opinion of this crummy hole. The clock on the wall said two minutes past nine. Eighteen minutes later she was still leaning against the wall, the phones were still going mad, the secretaries were still trying desperately to cope.

"Listen, I'm going to be late for my second class, too, if you guys don't get the lead out!"

"I don't have to take that from *you!*"

Sally came off the wall, stiff with fury. "I'd really like the opportunity to take a late slip from your lily white hands and carry it down the hall to my socials teacher so I could at least get myself *started* today!"

"You can see the vice principal, instead, young lady!"

"Jesus Christ what is *wrong* with everyone today?" And of course she had to wait her turn to see the vice principal. "What is wrong with everyone?" she repeated several times.

Whatever it was, the vice principal was affected, too. He tried to be patient, but Sally was, by now, on the prod.

"What can I do for you?" he asked pleasantly enough.

"I need a late slip," Sally said, ice hanging from her words. "The bus got held up in traffic because a trolley had . . ."

"You know you get the late slips from the secretary in the office! You don't bother the vice principal for a late slip."

"I know that, you know that, but someone forgot to tell that dipshit broad out there. She told me to come *here!*"

"Who do you think you're talking to like that, young lady?"

"Leave me alone! For God's sake will you all just leave me *alone!*" and she went out of the office and over to the secretary. "Gimme the effin slip, the man says you're wasting his time!"

There was no use bothering to go to socials. She headed to her next class, Girls' Mechanics. She walked in and handed the late slip to Mr. Gerard, her favourite teacher.

"What's this?"

"A late slip."

"But you aren't late!"

"Not here. But I was late for socials. So I had to waste an entire period in the office. And if I take the slip to Jonas I'll be late *here*, too, then I'll have to go back down to the office for another fuckin' slip . . ."

"Easy, Sally, easy, you know me better than . . ."

"Want to know what I know Mr. Gerard? I mean do you really give a shit about what I know? I know I've just about had it to *here* with this crap! Jonas has his usual hangover and I didn't have anything to do with that, but I catch it because he feels like shit on a stick." She worked herself into a full-blown temper tantrum. "The secretary is a wuss, the vice principal didn't get any breakfast before he left home, and now *you're* on my case, too. Well, *fuck it!*" She tossed her books to the floor. "And fuck you, and the horse you rode in on!" and she stormed from the room.

Mr. Gerard gaped, then headed after her. Halfway down the hall he decided he wasn't taking any of it out on Sally, she'd obviously had enough. He wound up yelling at the vice principal. "What in *hell* is going on anyway? What have you been doing to that kid? She's got a solid A-plus in my class and all of a sudden she's throwing books and leaving. Damn, I wish I was still fixing engines in a machine shop! At least there the dipsticks aren't in charge."

Sally didn't even try to clean out her locker, she just grabbed her gym bag and her jacket, and turned to leave. She almost fell over the hall monitor, who loftily demanded, "And why aren't *you* in class?"

"Same reason you're not in the zoo where you belong, zit-face," Sally retorted.

She was almost at the front door when the vice principal stopped her.

"Sally . . . let's talk about this . . ."

"Outta my way. I'm leavin'. I don't *need* this crap!"

"Sally, please."

"Get your freakin' hand offa me! I'm goin to the freakin' store to get some freakin' tampons because obviously the whole freakin' world has got pee ehm ess this morning, okay? Or do you want to come with me and pick which brand to buy just to demonstrate how freakin' helpful you can be, especially when your help isn't needed because it wasn't there when it *was* needed!" and she pushed past him, free, free, free at last, great God almighty free at last.

She didn't get ten steps from the front door when two cars squealed onto the school parking lot, practically colliding. All the car doors opened, combatants piled out of each car and the fight was on, all over the schoolyard, bats, sticks, bits of chain, one gang hammering on another. Sirens wailed, cop cars came from six directions and the student body followed Sally out the door and onto the schoolyard.

"Hey, what's shakin'?" Mark asked, coming to stand next to her.

"Fuck, man, I don't know. The last thing I understood was that the trolley hook had come off the overhead cable. Since then it's been nutsy time."

"Yeah," he grinned, "I heard. Is it true you offered to kick the vee pee in the nuts?"

"No," she laughed. "But I'd pay a quarter for the chance. My God, here comes the ambulances! *Look* at that guy over there . . . Jesus, he looks like something ate half his face! Guh-rosss!"

And of course on the six o'clock news there they were, the two of them, Mark and Sally, onlookers front and centre. Jean groaned and blew her nose. "Just can't keep this family off TV," she said.

"Yeah, the big dee-butt. Mark as Steve McQueen number two and me as . . . who'll I be? Meryl Streep?"

"You act as if this is all just a big show, as if it isn't real. That boy is *hurt*," Jean protested.

"Nobody forced him to join a gang, you know. If you can't hack it, don't play games with it," Mark said coldly.

"Dumb shit," Sally agreed. "Everybody knows if you join a gang you wind up hurt. Just like everyone knows if you go out in the rain you get wet. Stew-puhd!"

"Stew-*pid*," Jean corrected, not really caring one way or another how her kids pronounced the word as long as they kept themselves focussed on the issue.

Jean was lying on the sofa in the living room watching TV and enjoying the sensation of being able to move her head without having her sinuses drain down the front of her shirt. The antibiotic made her a bit sleepy, but she could feel it winning the battle in her head. She wondered why she hadn't phoned her doctor and demanded something herself. Maybe an infection in your head affected your brain before it affected your stomach or bowels. Mark was just home from school, Sally was still refusing to ever, as long as she lived, set foot, even one foot, back in the hallways. When the phone rang Eve answered it, as much because nobody else seemed inclined to as because she was closest to it.

"Mr. *Whom*?" she asked in a perfect imitation of the Queen Mom.

"And who might you be, may I ask?" she tilted her head to one side, as if Mr. Whom could not only hear her, but see her. The honey blond wig swayed as stiff as a branch in a high wind, as natural as a styrofoam Christmas tree. "Ah, the vice principal." Sally stiffened, immediately ready for a set-to, a go-round and a furor. "Yes. Yes. Yes, I'm quite aware. Yes," and Eve winked at Sally in a way that made the kid's shoulders lose at least a touch of defiant stiffness. "Oh, yes, I'm sure I know what happened. In the time I've known Sally I've had no reason to suppose she embroidered events any more than any of the rest of us do." She paused, smiling slightly, looking more like the Queen Mom than ever. "Well, yes, actually, I do have some ideas of my own as to what happened and why. Have you spoken to any of the youngsters who were in that class at the time? Oh, you haven't?" Her tone suggested a kind of amazement reserved for kangaroo courts. It also suggested, without actually saying, that she herself had interviewed every one of them. "I'm sure I don't understand why not, we have no reason to suppose they are all of them unregenerate liars, surely," and again she winked at Sally who by this time was totally relaxed and exchanging admiring glances with Mark who seemed to have just received proof his grandmother was directly related to God.

"I don't know whether or not you're aware of the situation in our home," Eve said smoothly, as if she herself had spent years as part of it instead of a mere couple of weeks. "You see, Sally lives with women. Sober women. The only man in her immediate reality is her brother, who is also sober. She has practically no experience at all in dealing with adult men who are, well, one doesn't want to slander anyone or appear in any way judgemental so let's just say 'influenced', shall we? Influenced by alcohol consumption." She paused and listened, her eyes slitting, her face assuming the air of someone ready to send the stiletto to the brain. "No, I am not saying the man was drunk at the time," her tone oozed like corn syrup, thick and golden, "but I am saying he was still suffering the effects — or perhaps after-effects — of what can only be thought of as overindulgence. In brief, and to put none too fine a point on it . . . in fact to be as blunt as one can be without being crude . . ." Dropping the Queen Mom, Eve went right into Rambo. ". . . the asshole had a hangover."

She straightened then, and to the silent cheers of her grandchildren, let loose with the salvo. "And I see no reason we, as parenting figures and caregivers, should be required to give our kids a course in how to deal with a hungover power-tripper just to enable them to attend public school which is, after all, supported by our taxes. Before I'll do that, sir, I will personally appear in front of the Board of School Trustees with every member of the class who was present at the time, and if I have to do that I might as well have the newspapers and television with me, and we'll just see who is going to have to apologize to whom before she is allowed back into school!" One hand reached up and adjusted the wig, as if settling it more firmly on her head were tantamount to re-aiming the cannon. "And, good buddy, if I have to do that I might as well clean house all the way to the top because in all my years I've never stood by and watched while some barroom bozo made life miserable for anybody, let alone for a kid who was only trying to get to her seat before the buzzer quit ringing. Thank you so much for your kind interest." She hung up, and they all knew without her saying, the vice principal would be staring at the dead receiver still in his hand.

"Aaaaahhhl right!" Mark cheered.

"Thanks, Gran," Sally sighed happily.

Jean almost asked Eve just who in hell she thought she was, but the thought of what it would kick off in the living room changed her mind. She rolled on her side, the back of the sofa supporting her cough-fatigued lungs, and returned her attention to *Donahue*. Phil was interviewing a mass murderer who had been sentenced to three consecutive life terms with no possibility of parole. The hatchet man was upset because he had written a book and the law didn't allow him to profit from the sales. What, he asked, about the first amendment and my constitutional rights?

Well, really, when you thought about it, what *about* the constitution and the first amendment?

Sally headed back to school the next morning with much the same expression on her face Doc Holliday must have worn as he headed down to the OK Corral to get in on the big fight.

Nothing happened.

No trip to the office, no apology, no late slip needed, she just went to her mechanics course, slipped into her usual place and picked up where she had left off.

Einarr phoned every second or third night after supper, ostensibly to check on how Jean was progressing with her cold and her sinus infection. He spoke to the kids, he asked about their lives and interests, and worked so hard at ignoring the fact his ex-wife was back in their lives that he made it obvious he was flipped right out about it. For years he had been the only grandparent. All the kids' attention was focussed on him. He could do no wrong. He was the one who sent money for them to go to the PNE, he was the one who arrived in a taxi with so many Xmas presents he made Santa look cheap, he was the one who got the school pictures and the copies of prize-winning school compositions, and suddenly, instead of being the big cheese, he was just this old guy they'd known forever, an old guy who lived hours away, and the person he disliked the most was right in front of them, hogging the spotlight.

"He's sure worried about your sinus infection." Mark shook his head wonderingly. "I told him you were feeling better, but . . . he's going to have a phone bill as big as the bathtub."

"He's an old man," Sally said quietly, "and he's far away, and she *is* his only kid. Stands to reason."

"Just be nice to him," Jean sighed, "and be sure to tell him you love him. He's very upset right now."

"Because you're sick?" Mark asked, and Jean realized Mark knew there was more to it than that.

"No," she levelled with her kids, "he can't handle the fact Eve is here."

"Gran?" Sally laughed softly. "Why does that bother *him*?"

"Because she walked out on him." Jean gave it to them baldly, with no frills and no foam rubber to pad the edges. "He came home from a week's fishing and she was gone. No note, no kiss-the-kid-at-bed-time-for-me, no nothing, just gone. Clothes gone. Bank account cleaned out. Gone. And the whole town knew about it before he did."

"Oh," Mark rolled his eyes. "Wow. How to make a guy feel dumb, huh?"

"Worse then than now," Jean agreed.

"Why?" Sally puzzled.

"Nobody ever told *me*," Jean tried to joke. "I was just the rock got hung around my Nana's neck. Nobody explains anything to rocks, right? I wasn't quite five years old. Nobody explains anything to rug rats, either."

"And you still don't know?"

"Nope." She dared to light a cigarette. When it didn't make her cough and throw a lung across the room she took another grateful puff. "So try to make sure one of you answers the phone after supper, okay? It must about freak him out to hear her voice after all these years. He just doesn't want her to steal his kids, is all. He just needs a bit of reassurance and some attention."

And then Einarr found the one certain way to pull the attention away from his ex-wife and back onto himself. He had a heart attack. One of his buddies found him on board the *Old Woman*, sitting slumped over the wheel, already cold.

Jean was so taken aback, so utterly amazed when Eve said she was going up with them for Einarr's funeral, she couldn't even find a way to say she didn't think it a good idea. She just stared, feeling her jaw hanging open like a flycatcher.

"Why not?" Eve demanded, sounding angry. "He *was* my goddamn husband!"

"Hey, I didn't say a word."

"You *looked*."

"Mulroney passed a law against looking?"

"You don't think I should." Eve took most of the chain saw out of her voice.

"Listen, you know what that place is like. You know better than anyone; if you figure you can take it . . . fine."

"You mean their snotty looks and snoopy questions? Hell, I grew up knowing how to take it! You just bet your blue-blooded bippy I can handle *them*," and she headed off to Sally's room to pack her gear.

"Holy wow," Mark breathed, seeing a side to his dear sweet Gran he hadn't before seen.

"Yeah?" Jean sighed. "Just wait until someone looks at her sideways and she dips into her warbag and brings out the heavy artillery. Mark, you are not dealing with the little old doll who makes gingerbread cookies while wearing her designer apron, okay? Even if nobody told me what had gone on that sent her down the pike, I heard more stories than you could shake a stick at about What Eve Did This Time Har-de-Har. I grew up determined not to quarrel or argue because each time I did someone would say Be Careful, she might be another Evie and break your neck."

They took a city bus to the depot, then bought their tickets and went to the bus bay where Maverick Coach Lines was loading for the trip upcoast. Patsy was red-eyed and miserable. As long as she had something to do she could hold it all together but as soon as there was nothing to keep her focussed, her eyes began to leak again. Jean tried to find even one comforting thing to say, and only managed to make Patsy bawl. "Leave her alone," Eve snapped, "There's nothing better than a damn good cry when you're up against something you can't change no matter how badly you want to. She's got every right in the world to cry, he was her Grandpa! You go for it, honey." She gave Patsy a one-armed hug. "Shed a few for me, too. It's been years since I was able to cry for anybody, not even my own self." In honour of the gravity and seriousness of the situation her wig was subdued, almost looked real, might even be mistaken in the gloomy interior of the bus for something that had actually sprouted from human tissue.

They got on the bus and stowed their packs in the overhead bin. Eve sat by a window with Patsy next to her, Sally and Mark sat across the aisle, and Jean sat alone, behind them, where she could keep an eye on Patsy who had a brand new box of tissues on her lap and a paper bag at her feet.

They drove from the depot, through early morning city traffic to the ferry terminal, then waited a half hour until it was time to drive into the belly of the ship. As soon as the bus was parked and the doors open they got off and went up the escalator, turning almost immediately into the coffee shop-cum-cafeteria.

The coffee was dreadful, but they drank it and sat in the cafeteria only occasionally looking out the huge glass windows at the breath-taking scenery sliding past. When the voice crackled from the ceiling, they rose obediently, tossed their disposable cups in the black plastic garbage bags lining the waste bins, and went down to the car deck to reboard their bus.

The drive from one ferry terminal to another could have been enjoyable if they had been making it for any reason except the one they had. The road snaked and twisted along the coastline, flanked by sheer cliffs, cutting through tall stands of towering trees, winding past farms and small holdings, past marinas and charter boat rentals.

They had three-quarters of an hour to wait for the second ferry and spent the time in the chalet-style restaurant near the terminal.

Jean ate a hamburger but couldn't manage her fries so Mark and Sally ate them for her. She smoked as many cigarettes as she could because you couldn't smoke on the bus or on the ferry. Unless you wanted to stand out on the deck and catch bronchitis, because everyone was so health conscious, so freaked out about secondhand cigarette smoke, although they seemed totally unconcerned that the interior of the ferry was entirely swathed in asbestos insulation. Patsy packed away a bowl of chowder and a hamburger, Eve matched her bite for bite and while it was obvious she would have killed for a cold beer, she settled instead for a slice of pie.

Then back onto the bus and into the belly of the ferry. When it pulled away from the dock they were on the deck, pretending to admire the view. But the breeze was stiff, the air cold, and they quickly gave up and went inside, sat at a table and stared at their hands. Eve kept them from going insane by reaching into her enormous purse and pulling out a deck of cards. "Who's for poker?" she asked. The kids stared. "You're kiddin' me," their grandmother said, shocked. "You're not telling me you don't know how to play poker?!" She shuffled the cards expertly. "It's a damn shame, and I don't care who knows I think so," she announced. "Anyone that can't hold up their end in a poker game is a person who's been subjected to child abuse," and she started dealing.

"Not me," Jean said firmly.

"Why not you?"

"Because," Jean said clearly and firmly, "the whole thing bores my ass numb."

"You're kidding."

"I am not kidding."

"You mean you don't know how to play?"

"I know how to play. Einarr made me learn before I was six. I've played more games of poker than most people have had cups of tea, and I vowed, years ago, that I'd never waste my damn time again, not that way."

"Jesus, and all these years they never told me I had a retarded child," Eve laughed, scooping up the cards she had dealt to Jean and adding them to the middle of the pile in her hand.

"How could they tell you?" Jean snapped. "Nobody knew where in hell you were!" and she rose abruptly and walked over to buy a newspaper.

When she got back to the table with it nobody would look at her.

They were too busy making sure they gave their full attention to Eve, who steadfastly refused to rise to the bait Jean had thrown so rudely onto the surface of the family pond.

"So what's the news?" Sally tried to be peacekeeper.

"Well, the leaders of the world have gathered to discuss the problems of children. Again," Jean said, then coughed harshly. Her chest still ached when she coughed, and it still sounded as if there was a ton of something ugly lodged in her lungs. "They've got pictures of them all standing around in two-thousand-dollar suits, shaking manicured hands with each other. I guess they'll dine on oysters Rockefeller and pâté de fois gras, probably put away a case or two of three-hundred-dollar-a-bottle champagne, then hear a report about widespread rickets among children."

"The cost of the fuel to get all those private jets to the same place would probably feed all of Brazil," Sally agreed.

"Yes," Patsy blurted, her eyes blazing with intensity, "and they'll *all* sleep in *lovely* suites because *they're* too important for a mere *room*." Her voice rose, the people at the next table half turned. Patsy raised her voice even more, including most of the other passengers. "And of *course* they'll have to be driven in a *fleet* of limos to *breakfast*, and from there to the *meetings*, so they can get their *pictures* taken and at coffee break there will be *more snackies*, and then of course *lunch*, which will probably be *roast beast* and in the *meantime* the rest of us get to *pay for it* and the kids just go on *starving, starving, STARVING*, and it makes me *sick!*"

"Right *on!*" Mark shouted, pumping a powerfist. "Put 'em up against the wall!"

"Motherfuckers all!" a guy in dirty work jeans and thick dirt-smeared work shirt stood up grinning, yelling from across the lounge. "Anarchy *TODAY!*"

"Now ya done 'er!" Eve said proudly. "Now ya done 'er, Patsy, they's all gonna join in."

The slander and sedition occupied the attention of everyone for the rest of the trip to Saltery Bay. The lounge became one huge living room, the passengers united in their distrust of all politicians. "How'n hell can they claim to be honest if they're in politics?" someone sneered. "It's like military intelligence or peaceful weapon. The thing is self-contradictory."

"Cocksuckers," a woman agreed. "Put 'em in a sacka flour, shake three times, let 'em out and then try to tell one bastard from another!"

Jean tried to bury herself in her newspaper. This was part of why it was she had never regretted leaving. She would have preferred just to leave, not leave and leave and leave one town after another, one house after another, one job after another until it all got so boring she felt she was living inside her own packing crates, but this part of it had never felt like something she had wanted or needed. They all of them took such deep personal pride in hating the government. Any government. Even the one for which they themselves had voted! It was a stance, a routine, a vaudeville act with the audience writing the lines, and her own kids leaping into the middle as if they had cut their teeth on it.

"Oh, *sure*," Patsy said clearly, "it's *fine* for *him*. I mean isn't *he* the one wants *special status*, and isn't *he* the one wants to *separate?* And isn't *he* the one calls out the *army?* For which *we* have to *pay?* If he wants to go *his own way* why doesn't he *pick up his own tab?* I mean *really*, can you *believe* it?"

Just before the ferry pulled into the dock at Saltery Bay the young workie in the stained work clothes smiled at Patsy and stuck out his hand. "I'm Terry Dugan," he offered. "You live around here?"

"Patsy Pritchard." Patsy took his hand. They didn't shake, they just sat there grinning and holding hands. "No, I don't live around here, we're just going up for my grandfather's funeral."

"Ah, hey, I'm sorry about that. Did I know him?" and then before she could answer, his expression changed. "Einarr?" he guessed. Patsy's eyes flooded, she nodded miserably. "Well, hey, will wonders never cease." He squeezed her fingers gently, "I'm off work early myself for just that very thing."

"You knew my grandpa?" a tear slid down her face, she wiped at it with her free hand.

"Who didn't?" Terry Dugan laughed. "There's gonna be more people standin' around that open hole than you'll be able to count, Patsy! I just hope to God when I go people give me as good a sendoff as this is gonna be."

"I'm sorry." Patsy freed her hand from his, used her tissues, wiped her eyes, her nose. "I just keep *crying* about it," she managed. "I try *not* to and . . . I just cry anyway."

"Yeah," he nodded, then patted her knee. "You do 'er," he smiled, "Just do 'er until you don't have to do 'er no more." He pulled a filthy little note pad from his shirt pocket, dug a pencil stub from somewhere and scrawled busily. "If you need to take a walk or anythin' you just phone here. If I'm not there they'll know where I am. I'll come'n'get you and walk with you, okay?"

"Thank you," she sniffed.

Back on the bus Jean sat with her arms crossed, her back to the window, glaring at the rubber mat in the aisle of the bus. She tried to figure out who or what she was mad at; not Patsy, not Sally, not Mark, not even Eve, and certainly not Terry Dugan who had driven off the ferry in a dust-covered mud-smeared near-new four-wheel-drive pickup.

The bus took them as far as what was generally called the depot but was, in fact, nothing more than the parking lot of a small mini-mall where one of the shopkeepers looked after incoming and outgoing freight.

Half a dozen people waited under the overhang of the roof, leaning against the wall, as patient as cows under an apple tree waiting for another wormy one to fall to the ground. They straightened expectantly as the bus slowed, then stopped.

Bill Fergus was one of them. Uncle Bill. Einarr's brother-in-law, married to Einarr's sister, Alice, who obviously hadn't come to wait for them. Maybe she knew Eve was coming. That would be enough to keep Alice away from her own funeral! He tugged at his jacket nervously, then rammed his huge hands in his pockets. The corners of his pockets had been reinforced with little triangles of canvas and almost solid patches of strong machine stitching. Aunt Alice knew how many pairs of otherwise good pants had been ruined because the pockets had been frapped by Bill's huge hands and his habit of stuffing them out of sight.

"Hey," he said by way of greeting.

"Hey yourself." Jean moved into his hug, rested her face against his barrel chest.

"You okay?"

"I'm okay. You?"

"Yeah. Alice is bust up about it, but not so bad today. Soon's she knew you were comin' she felt better."

Jean watched Bill with the kids, saw how pleased they were that he didn't say My How You've Grown or I'd Have Known You Anywhere. He treated them like strangers from a far-off planet, but strangers deserving of respect. And then Eve stepped forward and Bill straightened slowly.

"Bill. . ." Eve sounded calm but Jean wondered if she really was or if she had just, over the years, learned how to out-act Katherine Hepburn.

"Evelyn," Bill's voice was so noncommittal Jean wondered if he'd understudied Spencer Tracy.

"You're looking well," Eve smiled coolly.

"I am well. Yourself?" but he turned just a fraction of a second too soon for her to be able to say more. Unless she wanted to talk to his right ear. "Plenty of room in the trunk for luggage." He moved to his car, opened the trunk and waited for the kids to bring the packs. The driver had the luggage and freight bays open, was slinging stuff to the damp blacktop for others to claim or deal with.

Eve sat in the back with Sally and Patsy, Mark sat by the door with Jean between him and Bill. "Is it far?" he asked. "I don't remember."

"Twenty minutes, twenty-five," Bill answered calmly. "Been a long long time since you were up here, Markie."

"Mark."

"Sorry," he grinned. "Shoulda known better. Nobody quit calling me Billy until I was big enough to kick ass and had actually done it a few times."

"Yeah," Mark laughed softly, "well, I'll be big enough soon. And then," he dug Jean in the ribs gently, "then, by God, look out!"

The pulp mill was brightly lit, the plumes of smoke rising thick above the bay, blowing back over the town, gathering in the little bowl of a valley that formed the lake where everyone's drinking water was collected. One minute they couldn't smell it, the next minute they could. "Holy old lordy!" Mark gasped. "Did something big *die?*"

"Hey, that's the smell of money," Bill teased. "That's bread'n'butter in this town. . ." He glared at the lights, the scunge, the noise hammering them from inside the concrete walls. "Biggest and most filthy mill in the entire country," he pretended to brag. "Not many places can make that claim!"

In the back seat Eve sat quietly, not looking at the mill or at the scenery. Anything she might have been thinking and feeling was stored safely behind a calm facade, and if Jean hadn't known the history, or at least some of it, she might have thought everything between her mother and her uncle was fine. But she did know the history, and she knew that whatever else their relationship was, it was not fine.

And yet Eve sat in the back seat between her granddaughters, looking as if the Queen Mom had learned from her how to appear regal in a gas guzzler. And Bill steered the car with a casual grace that belied any hint that beneath his skin a volcano was simmering.

Closer to half an hour than twenty minutes later, Bill parked the car in the old man's driveway. Jean just sat, staring at the place, the one that had been "home" even after she had left it as far behind as she could.

No fence, not even any real walkway to the door, the house snugged behind a couple of lilac bushes almost big enough to be called trees, even here where *tree* did not mean what it meant in the stunted interior. Foxgloves grew where they had decided they wanted to grow, especially along the waist-high wood board fence between the old man's place and the smaller place next door.

"You ready for this?" Bill asked quietly.

"Sure. As ready as I'll ever be, I guess." She reached for the doorlatch and took a deep breath.

The lights were on in the kitchen and hallway. You'd have thought the old man had just stepped outside for a few minutes and would be back any time now to put on the kettle, make tea and welcome them all. She could smell all the things that had always meant home: those sniffs, scents, and smells which nobody would ever be able to identify individually, but which together meant warmth, light, safety and stress.

The neighbours had been there. Someone had placed a large bouquet of flowers on the table. She knew there would be food in the fridge. Probably a casserole or two, undoubtedly a big bowl of potato salad and a platter of sliced meats.

"Oh, God." She sat down suddenly, her eyes flooding. "Oh God, damn!"

"Yeah," Bill nodded, moving to turn on the gas under the kettle. "Doesn't seem real until . . ." He didn't finish, but she knew what he meant. "Why don't you show the kids where the bedrooms are," he mumbled. Jean got off her chair and left the kitchen, suspecting Bill needed time alone to haul his big red-with-white-spots hanky from his back pocket and wipe the mist from his eyes. Eve followed Jean and the kids trailed after them, bringing the luggage.

She took the old man's bedroom for her own. If there were ghosts to be faced down, better she do it than leave them for the kids to deal with. And somehow it seemed too bizarre to expect Eve to stay in that room and sleep in what might once have been the marital bed.

Jean half expected Eve to stay upstairs, unpacking or something, rather than try to keep herself intact in the face of Bill's total refusal to acknowledge her presence. She might have been invisible for all the notice he seemed to take. He had said hello, and then she might well have dropped into the Grand Canyon, without a sound to signify her fall. But Eve was first one back downstairs, and Eve was the one bringing out the tea canister, rinsing the brown betty tea pot in hot water, getting ready to make them all a relaxing warm drink which, from the look around his eyes, Bill thought might poison him.

"Einarr's down to the funeral home," Bill blurted. "They've got what they call 'viewing' tomorrow. Some kind of little prayer service or something tomorrow evening. Funeral the day after. I guess they kind of expect some members of the family to be present for the viewing and the prayer service. But I guess folks would understand if you didn't. The trip and all. . . ."

"Who made the. . .the. . ."

"Alice'n'me." He looked down at the table, his thick fingers tracing the red pattern of squares on the white oilcloth. "Einarr had been pretty outspoken about what he did and didn't want. No church service. No big fuss. For a while he talked of cremation, but then decided he wasn't going to do that. Said he'd already paid for space next to the rest of the family and he wasn't going to buy six by six by three and then plant a little jug in the middle and waste the rest of 'er," he grinned crookedly. "God alone knows what his real reasons were, you know how he'd say those awful damn things just to get a rise out of people."

"Like the time people were going door-to-door collecting money because the minister had been transferred," Jean laughed suddenly, turned to Patsy. "I guess what they really wanted was to buy a going-away gift or something but we're just finishing supper and knock-knock at the door and I answer and here are these nice ladies standing there and they're talking away about how the minister has been transferred and they're collecting money and Einarr hollers from the kitchen Let the goddamn church buy his ticket, they're the ones transferring him!" She laughed and Patsy grinned faintly.

Eve poured tea all round and only Bill ignored it. Jean knew Eve knew Bill was refusing to drink it simply because Eve had made it.

And Jean knew Bill knew Eve knew. She wondered if they both knew she wished they'd just put a cap on it. Any kind of hatred mutually sustained for more than a year or two becomes a total bore to the rest of the world.

"Buncha papers on the sideboard in the living room. Need to be signed." Bill pushed back his chair, patted Jean's shoulder. "Lawyering stuff, funeral stuff, things like that. Sorry to burden you but they wouldn't accept Alice'n'me's signatures."

She walked him to the front door and kissed his cheek gratefully.

"Thank you," she whispered.

"Why'd you bring 'er?" he demanded.

"You ever try to say No to her?" Jean countered, knowing she was avoiding years and years of crap.

"Why'd she come?"

"If you'd bothered to talk to her you might have asked her yourself," Jean said, but he shook his head, then shrugged.

"See if I give a shit," he invited gruffly. "You take care, okay? I'll be round tomorrow morning to check on you. Alice'd prob'ly like to come." He moved faintly in the direction of explosion. "Don't know if she will with Eve makin' the tea, though."

"I'll make the tea," Jean promised.

"Too bad you couldn't deep-six her," he grumbled.

Jean lay awake staring at the ceiling, her mind racing around like a mouse looking for a way into the cheese cupboard. Any time she, herself, had felt the least bit out of place she had wanted to leave immediately. And hot on the heels of wanting to leave came needing to leave, a physical urge probably rooted in the fight-or-flight instinct. That need to leave did not subside, it grew, feeding on itself and on her own paranoia until her hands were sweating, her fingers trembling, her brain unable to keep track of conversations, the clenched knot in her stomach radiating nausea. How could Eve just sit there, smooth as cream, smiling that gentle little smile she had taught the Queen Mom, nodding her head slightly whenever the person who hated her most said something the least bit sensible.

Christ, she had to know! Eve had been born here, grew up here, if indeed she had ever really grown up. She knew the rules, and she knew the ways those who broke or ignored those rules were regarded, and treated. You could fuck around on your spouse until hell froze over and as long as you kept it quiet and didn't rub the spouse or anybody else's nose in the mess, nobody would care. In fact, they would work just as hard at keeping it all quiet as you did. Harder, perhaps, depending on whether or not your play-partner was married, and if so, how many kids he or she had. You were supposed to keep the kids from knowing. Everybody knew, or at least everybody said everybody knew, that kids were mean little fucks and would make life miserable for any kid whose parents were out of line. So don't let the kids know. But Eve hadn't cared who knew. Eve didn't bend the rules, she didn't break the rules, she didn't even smash the rules, she just grabbed hold of the rules and heaved them in all directions at once and then left the Devil to laugh at the losers.

She had to know she was about as welcome as a wet toilet seat, especially now, with all of Einarr's friends feeling raw and abandoned. And still she just sat at the table and put on her Canasta Queen imitation, with her unwitting grandchildren pouring diesel on the inferno by doting on her. When you gave society's rules a kick in the slats you were supposed to pay for it, especially when you got older. You were supposed to look around one day and realize you were old, and lonely as hell, and it was all your fault for having been a tacky shit. Any time anyone got served a pile of shit sandwiches, what was the consolation they got from everyone around them if not the assurance that one day the chickens will come home to roost and vengeance will be done. Instead, there was Eve, with Patsy asking if she needed a pillow for her back and Sally leaping up to get it as if the safety of the world depended on dear old Gran's comfort. That wasn't how her life was supposed to be. She was supposed to be sitting in a third-floor cold water walk-up in Chinatown, living on weak tea and aged crackers, slopping around in a faded and half-bald chenille bathrobe, and no slippers, just fifty-cents-on-sale dark blue canvas sneakers from Taiwan on her feet. She was supposed to hobble because her legs were roped with varicose veins from hours and hours of streetwalking, she was supposed to sit at a filthy window, her grey hair straggling past her shoulders, hanging untidily in her face, falling over her forehead and into her eyes while she stared out past the pigeon shit at the rubbies like herself lurching sideways past the gin mills and dope dens. Weak tears of self-pity were supposed to slide down her faded harridan face and soak the front of her robe, and she was supposed to light another home rollie cigarette and hold it in fingers stained orange by nicotine while she sobbed remorse for a life of sin and low-rent shit.

Instead she was at her dead ex-husband's table, with maybe three hundred fifty dollars of Eva Gabor wig heaped in gravity-defying swirls and loops on her head, pouring tea with the kind of kiss-my-ass-you-fuckin'-peasant hauteur the governor general's wife displayed. Up your nose with a rubber hose you fuckin' loser. May the bird of paradise fly up your gee-gee, and would you like another cup of tea.

And Uncle Bill just sitting there, waves of fury coming from him, his hands clasped around the cup as if he were cold and needed to warm them. But he'd die of thirst in the Sahara before he'd have so much as one sip.

Why hadn't she just stayed in Vancouver? God-Jesus-Mary'n'the Angels they'd come to bury Einarr not disinter the scandal! But the scandal was unburied again. The scandal had on its black fishnet stockings and its bright red skin-tight above-the-knee red satin dress. Its hair hung past its shoulders, it had a deep red rose clutched between its pearly whites and it was sauntering down the main street humming Love For Sale. And Eve had turned the scandal-bitch loose on purpose! The entire town had once told her kiss my ass. Now she was back, smiling widely and saying Take your ass off your shoulders, put it where I can reach and I'll kick it over the moon.

It was Einarr, no doubt about it. It wasn't true that he looked as
if he'd just gone to sleep. He had always slept on his side, his
knees drawn up, his hair rumpled, his face relaxed. Here he lay flat
on his back, his hands folded across his little paunch, legs straight,
hair combed more neatly than Jean had ever seen it in her life. And
there was a faint blue to his lips and chin the undertaker's skill had
not been able to remove. She wanted to throw her arms around him,
lift him from that awful damn box, sit with him cradled against her,
and love him back to life again. She wanted to put her head on his
chest and sob for all the times she could have come to visit and hadn't.
She wanted to at least kiss his cheek, but her horror of dead flesh kept
her distanced. "Oh, Poppa," she mourned.

"Even if you didn't know he was dead, you'd know he was dead,
right?" Mark took her hand, held it gently. "I mean. . . if you just
walked in out of the rain or somethin', you'd take one look and know.
I never saw a dead person before but. . . Gramps looks dead. Not like
in the movies at all."

"You going to be okay?"

"Yeah. Yeah I thought I'd, well, you know, puke or something
maybe," his face was white, and he was sweating, the hand holding
hers trembled, as did his voice, but she believed him. She knew her
son, the baby of the family, would be okay. "I was kind of bent outta
shape before we left the house, but Gran, she said everybody who
gets born is gonna die, and I thought about that, and it's true, and I
don't know why, but that helped."

Good old Gran the eastern philosopher, maybe change her name to Mahatma Grandma, she there in the auburn wig, the auburn almost-afro wig, Jesus Christ she looks like a brillo pad gone rusty, doesn't she have any idea how to dress, how to act, how to *be*? Where in hell was the geriatric guru when it was Nana they were burying? Where in hell was old Metaphor of the Mountain when I walked in from school with my grade ten stuff under my arm and there she was on the kitchen floor with the spatula not three inches from her outstretched hand? And Einarr at sea. And everyone whispering to themselves that she might have lived years longer if she'd ever been given any chance at all to rest, but no, poor old thing, all the work and responsibility . . . except by then, and for more than a couple of years, I'd been babysitting her instead of the other way around, and damn it, they all ought to have known that. Part of her had gone to la-la land, I had to make sure she was dressed before I left for school or she'd be as apt as not to push her shopping cart down to the store wearing nothing but her nightgown. If that.

Patsy wanted to scream. Patsy wanted to open her mouth and just let 'er rip, but she was the oldest, and if she flipped her wig the other two might do the same, and that would be a great howdy-do. She wanted to scream, and then tell the whole world that whatever was lying in that coffin, it had nothing at all to do with her Grampy. It didn't even *smell* right. Grampy smelled of Juicy Fruit gum and Mennen Aftershave, and sometimes, when he swooped you up and swung you, he smelled of those big round Scotch mints, too, because he had a bag of them in his left front shirt pocket, and when you'd gone around the world two or three times he'd sit you on his left hip and you could rummage for your treat. And when you were older, and too big to swing around the world, he hugged, hard, and tight, and slipped money into your pocket. He didn't smell like disinfectant!

"You okay?" Eve asked.

"Yes. It's just . . . saying goodbye is so *hard*!"

"Sure is," Eve agreed.

"For you, too?"

"Of course for me, too." Eve dabbed at her eyes with a tissue. "Hell, I thought I'd already said goodbye to him!"

"Is this harder?"

"No." Eve stuffed the tissue back in her shiny black purse. "No, this is a piece of cake compared to the last time."

Jean and the kids took turns all day sitting in the little side room, listening to the dreary recorded music, on tap like cheap beer, in case any of Einarr's friends wanted to come over, shake hands, give words of cheer or comfort. Einarr had more friends than anyone else in the world, and they all did their best to help hold the family together. It was exhausting. It was half a step away from macabre. It was a short quick course on how to put behind you what needed to be put in its place. By mid-evening they were all drained. The tears had been shed and a numb, tired acceptance had taken over, leaving them calm. Eve, thank God, had not offered to spell any of them. Even she, with bones and blood of brass, knew there were limits.

What she did do was start at one end of the house and move through it like Mrs. Clean. The neighbours had tidied up, but respecting the family's need for privacy, had made no move to sort, discard or pack any personal stuff. Eve had no such hesitation. Anything and everything that could possibly be tossed away she grabbed, folded neatly, stuffed into boxes, then carried out to the garage and stacked, ready to be taken off to the Salvation Army.

When Jean got home at nine that night and went to lie down for a half hour or so, the room which had been Einarr's smelled of Mrs. Murphy's wood soap. The closet was bare, the dresser drawers empty, and the room suddenly as impersonal as if she had been staying at the Alcazar.

"Why?" she asked.

"Think about it," Eve answered briskly "while you're bringing your stuff for tomorrow down for me to sponge and press."

"Evelyn . . ."

"Just do 'er darlin'." Eve's eyes sparkled with unshed tears.

"There's some stuff of his Mark might like to have."

"It can be gone through later," Eve snapped. "But what you don't need to do right now is have a bath, then go up to that room and sit on the floor of the closet holding his jacket against your face and bawlin' yourself into a goddamn nervous breakdown!"

"Oh." And she wondered if Eve had done that very thing while everyone else was down at the funeral home.

Rituals are handy. Rituals give you something to do at a time when there is really nothing for you to do. There aren't any professional mourners to hire any more, no public tearing of hair or rending of garments. Nobody has to get all the stuff together to chop off fingers or hack off noses or sacrifice animals and smear the blood around for the appeasement of the departed. All you have to do is put one foot in front of the other and follow what shreds of ritual are left.

And then there you are in a graveyard at the top of a hill, looking out over the roofs of the town, concentrating on watching the sunlight sparkle on the water, listening to someone you don't know drone on about life eternal and everlasting and the soul of the faithful departed.

She heard something that cut across the words of the young minister like a battle-axe going through a plate glass window and setting off the burglar alarm. The mourners jerked around, surprised and shocked. The young minister stopped talking, his mouth still open, and across the graveyard came Bill, his bagpipes yowling.

"The catawumpus!" Jean blurted. A giggle burst from her throat. Someone else laughed, several grinned, and then everyone began to clap. Bill just kept playing, walking toward them, bringing the yowling closer and closer until it was almost more than the human head could endure. Jean wondered if bagpipes ever got out of tune. If they did that might be part of what was so awful about Bill's music, if anyone in her right mind could call it music. And then Terry Dugan began to sing, very very softly, too softly for the young preacher to hear and take offence but loudly enough for Einarr's friends to hear and smile appreciatively: "Some had their boots and stockin's, some had nane at'a, some had naught but big bare airses, comin through McGrogan's draw."

Bill Fergus walked slowly back and forth in front of the mourners, the catawumpus yowling, tears slickering from his eyes and down his tanned, creased face. The screeching and wailing strengthened, took its own form, grabbed itself by its own sox and changed from something to send every dog in the district running for the bush to something so sad you could believe, for a few minutes at least, the banshee was real, and had come with the clans across the sea to a new land. And then they were all singing "Amazing Grace" and Jean could let Einarr go, really let him go, singing in a harsh whisper because her throat was tight with sobs. Terry Dugan didn't sing in a whisper, he tilted his head back and just let 'er rip, and so did Aunt Alice, and all the others who had known Einarr, laughed with him, argued with him, fished with him, got drunk with him, maybe even fist-fought with him over something totally unimportant, like politics or who had dared cork whose nets or lines.

Eve stood with her grandchildren, and did not sing. Nor did she cry. She just stood and watched Bill Fergus, and when the last wheezing notes had faded she said, loud enough to be heard by all, loud enough to insult most, "Thank you."

Bill turned slowly, his eyes focussed on her briefly, then passed, as if there were nothing there except maybe a shadow, probably the shadow of a large pile of manure. He rested his eyes, finally, on Jean. "Time to go home, honey," he said.

"Yes," she nodded, and turned and walked away from Einarr's grave. The kids followed, Mark and Sally solicitously holding their grandmother's arms, as if Eve were too feeble to walk by herself. The little buggers are doing it on purpose! Jean realized. Rubbing Bill's nose in it. Rubbing everyone's nose in it. And Eve, damn her, is playing it right to the hilt. You'd think she'd been entwined in their lives since birth! Since before birth, for God's sake.

Maybe since before the birth of the Gods themselves.

And it continued back at the house. Nobody could ignore Eve. Nobody could pretend Einarr had never been married. Nobody could try to continue the conspiracy. The kids hauled platters of sliced meat from the fridge and put them out, they produced potato salads, green salads and six-bean salads. A roast turkey was hauled out of the oven and sliced, a bowl was filled with stuffing, another with cranberry sauce. Eve had been doing more than cleaning house, and everyone knew it. While the others had been going through their ritual during the viewings, Eve had been up to her pencilled eyebrows in another sort of ritual. And since nobody knew which potato salad Eve had made and which ones other women had made, there was no way they could ignore hers and only touch the ones made by decent, respectable, socially acceptable women. Nor could they tell Eve's sliced ham from someone else's sliced ham. If any of it stuck in their throats only they knew. Or cared.

"Come on," Terry Dugan said firmly, "get some of this down you."

"I'm not hungry," Patsy smiled faintly, sniffed back tears.

"Didn't ask if you were hungry, babe," he shook his head and smiled, "just told you to eat it, is all. Come on, you might not feel hungry, but you know what they say, if you don't eat you don't shit and if you don't shit you get sick as a pig and maybe die."

"Christ," Eve said at Jean's elbow, "they don't get any smoother, do they? I remember Einarr saying something very similar to me, once."

"Yeah. But you notice she took it and she's picking at it."

"You okay?"

"I'm okay. You?"

"I'm fine!" Eve laughed softly. "There's a few others here who are just about ready to shit themselves blind, but I'm doing just fine."

Mark stood by the fridge hauling out beer, twisting off the caps and handing bottles to the thirsty. Sally reigned over the wine and filled little plastic glasses to the brim for women who nodded, smiled and spoke quietly to her. Patsy moved around the room with Terry Dugan filling in for Spike the Faithful Guard Dog and Eve just kept rubbing other people's noses in something Jean wished had been buried with Einarr.

Aunt Alice one-upped her hated once-sister-in-law, however. She did not come to the house. Nobody could remember a time a close member of the family had refused to go from graveside to house. They'd talk about it for at least another generation.

Mercifully, time passed, people left, and Jean was able to find a quiet place to sit, blessedly alone. She read the heap of papers Bill had warned her about, signed what needed signed, and stared at the pattern in the carpet on the floor. Big pink roses against a background now faded but once rich blue. She had never thought it was lovely, or even very nice, and yet tonight it seemed almost beautiful.

She heard Terry Dugan's pickup stop outside the house, and waited for long, very long minutes before Patsy came in the front door. "You okay, Mom?" Patsy asked from the doorway.

"I'm fine, dear."

"Why don't you turn on the *light*? Why are you sitting in the *dark*?"

"I'm fine," Jean repeated, sighing. "I just wanted to have some time alone, to think."

"*Think*?" Patsy made it sound like something nobody in their right mind would bother doing. "About what?"

"About what to do with the house, the furniture, all that stuff."

"Oh, that's *easy*," Patsy laughed softly. "Just *sell* it, Mom. Everything."

"Sell it, huh."

"*Sure*, why not? Then you can *sit* me *down* and have that *talk* you enjoy so much, about how I have to *figure* out what I *want* out of life and go for it. Only *this* time, instead of saying I need *time*, I'll say *great*, and give you the scoop on *computers* and *college* and all that *good stuff*."

"You will, huh?"

She didn't bother telling Patsy the alternative idea she was toying with. She kept it to herself. She waited, patient as a sunning snake, letting her mind take all the time it needed to come around to what she knew she had already half decided to do before she had even hung up after that awful phone call. They were back in the city before she dropped the bomb on them.

"You're out of your *mind*!" Sally shouted angrily. "I am *not* going to *do* this."

"You sound like *Patsy*!" Jean laughed.

"And *you* sound like someone just turned loose from the fruit-and-nut farm! Give your head a shake, Mom. A good hard shake."

"Ah, Mom, you're kiddin', I hope," Mark moaned.

"I'm not kidding. You can stop screaming and yelling and sit yourselves down and look at the figures if you want. If we got top price for everything, which we probably wouldn't, by the way, it would only make things a bit easier for maybe five years. And then there we'd be, where we are right now."

"Five years from now," Sally screeched, "will I care?"

"Then why should I care now?" Jean countered. "If you don't care about *me* am I still under some moral obligation to give two hoots in hell about *you*?"

"Mom!" Sally gaped, shocked.

"I'm tired, Sally. I'm tired of moving, I'm tired of coming home from work and facing a house that looks as if the roaches are moving out before the place falls down, I'm tired of knowing that there isn't anywhere within two hours of this shitty place that's any better, and I'm tired of knowing any job I get could be gone the day after tomorrow. I'm tired of noise, and stink, and rudeness, and I'm tired of wondering if the next time they blow the window apart with their toys they might take my head as well."

"But Mom, my God, to move? *Up there*?"

"What if I won't go?" Mark asked defiantly.

"Don't," Jean shrugged. "I'm sure if you'd rather stay with your dad I could learn to live with your decision."

"You mean that?"

"Think about it. Think about everything I've said. Then answer your question yourself," and she walked out the room, leaving them to moan and bitch to each other.

"What in hell *for*?" Eve asked.

"I sat in that living room and looked around and knew that unless I won the 6/49 I'd never have that kind of comfort and security. Put that house down on any lot in this city and only the doctors and lawyers would be able to afford it."

"But there's no *work* up there," Eve argued.

"What the hell is there for work down here? What in hell is there that's worth getting out of bed to go and do?" Jean shouted. "Out of work down here I have to pay *nine hundred a month* just to live in a rat's nest. Out of work up there I'm comfortable and have nothing to worry about except getting together a couple of hundred dollars a year for taxes! What *is* it with everyone all of a sudden that they think I'm made of money?"

"Easy, easy," Eve soothed. "No need to get upset."

"What about *me*?" Patsy shook with fury. "What about *me* and *college* and the *computer course*?"

"What about it?" Jean parried. "Aren't you the one stood in the doorway and told me you were *free, twenty-one* and *capable* of making your *own* decisions? And didn't you make them? And aren't you on your own, now, with your own little crackerbox apartment and everything?"

"Well, isn't that *nice*!" Patsy blustered. "Isn't that just *too* nice!"

"You want to learn computers? There are night classes."

"After a hard day's work I should go to *school*?"

"Why not? *I've* done more than that after a hard day's work. You can go dancing for six hours, you can sit in a classroom for two!"

"And go forever, I suppose. Two hours here, two hours there . . . full time is how you learn!"

"Then go to the retraining people. Get them to sponsor you."

"Oh wow!" Patsy went into high gear. "I just *love* the kind of *help* and *support* you get around here! A person could *die* and would anyone care?"

"Probably not," Jean agreed, "especially if you'd been in one of *these* goddamn moods just prior to the heart attack."

Sally walked around looking as if she was ready to chew out someone's throat. "Great," she muttered, "just great. Get to live like a toad under a leaf. Marrrr-vee, as they used to say. Be lucky if the school has joined the twentieth century. Probably wear ankle-length skirts and those funny little bonnets. Probably no soccer team. Get to bake brownies in home ec, instead."

"She said if I didn't like it I could live with *him*," Mark agreed. "Wouldn't that be more fun than you'd want to have to describe. Get to listen to him blow hot air and good old wotzername smilin' around and treating me like I was still in kindy-gardy with those rug rats of hers."

"Maybe we could stay with Gran?" Sally dared hope.

"Yeah. Sure. I can just see her making ends meet on her pension. And it would mean we'd wind up having to live with Patsy, too. . . Pardon me," a ghost of a grin managed to surface, "*and* it would *mean* we'd wind *up* having to *live* with *Patsy*, too."

"Probably her *voice* is what's putting the *holes* in the *ozone* layer," Sally growled.

They nodded at each other, and reached for their jackets. When in misery seek company.

Sally insisted she wasn't going, but she went. Mark looked as if he expected at any minute to be lined up against the wall and told to face the firing squad but he packed his things and got ready to go, too. Patsy wasn't talking to Jean but she would still talk and listen to Sally, so Jean got Sally to pass on the invitation for Patsy to choose any of the furniture for herself. When Patsy said she wasn't interested because she didn't have any place to *put* it in her *little* crackerbox Jean said fine, and went down to talk to the young couple who rented the bottom suite. They were overjoyed. Of course when Patsy found out she had another fit, but by then nobody was paying much attention to her dramatics. They didn't even have to lug stuff down the steep and rickety stairs because the young couple were moving up into the place as soon as Jean and the kids moved themselves out of it. Friends were moving in with them, and they would share all expenses. "She's got a kid, too," the young mother confided, "but she's got office experience, so she's going to get a job and I'll stay with the kids and make supper. It'll work out," she said stoutly, and Jean could only hope it would.

Except for the constant insurrections, rebellions and minor civil skirmishes, it all happened much more easily than Jean had dared hope. A month and a half after Einarr's funeral Jean, Mark and Sally, with their clothes and personal treasures packed in sturdy boxes and stowed beneath the bus, were on their way back upcoast.

"I'm glad Gran and Patsy decided to get a place together," Mark mumbled. "I can't see either one of them making out very well on their own. Not really on their own."

"Patsy's been on her own for almost two years!" Sally argued.

"Nah, anytime she wound up painted in a corner she just had to reach for the old blower and she got bailed out."

"Well, yeah, but, still,"

"Gran'll look after her."

Jean rolled her eyes, pulled her collar up around her ears and scrunched down in the bus seat, closing her eyes and concentrating on paying as little attention as possible to the conversation in the seat behind her. All she had to do right now was let the bus deliver her, get off the bus, grab her boxes, stuff them in the trunk of Bill's car and let him deliver her to the old house. She had done what she could do, she had done what she needed to do, she'd done as much as she could do and now she was a parcel herself, being delivered.

It felt so good to let go that she fell asleep.

They left Vancouver at eight-thirty in the morning, got off the bus at two in the afternoon, and were in the old house by four. The nittering and bickering over who got which room took less than half an hour, the unpacking and putting away took another hour and a half. By six-thirty the empty boxes were in the garage, stacked neatly along one wall, and Mark and Sally were ooohing and aaahing over the fifty-six Chev Einarr had seldom driven.

Jean made supper, and the kids came in and ate like dragonflies, which consume the equivalent of their own body weight every day. Then finally, blessedly, the dishes were done and they could all head off to bed.

It didn't seem like her own room yet, but it didn't seem like a motel, either. She turned off her light and lay on her side watching the rain stream down the windowpane. Faint light softened the night, the lights of the marina beaconing in the storm. A gentle tinkle tinkle wafted from the bells on the stabilizer poles of the fish boats and somewhere out in the misty dark a buoy ding-ding-dinged regularly. The foghorn squawked from Rebekah reef, and something with a set of big engines was moving downcoast, the rumble muted by the damp, reassuring and soothing. The oil furnace kicked in, startling her, and she sleepily considered getting up and turning down the thermostat to save on fuel. Somewhere she had heard you could save one-third your fuel costs if you turned off the heat at night. She'd do it tomorrow. She was too warm, too cozy, too snugged down to get up and pad barefoot across the floor. It would wake her up and she didn't want to be awake, she was tired. You sleep on a bus and it's more exhausting than if you'd stayed awake!

The *Old Woman* was moored securely to the dock, her decks wet with last night's rain, her paint only slightly faded. Einarr had always taken good care of her, and it showed.

Jean stood with her hands stuffed deep in the pockets of Einarr's warm jacket, her feet snug in two pair of socks inside her gumboots with the tops turned down. Tommy had always teased her about it, said you could always tell a real coastie because they wore gumboots with red soles and black tops, and, like the Indians, turned the tops over, exposing the grey lining. "It keeps the gumboots from rubbing your leg and leaving little purply chafe marks," she explained over and over and over, while he laughed as if the explanation was as much something to be as mocked as the thing being explained.

She stepped from the dock to the deck and walked around looking at what had become hers. Of all the things in the world she had never thought of wanting, getting, owning or having, a fish boat was at the top of the list.

The wheelhouse door had a lock and she had a key but didn't need it: Einarr never locked up his boat. Jean went inside and rubbed her hand along the wooden dashboard, stared at the glass faces of the dials, gauges and thingamajigs, some original, some installed later. Enough electronic crap here to navigate your way around the world. Twice.

Out the window she could see the general store and post office, the pub and hard bar, the marine sales, service and fuel distributors, and enough dogs to fill the needs of a major city. Big dogs, small dogs, fat dogs, too many skinny dogs, shaggy dogs, shivering dogs and all of them wandering back and forth on the beach sniffing at dead crabs and tide-stranded flopping fish. Not one of them seemed to belong to anybody. Not one of them seemed to have eaten recently. A big shaggy black mutt that looked as if somewhere in its background lurked a Newfoundland and somewhere else lurked a Bouvier came sauntering down the tidal line with a string of unidentifiable guts trailing from its jaws. The sand-sniffers caught sight of the mess and raced off eagerly, snatching bits and ripping them loose. The big black mutt gulped what he could and when the whole pinkish-grey mess was gone he turned around and headed back in the direction he had just come, probably in search of more. Half a dozen others followed.

Above the console, framed and bolted to the wall, was the official paper that went with the metal "B" licence screwed to the outside wall of the wheelhouse. Jean stared at it and sighed deeply. Way to go, Einarr. A "B" licence. Worth about half the price of the paper it was printed on. She'd had the story, chapter and verse, from the Fisheries asshole. Whoopyding and nobody had told her. And why not? Had they assumed she already knew? Had they decided to let her find out for herself because what you learn the hard way you remember? Or did they just need a good laugh to help November on its way?

A "B" was non-transferable.

"You could sell the boat," the Fisheries idiot had suggested.

"Sell a fish boat with no fishing licence?"

"A lot of people are buying them up and turning them into pleasure craft." He smiled as if he thought this was something great, something of which the feds ought to be proud. "They're very seaworthy and when you haul out the fish hold and put in some living space, well, you've got a fine little yacht."

"Yeah. And you've got one less workie out there making wages."

The ay-hole yammered on about diminished fish stocks and the need to cut down on the number of boats, as if it were the fault of the little guys the fish had nearly vanished. Instead of a thousand boats supporting a thousand families we wind up with five big bastards out there scraping the bottom, pulling in more fish than ever, driving down the prices and sending the profits to the corporations while the people who used to feed their families in this industry sit on welfare and watch numbly as their boats rot on the beach. And they call it progress.

Progress, she figured, was what happened when people who not only didn't live here but probably had never even visited gave orders which sent other people's lives into nosedives. Progress was what happened when some lugan in an air conditioned office somewhere comes back from drinking his power lunch and decides to lean on the gomer two rungs below him on the ladder. And the gomer leans on the jerk who in turn leans on the dipper who can't go home feeling manly unless he leans on the next guy down the pyramid. And after all that leaning, progress happens, and the guys who never got to make any of the decisions or do any of the leaning, or even any of the drinking of the power lunches, get told to go out and clearcut all the way to the edge of what had been for thousands of years a productive spawning creek. Never mind the regulation which requires a strip of trees be left to protect the bank from erosion, never mind that the machinery is never supposed to go into or through the creek, never mind all that damn tree-hugging bullshit nonsense, just rev up the old Stihl and hack 'er down, gnaw off the limbs, load 'er on a truck and haul 'er off to be graded, then send the raw logs off to Japan or some other fleabite on the ass of the world. Progress is when the same downward decision making happens in other places and roads get put where no road ought ever go, and the oil sprayed to keep the dust from blinding the drivers of the trucks hauling out the old growth is washed by rain into creeks and streams where it poisons the young fish. Progress for Christ's sake is when you can use their own figures to prove there was more money taken out of the taxpayers' pockets and pumped into the board rooms than ever came back to the people by way of stumpage fees or taxes. Very much more fuckin' progress and we're all going to be walking around with our ass ends hanging out of our worn-out jeans and our stomachs asking our spines if our throats have been cut.

But sitting glaring at the depth sounder isn't going to solve anything. You can't use your "B" licence and go out and catch salmon. You can't live forever on unemployment enjoyment. So think, you dumb shit, think. Maybe you can fix this thing up and get a permit to take tourists out sports fishing. Maybe you can run a charter boat. Maybe you can run drugs and actually feed your kids! Already Jean had heard about the so-called fish farm where salmon were raised in pens, fed additive-enriched pellets, then harvested, cleaned, frozen, and shipped off to select customers some of whom were more interested in the condoms of cocaine secreted in the body cavities of the fish than in the fish themselves.

The way her luck was going lately she'd no sooner get the whole thing lined up than the market price for cocaine would bottom out, she'd lose her shirt and be worse off than she had been.

The big shaggy dog came back down the beach. He wasn't dragging anything this time. The dogs coming behind him were, however. Maybe he'd already eaten his fill. The fish processing plant was just around the headland, in the next bay. Probably the dogs were feasting on what the plant was supposed to have buried in lime-lined pits and all too often just pitched into the chuck for nature to take care of, instead. Oh well, commercial dog food wasn't much more than fish guts cooked in a can, with a generous portion of racehorses that had been ruined by being ridden too fast too young in pursuit of more money for the ay-holes who owned them. Maybe this pack of motley mutts were actually onto a good thing, the canine version of the back-to-the-land movement, cut out the middlemen, fish guts or granola, do it yourself and devil take the leaders.

She poked around the *Old Woman*, remembering all those summers out with Einarr, setting trolling lines and scrubbing fish slime off the decking so that when you hauled in the lines you could sit and clean fish, getting the deck all slimed up again. And when the last of the catch were cleaned and iced you could clean the deck off because it was damn near time to haul 'em in again and start all over again with the thin, sharp gutting knife. From grade six on she'd gone out with him; he told everyone she was his deckhand, that he couldn't get along without her, she was like some kind of good luck charm, and he caught more fish and bigger ones with her there. Until grade nine she had swallowed it all. After grade nine it was just another chore that cut into her life, about on a par with cleaning the toilet or doing the dishes.

She went out on deck and leaned on the railing, looking down at the grey water between the pilings supporting the dock. A big blackish shape moved slowly over the mud, stopped near a barnacle-encrusted deep-sixed bike frame and hovered, sucking, trying to slurp some barnacle out of the pyramid shells. Unsuccessful, the big cod moved on, cleaning rotting crap from the sea bottom as he searched for food. Something originally from the fish processing plant drifted up from the mud, disturbed by the finning motion of the cod. The black-skinned scavenger stopped and swam backward, the disgusting whatever-it-was wavered in the water, then vanished into the cod's mouth.

"Hey, guy," she whispered, "there's lots more in the next bay. Swim over and feast."

In the city that black bugger would be worth fifteen dollars if he was worth ten cents. The Szechuan restaurants would fight for him. She could almost imagine him served up with black bean sauce and hot chilis.

They'd probably use him for advertising, put him in a thousand dollars' worth of aquarium and water pump, let him swim around with the smaller ones destined for the bean sauce and chilis. Call him Oscar or Conrad-the-Cod, maybe tell little kids if they were feeling sad they could talk to the fish and he'd take their troubles away for them. Just put a dime in the little fancy cup, sweetheart. Oscar will take your troubles away and the money will go to buy milk for little children who need our help.

"Wanna hear my troubles, Oscar?" she asked. The cod flipped his tail and went deeper under the pier. Obviously he wasn't the least bit interested, she could keep her troubles to herself. "Well, up your nose, too," she decided, "find your own way to get to the city and become a minor celebrity! See if I'll give you a ride, the attitude you've got."

She stepped to the pier, walked the wet planking, and was almost home before the dime dropped. She spun on her heel and headed back down the hill. The Fisheries asshole was having pie with ice cream in the coffee shop. The last time she'd talked to him he was having coffee and jelly-filled doughnuts. No wonder his gut folded down over his belt and kept the buckle warm.

It was actually much easier said than done. It was also much more expensive than she had expected. But in for a dime, in for a dollar.

They hauled the *Old Woman* out of the water and set about changing her innards. Every bit of ballast in her belly was jack-hammered into small enough pieces to lift out and dump in a heap on the beach. When it was all gone the place it had been was rebuilt, sealed and called something else. Instead of ballast it was live tanks. The licence she couldn't get for salmon she got for cod. She would still have to set lines, bait hooks, catch fish, but instead of cutting them open and putting them on ice she would take the hooks out of their mouths and drop them through a hole into her glorified aquariums. Pumps brought fresh sea water into the tanks, other pumps pulled dirty sea water off the bottoms of the tanks. And the entire town thought she was playing with a short deck.

"It'd break your grandpa's heart if he could see what you done to his *Old Woman*," Bill said sadly.

"It'd break his heart even more if she wound up sold to some damn yuppie for a weekender," Jean answered tartly.

"Cod, for Chrissakes, is no load for a salmon boat."

"Did I invent the licence system? Am I the one downgraded her to a 'B'? Was it my idea to beach the fleet? Do I own the big fish company? Cut me a bit of slack on this Uncle Bill, I'm doing as best I can with what I've got, okay? If I don't do cod," she shrugged, "what do I do? They've got more damn rules and regulations on prawns than you can shake a stick at and anyway most of the prawn grounds are closed because of contamination from the pulp mills. Besides which, if you didn't fish for prawns last year you can't get a permit to fish this year."

"I know, I know," he said hurriedly, "I know it isn't your doing, but still and all it would break Einarr's heart."

"Yeah well, you know what they say, life's a bitch and then you're dead. Except," she added, winking, "except for the Buddhists and they say life's a bitch and then you come back again."

She walked off, leaving Bill to stand on the roadside glowering at the *Old Woman*. Outwardly she seemed no different. The look on Bill's face said she would never be the same again. Well, Bill could afford to be choosy, he had a highliner with an "A" licence.

It seemed to Jean everyone she knew had a mad on for her these days. Sally and Mark came home from school each evening with expressions on their faces that put a person in mind of the stench issuing from the public outhouses in the provincial parks. New-kid-in-school syndrome was hitting them and they didn't like it. God knows they were used to moving, used to switching schools, used to finding a place to slide into and a way to do the sliding, but where they had wimped or grizzled in the past, now they were vicious. Jean often felt like sitting down and doing some wimping and grizzling herself, but she was too busy, too pressured, too much like a one-armed paperhanger to be able to afford the time. Somehow, her very busyness offended them and made them all the more ratty, shitty and generally unbearable.

"I can't even get the same courses I was taking at home," Sally yelled, so often and so accusingly Jean stopped listening. "Can you imagine? I mean can you *imagine*? Almost Christmas and I wind up in classes I've never even thought of taking, and I'm expected to catch up! And other classes I was taking, in which, I might add, I was getting good marks, don't exist at all in this flyspeck! I should have gone to live with Dad!"

"It's not too late," Jean agreed.

"No girls' mechanics course," Sally raged. "Oh, they say, we offered it, once, but didn't have sufficient enrollment. My best subject!"

"They've got a mechanics course," Mark contradicted. "I'm in it."

"Oh, yah, sure, they've got a mechanics course. For *boys*."

"Jesus, Sal, an engine is an engine is an engine, you know. It doesn't care if you sit down to pee or stand up to pee."

"How badly do you want mechanics, anyway?" Jean asked.

"How badly? How *badly*? Do you ever listen to what I say to you?" Sally was so angry she was shaking. "It's merely what I plan to do with my life, Mom. It's *only* on the same list as eating, breathing, shitting and sleeping, that's all."

"Then take the same course as Mark," Jean sighed. "And if they give you any flack, phone me. Believe me, I'd far sooner fight with the board of school trustees than fight with you."

Sally stared. She turned and stared at Mark, then at Jean, then, finally, at her own battered Nike high-top sneakers. "You mean that?" she asked in a voice so small Jean knew she was frightened.

"Sally, I mean it." Jean grabbed the masher and started to pound hell out of the potatoes in the pot. "I didn't decide to move up here just to kick the shit out of your social life, your education and your future!" She sniffed back tears, grabbed the bowl of chopped onion and tossed it in the pot, hoping the kids would think her tears were because of the onion fumes, then cracked an egg into the potatoes and threw the shell into the sink, almost disappointed it didn't crack the porcelain. "This is our chance," she shouted, slamming the masher into the mess and stirring violently. "We might even wind up somewhere better than marginally poor!" She kept stirring, mixing egg and onion in with the mashed potatoes. She dropped in a big gollup of margarine, splashed some milk into the mix, and started stirring again. "I know it sounds as if Grandpa left us a friggin' fortune, and I know you've decided we could have stayed in the city and lived off the stocks and bonds coupons we clipped every year, but it wouldn't have been a fuckin' down payment! With no 'A' licence we'd have been lucky to get fifteen or twenty thousand for the *Old Woman*! Maybe we'd have come up in the Celestial lottery and a yankee tourist would have put out twenty-five, but how often does that kind of luck happen to *us*? Add to that the maybe forty-five thou we could have got for this house and we don't have a bloody down payment on that rat hole we lived in! And if it *was* a down payment, where do we get the monthly payments, plus the taxes, the new roof, the drain, the windows that need fixing and the wiring that's about due to electrocute everyone? *Jesus Christ almighty* we are *broke*, we have always been *broke* and this is how we might one day *not* be broke!"

"Oh." Sally's eyes flooded with tears.

"Then there's the little matter of a job. Know why I'm on pogey? Because I'm not twenty-two years old, they can't put me on roller skates so I can cover ten times as much territory in one-tenth the time, and I'm in the union so they can't pay me bugger-nothing and play games with my benefits. And yes, I might have been able to find another job; for the six months or a year it takes them to pull the same stunt at another supermarket. My job is *dying*, Sally!" She continued stirring, whipping and occasionally pounding the mashed potatoes. "How often can I go on pogey before I don't have any pogey left to go on? How long can I stay on pogey? A year, kiddo. One lousy stinking goddamn *year*!" She whirled and threw the masher into the sink, breaking two drinking glasses. "And in that year . . ." She felt it all drain out of her. "In that year, I have to set things up so we at least don't starve if we wind up on welfare."

"Oh," Sally swallowed. "You mighta told me."

"I did. You weren't listening."

"Boy," Mark forced a wide grin, "are those potatoes ever *mashed*!"

They ate supper in a heavy silence. Mark kept looking from Sally to Jean as if expecting the purple balloon to go up again. "There's a sign on the wall of the pub," he dared. "They're looking for part-timers for the clam stuff."

"What do you know about the wall of the pub?" she teased

"The outside wall." He didn't smile and she knew this one couldn't be defused or sidestepped, this one was going to have to be talked about seriously.

"That's mean, miserable work," Jean warned.

"Maybe I'm a mean, miserable guy."

"You? I thought you meant me."

"You?" he laughed shortly. "Mom, I can't see you bent over with your bum pointing at the sky and your nose pointing at the sand raking up clams."

"Funny," Sally agreed, "I can't see *you* doing it, either."

"You know that kid lives next door? The Vietnamese kid?"

"You mean Jonas? Or whatever his name is."

"He does it. Him'n'his mom'n'dad."

"How'd you know?"

"He told me."

"When?"

"Lunch time."

"You were talking to him at lunch time?" Sally stared.

"Yeah. Why not? Nobody else talks to me. Nobody talks to him, either. So," Mark shrugged, "so we talk to each other."

"No wonder nobody talks to you." Sally poured more milk into her glass.

Jean stared. It was a remark she would have expected from Patsy, not from Sally.

"He's okay," Mark shrugged. "Talks English as good as you or me. Actually, he talks English as good as I do and better'n you."

"Oh, I just *bet*." She pretended to aim a forkload of potato at him. He grinned and picked up his clean-picked pork chop bone.

"Put it down," Jean droned, knowing they had no intention of throwing food at each other.

"Anyway," Mark continued, "he said if I was interested, I could go over with them. You do the best if you work as part of a gang. That way some rake and others pick, then switch about when the rakers get tired. Might be a dollar or two, anyway." He looked at Sally, his face expressionless. "I could ask about you if you want."

"Sure," she nodded. "My reputation at school doesn't exist anyway, so what have I got to lose?" She rolled her eyes. "I can hear it now, all the jokes about rice bowls and paddy-whackers."

"Sally!" Jean gaped.

"That's how it is, Mom. I didn't make it that way, don't blame me. I didn't say *I'd* be making the jokes!"

Jean did the dishes. It wasn't her turn but she did them anyway. She needed something to do with her hands, and she'd never learned to knit or crochet. The kids went outside, probably to organize a window smashing raid on the neighbours or to nail two-by-fours into a cross, wrap old burlap sacks around it, soak the mess with gas and burn it on the front lawn of the first person looked different than they did.

But then they came back in the house again. She heard them giggling in the living room. Maybe they were nailing a cat to a shingle or making molotov cocktails out of old Coke bottles.

"So what do you think?" Sally asked from the doorway. Jean turned. She stared.

"My God in heaven," she blurted. Sally and Mark had regressed totally, they were back to playing dressup in the attic. Einarr's best and next-to-best suits, shirts and ties hung off their juvenile frames. "You put them back," she breathed.

"No way!" Mark laughed, rolling up the sleeves of the jacket. "No way at all. This stuff is neat!" He bent over and rolled the cuffs above his high-tops. "They're charging big money for this stuff in the Second Time Around," he crowed, "and if they're going to ignore me at school they're going to have to ignore the best-dressed dude in the lunchroom."

"You're not wearing that to school!" Jean shrilled. "That's *awful*, Mark! That was your grandfather's best suit!"

"So?" he shrugged. "What's the difference? Wear his suit or eat at his table? Wear his shirt or sleep in his bed? The man," he said carefully, "is dead, Momma. They bought him a brand-new dark blue suit and buried him in it. But they didn't bury him in this one. And I'm wearin' it, see."

"Boy, Mom," Sally sighed, "you've sure got some weird and strange ideas! It's okay to rip the guts out of his boat and turn it into something else but it isn't okay to wear his clothes? You wear his work jacket!"

"Yes, but . . ."

"*That's different!*" they shouted, suddenly laughing, and she knew they were going to do whatever they had already decided to do. With or without her permission and approval. She also realized the only reason she had any authority over them was because they politely granted her that pretence of authority. The realization went a long way toward easing her guilt over disrupting their lives, uprooting them, moving them and bringing them to this totally different environment. They could, after all, have dropped the charade, told her she had no authority and stayed in the shitty.

"You can have the hats," Sally smiled. "I don't want 'em."

"I wouldn't either if they made me look like a badger poking his head between the pickets of a fence," Mark agreed. He put Einarr's favourite hat on his head, tipped it back and smiled widely, and his mother finally realized her son was what could well be called a Hunk.

"Stuff yourself." Sally pushed him, then hurried back to the living room to claim the old-fashioned ties.

"I should take tap dancing lessons." Mark pushed his hands into his grandfather's pockets, bopped awkwardly, smiled widely. "Get a stick instead of a cane, do the old Bojangles thing."

"Yeah," Jean found her voice. "Go on TV, make a fortune, live in the style to which we all wish to Jesus we could get accustomed or even introduced and support your poor old mother all the days of her life."

"Right on!" He gyrated back down the hall to try to wrench some of the ties from his sister.

Jean finished the dishes, wiped the countertops, looked around for something else to do, couldn't spot it so got out a deck of cards and sat at the table laying out the pattern for Solitaire. She heard the front door open and close, heard Mark clatter down the front steps and five minutes later come back again. Probably off stealing dynamite from the construction shack, maybe turning the clock radio into a timing device so he could blow up the post office.

"Mom?" Jean looked up. Three kids were in the doorway, her own two and another the goddess of chance suggested might be Jonas. "You know that stuff in those boxes? The ones Gran packed away?"

"The ones you hauled out and opened tonight, you mean?"

"Yeah. There's lots of stuff in there. Shirts and a box of dresses and stuff. Maybe they were Gran's. Or *your* Gran's."

"Stuff."

"Yeah. What you got in mind for it?"

"Nothing," she shrugged. "I guess we were supposed to drop it off at the Sally Ann and didn't get around to it. Why?"

"Well, Joe's mom does sewing, right? And if we don't need it, maybe she could, like..."

"Sure," Jean agreed. "Why not? It'd probably mildew in the garage before we got around to remembering to take it in," she smiled at Joe. "If you guys want anything..." She let it drop, meaning it more as a welcome than an actual invitation to deplete the groceries. Joe grinned shyly, apparently voiceless, and the hear-no-evil, see-no-evil, speak-no-evil crew turned and hurried back down the hallway to the living room. Jean went back to her Solitaire. But she couldn't remember where she'd been in the game, and it all seemed incredibly stupid, so she piled the cards, put the elastic band around them and returned them to the Hell Drawer. She sat at the table staring at the pattern in the oilcloth, listening as the kids clattered upstairs to the bedrooms, then clattered downstairs again. They went into the linen closet and opened the trap door down into the basement, clattered downstairs and started giggling. A while later they came up from the basement and went into the living room, then hurried back down into the basement, rummaged noisily, came back up, closed the trap door and bumped back into the living room. What in hell were they up to? Getting ready to launch a full-scale land and sea assault on the pulp mill?

"What about this stuff?" Sally called.

"What stuff?" Jean moved to the living room.

The sofa, both stuffed chairs and the rocking chair were draped with clothes. Half a dozen empty cardboard boxes were pushed messily against one wall.

"Oh, for crying out loud," Jean breathed. "He must have saved everything since the year zip." She picked up a faded cotton dress. "This was my Gran's. And so was this...I don't remember seeing this before but my God, look at the style of it!"

"Maybe it was Gran's. My Gran, not yours," Sally grinned. "Whoever wore it was about half the size of a shirt button. I'd have to lose ten pounds just to fit in it and I'm not exactly what you'd call large."

"No, you're not," Mark agreed. "Not exactly what I'd call smart, either."

"Stuff it," Sally invited.

"You don't get into trouble for talking to each other that way?" Joe marvelled. "Boy, at our house it would be Instant Death!"

"I have no control over them," Jean told Joe. "They're totally uncivilized, impolite and disrespectful."

"That's what my dad says about us, too," he agreed.

"You want any of this?"

"No," Jean said firmly, "I do not want any of that. Well," she amended, "maybe the baby clothes."

"Why, you going to have a baby?"

"No, I'm not going to have a baby," she laughed, "But you never know, Patsy might. Sally might."

"Not me!" Mark bragged. "I will *never* come home pregnant."

"Right," Sally agreed, "especially not with an idea!"

"You're sure your mom won't be insulted or something?" Mark stuffed clothes back into boxes, making no effort at all to fold them neatly. "I mean, you know, like she might think this is just junk or something."

"She won't be insulted," Joe said confidently. "It's almost impossible to insult my mom. She says that when you've lived with people throwing hand grenades at you it's easy to overlook a few insults tossed your way."

"You remember any of it?"

"No, I was born over here," Joe laughed. "What you think, dim-bulb? How old am I? It was all finished and done with before I was born." He winked. "I'm too smart to show up while the walls are still falling down. The only mistake I made was in not choosing rich parents."

"Yeah, I made the same dumb mistake," Sally agreed. "Just one little mistake and it's going to affect my whole life."

Jean went back to the kitchen and sat staring at her own reflection in the window, wondering if anyone would notice if she started kicking her own backside. Sally had said it very clearly and Jean had not heard it at the time. She heard it now and wished she could think of just one way, please God, just one little temporary way, to apologize. Sally's scorn had been directed at the ones making the ugly remarks, not at the kids who had to learn early how to survive them. She wondered why it was so hard to hear what your kids were actually saying.

With the house quiet, even temporarily, she moved to the living room and turned on the tube, then dropped into Einarr's old recliner and focussed herself on the glowing screen. All you had to do was find the right number on the dial and you could have news around the clock. News from here, news from there, news from everywhere. Of course, you did need to have the energy to focus your eyes, but if you could summon that, you had it made. You could watch the guys in two-thousand-dollar suits coming off aircraft capable of delivering three hundred and fifty refugees to some safe place but chartered just for them and a few chosen cronies. Tired after several hours of sitting on their asses sipping champagne and munching little snackies, they still managed to pull together the energy to smile at the cameras and come out with the five-second clip for the TV people. Then into the air conditioned limo to drive to the God-knows-how-much-a-night hotel suite to rest up, sipping Napoleon Brandy and nibbling delicately at smoked salmon while someone else ran the bath and laid out the clothes and Gucci loafers. A quick dip in scented water, a gentle rubdown with a brand new fluffy towel, then into the duds and off to the limo to be delivered to the conference where we'll all sit around in those antique chairs hauled out of some castle or other. And what will we discuss today, gentlemen? The destruction of the ozone layer? The desertification of what was once the British Columbia rain forest? Oh, no, not that same old thing, not the millions of starving children in Africa. Ah, c'mon fellas, we talked about that *last* time. Let's talk about something new. Let's talk about Peace. That's new. So new there hasn't been any of it in living memory. Peace. Oh, just a piece of this place and a piece of that place and maybe a tiny little piece of the Canadian Rockies where all the water for North America originates. And a piece of the Alberta oil field and a piece of the Saskatchewan uranium fields and a piece of this lovely smoked eel. Mmmm, nibbly nibbly chomp chomp. Oh, well, if we *must* talk about those skinny brats, fine. Trot out the statistics. Fifteen million a year will die of avoidable causes, thirteen million of them under the age of five, but as Scrooge said, how the fuck *else* are we going to ensure the status quo remains properly quo'd? Which is, after all, what keeps us in our nice niche here at the universal trough.

"May your assholes move to your ears and shit drip freely upon your fat shoulders," she grumbled. There he was, by God. Good old Joe. Not only can't walk and chew gum at the same time, he falls getting off aircraft, loses his fuckin' luggage and *then* seems to have misplaced the capital city of the country he is visiting. Way to go, Joe. You look more and more like a pug dog with the mange all the time. Does anyone ever understand what you say? Who could understand what you mean?

"Jesus Lord God in Heaven, did you ever think the day would come when you would actually *pray* for that insufferable little vinyl imitation of Cardinal Richelieu to return to political life? Where, oh where *are* you now that we need you, Pete Turd-oh?"

Nothing prepared them for the reality of clam digging. It was basically hour after hour of cold, damp and misery. By the middle of the second hour a band of fire had settled across the small of the back, by the end of the third hour hands and arms ached, and by the fourth hour feet were so cold and so sore, stumbling replaced walking. Not all the clothes in the world could have stopped the wind from making their ears ache. The earache spread up into their heads, down into their faces, until discomfort was forgotten and pain was the name for what they felt from tip to toe.

"So this is why they call it 'work'," Sally sighed.

"C'mon," Jonas panted, "you're falling behind."

"What I'm falling," Mark answered, "is down, flat on my fuckin' face."

"C'mon, my old man will get mad," Jonas grinned. "You think life is miserable now, wait until the old fart gets to yelling at you in two languages."

Everything depended on the tide. They were on the beach as the tide began to fall and stayed there until the tide came back in and chased them home. Jean wanted to put her foot down and say No to any idea of them going out on school nights but they cut her off at the pass and before she could squash the idea they gave her the sales pitch about how Jonas had one of the highest averages in school and still went out clamming.

"You don't have high averages," she snapped.

"I will, though," Mark answered, "because Joe's gonna tutor me."

Sally didn't even enter into the debate, she just announced she was going to do it. "And if you try to stop me I'll quit school and dig clams full time," she said defiantly.

"Oh, and won't that just show *me*," Jean shouted. But she was ever more aware of how thin her hold was on them, and anyway, every now and again you just step aside and let Fate, Chance and Luck do the parenting for you. Let them find out the hard way.

They found out. Jean found out, too. Found out her kids weren't spoiled jam-tarts after all. They weren't the fastest, they weren't the best, and God knows they bitched constantly about it when they were home, but they stuck it out and brought home paycheques they seemed to find satisfying. But sometimes, when they were back from clamming and had thawed themselves in a hot bath before falling into bed aching with fatigue, Jean stood in a bedroom doorway and wanted to weep.

"Shit, I missed the bus!" Mark screeched.

"Go back to bed," Jean answered. "You look like hell."

"Where's Sally?"

"Make any more noise and wake her up and you're sure to find out where she is. She'll be up your nose with a wire brush. Go to bed."

He did, and fell back into a deep sleep. Jean checked on them both a couple of hours later and could have sat on the floor and bawled into her apron, if she'd had an apron. They looked worn to a nub, and so totally limp they no longer seemed three-quarters grown, but more like they had looked when she had brought them home from the maternity ward. She wanted to give someone a dose of something in protest, and knew whoever she was angry at didn't care at all. And as mean as the work, as miserable as the weather, as unused as they were to such toil, most of the rest of the world would gladly stand in line for the chance. There wasn't as much jam in the jar as there had been, and it was harder to get at, but it was jam, and nobody was dropping bombs on their heads.

She tried to unwind by watching CNN but none of it seemed connected to anything at all, especially not to her brain. What in *hell* were they going on about now? There he was, trying to pull at our heartstrings, some bewhiskered peasant from some ungodly hell hole, sitting in the rubble, holding the body of his poor old dead mother, rocking back and forth and howling with grief, tears sliding down his weathered face. The noise coming from his throat was the noise of a mourning soul, a wordless thick bellow that would have wrenched your guts if it hadn't been for the very modern and doubtless expensive-as-hell automatic weapon slung over his shoulder. Get rid of the gun, chum, and *then* ask me to mourn your dead mom. Because I know as soon as you catch your breath you'll be up on your feet, dropping the poor old corpse back in the mud, racing off over the horizon to shoot the shit out of somebody else's mom. Or dad. Or teenager. Or three-year-old. Hard to feel sorry for some guy with a thousand bullets strapped across his chest in crossed bandoliers which remind us all of Pancho Villa.

And aren't *we* in one helluva mood tonight? Better to turn it off and go to bed and try to think of something you can *do* something about instead of flogging yourself with all this stuff that is absolutely, positively, undeniably not, repeat *not*, going to change in your sorry lifetime.

Election year is a wonderful thing. Not many weeks ago the news was full of stuff about the millions of homeless families, kids living in abandoned cars, eating food provided by church soup lines, shivering in doorways, with eyes like holes burned in styrofoam cups. And now it's time to snowjob the electorate into casting their purportedly precious ballots and the media, as obedient as any lapdog, is trying to tell us all that out of the clear bloody blue vast numbers of these lost folks have suddenly found jobs. At a time when we are also being told unemployment is at an all-time high, the poorest in the country have cornered the job market, I suppose. Showed up in their Goodwill bin clothes, shoes held together with strips of torn towel, and convinced the employment manager they were most suited for the best jobs. Not only found jobs, but managed to buy houses. There you have it, proof positive, the very best thing to do with the problems of technological change, unemployment, rising crime rate and falling economy is kick off a war in someone else's back yard while ignoring the sad conditions at home. God, but those guys are smart. Make a person humble.

Patsy came up for Christmas with the family. And brought Eve with her. They weren't in the house an hour and Terry Dugan was standing in the doorway grinning. "Merry Christmas," he beamed, handing Jean a huge basket of grapes, cheese and fancy biscuits.

"Why, thank you," she smiled. But he didn't fool her. She hadn't fallen with last week's rain. It wasn't her or the spirit of Christmas brought him to the door, it was Patsy.

So, of course, she had to invite him to Christmas dinner. And he, of course, accepted gladly, which was what the basket of goodies had been all about anyway. Even knowing that, she had to admit the kid was nice. More than nice, he seemed to fit, somehow. When he matter-of-factly slipped off his shoes and padded into the house in his thick warm wool socks, she knew more about him than she'd have known if she'd spent an hour talking to him at a party in the city. He wasn't wearing *fibre inconnus*, he was wearing thick grey wool "polars," and that meant he was all dressed up in his finest low-key garb. His jeans weren't brand new, but almost, and his tee shirt and deep green flannel shirt had been washed just often enough to make them soft.

The tree was already up and decorated, the presents already stacked temptingly. Jean had even managed to do some baking. Eve looked at the cookies and pies, shook her head and lifted her painted eyebrows patiently.

"Where's the shortbread?" she asked.

"I'll buy some tomorrow."

"Buy shortbread? Nobody buys shortbread!"

"Everybody buys it, for God's sake. Nobody makes it any more."

Eve did. She made it by corralling everybody else in the house, snapping orders and putting them to work. "They made the atom bomb without this much fuss," Jean snarled.

"You shut up," Eve told her. "Just go find a toadstool and park under it for a while. If you're going to be an ogre you might as well live with them."

The kids waited for an explosion. Nobody talked to their mother that way. Jean glared at Eve, then turned and went into the living room, turned on Einarr's TV and stared holes in the screen. Jolly ho ho ho. Bah humbug, more like it. She knew from comments Joe had let slip things weren't much better next door. She hadn't asked many questions, but had gathered from dropped hints and muttered oh-woe-is-me's that Mr. Nguyen agreed with those who thought the younger generation was going to the dogs. He also thought it was a direct threat to his own comfort that Mrs. Nguyen had started dropping over for coffee with Jean of an afternoon. "The women in this country," he had lectured, "smoke cigarettes! On the streets!" "Yes," Joe's mother had replied, "and the men do the dishes." The threat of dishes had shut Mr. Nguyen up for the time being, but he was beginning to sound as if he thought bullets and bombs easier to live with than some of the things his family was doing.

"It's very hard for him," Tran told Jean. "Family, for us, has always been important and we are all we have left."

"Maybe the Red Cross could find some relatives back home?"

"They haven't yet," Tran shrugged. "It no longer seems very important to me, but for him . . . he had a wife, he had four children, he had parents, brothers, sisters, and then he was made to join the army and when he finally got home again, everything and everyone was gone."

"Which army?" Jean asked. Tran just shrugged and looked away, and Jean took the hint.

"He had nothing. Not even identification. So . . ." She looked down at the oilcloth covering the table. "He got some. Papers. And he left. I met him later."

"You're his second wife, then?"

"Third." Again the shrug. "His second wife died in a refugee camp."

"Jesus Christ almighty."

"So sometimes, when he is angry with everyone . . . well, there are reasons."

Jean wanted to ask Tran about her own history but couldn't bring herself to do it. Maybe she didn't really want to know. Maybe she was afraid Tran would just invent something. At what level of desperation would Jean, herself, decide to steal identification papers and live a lie?

Who was who, anyway? Bunkhouse Betty was out in the kitchen pretending to be Madame Benoit and the kids were imitating Dick'n'Jane'n'Baby Sally, licking spoons, washing bowls and getting in each other's way. Patsy and Terry were casting calves' eyes at each other, and on television yet another good angel was fixing up the lives of the good little chilluns, filling stockings that would otherwise have hung empty, finding a job for brave old Dad, putting faith back into the heart of dear harried Mom, getting ready to fix it so everyone could live happily forever after in a split level in the suburbs. Joy to the world. Gimme a G gimme an R gimme an I N C H

YAY GRINCH!!

Finally the shortbread was done, the butter tarts were done, the mince pies cooling and the self-congratulations finished. Jean went to bed leaving the festive crew in the living room. When she wakened it was morning, and she had a full hour in the kitchen by herself, drinking coffee and loving the peace and quiet. Terry Dugan was snoring in a sleeping bag on the floor in the living room and had rolled so close to the tree you'd have thought he was one of the presents. She would have placed a stick-on bow on his forehead but she was afraid he'd wake up and then she'd have to talk to him.

She peeled onions, crumbed bread, and had everything mixed and rammed it into the turkey by the time the first of the pack wandered in, yawning. "Need any help?" Mark asked.

"None at all, thank you," she made herself smile.

"Good." He poured a coffee and sat at the table, his bare feet looking big enough to paint white and call herring skiffs. They had once been small, pink and chubby. Now they looked as if they belonged in steel-toed boots, and he had dark hair growing along the top of his foot, like a hobbit.

The turkey was trussed and in the oven before Sally and Patsy came down. Patsy poured two cups of coffee, took one into the living room for Terry, then sat on the sofa drinking her own. Sally rolled her eyes, poured her own coffee and sat at the kitchen table. Mark ignored her. She ignored Mark. They did such a good job ignoring each other that Jean noticed immediately.

"What?" she demanded.

"Nothin'," they answered.

"What!"

"Okay!" Mark's face flushed. "We had a big fight, okay?"

"Well, Merry Christ Mess to the both of you."

"She thinks *I'm* gonna move into the crummy basement!"

"Move into the basement? Why?"

"Because Patsy and Gran want to move in with us and I'm *not* sharing a room with either of them!" Sally gritted. "He obviously can't. So he can go down to the basement and they can have his room."

"Fuck you too, when did God die and put you in charge of creation?"

"Don't tell your sister fuck you," Jean snapped. "Neither of you are moving down into the basement."

"Well, what about Patsy and Gran?"

"Let *them* move into the goddamn basement!" Jean poured the last of the coffee into her mug, rinsed the pot, filled the coffee maker, then added sugar and cream to her own brew, stirred it and went back to the table. It was still sticky with dressing, bits of onion, flakes of sage, and she didn't care.

"You can't make an old woman like Gran move into the basement like she was a toadstool or something," Sally protested, shocked.

"Why not? Whose idea is it for her to come up here and drive me crazy anyway? Patsy said she wouldn't be caught dead up here and now all of a sudden she's ready to kick people out of their bedrooms? Let her live in the basement. Better yet, let them both stay where they are."

"You can't deny your own family!" Sally argued.

"I could," Mark countered. "I'm outnumbered around here as it is. Another week or two I'll be sleeping in Gramps's old car."

"You stay away from that car," Sally warned, "because *I'm* the one going to fix it up and *I'm* the one going to drive it, see."

"Correction," Jean growled. "You might fix it up but that's as far as that idea goes."

"That's not fair! I do all the work and . . ."

"Oh shut the fuck up, will you? Merry goddamn Christmas, Sally!"

"I'm sorry." Sally's eyes filled with tears. "It's just . . . it's just such a WEIRD Christmas!" and she started crying.

Jean moved to sit next to her, put her arms around her and hugged her tight. "Come on, baby," she whispered, "the coffee's ready. Let's take it into the living room and have the big demonstration of greed and avarice, okay?"

"Oh, Mom," Sally sobbed. "I wish once, just once, when things changed, they'd change into something nicer."

"Any kind of change, even nice change, is scary." She stroked back her daughter's hair and put a peck-of-a-kiss on her nose. "It's okay. Really it is. We just get ourselves so hyped up for the baby-in-the-hay stuff, and probably right now half the town is bummed out, everybody just about convinced they and they alone are feeling crummy while the rest of the world is having one helluva great old time. So let's us put on a good show and fool 'em all, okay?"

"Oh sure," Sally sniffed. "Sure, why not, eh?"

"Come on, Sal," Mark grinned, "I want to see your face when you open the present I got you. It's the nicest little Barbie doll I could find."

"Asshole," she grinned, and it might have been more than a bit forced, but it was still a grin. "It ought to go real good with the GI Joe doll I got you."

Eve drifted into the living room just as the first of the wrappings hit the floor. She pulled a flash camera from her pocket and started snapping pictures. By the end of the third roll of film Jean was ready to ram the whole jobby where the sun hadn't shone in fifteen years. Or if it had, it shouldn't.

Mark really had got Sally a Barbie doll. It was lying on its back on the lid of a socket set. GI Joe was taped to the box in which was packed a walkman. "So you can listen to your ugly music while you're digging clams," she teased.

Neither Eve nor Patsy said diddly about moving in with them. Maybe they'd overheard the snarling match in the kitchen. Or maybe they were waiting for the true spirit of Xmas to take hold of the hearts, minds and souls of the others. If they weren't going to mention it, neither was Jean.

Still, it took any glow there might have been off the day. Eve didn't seem to notice. She was making up for all the Christmases she had missed. She continued to snap pictures and she got overwhelmed with emotion, grabbing one or another of the kids and hugging them. She said "oh what a perfect day" so many times Jean wanted to choke her. And then Eve grabbed Jean and hugged her. Jean stiffened.

"Oh, don't *be* that way!" Eve protested. "A mother has every right in the world to hug her own daughter."

"Easy," Jean said softly, "Don't push it."

She didn't have to say anything else, Eve understood totally. She stood, and for a minute Jean almost felt sorry, then Eve lifted her head. "You don't know what you think you know," she said gently, "and you haven't asked a single question so I guess that means you aren't interested in finding out. And that, as they say, is the screwing I get for the screwing I got. Fine. But those are my grandchildren. So don't *you* push it, Jeannie, because I'll go right over top of you if I have to."

Jean smiled the iciest grimace she could manage. "Did I tell you to get on your bicycle and pedal your ass out of our lives? No, I did not. You walk in after who knows how many years and Jesus Christ if you don't have your suitcases with you, set to stay for life, and did I tell you Eff Oh? They've seen you maybe four times since they hatched out of the egg, usually in a coffee shop or a chow mein house, but did I say fuck off stranger? No, I did not. Because yes, they are your grandchildren. And your relationship with them is your business, their relationship with you is their business, and none of it is any of *my* business. But don't you push 'er with me, lady."

Eve nodded, her Christmas wig so elaborate a person could be forgiven for thinking Whoopi Goldberg had changed her skin colour and aged thirty years. The troops retreated on both sides, the bugles quit blowing, the cavalry took their horses back to the stables, the artillery unloaded the big guns and everyone settled down to enjoy what was left of the Ghost of Christmas Present.

For three lovely, blessedly quiet hours in the afternoon Jean had the house to herself. Patsy and Terry went off in his truck, probably to make out up a skidder trail somewhere. Sally and Mark went next door to show their loot to the Nguyens and see what the Jolly Old Man had dropped off at their place. God in her heaven alone knew where Eve went, she just put on her fake fur coat, slipped her feet into her lined city winter boots and with her purse over her shoulder sallied forth into the December gale.

She was back in plenty of time to help set the table, make gravy, mash potatoes, haul stuffing out of the turkey and pile dark meat on one platter, white on another.

"We should say grace," she announced, "and give thanks to the good lord that we're all together."

"Are you out of your mind?" Jean snapped.

"Why not?" Patsy protested. "I think it would be *nice*," she smiled at Terry who turned brick red and smiled back at her. "I think we've got a *lot* to be thankful *for*."

They sat at the table, joined hands and tried to pretend one of them knew the words of a prayer of thanks.

Finally it was Terry Dugan who saved the day "For all the blessings in our lives," he said firmly, "we give thanks in our own way to our own personal vision of the Creator. All my relations," he added.

"All your who?" Sally asked.

"It's a thing the Indians say," he confessed. "It means you call on all the people who were here before you to join their spirits with yours."

"I didn't know you were religious," Sally marvelled.

"I'm not," he grinned. "Not if religion means churches and collection plates and original sin and all that other bullshit." He started piling food onto his plate, passing platters and accepting others. "But sometimes, I tell you, I look up from what I'm doing and I see the light on the water, maybe, or some big old cone-covered fir and I just feel so . . . so damn good, eh . . . and I know I don't have to pretend to be the apex of creation. I'm no more than a skink under a rock. And that feels real safe to me."

Eve winked at him. "Your old man was crazy, too."

"Musta been," Terry agreed. "My momma was sane, though. She packed us up and hit the old trail with us."

"I didn't know that," Eve answered. "Can we take a minute here while I get my foot outta my mouth? When I knew him he was about the same age Mark is now. I actually knew your grandpa better'n I knew your dad. And your grandma," she added hurriedly, "she and me were good friends for a while."

"Yeah, where was that?" He was busy with knife and fork, but listening intently.

"I was cooking up Fathead Bay and the bullcook took the DTs and had to be sent out on the freight ferry. Hungarian guy, big scar on his face, ran out of booze and got into the vanilla extract, then when he'd drank that he started in melting shoe polish and straining it through a slice of bread...went absolutely asshole and decided the German army was comin' through the toolies after him. Grabbed a three-oh-three and put a couple of slugs through the yarder before they got it away from him. So your grandma she filled in, supposed to only be until we got another bullcook but she did such a good job nobody looked for a replacement. We'd sit after supper while the next day's pies was baking and we'd play cards. After a bit a few others got to dropping by to take a hand. Next thing you know we've got a bloody casino going !"

"And you knew my dad, huh?"

"Yeah. Crazy little bugger, that one," she laughed softly. "He was supposed to be doing correspondence courses but he'd been mucking away at the same ones for a couple of years so finally your grandma agreed he'd be more use working. He played the harmonica, as I recall."

"Yep," Terry speared more turkey, piled it on his plate, drowned it in gravy and cranberry sauce, and dug in. "And the fiddle, too. That man could do just about everything except keep his pants zipped shut, I guess."

"There's lots in the world got the same problem," Eve agreed, apparently quite willing to overlook the fact that in the opinion of a number of people she suffered from the same affliction.

"Won't your mother miss you over the holidays?" Jean dared.

Terry grinned widely, and shook his head, swallowing ten pounds of food. "She's lying on the beach in Hawaii, probably right smack under the hole in the ozone layer, flirting with skin cancer. I asked her what she wanted for Ex-Mess and she said she wanted three weeks at Waikiki. So," he laughed softly, "I shocked the hell out of her and give it to her."

"There!" Jean said loudly, pointing her finger at Mark. "*That* is a son."

"Gonna get you, fella," Mark warned quietly. "Any more of that kind of talk and you'n'me's gonna get down and dirty. Don't you know mothers are people you treat like mushrooms?"

"Keep 'em in the dark," they all chimed, "and feed 'em shit!"

Later that evening, with Patsy and Terry once again off together in the pickup and Sally and Mark gone who-knew-or-cared-where, Jean took a can of beer into the living room and sprawled on the sofa, ready to dive into the copy of *Lonesome Dove* Sally had given her. Her old copy, which she'd read from start to finish more than once, had taken a hike in all the moving and packing. She hadn't realized how much she'd missed it until the new copy was in her hands. God, life was so much easier in that book. Diving into it was like diving into the answers to all the questions you didn't dare ask any more. Just sit on your horse and follow the herd. Of course that meant you were riding through cowshit all the time but maybe you learned to ignore it. She'd made this trip with the blue shoats for company often enough to invent for herself entire episodes which hadn't made it to the pages of the book and she still hadn't grown tired of it.

Eve came in with a glass of something dark brown and sat in one of the big stuffed chairs swirling her ice cubes and looking thoughtful. "You really got a mad on for me, don't you," she said finally.

"Not any more. At least, I don't think I do."

"Seems like it."

"If you say it seems like it to you, then I'll accept that. It seems like it to you. Just don't make the mistake of telling me what I feel and don't feel, okay? And I don't think what I feel for you can be called 'mad'. Maybe it used to be. But now, it's more like . . . well," she laughed softly, "the truth is I don't know exactly what it is. But I do know I'm not standing in line with my heart on my sleeve waiting for a big lovey hug, okay?" In Lonesome Dove they didn't need entire paragraphs to explain anything. Yep. Nope. Pull out the gun and blow away the problem, then feed it to the pigs.

"What harm does it do you if I give you a hug?"

"I don't know. I've never felt that because someone else wanted to hug me . . . or kiss me . . . or, for that matter fuck me . . . I was under an obligation of some kind to go along with it."

Eve just stared, then shrugged. "You and Bill must get along just fine. And you'n'Alice, too."

"We get along real fine. Always have. We don't always agree, but we get along just fine."

Eve nodded, sipped her drink, then obviously decided to barge in further. Jean sighed and put Lonesome Dove aside, wishing she could scream for five minutes, then join the cattle drive. Maybe she and the pigs could live together under the wagon, eating snakes and dodging kicks. How do you look someone in the eye and tell them that it isn't true that when love dies hate replaces it? How do you tell them that what replaces the aborted love is complete indifference?

"You know you never call me Mom? You aware of that?"

"I wasn't aware of it, no. I guess it wasn't a conscious decision. Why, what do I call you?"

"You say 'you' a lot. Or Eve. Never Mom."

"Well, there you have it. I guess what we don't say is often just as important as what we do. Probably holds true for the things we see and hear, too."

"Meaning there's stuff you're not saying?"

"Maybe so." Silence grabbed hold of the entire living room and squeezed it for long minutes. Jean was just reaching hopefully for *Lonesome Dove* when Eve started in again.

"What did they tell you?"

"Not much," she admitted.

"They tell you I left with someone else?"

"Not at the time, they didn't. I learned that the hard way. From other kids."

"Guess you heard a lot from the other kids over the years."

"Sure did. And I vowed my own kids would never hear shit like that about me from anybody." She felt her face harden, her eyes slit. "Can we drop this soon?"

"So why didn't you slam the door in my face?"

"Oh, maybe I should have done. But I'm slow off the mark, you know. And if you remember, the way it worked out, one of the kids answered the door and let you in. By the time I even knew you were under my roof they had jumped feet first into the grandma-ginger-bread-apron-shortcake bullshit. Do I want to fight with them about something like that? Hell, I've got all I can handle to put up with their constant dream-disillusion shit with their own father, I don't need to get into it about their poor little old grey-haired grandma!"

"All alone in the rain with holes in her plastic overshoes," Eve grinned, "and nobody in the world to love her." She drank thirstily, then popped an ice cube in her mouth and crunched it. "You want to hear my side of it?"

"No," Jean yawned, "I'm not interested in sides. You have to understand, Eve, that if you've got something to say you'll have to find someone who gives a shit."

"Fuck, you're hard."

"No, if I was hard I wouldn't have to come on strong. If I was hard I wouldn't have to protect myself."

"Well." Eve sat straighter, reached up, scratched delicately under her wig. "I'm sorry you got the dirty end of the stick, kid. I never meant it to be that way. I didn't leave you because I hated you; I knew Einarr would hunt me to the ends of the earth if I took you with me. Then probably snap my neck when he found me so I couldn't come up and steal you back. I knew I either had to leave you behind or stay here with you. And if I'd stayed, life would have been about ten times worser for all of us."

"So you say," Jean smiled. "And I bet you even believe it."

"I've been out looking." Eve's voice was firm, almost hard. "There's about three places within two minutes' walking distance that I can rent." She paused, but Jean didn't say anything. "I'd rather just move in here and chip in on my share of groceries, utilities and such. Pay you some rent, help with things. Get to know the kids. . ." Still Jean didn't say anything. "But I guess you knew I was thinking about it, eh?"

"What I heard was you and Patsy were moving in and everyone expected Mark to move into the basement."

"He don't got to move into no basement!" Eve flared. "Jesus Christ, I never said nothin' about no basement! There's space in this house hasn't even been looked at yet. That whole back area, mud room or whatever they're calling them these days. Move the washer and dryer to the basement, do the ironing in the kitchen where it's always been done anyway. There's easy room for two out there!"

"Got it all figured out, huh?" Jean could feel the net closing around her head, and wanted to flail out, hurt someone, hurt anyone, hurt this boozehound with the nylon headpiece. And knew if she did Eve would do what she had hinted at, she'd rent just down the road somewhere and the kids would as good as live with her. "If I say no I'm the black wolf. If I say no I'm going out of my way to be unreasonable and break everyone's heart. Well. . ." She stood up and grabbed her book. "I'm not going to give anyone that satisfaction. You do what you want. I'm not giving up *my* room, Sally's not giving up *her* room and Mark isn't giving up *his* room. Nobody is moving in with any of us. We've all pissed on our posts, Eve. If you can find one or two that hasn't been pissed on, go for it, turn your bladder inside out, all *I'm* doing is getting my sails out of the goddamn typhoon!" My dear lord God in heaven, son of the creator of heaven and earth, hell and damnation, and all other stuff that goes bump in the night, all she wanted to do was sit down and reread for the umpteenth time a book she knew was her escape. They say nobody else makes you mad, you just give yourself permission to get mad. But it sure does seem that with some people if you don't pitch a fit and holler down the sky you'll wind up sitting with a smile on your face trying to pretend the rough cob shoved up your ass is not only comfortable, but pleasant. "Push push push push fuckin' push," she breathed to herself once she was safely out of earshot and halfway up the steps, "push push push."

Terry Dugan rented a truck in town and drove it to the city with Patsy talking italics beside him the whole way and Eve sitting over by the passenger's door with the window half rolled down so her cigarette smoke wouldn't fog up the interior of the cab. They were gone three days. When they came back the truck was half stuffed, and Patsy was sporting a big weight on the third finger of her left hand. "It's not a diamond," Terry admitted, "it's prob'ly just glorified milk bottle glass, but we'll get a better one later on."

"No we *won't*," Patsy vowed, "or if we *do* it won't replace *this*. I *love* this!"

"What a sweetie," Terry breathed. "Jean, I gotta tell you, you did the world's best job on her. She's perfect."

"Nothing," Jean shook her head, "and nobody is perfect."

"Oh, *Momma!*" Patsy laughed. "You're such a *tease!*"

Jean did her impersonation of the Mona Lisa, a little smile that told nobody anything of what was going on behind her mask. Maybe they'd find out one liked Coke and the other liked Pepsi. Maybe one or the other, preferably both, would meet someone else and fall madly in lust and call off this lunacy. Maybe they'd realize they were better suited to be good friends. Maybe the blue shoats would learn to fly.

Sally said little about the changes. She was more than content to have her grandmother living with them, she was happy. It was having Patsy back in her life full time that stuck in Sally's throat. She had never been able to stand being around her sister for very long at a time. Mark seemed amused by the whole thing. Jean thought often of pulling out all her hair but figured the wind would be damn cold on her bare skull. Eve just beamed constantly.

Terry and Mark moved the washer and dryer down to the basement, they ran the 220 wiring, they installed the plumbing, and they moved the other stuff in the back room, too; the shelves for canning jars, the shelves for spare extension cords, the shelves for bits and pieces of stuff that didn't fit in the Hell Drawer. They took everything back to the very walls, then started in on the walls. Jean preferred to leave them to it and spend her time watching the *Old Woman* being gutted, refitted and tested. Everything was being stripped down to the support studs, why not her own brain, or what little was left of it.

When school started back up again Patsy went into town and signed on at the college for computer courses. "It's the thing of the future," she assured Jean.

"Darling," Jean corrected, "it's the thing of the present. It was the thing of the future fifteen years ago."

"Oh, you *know* what I *mean*," Patsy laughed. You couldn't get through to Patsy. God knows she'd been thickly enough insulated before, but now that she and Terry Dugan were walking around in pink clouds it was worse than it had ever been. She was so constantly cheery it was almost an overwhelming urge to just strangle her.

"A month ago," Sally said quietly, "I was almost an adult. Today I'm in kindergarten again."

"Oh, sweetie." Jean grabbed Sally, hugged her fiercely, briefly. "I know this isn't going to seem like much help to you but...it isn't all Patsy's doing. I know she treats you like a baby, but...if you refuse to play into it she'll have to find a new way to relate to you."

Sally stared, then leaned forward, her hands in the dishwater, her elbows resting on the edge of the sink. "Momma," she addressed the suds, "you could get a job writing one of those awful fuckin' columns. 'Be good sweet maid and let who will be clever' and stuff like that."

"No!" Jean was fighting for her kid. "No, don't you *ever* be 'good', don't you *ever* let other people be clever! You be you! Even if the only way you can be you is to develop the personality of an enraged viper, which you seem very close to doing, by the way. She might want to treat you like a baby but only *you* can decide you'll behave like one and be treated like one."

"Yeah?" Sally grinned suddenly. "An enraged viper, eh?" and suddenly Jean was wiping dishwater suds off her face and Sally was laughing freely.

"What*ever* are you two *doing*?" Patsy shrilled from the doorway. "Just *look* at the *mess*."

"You don't like it?" Sally shrugged, still laughing, "clean it up yourself," and she flipped another handful of suds. Jean caught the foamy bubbles and put them on Sally's head.

"Queen of the sink."

"Yeah. Right. The Enraged Viper Strikes Again."

"Oh, you *two*, really, you're *always* so *silly* when you're *around* each other!"

Sally did not smile. "If you'd stop telling us how silly we are and be a bit silly yourself you wouldn't be on the outside looking in."

"I don't *want* to be *silly*, Sally. *Silly* is for *immature* people."

"Yeah? Well let's give a cheer for immature people. Nobody's ever going to take us immatures and sillies and promote us to Chief of Staff so we can make no-fun-at-all decisions and send serious people like yourself out to drop bombs on little kids. Us sillies are never going to hi-de-ho down the pike and join up with some group of Pentacostal evangelicals who think having a good time is a sin. And nobody's gonna take us sillies seriously, especially not our silly selves. We'll leave that to the self-appointeds."

The kids headed off on the school bus but because Patsy was going to college, not to high school, she couldn't ride with them. Patsy had to make arrangements for a ride in every morning; then, because some days she was finished class by two in the afternoon and other days she had to stay late and catch her evening class, she had to arrange different rides home. When she couldn't arrange a ride home with someone else, and Terry Dugan was out of town working, she would phone, half hysterical. Jean would back the tired old Chev out of the garage and poke it along the road, windshield wipers slapping ineffectually at the rain, headlights doing their aged best against the darkness. The entire ride home Patsy would complain about how slow and pokey the old car was. "Why don't you get a *new* one?"

"You're the one whining, moaning, complaining and bitching, *you* get a new one!"

"I don't have any money and you know it!"

"Yeah, well the bad news is, sweetheart, I've only got an account at the Bank of Montreal, I don't own the assets."

"You've got money! Grandpa left you lots of money!"

"Isn't it weird he decided not to leave it to you. I mean you've got all these great and swell ways of getting rid of the burden within six months, I wonder why he decided to leave it to someone he could be pretty sure would hang on to a bit of it."

"There you *go*. I'm not talking about *wasting* it, I'm talking about *investing* it in some *decent* transportation."

"This old bazoo is getting you home tonight, don't knock it or the next time you're stuck either the car or driver may be unable to co-operate."

"Oh, there you *go*! Gee *whiz*!"

"Patsy, for Chrissake shut up. I can't take a lot of this, okay? *You* are the one decided you weren't going to go to college, you were going to get a job. Then *you* decided you'd get your own apartment. Now *you* have decided to move up here, and *you* decided to move in with us, and *you* decided to go back to college. If *you* can't accept the price tag, do something about it. Move into town. Live next door to the college. Then you can *walk* to class."

"Well, *gee whiz*, eh? That's nice, Mom, that's really nice."

"What would you know about nice? You, the queen of passive aggression! And don't give me that shit about how we should all sit down and *discuss* things so we can arrive at a *consensus* because talking to you or with you is a waste of time. All that happens is talk. Nothing gets resolved because you just go back to doing what it was you were doing before the talk."

"Then I'll hitchhike home. *Someone* will give me a ride. Of course they might slit my throat, too."

"For that matter I might slit your throat. Shut up."

Then, finally, blessedly, the waiting was done. The *Old Woman* was ready to be slid off the ways and down into the water again. Jean decorated the old girl with coloured paper streamers and big multi-hued rosettes, even ran a string of outside Xmas lights along the edge of the wheelhouse roof and plugged the extension cord into the adaptor Einarr had rigged up so he could play his portable radio without always having to fritz with battery connectors.

"Glad to see you did 'er up proud," Bill grinned. "I mean it's nothing I'd have done to her but I guess I have to agree you didn't have much choice, all things considered."

"She looks lovely," Alice smiled. "Are you sure you'll be able to handle her yourself?"

"Auntie Alice!" Jean laughed. "Cut me some slack, okay? I might be a bit rusty but I grew up on that old girl."

"She'll do okay," Bill agreed, stuffing Juicy Fruit into his cheek. "Don't know as how the rest of us will easily survive, but Jeannie'll do okay. Guess as long as we keep one eye peeled for her and stay out of her way . . . women drivers, y'know."

Alice ignored him and so did Jean. Bill laughed. He loved getting a rise out of them, even a silent one, and there was no better way of getting one than to crack what Alice called Another Damn Piggy.

Jean had no excuses left, no way to convince herself if a thing is worth doing it's worth putting off another week or two. All the licences, permits, and permissions were in place, the market was assured, all she had to do was get off her keister, go out, catch cod and have them delivered, live and still kicking, to an eagerly waiting market. Nothing to it. Piece of cake. Full speed ahead. If not fame at least fortune.

So why was she scared spitless?

She said nothing to any of them. She waited until the kids were in school and Patsy was in computer class at the college. Only then, with nobody along for the ride, did she very quietly pack a big bag of sandwiches, fill two thermoses with coffee, take a small bag of extra clothes, leave a brief note on the table and exit the house by way of the back door. Eve was in the bathroom getting herself ready to face another day, that was good for at least three-quarters of an hour, plenty of time to get to the wharf and start making a fool of herself with nobody to watch, criticize, kibitz, or offer advice. Unwanted, unwelcome and totally ignorant advice at that.

It was so easy she wondered why she had been so apprehensive. With or without the live tanks, she was still the *Old Woman*, still the sturdy, reliable old wooden bucket Jean had first learned to handle. Other boats had come later, most faster, many fancier, some actually better, but none as reliable and as forgiving. Maybe she rode a bit lower, maybe she rode a bit slower, or maybe she didn't and it was just that same thing that happens when you go back to the scenes of your childhood and realize that Suicide Hill isn't really all that tremendous after all, Devil's Hole isn't as deep as you remembered and the garage roof isn't a mile up from the lawn.

In many ways it was nothing at all like it had always been and yet it was exactly the same. Fishing is fishing, especially to someone who cut her teeth doing it, and some things you just don't forget. You may change your sink, replace all your water pipes, buy different detergent, but when it's all been said and done, once you know how to wash dishes, you know how to wash dishes.

She baited her hooks, set her lines, then sat in the wheelhouse sipping coffee and playing at being the next best thing to a tourist. She wasn't really sure what the proper speed would be for cod, but she'd mooched enough of them in her life to know you probably wouldn't even try to hit salmon trolling speed. Cod don't like to do anything in a hurry, they like to take their time, consider the situation, study their options, and then, maybe they will bite and maybe they won't. Like any other fishing, no matter how much you think you know, the fish are under no obligation to co-operate. Some people ignore all the supposed rules and highline, others are so persnickety it could make your head ache. A few honest ones admit it's all in the way you hold your mouth — if the fish approve they bite, if they don't approve you might as well take up driving truck.

She ate some sandwiches, burned some gas, then turned off the motor and went out to bring in her lines. You could get away with that on a good day. She wasn't sure what she was going to do on a not good day. But she wasn't out here to make her fortune on the first try, she was just trying things out.

Time slipped into neutral and for the first time since Einarr's funeral, Jean felt as if there was actually time enough to do what needed to be done, with plenty of opportunity to put her bum on the yellow plastic milk crate, and actually use her eyes to see. The feeling of pressure and dread was just suddenly gone; it didn't fade, it didn't subside, it didn't recede, it was just suddenly gone. Nobody could get at her here; no kid's problems, no Patsy's italics, no wrinkled old tart wearing hair which belonged to either Whoopi or Cher. She didn't have to calm anyone else's insecurities before she could face up to her own. She could just sit here and feel the chill breeze on her face.

She knew Einarr wasn't sitting next to her, she knew she couldn't turn to him for help if the world began to come apart at the seams, she knew it was still up to her and only her to keep her kids fed, clothed and housed. And she knew it wouldn't be any easier to do that than it had ever been. But they weren't bunched around her, and she didn't feel as if her ankles were being gnawed to the bone by salamanders, no one bite big enough to really hurt, but over enough time you're walking on ankle stumps.

Vancouver Island looked as if it was floating four inches above the surface of the chuck. The blue green bulk of it was truncated, the tops of the mountains obscured by long grey-white clouds. The sun behind the cover broke through and turned the surface of the water glittering silver and a flock of wave riding birds took to the air, breaking the sea and sending zillions of droplets of light flying upward.

It was a damn good job she hadn't decided to make her bundle and retire. She only got three, one of them a red snapper, but the cod were a decent size, and the day hadn't died yet. She wrenched the hook from their mouths, dropped them through the hatch into the live tanks, re-baited the hooks and set the lines again, deciding to try a bit deeper. Maybe they were feeling shy.

When she went back in to dock, the early spring darkness was spreading across the water. She had a dozen, not enough to bother trying to ship to the city but enough to make her feel she'd at least made gas and moorage. Maybe not wages, but at least the *Old Woman* wasn't costing her money, not today.

She tied up in her usual place, got her dip net and went down to scoop out the big red snapper. Nothing better than red snapper for supper. Fillet it, dip the fillets in seasoned flour, drop them into a decently hot frying pan with some vegetable oil, and stand back. With properly creamed potatoes and a good herb-and-spice salad you've got a supper the Queen of England doesn't get many chances to eat.

As she expected they were all disappointed she'd gone alone. "Well, gee *whiz*," Patsy protested, "you might have *said*. I'd have liked to go *too*, you know."

"Yeah, but you've got computer class."

"It's not as if I can't *miss* once in a while."

"Try missing work once in a while and see how long you keep the job."

"If you didn't *want* me you only had to *say*."

"Okay, I didn't want you there."

"Well, *that's* nice, *isn't* it!"

"And you wonder why I didn't say anything? Jesus, Patsy, don't you ever listen to yourself? If I'd said anything beforehand you'd have done this thing of yours until I gave up, gave in, gave over and said yes, just to stop the yammering. And if I'd said yes to you everyone would have gone, it wouldn't have been fair otherwise. And I didn't *want* the whole kit and caboodle out there with me, okay? Gimme a break!"

"Scared we'd see you goof up, eh?" Mark teased. "Didn't want us to know you took off dragging the dock with you, eh?"

"She wouldn't drag the dock with her, you fool," Sally countered, "she'd leave the dock there so she could smash into it on her way back in."

"And you wonder why I didn't take you? Do I need your supportive attitude?"

"You don't have to worry about your mother taking out the dock," Eve said suddenly. "Her dad had her out there when she was still in diapers and if Einarr's the one taught her to handle a boat then you can bet money she's at least as good as the best. I never worried about her on a boat. I worried about her on dry land, I worried about her in a car, I worried about her in a plane and on a train, but I always knew if she was on a boat she was fine."

Jean didn't have any idea at all what she ought to say. But it didn't matter, she didn't seem to be expected to say anything. Eve was busy, and pulling the kids into it so smoothly even Patsy's sulk had begun to vanish. The idea of Eve worrying about her was so foreign to Jean she couldn't even look at it, and had no idea where to put it.

She stared at Eve, busy expertly filleting the red snapper. "You go take a good hot bath," Eve ordered, "or you'll get the shivers. Sally, honey, you can take that stew off the stove and set it on the counter to cool; we'll have 'er tomorrow night. Stew's always better the second night anyway. We're having us First Catch here tonight."

Life assumed a kind of irregular schedule inside which each of them had their individual routines. Jean went out with the *Old Woman* depending on tide and Fisheries regulations, but made no attempt to go very far or stay out very long. She was not so much fishing as she was practising and honing skills she had thought she would never again need. Before she went gallivanting off on two- or three-day heavy duty expeditions, she wanted to know what every creak meant, what every shift in pitch and tone of the engine meant, whether the *Old Woman* was sneezing or getting ready to blow her top. Jean still felt a hollow ball in the deep pit of her stomach when she loosened the lines and got ready to take the *Old Woman* out, and until that cold emptiness went away and stayed away, there was no way she was getting adventuresome.

Eve putzed at home, playing Suzie Homemaker with a dedication that amazed everyone. Wasn't she the one who had turned her back on brownies and pecan pie, wasn't she the one had told the washing and ironing to go to hell and taken a hike as far from all that as she could? And yet there she was, with the CBC radio tuned in and turned up, and if she wasn't washing and waxing she was ironing and folding. "My grandchildren," she said fiercely, "are not going to have to take goddamn Twinkies in their lunch pails! They'll take good made-from-scratch or I'll know the reason why."

If Patsy launched herself into computers the way she launched herself into being apprentice Suzie she had a fine, stable career ahead of her. There she was, still talking italics, busy mixing, stirring and checking the oven temperature as if she weren't the one had loudly and often argued, fought and even cursed the idea of having to take home-ec in grade ten. "It's not the *same*," she insisted, "at school they only taught *dumb* stuff. I mean, *really*, how often do you need to make *one* cupcake? I mean...*one*?"

Sally and Mark dutifully did school. They left in the morning with Joe and his siblings, walked to the corner and waited for the school bus. Jean didn't know they waited in a group visibly distanced from the others waiting for the same bus, nor did she know that once on the bus they sat together, ignoring and ignored by the rest of the kids, and if she had known she wouldn't have had any suggestions for bridging the gap. It was more than the new kid syndrome, it was even more than the fact Joe's family were what the rest called Veets. They could have forgiven the Veets part, what they couldn't forgive was that the new kids obviously preferred the company of the Veets.

And then the kids came home with torn clothes, and Sally had a shiner that started at her eyebrow and went down past her cheekbone. She also had a grin that was maybe a bit tight at the corners, but totally sincere.

"My *God*!" Eve shrieked. "My God what happened?"

"I was talkin' when I shoulda been listenin'." Sally tried to pass it all off as nothing at all but Eve was in high gear, getting ice cubes, getting tincture of benzoin, getting ready to take hysterics.

"Yeah." Mark took Sally's hand, squeezed it gently, his smile stretching his swollen lower lip. "And you should see the other guy, eh Sal?"

"What other guy? What happened?" Jean decided Eve doing the fuss-budget hysteric was enough for any household. She sat down and pretended to be calm.

"Oh, you tell 'em," Sally winced, blinking rapidly, fighting the need to cry as Eve's first aid skills blundered away at the eye.

"Well, we're waitin' for the bus at school, to come home, eh, and they start in on Joe, eh." Mark was obviously going to make it all as unimportant as possible. "So first it's the townies, but then the bus kids pick up on it. You know, Buddha-eyed bastard and goddamn boat person and that shit. So then the bus comes, eh, and we get on, and it just gets worse. The joke shit, eh. How can you tell how many Veets live in a house? Count the windows and multiply by thirty; stuff like that. So we get off at the regular stop and don't they *all* get off, and so it's either let them pound on Joe and stand around as much use as a cuppa warm piss, or try to make 'em stop. So, they go for us, too. And I'm gettin' my clock cleaned real good and then *whappo!* and it's Old Sal, here, right in there like a dirty shirt, only this guy grabs her from behind, by the arms, eh, and this other guy gives her that shiner and Joe went nuts."

"So did you." Sally took the tea towel with the ice cubes wrapped in it away from Eve and held it against her own eye in self-defence. Eve was so fraught she was practically ramming it through Sally's skull.

"Yeah. And so I get the guy who's holding her and Joe gets the guy who hit her and then *Sal. . .*" He shook his head, grinning widely. "Listen, don't you ever get noisy again about how we turn our brains to train oil watching Rambo movies because Rambo has nothing on Salbo, here. Yah-*hoo*! Dumbshit Mikey Tyson has nothing on Sally. Except the lisp."

Sally came off her chair, clowning, foolish, pretending to go for Mark who pretended to cower back in abject terror and the two of them cavorted around defusing the anger, insult and belated fear of the others.

And then Mr. Nguyen arrived. And the guy who hardly ever said anything to anybody had his jaw in gear. The man who made everyone feel as if his opinion of them couldn't be much lower was carrying a small black lacquer bowl with two brilliant gold fish painted on the sides. He didn't even knock at the door, he just came in. Into the kitchen, right into the middle of the foolishness of the release of nerves and adrenalin. The kids froze, half expecting him to ream them out the way he had probably already reamed out Joe and the younger kids.

"Thank you," he said quietly. He very formally handed the bowl to Sally, looked at her eye and winced, then turned to Jean. "Cold tea," he said gravely. "You make tea. You drink tea. You settle nerves. Put cold tea bag on eye," and then he grinned, too. "My son says they kicked ass." He turned to Mark. "That true? You kick ass?"

"Yes, sir, Mr. Nguyen. And we'll do it again tomorrow if we have to."

"Damn kids," he decided. "Drive me crazy one day." He smiled and nodded all round, bobbed his head a few times, and then was gone. As he closed the door they heard him chuckling happily to himself.

"Boy," Mark said, "he's an odd bird. I thought he'd raise holy old hell about fighting."

"Probably would have done if you'd lost," Eve said softly. "It's hard to argue with the winners."

Popular mythology says it only takes one good fight to settle things down and after that everyone moves rapidly into friendship. It didn't happen that way. It didn't happen the least little bit that way. There were no fights on the way to school, bruises and swollen lips are too hard to explain when you walk into class. But the bus stop and the short trip from there to the front door became a war zone.

Everyone else had routines, more or less, to hold the edges of their lives together. The school bus arrived at a particular time, and returned at another particular time, Patsy's several rides to and from college were geared and timed to other people's shedules but became her routine. Eve was so into Dora Domesticus she was washing on Monday, ironing on Tuesday, brownies on Wednesday, oven cleaning on Thursday, floors on Friday, and only Jean drifted around loosely, depending on tide, weather, Fisheries regulations, dawn, sunset and how strongly the winds were blowing and from what direction.

She came in because the wind was blowing too strongly from the wrong direction and threatening to get stronger. She didn't mind, though, the tanks weren't full but they were so far from empty she felt cheered. The packer was waiting in the cab of his truck when she arrived. He waved and stubbed out his home-rollie cigarette, then got out and moved to help with the ropes.

It only took fifteen minutes. They lowered the fibreglass tub, dipnetted the cod from the live tank into the waiting water-filled container and when the live tanks were empty, Jean turned off her pumps and watched while the packer went back to his truck and winched his tub to the weigh scale. They both grinned; even when he subtracted the weight of the tub and water from the poundage indicated on the dial there was money, good money, being made.

He winched the tub into place, tied it down, signed the chit and handed it to Jean who tucked it very carefully into her wallet. The truck drove off. Jean walked over to the packers, presented her chit and waited while the bookkeeper made out a cheque.

She was in a good mood as she walked home. She had fewer worries right now than she'd had in four or five years. She was tired, sure, but tired can be overcome. A hot bath, a meal, a few hours sawing logs and tired is gone. Terry Dugan would be lead-footing it to the house soon to collect Patsy and head off, probably up a back road to neck until the cab of the pickup was steamed; maybe, after a nap, she'd suggest the rest of them go into town for a pizza and maybe catch a movie. The movie. The only one in town. The only one for sixty miles.

She topped the hill and started down the other side, heading for the corner and the road home. That's when she walked into the brawl.

Joe was rolling in the mud, fighting desperately, Mark was pinned against a tree catching punches groggily and Sally was flailing and kicking while two bozos big enough to be on a chain gang laughed and slapped her repeatedly. Joe's siblings were racing down the road toward home yelling for their mother to come and help.

Some things you do before you even think about how to do them. Jean hadn't been in a fight for probably twenty-five or thirty years. She neither knew nor cared who was right and who was wrong.

One of the several taking turns turning Mark's face to mush had his back fully turned to her. Jean ran as quickly as she could and two and a half feet from the broad jean-clad backside she fired a kick that connected squarely between the muscled thighs. Someone's pride and joy gasped and dropped to his knees. So she kicked him again, this time on the side of the neck.

There was a stick lying in the gravel on the side of the road. It wasn't a club, it wasn't even a baseball bat, it wasn't much of a stick, really, but when it landed on the head of one of the jerks giving Sally a hard time it did exactly what Jean wanted it to do. Suddenly the fight was withering on the vine. One of the valiant turned threateningly and Sally screamed, "You just dare touch my mother you fuckfaced asshole, you just dare!"

The word *mother* hit harder than any kick, harder than any stick, harder than the club Jean wished she had. They just froze. The expressions on their faces changed. They stared.

"Come on," Jean puffed and panted, her heart thudding in her ears, "let's go home before the cops arrive."

The word *cops* finished what the word *mother* had started. Within seconds gladiators were drifting away wordlessly. Jean grabbed the groin-kicked pride and joy by the shoulder, and helped him to his feet. "Do anything like this again," she said quietly, "and you are going to be one very sorry little boy. Do you understand?" He nodded, too sick to be angry. "Seven against three," she rubbed his nose in it, "and one of them a girl. What would your mother say if she knew?"

Sally didn't cry until they got into the house, and then she just sat on a chair, put her head on the table and let 'er rip. Jean was so upset she wanted to sit with her and join in but all she could do was take off her work jacket, sit on the bottom step, take off her boots and put them on the newspaper on the hall floor, then pad upstairs in wool socks to change her work clothes for clean ones.

When she came down Mark was washed and changed. Without the blood from his nose smeared all over his face he looked not too bad. Sally didn't have any marks on her, she had been pushed and shoved more than punched or hit.

"Looks as if Joe got the worst of it." Jean forced some calm into her voice but it still shook and quavered.

"You should call the cops," Eve's voice trembled. "This is starting to go too far."

"No," Mark said quickly, "no cops."

"Christ." Jean sat in a chair, and Eve put a cup of tea in front of her. "They all think they're John Bloody Wayne or someone."

"Joan Wayne." Mark pointed at Sally and tried to grin. Sally didn't answer, she just got up from the table, sniffing, and moved to the stairs. Jean left her tea untouched and followed.

Sally was at the bathroom basin, sponging water onto her face, still hiccoughing and sniffing. She turned and Jean folded her into a tight hug. "Oh, baby," she mourned, "Oh baby, I was so scared for you."

"I was scared for *you*," Sally wailed. "What if they'd hit you, too?"

"When are they going to leave Joe alone? Poor little guy."

"It wasn't *Joe* this time." Sally looked as if she wished she'd kept her mouth shut but you can't let a cat half out of a bag, it's either firmly hidden or racing around yowling in the face of the entire world. "Oh, Momma," and she was sobbing.

It took ten minutes to get the story from her. Maybe the fights had started because of Joe, maybe Joe had only ever been the excuse. "They said Gran was a . . . a . . ."

"Bunkhouse Bertha," Jean guessed. "Loggers' whore."

"You knew?"

"No. But it's what they said to me when I was younger than you are. And I wasn't a very good fighter. It wasn't so much I was afraid of getting hurt, it was that I was sick at the thought of hurting someone else! So instead of fighting with my fists, I fought with my tongue."

"Yeah?"

"Yeah. You just tell 'em Oh yeah? Well at least *my* Gran doesn't give it away for free like some cheap shits I could name but won't. I think I won when I told 'em all that the only reason they were raisin' hell about my mom was they knew their own fathers were at the front of the line, waiting in the rain for the one chance of their lives."

Sally stared. Then she nodded. No grins, no giggles, no hugs, no kisses, just a nod and total understanding.

They both heard the quiet gasp at the doorway. They both turned, startled. Eve stood, her face pale, her eyes suddenly sunk deep in her head, her lipsticked mouth half open with shock and pain. She tried to speak and couldn't, just shook her head, unable even to weep, and Jean knew every party Eve had ever attended, every fling Eve had ever flung, every don't-give-a-rat's-ass laugh Eve had ever uttered had come due, the bill was staring her in the face, the piper wanted paid. But she had no time, no energy, no interest in Eve, her problems, or her obvious pain and regret. Sally was sobbing heart-brokenly, and Sally was who was important. The sins of the mothers ought not be visited upon the children, even to the second and third generation. But they are. What's sauce for the goose is excused for the gander, the sins of the temptress outweigh those of the tempted. The double standard is alive and well and the innocent catch the shit.

She took one step forward, put her arms around her devastated child and held tightly. "I love you, baby," she said. "And that might not be much, it might never be enough, but it's just about everything I have. I'd give my right arm for you to never be hurt again, and we both know I can't stop the hurts. But we can stop this one. Fuck it. I'll sell the house, sell the boat, if I have to I'll sell my gumboots, but we'll get you away from all this generational bullshit."

Supper was quieter than the average funeral. Nobody spoke, not even to say Pass the bread or Please hand me the pepper. Jean almost felt sorry for Eve. She sat with her bright auburn wig defiantly glommed on her head, picking at her food as if she didn't know what it was and wasn't too interested in identifying it. The hand holding the fork trembled, more than once she looked as if she wanted to say something, and couldn't.

Patsy reached over, patted her grandmother's hand, and a look passed between them that rocked Jean to her socks. There it was, in that look, and it said everything that needed to be said. Patsy felt about her grandmother exactly the way Jean felt about Sally. Mine, right or wrong, good or bad, socially acceptable or not, mine, mine, mine, and I'll fight and die to protect it. And Eve knew it. But also knew it wasn't deserved and wasn't enough. Not enough for Patsy, not enough for Sally, not enough for Mark, certainly not enough for Jean, and not anywhere near enough for Eve herself.

"I don't want you to sell the boat," Sally said quietly.

Jean stared. "I thought you hated it here."

"Fuck 'em." Sally even smiled. "Fuck 'em all with broomsticks."

"But..."

"I'm not running away from a bunch of small town losers!" Sally almost started crying, again, but forced it back. "They'll either stop it or they'll eat it."

"Absolutely," Mark nodded. "There's more than one way to fix 'em."

"But..."

"I'm going into the cop shop," Sally announced, "and I'm going to lay assault charges on each and every one of the goddamn fuckers!"

"Me, too." Mark put his fork down with such force Jean knew he really wanted to throw it across the room. "And I'm gonna ask Joe to do the same thing."

"But..."

"You sound like an outboard motor." Mark twisted his mouth in what he thought might look like a smile. "But-but-but-but vroooom!"

"I'd like to say some stuff." Eve's voice was that of a very tired, very old woman.

"It's okay, Gran," Patsy said hurriedly.

"I can leave for a while if you'd prefer." Terry Dugan pushed back his chair, his face red. "I mean, fam'ly stuff and all..."

"Sit," Jean ordered. Terry sat, his big hands picking little bits from his slice of bread, rolling the bits into balls, dropping the balls on top of his mashed potatoes.

"I shoulda maybe talked sooner," Eve sighed. "I thought I'd done 'er right, but I guess no matter what you do, if you keep your mouth shut, you're doing 'er wrong. I always thought least said soonest mended." She looked at Jean, and Jean knew Eve didn't really care if Jean believed her, understood her, or would even try to do either or both. "I didn't take you with me because Einarr woulda hounded me into the loony bin. You were always *his* kid. First time I ever slapped you he just about went through the roof. Told me if I ever hit you again he'd beat me senseless. And he wasn't a man to talk like that, so I believed him." She sipped her tea, and for a few moments her eyes were blank, turned inward, watching an old movie, one she had seen a thousand times without enjoying it once. "He was about as good a husband as any woman coulda found and I knew it, even dumb as I was at the time. Gentle. Quiet. Never bitched or nagged. And all he wanted was what anybody woulda called a normal life." She shook her head, looked at each of the others, shook her head again. "I don't know how to say it," she admitted sadly, "so I guess there's nothing for it but to get on with the hard part." She reached up, her fingers fumbling at her temples, tears streaming from her eyes, her face suddenly haggard and ugly.

Eve removed her wig. They stared, wordless, at the totally bald skull. Jean could think of nothing other than a huge flesh-coloured egg. The sound of their breathing was loud in the silence, she could even hear the humming sound the kettle made as it simmered. The plumbing gulped and rattled, the fridge trembled as the thermostat kicked the motor into gear.

"It just started coming out," Eve said quietly, her voice thin and trembling. "Every time I brushed, more of it came out. It got so bad I took to wearing a bandanna most of the time, and I went to the doctor so often I almost felt I owned his waiting room. They did tests, and then they did more tests and then they told me the name of it. Name about as long as my leg. But all any of it meant was there was nothing they could do about it. So I took to wearin' a wig over what was left of my hair. People thought it was just some kind of fashion bug I'd got in my head, eh. Didn't know how carefully what was left of it was brushed over the naked spots and patches. But Einarr knew. You can't sleep in a damn bandanna! Even Aunt Jemima must take hers off when she gets into bed. He knew. And at first he said oh, it'll go away, it's just some chemical imbalance thing. Even the doctor said it was maybe connected in some way to chemical changes from having a baby. Told me maybe it was nerves," she tried to smile and failed utterly. "I guess they didn't know the word 'stress' back then. Just nerves. And like I said, Einarr, all he wanted was for things to be ordinary, to have a normal life, and I don't think that was a lot to ask. I think we're all entitled to a normal, ordinary, everyday life. And how normal is this? He *said* it didn't matter, but it did, and I knew it, because I was one of the ones it mattered to. So...every-thing started going to hell. You couldn't say bugger-nothing to me, I was as edgy as all get out and I'd get insulted over nothing and ride his case. So that made him snarky and Jesus, Einarr snarky was something that went on for days. And while he was bein' snarky I'd get my feelin's hurt and ride his case and it was just stupid, but it was one thing after another and it didn't take but a year or so and we couldn't be in the same room. Sure as hell not in the same bedroom! So..." She picked up her wig, and stroked it as if it were a living creature, a cuddly, loving living creature. "So I took off. And yeah, I got me a pogo stick and hopped it in and out of a lot of beds. Because when you feel ugly that's one way to try to convince yourself you aren't ugly at all. But none of 'em could handle it any better'n Einarr could. Or maybe I wouldn't let them handle it no better. Some of 'em I suspect I didn't give a chance to even try to handle it. And I'm not makin' excuses. Or maybe I am, I don't know! But I didn't do any of it to hurt anybody but myself, and about all I can say in my own defence is I wasn't thinkin' exactly straight at the time!" She reached up and rubbed her own bald dome. "Would you?" she challenged.

Patsy got up suddenly and ran to the downstairs bathroom, sobbing loudly. Sally almost got up to follow her, then settled back in her chair. Mark looked at his thumbnail as if he'd never seen it before, then, unwillingly, reached up and scratched his head.

"What about transplants?" Terry asked.

"Tried that," Eve grinned sourly. "They fell out, too. And thank God they did because they made my head look like a fuckin' patch-work quilt!" She laughed softly. "I didn't have to pour good money after bad to look like the Freak-a-the-Week! I could do that without spendin' a dime."

"Must be a bugger." Terry blew softly, a sympathetic whooshing sound that did more than anything anyone could have said to ease the tension.

"Jesus," Mark sighed. "I guess it's inherited or somethin', eh? I guess I kind of always knew that sooner or later I'd lose my hair. I mean, well, most guys do, I guess, eh? But...well..."

"I don't know. Some say yes, some say no. I don't know anybody else in *my* family went as bald as this," Eve tried to make light of it. "I think I hold the record for billiard ball heads. There isn't even peach fuzz up there. The up side of it, if it has one, is that I got no hair anywhere else, either."

"You're kiddin'!" Mark stared.

"Not so much as one fuckin' follicle," Eve laughed. "Prob'ly saved three hundred dollars just on razor blades I didn't need to shave my legs."

Sally stood up, leaned over, kissed Eve on the top of the head and even managed a wink. "Helluva way to save money! I think I'd rather stick to a porcelain piggy bank."

Jean could have stood up and cheered. The kid collected the plates, scraped the uneaten suppers into the compost bucket and, as if it were any other night of her life, started doing the dishes. "Get up off your ass, Mark," she chided, "and finish the table, will you. I'm not doing everything by myself for the rest of my life, you know."

"'Scuse me," Eve sobbed. "I got to go to the can, talk to my kid and get this rug in place again."

Jean moved behind Sally at the sink, put her arms around her daughter's waist, then leaned against her, squeezing gently. Sally bowed her head and nodded. Not one word got said. Mark looked at them, then put his dish towel aside, stepped forward, put one arm around Sally and one around his mother and hugged gently. "Fuck, eh?"

"Fuck for sure," Jean agreed.

She left them with the dishes, got her gumboots and jacket from the hallway and walked out into the velvet dark night. You think you know something, and you feel secure in what it is you think you know, and then in two minutes you learn what you thought you knew isn't true, wasn't true, won't be true, has never been true. And where does that leave you?

It leaves you right where you were before you lost what you thought you knew. It leaves you with someone you don't know or love firmly implanted in the middle of your life. Whatever the reasons why nothing altered the fact Eve was a stranger. Nothing would fill those empty holes, nothing would bridge the years, there was no way to alter one single hour of any of it. Nothing changed. Eve had still hit the pike, there was no sudden rush of stuff to patch the rip, no surge of daughterly emotion, no Mormon Tabernacle Choir singing paeons of praise and that, as they say, was that.

Sometimes, when she should have been doing something else, Jean would find herself staring at nothing the least bit important, and thinking of what it must have been like for Eve when her hair began to thin. She knew from bitter personal experience what it was like when your marriage began to fray. Things you would have overlooked only a few months before suddenly seemed to loom overwhelmingly. Words you could have said easily suddenly stuck in your throat, words you would have kept to yourself leaped out, unbidden and unconsidered.

All those things you would have been willing to believe, even eager to believe, rang hollow when he said them, and things you thought you had put behind you suddenly jumped up and bit you on the nose, forcing you to see, whether you wanted to or not, there was a pattern, and it was once again repeating itself all over your life.

It wasn't just the constant moving, it wasn't even that the moving began to seem terribly like running away from something you wound up taking with you anyway. It was something else, a boulder perhaps, which fell into a clear crystal stream and changed the flow of the current until what had been one stream became two small creeks running parallel for a while, but then each creek had to accommodate other boulders, a stump or two, perhaps a huge tree, and then there were two streams, no longer parallel, winding their own courses, and they might meet and touch again at different times and places, but they weren't a single stream any more, and each separate one had a very different composition of minerals.

Jean didn't know about losing your hair, but she knew about losing your own deep inner desire to believe and to trust. He'd come home late, only two or three hours late, and if there was a very faint smell and taste of beer on his breath when he kissed her, it was nothing more than was usual because he often stopped for two draught when he got back from a trip. But the boulder had already settled into the creek, and the taste of beer triggered something. She smiled, she said I'm glad you're home, she got his supper out of the oven where it had been staying warm and slowly overcooking, she even sat on a chair at the table with a cup of tea to visit with him while he ate hungrily, and all the time she was remembering how angry and hurt she had been the time he nearly missed Patsy's Christmas concert.

She didn't drive a car then, and even if she had been able to drive, the car wasn't at home because he drove it to the company yard and parked it behind the freight shed. He was due back from his run at noon, should have had his truck serviced and parked, his waybills checked and turned in and been home easily by three, plenty of time, beaucoup the old tick tock as he liked to tease. And there they were at six-fifteen, and no car, no ride, no nothing except three kids all dressed and ready to go and Patsy on the verge of tears. Jean didn't have the money for a taxi. So there was nothing for it but to steel herself, leave the kids sitting round-eyed and worried, watching television, and go to the neighbour's. She remembered standing in the doorway, explaining, the smile on her face feeling stiff and phoney. The neighbour woman just nodded as if every day of her life someone she barely knew came to the door with a problem, and ten minutes later they were being driven to the auditorium. Anything else she could have managed on her own, but the concert had been moved to the junior high school, too far to walk with the kids, too late for a municipal bus. The ride was a vital necessity.

Patsy was so worried she wouldn't get a chance to be one of the three wise men she was almost sick to her stomach, and Jean barely had time to thank the neighbour for the ride before Patsy was racing off to get her costume pinned together. The overworked teacher gave Jean a look she probably reserved for things she found in old cheese in the science lab and snapped, "We asked the parents to be here early!" Jean wanted to say Hey lady, you're lucky we made it at all, but she just nodded miserably.

Nodded and felt, somehow, that unreasonable as it was, she was guilty of something. Somehow her fault that he hadn't come home, her fault she and her kids had been caught stuck in a bind. Her fault the overworked teacher had more last-minute rush pushed on her. Her fault, her guilt, her inadequacy.

The first half of the concert was behind them, the parents milling around in the foyer, buying UNICEF cards or decorations made in the home ec or IE classes, profits and proceeds to the Salvation Army Christmas Cheer and then there was Tommy, half cut, of course, dressed to the nines, in his best suit, with his shoes gleaming. He had spotted her where she was standing by the open window having a cigarette, carefully blowing the smoke outside. He came over, kissed her cheek, said Sorry I'm late, the traffic was a bitch, and she smelled the booze. She was sure everyone could smell it. She knew everyone knew he had just arrived, she knew everyone knew he had missed the first half, she knew everyone knew as well as she did that he had been sitting in the pub swilling it back, the company of others more important to him than his kid and her first Christmas concert.

And it wasn't just the smell of beer that filled the air around him, it was the smell of whiskey, too, he'd been in the hard bar, and not for a couple of fast draught, either. He'd been there for hours.

When she hissed at him that he was late he just grinned and said Hey, I'm here aren't I, settle down for Chrissakes. She didn't settle down but she did bite her tongue. Two more words and she'd plant the ashtray between his upper and lower jaw.

She sat through the second half of the concert with him sitting beside her, the beer and whiskey fumes wafting. And then it was pageant time, and there was Patsy in a bedspread burnoose, piping her lines clearly, and Jean's eyes filled with tears. The kid didn't even know her dad had made it but she went on anyway, and remembered all twenty words, in the proper order. Jean wanted to stamp on Tommy's foot, right on the bunion beginning to form on the joint of his right big toe. Sally cheered and Mark, half asleep on his mother's lap, sat up, saw his big sister and laughed happily. And Tommy grinned as if he'd been there all along, as if he'd written the playlet himself, as if he had any reason at all to feel any emotion but ashamed of his bloody self.

They waited until they got home and the kids were sound asleep in bed before they had their fight about it.

"What's the big deal?" he yelled. "Jesus, so you had to bum a ride . . . did it *kill* you? You're my wife, you're not my fuckin' *mother*, okay?"

"That's right, Tom, keep yelling. The guiltier and shittier you feel the louder you yell. Break the sound barrier one day."

"Break *you* one day if you don't stop. If I want to stop in for a beer after a damn hard trip, I'll stop for a bloody beer, and it'll take more than some nagging bitch to stop me."

"You had *a beer*? On top of everything, you're a bloody liar."

"I'm not pussywhipped, though! Bloody see if I am! It'll take more than anything *you* can come up with to slice mine off and keep 'em in a jar. Just shut the fuck up before I give you something real to bitch about!"

The violence she had always known was simmering behind his smile surfaced and she knew he wasn't trying to communicate with her, he was bent on controlling her. Push him much harder and something was apt to happen that she didn't want to admit could be true. It wasn't so much she was afraid of him as she was afraid of what she would find out. Even at the time she knew if he did hit her, he — and she herself — would later say she had made him do it. But nobody makes someone else hit and punch. She knew that. And knew she was going to shut the fuck up before he did, in fact, give her something to bitch about. Because she knew she'd do her bitching to the police and that would be the end of everything, Tom Pritchard would never forgive her for busting his ass and putting him in the crowbar hotel, not even overnight.

She'd put it behind her, she thought. And it stayed behind her. Until things were tight between them, until there'd been two or three moves too many, a couple of fights too many, suspicions about girlfriends in towns at the other end of his run, and then, sitting there finishing a happy supper with the kids, not giving two hoots in hell if he was an hour late or not, it all came flooding in on her, not only did the dime drop, the whole thing dropped in place, and she had to excuse herself, get up from the table and go to the bathroom to run cold water and splash it on her face. She let the cold water run on her hands and wrists and realized no talk was going to alter anything, no discussion was going to do what we all hope discussions would do, and no agreement would ever be anything other than very temporary, made to appease her but easily ignored. Throw the geek another raw chicken, feed it and maybe it'll calm down, give it something so it'll stop rattling the cage, then we'll get on with life as we have decided we will live it.

The son of a bitch. The selfish son of a bitch. This is what I am going to do and you can like it or lump it.

Well, she hadn't liked it and she refused to lump it. She waited, patient as any lizard, and carefully considered all her options. She wasn't about to take a flying leap out of the frying pan into the blaze. She wanted to get a job but Mark was too little, and there wasn't any decent daycare to be found. There was one woman five blocks away who babysat, but only for kids who needed someone to be with them between the time they got out of school and the time someone got home from work.

A few days of fretting and fuming and Jean woke up one morning knowing that what seemed like a detriment might be something else. Less than a month later the kids were arriving at her place as their moms went off to jobs they probably would rather not have needed.

"Christ Jesus," Tommy complained, "it's like living in a bloody orphanage around here. I get home after a trip and I'm up to my nose in fuzzy heads. Why can't their own mothers look after them?"

"Oh, listen to you," she laughed easily, "and you're the one said he wanted to have a kid a year for twenty years before he even thought about slowing down!"

"I didn't mean *this*. It's like a friggin' zoo!"

"It'd be worse if they were your own," she teased. "These ones at least *leave* after a while."

"Couldn't leave soon enough for me!"

But it eased the financial pressure, and with that worry gone it was easier for her to wait her chance to do something more about what was a less and less satisfactory situation. Just knowing she was doing more than sitting and eating crap salad stilled the angry words; the arguments hardly ever bothered happening any more because frankly, my dear, she didn't give a damn.

Right up until Mark was in grade one, and by then she had some decent clothes, her own car and correspondence courses to keep her brain alive. And she went out and got herself a real job. "What in hell *for?*" Tommy raged. "I can support my own damn wife!"

Except they both knew he couldn't. There were too many poker games to get into, too many cases of beer to be bought, too many cars he decided to trade in before they were paid off so he could sign on the dotted line for bigger monthly payments over a longer period of time. Thread by thread it frayed, until it wore out completely, the day he said he had a line on a better job and she told him she wasn't going with him.

Had any of it been like that for Eve? What did she feel each morning when she brushed her hair and found more of it stuck in the bristles? Did she buy and take every possible kind of vitamin pill? Did she send off to addresses she found in the back of pulp magazines, Stop Hair Loss Now? Did she rub warm oil on her scalp and pray? Did she sit in the bathtub with tears sliding down her face and curse?

Tommy had sat up in bed one night and said, "I'm human, too, Jeannie, and just once in a while it would be nice if you reached out for me."

"Why?" she asked, knowing she was sending a knife into his guts, "if I don't feel like it?"

"Don't feel like it," he echoed dully.

"When would I get a chance?" She sent another knife. "Even if I'm not in the mood you always are, and you won't take no for an answer. If a person feels like she's already getting used, like it or not, why would she reach out for more of the same?"

"Like it or not, huh?"

"Yes, like it or not." She sat up in bed, too, and looked him right in the eye. "You come home after being gone for anywhere from two days to four, and you come in stinking of beer with someone else's perfume on your shirt and I know you've been having a great old time somewhere, spending money we can't afford to be Mister Congeniality. And you come in the door with a hard-on you got dancing with someone whose face I've probably never seen and then I'm supposed to swirl around like Loretta Young and her goddamn refrigerator and be *glad*, Tommy, that you finally condescended to pay any attention to us! But you don't, you don't really pay any attention at all, we're like the old dog who will always be at home waiting to lick your hand. Maybe if you put one-tenth the energy into life with us that you put into being the Playboy of the West Coast, I *would* be reaching, but you don't, and you haven't done for a long time. Why should I reach for you when you're busy reaching for beer?"

"If it's too much bother. . ." He swung his legs over the side of the bed and reached for his shorts. "Then believe me, lady, I won't impose."

So he slept in the sleeping bag on the living room floor, but only for a night or two, and then he was back and she was left feeling as if she would have had more results if she'd gone down the hallway and talked to the umbrella someone had left hanging behind the door.

For Eve, it was Einarr who began to hesitate. It was Einarr who had to turn out the light before he could reach. And it was Einarr who had felt the thin thin wisps of hair against his cheek and not been able to deal with the mental image of a dome barely covered with downy tufts. It was Einarr who lay with his back turned until Eve got up in the morning, her wig askew because she had tried to sleep in it, tried unsuccessfully to hide what was under it. Eve who bought nightcaps with ruffles and lace, and knew they only made more obvious what was already far too visible.

And so Eve hit the road. How many times had she done it in her head before she actually up and did it? And how many times had she tied up with other men, trying so hard to convince herself of something she no longer believed, and then had her own disbelief proved right because they were no more able than Einarr to handle the truth when they discovered it. And what does *that* do to you after a while?

And how much worse would it be if, like Eve, you had more to lose than most people? Jean had seen pictures of Eve and Einarr and then cursed her own luck, and wished she had resembled her mother instead of her father. Einarr had been a fine looking man, but Jean would have preferred to look like her beautiful mother. Now she knew why, when she had said so, her grandmother had given her a long hard look and said "Be careful what you wish for, you might not like it when you get it. All that beauty did her no good in the end." Jean thought at the time her grandmother was referring to the Bunkhouse Betty reputation, the Easy Ride reputation, the Town Bicycle reputation, the rumours, stories and near-legends that made people raise their eyebrows when Eve's name was mentioned and say ugly things like Oh, her. If she had as many sticking out as she'd had sticking in she'd look like a goddamn porcupine.

Why had Einarr never explained? He hadn't hesitated a minute when it was time to sit down and explain menstruation. He hadn't hesitated when it was time to go from the birds and the bees to men and women.

Was he afraid his own guilt would surface and slap him in the face or was he afraid Jean would look at him with scorn, pack her things and head off to find her mother, rub the bald head and say It doesn't matter, Momma, for heaven's sake don't make a big deal of it....

That's what Patsy was saying. "Oh, come *on*, Gran! I mean just *look* around you. People are shaving their heads for a chance to look the way you do."

"What kind of people? Drug suckers and Nazis!"

"No, *not* just those kind of people! Women are questioning *all* those old sexist standards of beauty! Who *says* you have to have *tons* of long curly blond hair to be *beautiful*? Who *says* you have to be so *tall* or so *thin* or so curvy or so...certain a way? And *why* do they say it? And what *happens* if you don't believe it? And why *not* just tell 'em to go fuck the moon?"

"I did. I spent my whole life telling..."

"*No!*" Sally shouted, on her feet, vibrating with something even Jean couldn't identify. "No you didn't! You believed something was wrong with you and you tried to hide it. You had it all, and you were beautiful, and you liked what being beautiful got you and then you thought you weren't and that was awful for you. Well," and she shook her head and pointed at her own darling plain face, "look at this mug. I've worn it all my life. I never even had, not for one minute, what you had for all those years."

"That's not a mug," Eve said stoutly, "that's a good face. An honest face. A lovely face."

vely," Sally said clearly. "But one day I will be. Me. Inside
/hen I stop being so goddamn angry at so many people! You
s, Gran, like beauty is in the eye of the beholder, and beauty is
only u.... deep, and stuff like that. You tell me it's a good face but. . . you
don't believe it. I don't believe it all the time. But one day I will."

Jean sighed. It was so much easier to just come out here and put
bait on hooks, fasten leaders to the mainline, ease the line over the
back end of the *Old Woman* and inch across the face of the sea, trolling
for bottomfish.

And where in hell were they all going, those never-wily bottomfish? In only a few years the species they had all called trash fish had
become marketable. The big-headed ugly lumps once eaten only by
those too poor to have a boat with a motor that allowed them to troll
for salmon, the ones who had mooched and handlined, the poor and
the bottom rungers, had become money with fins, given names a bit
less off-putting than Long Jaws and Blue Bug-Eyes and Spiny Backs.
And in only a few years the fish that had once literally swarmed on the
bottom of the sea, feasting on what would probably be called garbage,
growing fat and huge on the leavings of others, scavenging and being
the housekeepers, had diminished until six of the twenty-one identified
kinds were so few they would be put on the endangered species list — if
there was an endangered species list to put them on, that is.

Where had they gone? It wasn't overfishing. There hadn't been
time for overfishing. The commercial fishing had barely begun. It
was something else. Something that had to do with the currents
running northward and the pulp mills clustering to the south, some
dumping fifty metric tonnes of poison-contaminated crud into the
sea every day, where it could flow slowly northward, accumulating
in the mud, stuff mixing with other stuff to form new stuff not even
yet identified, killing off algae and shellfish, killing off the small things
on which larger things fed.

But there was no proof. You could go to a meeting and stand up and
point to a map and name the mills and show where they were, and talk
about all that water coming from farther south, going past the pulp
mills, picking up the shit in the water and bringing it north, and all the
good it would do you would be some buzzard in a suit who had just
flown in from back east would say there was no proof. They knew two
teaspoons of dioxin dropped in the drinking water could kill the population of New York and still dioxin-contaminated crud poured from
the mills at a rate that staggered the mind; but no proof.

No proof of any kind. Except more and more kids with allergies, more and more kids with immune system deficiencies, more and more kids born without livers, doomed to die. No proof. Except all the terrible algae blooms were happening further south. The water around the mill here was clear. Too clear, too clean, too lifeless. Hardly any algae, and only a few kinds of seaweed. Fewer herring every year. Contamination warnings where people used to pick oysters or dig clams. The Sliammons sitting bitter-eyed and fiercely silent on a beach that had once been their banquet table and was now denied them as a food source because of contamination. And some nice man saying all anyone had to do was wait, the mill was cleaning up its act, and when it did Mother Nature would do what she had always done, and in a year or two everything would be fine. Except the beach was poisoned and it would take a minimum of a hundred years for it to be safe again. One hundred years during which the children of people who had considered that beach to be their pantry would have to live on wieners and bologna instead of clams and herring.

First they closed all fishing from Saltery Bay to Dinner Rock, then from Saltery Bay to Lund, and now they had closed the area as far up as Bliss Landing. Jean could no longer get in the *Old Woman*, clear the harbour and drop her lines. She had to get in the *Old Woman*, clear the harbour and go north for three-quarters of an hour before she cleared the closed zone.

They'd all wake up one morning to find the fishing finished from the forty-ninth to the border of Alaska.

But until then, she could at least come out here and work herself into heavy fatigue, catching cod to sell so she could support her family. And the cod would be transferred live to huge tanks on the back of a truck and taken to the city so other people could buy it to feed to their families, and it wasn't too hard at all to smother the voice in her head that told her she was catching poisoned fish and selling them to people who didn't know what they were feeding to their children might not be fit for human consumption. Hell, it *looked* okay! It wasn't as if the poison coloured the meat. It didn't taste funny. You couldn't smell it. You just bought the poisoned food, cooked it, fed it to your kids and if the birth defect rate was skyrocketing, well, who could prove Jean Pritchard had contributed to it with her bottomfish?

The sound of sirens wakened Jean. Police sirens. She was out of bed and grabbing for her underpants and jeans before she was fully awake. She rammed her feet into thick wool socks, shrugged on a long-sleeved undershirt, then pulled on a thick red and black checked bush shirt and headed downstairs, slipping on the bare wood floor.

She shoved her feet into her gumboots, grabbed her jacket and, ignoring the sleepy "What the hell is going on?" from Eve and the equally sleepy "Mom? Is it a fire?" from Patsy, Jean ripped out the front door and headed toward the noise.

Sally and Mark weren't back from clamming. She knew that. Knew it because some part of her always knew, even if she was sound asleep, when they came back. However quiet they were, that mother part of her heard them and relaxed. And it hadn't relaxed, they weren't home, and not only were there sirens, there were flashing lights.

She rounded the corner and started down the hill. The cop cars were parked one behind the other, at an angle, blocking the road. And between the cop cars and the dock, a knot of people, two knots of people, pushing, shoving, shouting, swearing and cursing.

She couldn't remember a time in her life when there had been a riot in town. Couldn't remember one single story of The Good Old Days when there had been a riot in the streets. Chalk one up for historical progress because the town had just joined the modern age. A riot, complete with easy-to-hand weapons: clam rakes, shovels, broken handles.

She found Sally, Mark and the Nguyen kids standing by the cop cars, staying well away from the uproar.

"Thank God!" She hugged them all. "What's going on?"

"A buncha Veets showed up," Joe said tightly. "Whole busload of 'em. And there wasn't anything anyone could do because Fisheries had given 'em all permits to clam here."

"But they're taking undersized, too," Sally added.

"Or at least everyone says they are," Mark corrected.

"They are," Joe nodded. "You know they are. They've all got bits of stovepipe, don't they."

"What's stovepipe got to do with it?"

"They cover the bottom of the sack with legals," Sally explained, "then push in a stovepipe; and they put undersized in the stovepipe with legals all around it and when the sack is full, just before they close it off, they haul out the stovepipe and fill the top with legals.

But there's a core of undersized in there, too! Like maybe a quarter of what's in the sack isn't legal. So now, instead of just getting paid for the sacks when we hand 'em in, we get tags with numbers on, and they put other tags on the sacks, with the same numbers we've got. And you get paid later on, after they've sorted through the sacks."

"They subtract the weight of the illegals," Mark added. "But there's people say the Veets are changing the numbers on their sacks so someone else gets dinged with the subtractions."

"They can't do that," Sally argued. "How they going to do that when there's two tags and you're supposed to keep one yourself?"

"Yeah, and how many people *do*? How many people got tags in their pockets and how many others leave the tags with their gear by the fire, where the tags won't get wet and shred apart?" Joe countered. "They're doing it!"

Jean saw Mr. Nguyen in the crowd yelling in his own language, cursing out people who looked like him and spoke the same dialect. "What's he saying?" she asked.

"He's giving them shit," Joe laughed. "Telling them they're killing off next year's clams. Telling them that they're bein' assholes and making it tough for the rest of us. And they're telling him he's a traitor."

The three policemen and one policewoman were pushing and shoving, trying to clear a space between the two shrieking groups. Jean saw a shovel come down on the shoulders and back of one of the cops. He fell to the paved surface of the road, the policewoman bent to help him to his feet and the gangs surged forward.

And then the rioters were all around them. Joe got hit on the side of the head and fell to his knees. Mark grabbed him, pulled him upright, and Eve was suddenly there, in jeans, gumboots and bush shirt, her nightcap still on her head, as out of place as a parasol in a windstorm. The little Nguyen boy was wailing as if his heart was broken. Eve scooped him up, set him on her hip and began pushing her way out of the crowd. Someone gave her a shove, she tottered, someone else grabbed her to straighten her, and in the heaving and hauling the nightcap wound up on the street, trampled by muddy gumboots. Her bare head naked for all the world to see, she kept shoving, putting her shoulder down and fighting for every inch, determined to get the eight-year-old out of the press and shove of enraged people.

Someone fired a shotgun blast and the gangs split. One group ran for the dock, the other group surged uphill past the cop cars. Jean grabbed the kids and got them off the road, away from the cars, into the brush flanking the gravel strip on the side of the pavement. She saw Bill, then. He was staring, but not at her, staring past her to where Eve, totally uncaring of her bald head, was calming and soothing the sobbing little boy who obviously wanted nothing more in all the world than to go to bed and leave all this nutsiness behind him. His arms were wrapped tight around Eve's neck, his face buried against her, and his thick black hair only emphasized the pallid nakedness of her skull. But Eve didn't care. She knew, she couldn't help but know, and yet all she seemed interested in was the child, and calming him, soothing him, making him feel safe.

A policeman made it to one of the cars and turned on the siren. The shotgun blast sounded again, and everyone froze.

"We're going home," Jean said firmly.

"Ah, Mom!" Mark protested.

"We're going home," she repeated, "because it's always the innocent bystanders who wind up getting hurt. Come on." She herded the younger Nguyen kids ahead of her. "We're going to get some hot soup into these kids and get them warm. They're half asleep on their feet!"

The kids were fully asleep in warm beds by the time the uproar was stopped. Sally had the two Nguyen girls in bed with her, Mark and Joe had the little boy in bed with them and there was hot soup waiting for Mr. and Mrs. Nguyen. They sat at the table eating hungrily and recounting some of who had said what to whom, who shoved, who pushed, who swung the shovel and nobody knew who fired the shotgun but nobody got hurt.

"Make life hard," Mr. Nguyen cursed. "Everybody hate Veets."

"Oh eat your soup," his wife said testily. "Eat your soup and ask if 'everybody' hate why are you eating soup." She looked at Jean and shrugged. Mr. Nguyen looked at his soup and his face flushed.

"It's okay," Jean laughed. "One day we'll find out who this damn 'everybody' is and then we'll raise hell!"

They left the Nguyen kids sleeping where they were. The parents went home, Eve headed upstairs for an hour or two of rest, and Jean sat at the kitchen table drinking coffee and trying to get the cobwebs out of her mind. She checked the clock on the wall, sighed, emptied the last of her coffee down the drain and began to get ready for another day out on the chuck.

There was no sign of the rioters, but signs of the riot were everywhere. Broken rake and shovel handles, bits of torn clothing, someone's left gumboot, broken windows in some of the buildings on the approach to the wharf. The whole thing left a sour taste in her mouth. Not long ago there had been so many clams buried in the sand around here you'd have had to make an effort to find undersized! But that was back before times got so hard people started selling what they had once considered public property.

She checked the *Old Woman* for damage and found none. That was one of the blessings for which she knew she was going to have to give thanks. She poured herself some thermos coffee and stood on deck, looking under the pier at the big lazing cod. He nosed constantly on the bottom, finding nothing that looked the least bit like food. Jean reached into her bucket of bait, tossed a piece overboard and it drifted lazily downward. Less than halfway down, the big fish was there, huge mouth open, sucking in the bait. Jean grinned, carefully balanced her thermos cup, got a strong length of wire line, fastened a leader and hook, baited the hook and tossed it over the side.

The big fish bit and she jerked hard, setting the hook firmly. He fought like a mad bastard but she hauled him in by brute force, not by grace or angling skill. And then, just to be sure she'd know which one he was at all times, she slit the tough skin at the base of his back fin and slid in a piece of bright yellow saw-edged garbage bag twist-tie. "There you go, old guy," she laughed. "Now you can live in the live tank where there's a half chance of clean water. And you won't be living off garbage." She dropped him down the hatch, sent a handful of bait down after him, a housewarming bribe, and closed the hatch.

"What you up to?" Bill asked, surprising her. She hadn't seen or heard him approaching, she'd been so fixed on the big cod.

"Oh, to each her own," she laughed. "Some people have pet poodles, I've got me a sort of a pet codfish."

"Amazes me the bugger's lived this long," Bill agreed. "I been watching him the better part of a year, and he's about half as fat as he was when he moved in. You'd think an animal like that, born wild and surviving only by his own smarts, would have figured it out and moved on, but I guess you can't expect 'em to know more than we do." He looked over at the cluster of houses along the lip of the bluff at the far side of the bay. "There's fools every year buy a hunka bluff and sink their life savings into a house right on the edge of what they say is about to become an ecological disaster. Sink all that money into a place where you can't even have a workin' septic tank because of all the rock. Never figure it."

"Makes me feel strange," she confessed. "I feel like someone is busy stealing something away from me and I don't know who's doing the stealing or what it is they've got their grubby little mitts glommed onto."

"You get home okay last night?"

"Yeah, no problem," she nodded. "Fed all the kids and piled 'em into bed. They were asleep in no time flat."

"That neighbour of yours took a big risk." Bill rolled a cigarette and offered the fixings to Jean, who took them and began rolling. "There were people just about ready to pop him one before they realized it wasn't them he was yelling at. Takes all kinds, I guess." Jean just nodded. Mr. Nguyen might let the town off the hook one day but she'd have to wait for him to set the example before she would feel inclined to forgive much.

"Saw your mother." Bill's face was brick red, his voice apologetic.

"Yeah," Jean nodded, "she did good, got Peewee out of the way and not a minute too soon."

"Einarr never said." Bill studied the pale blue smoke coming from his cigarette. "Guess it kind of explains some stuff."

"Don't know what," she shrugged.

"Well, couldn't have been easy for her."

"Wasn't easy for anyone."

"You nursing a grudge?"

"Uncle Bill." She dragged deeply on her cigarette, picked a piece of tobacco from the tip of her tongue and flicked it down to the water. "I don't even understand one-tenth of what's going on today, right now, this very minute, how in hell'm I supposed to find the time or energy to figure out what happened before I could tell my ass from my elbow? All's I want is to make it through from one day to the next with as little BS and heifer dust as possible." She grinned. "I was listening to the TV news the other night and this man came on they said was an International Economic Expert. And he talked about how as they changed money from one currency to another, from yankee dollars to Canadian, from Canadian dollars to British pounds, from there to francs, to marks, to yotzis to ditherwimps, they lost a million dollars a day." She stubbed out her cigarette and put the dead butt in the breast pocket of her bush shirt. "And I thought of all the people who had their houses foreclosed by the bank, all the people who lost their fish boats because they were a payment behind, and I thought to myself, bullshit. They'll ruin a family's chances for one thousand lousy dollars, they aren't going to let a million glide off into the ozone, they're all in it together, stealing 365 million dollars a year from *us*. And I knew if I never figured out anything else as long as I lived, I was one up on the International Economic Experts because they think I don't know that, and I know I do know it. But I don't know much else."

"Miserly bastards," he agreed, his voice gentle. "Hooligans, the lot of them."

"I used to think I didn't understand stuff because I'd dropped out of school. So I figured okay, I can cure that, I'll go to night school. Took my GED, took some other courses, probably racked up enough time I could have finished a couple of years university, but I still don't understand stuff. I still get hung up on questions other people seem to ignore."

"Yeah?" He looked at her, his expression half amused, half inquiring.

"What's a peaceful weapon? How can we have surplus food if there's kids dying of hunger? How come I'm payin' taxes until it hurts and the biggest companies in the world are given deferred taxes and special exemptions and then get grants and subsidies so's they can make even *more* profit?" She laughed softly, and heard Bill chuckle. "When Einarr went on like this we'd say he was having another Communist Fit, remember?"

Bill stubbed out his cigarette, stuffed the cold butt in his pocket and winked at her. "I do know if we don't get the hell away from this dock we're going to lose daylight and some other sad bastard will catch our profit, leaving us with butterflies in our wallets. See you, Spunk."

"See you, Uncle Bill." She waved and took her thermos cup into the wheelhouse, fired up the engine, left it on idle and went back out to free her lines. Over on the *Lazy Daze* Uncle Bill was getting ready to head out in search of salmon. He looked up and waved. She wanted to holler *I love you* but knew she'd feel like a damn fool if she did. And Bill would feel like a fool, because he was her uncle and should have brought her up to know better.

Weekends and spring break, Jean took the kids out with her on the *Old Woman*, introducing them to the skills and mysteries of the chuck, the wind and the boat, the same way Einarr had introduced her. "Here, take the wheel, I have to go see a man about a dog," and it was steer or stand there looking stupid.

"The leader goes in here like this. A hunk of bait on the hook, like this... then, over she goes. Your turn," and it was almost magical how quickly they caught on, how easily they got past the fumble-fingers part of it and made it to where they could almost do it with their eyes shut.

"Easy, now, she's heavier than she looks. Use the net because the less strain there is on her mouth the less damage is done. And the less damage, the quicker she'll adapt in the tank. We don't want them dead!"

"Seems weird, Mom, shipping live fish! You could take them to the fish plant and not have to bother about all this."

"And get paid so little for them it would hardly be worthwhile putting gas in the tank. There's more work to it this way, but there's more pay to it, too. And if anybody's going to get paid for working it might as well be us as a bunch of people we don't even know."

When she didn't have to supervise constantly, when she knew they could actually take the boat out by themselves and catch fish without her, she made a point of paying them weekend wages. Regulations might require her, as the holder of the permit, to be on board with them, but she could at least lie down in the thin spring sunshine and nap. And they could make enough money they didn't have to ruin their backs bending over the clam beds, raking heavy wet sand, then sifting through it in search of ever-diminishing numbers of ever-smaller clams.

Even Patsy learned how to handle the boat. Even Patsy learned how to set lines and haul in cod. That didn't mean Patsy liked any of it, but she did enjoy the bit of extra money she could make.

"I'm going to *need* it," she gushed happily, "for all the *stuff* we have to get for our *place*."

"God, yeah," Sally muttered, "a girl can't have too many knick-knacks, bric-a-brac, fol-de-rol and ticky-tack."

"Beg *par*don?" Patsy hadn't heard a word.

"I said yeah," Sally called more loudly.

Terry Dugan seemed totally overwhelmed by the idea of marriage. He just grinned, as if it was all too mysterious for words. Jean wanted to grab Patsy by the front of the shirt and yell *don't do this* but she knew she would only be wasting her breath. She told herself the only part of it that was any of her business was the part about persuading the loving couple to wait until Patsy finished her computer course.

"I don't see why," Terry said mildly. "She can go to school as easy from the apartment we'll get as from here. Easier."

Jean was ready. "But she'll have her head in the clouds. The only thing that will be important will be you, the apartment, your life together. And if what you feel for each other is the real thing it'll be just as strong two months from now as it is today."

Terry arrived Friday night and left Sunday night because his job was in camp and would be, even after they were married.

"You could," Eve glared, "offer them to stay here until they've got the down payment for a house. That way Patsy wouldn't be alone all week."

"I don't want any more people in this house," Jean said flatly. "There are too many of us underfoot already."

But Eve didn't take the hint. You could have surgically implanted teeth in the hint and trained it to bite Eve on the ankle and she would still ignore it. She wasn't going an inch away from her grandchildren. "Oh, I know," she said more than once, "I know exactly what some people think. And you can all see just how much I care for their opinion."

At least people spoke to her in the supermarket now. Neither Bill nor Alice would actually Talk to Eve, but they did nod and say hello. Once in a while of a Friday night Eve would get herself gussied up, put on her war paint, firmly set her finest wig on her head and sashay off down to the pub for a couple of wet ones and maybe a game or two of pool, but she was always home before closing time and she didn't bring anybody home with her.

Jean never found out who brought it home. She came back late, so tired she ached, and there it was, sitting on the front porch, looking as if its heart had broken and the weight of the pieces had pulled its ears almost down to its ankles. It looked at her hopefully, stood up, shivering, and tried to wag its stub of a tail.

The tail didn't look as if it had been stubbed on purpose. It didn't look as if a vet had carefully docked it, stitched it, disinfected it. It looked more as if something had gnawed it. The tips of the ears were already tattered, and when it tried to wag its tail its ass-end went nuts and the scallop-edged ears trembled.

"What in *hell* is *that?*" Jean shrilled. Whatever it was came gallumphing hopefully, bent almost double, rump pulled up almost beside the front shoulder, mouth open, tongue lolling. When she didn't fall in love with it the black and tan horror flopped to its side, then rolled on its back, submission city, look look look and see how totally helpless I am, don't you feel compassion. "*Mark!*" Jean yelled. "*Sally!*"

The door opened immediately. They must have been peering out sneakily to see her reaction to the marvel on the porch. They both smiled as if life had suddenly become ten times as wonderful as it had ever been.

"Hi Mom."

"What the by-Jesus hell is *this?*"

"Oh, that's Brucie," Sally smiled.

"Brucie? *Brucie?* Brucie lived in our old neighbourhood and wound up *dead!*"

"Yeah, that's why we called her Brucie. Thought it would be kind of a nice thing, what with old Bruce going out so . . . you know . . ."

"You say 'heroic' and you're dead. Get rid of this fleabag."

"Ah, Mom. Come on, Mom," Mark wheedled. "Look at her. Who'd want her? Nobody else is going to give her a place to live."

"If she isn't good enough for anybody else she sure as hell isn't good enough for *me*. She? *She?* Do you know how much it costs to get them spayed?" Why was she talking about spaying anyway, what did spaying have to do with a fleabag you weren't going to keep for another ten minutes? "Do you have even the beginning of a clue how much it costs for vaccinations?" Who cared what it cost for vaccinations if the damn thing took a hike before nightfall?

"Mom, she was sitting in the ditch by the bus stop, just sitting in water up over her bum, terrified of the traffic."

"What goddamn traffic? Four cars in the morning, two in the afternoon and all six coming home at night between seven and eleven. That is not traffic!"

"So scared she was shaking and shivering."

"Too stupid to get up out of the water, probably."

"Not stupid, Mom. Brucie is *not* stupid. Look," and Sally snapped her fingers. Brucie was up off the porch boards in a flash, all signs of submission gone. She zipped over to sit next to Sally, looking up at her with absolute faith. "Shake a paw, Brucie," Sally ordered. Up came a positively huge paw. Sally shook, then released the paw. Brucie held it up and watched intently. "Put your paw down, Brucie." Down it went.

"Oh, great. Big fuckin' deal. Call the David Whoozerman show, we've got a surefire winner here, a dog so bloody stupid it'll sit until the crack of eternity with its paw in the air."

"No, Mom, look," Mark was almost shaking with need. "Look what she'll do. Brucie, listen; there's a burglar coming up the walk with a gun in his pocket and you're the only hope we have. Whaddya do, Brucie?" Brucie fell on her side and rolled onto her back, exposing her belly. "Way to go, Brucie. Sit." Brucie sat, quivering almost as needily as Mark himself. "Okay, Brucie, here's another. The house is on fire. We're asleep. We're going to *fry*, Brucie, if you don't save us. What do you do?" and again Brucie fell to her side, then rolled to her back in submission. "Way to *be*, Brucie!" Mark was laughing happily, Sally grinning widely, and Jean began to feel like a scabby form of lowlife. "Brucie, get my slippers!" and again she flopped. Every trick Mark suggested, Brucie fell to her side, rolled to her back and showed her belly. "She knows two hundred and sixteen tricks," Mark announced, his eyes dancing. "You should see her dance for her supper!" Brucie squirmed and wriggled, convinced she'd just put on a display of obedience no other dog was ever going to rival. "She can fight off a gang of terrorists, she can disarm a nuclear warhead, she can do things those hero-dogs on TV haven't even thought of."

"Yeah," Sally giggled, "you should see her play the piano."

Jean exploded with laughter. "You crazy fools," she managed. "How did I wind up with two such manipulative emotional black-mailers."

"Ah, you know how it is." Sally grabbed Jean in a tight hug, kissed her on the cheek. "Monkey see, monkey do." Jean knew she'd put up with more than ugly Brucie for a hug that tight, a kiss that sponta-neous.

"Okay," she gave in totally. "But get ready for the lecture about feeding it, cleaning up after it, and not whining to have it in the house because it is not coming in the house *ever*. Not tonight because it's damp, not tomorrow if it's cold, not next winter if there's icicles hanging off its anus! Never."

"Until the twelfth of never," Mark sang, "it's on the porch for you."

"Right," Jean agreed. "And for God's sake start saving your money for vet bills because I absolutely refuse to contribute one red cent to this lousy mutt."

Of course Brucie tried to follow the kids to school in the morning so Eve had to step in and take charge. Jean knew that meant no sooner would she leave for the boat than Brucie would be in the mud room, with her face buried in the bowl of oatmeal Eve and the kids had suddenly decided was an indispensable part of a good nourishing breakfast, although until Brucie arrived all three claimed to detest mush. Jean didn't want to think about how much time Brucie spent in the mud room, or how easy it was to get from there to the kitchen, or how likely it was the territory would slowly expand to include the downstairs hallway.

"If I find so much as one dog hair," she warned, "there will be loud wailings and howlings, many thumpings and bangings, and probably a sob or two as well."

"Gee, Mom," Mark winked, "why would you fling yourself down the basement stairs that way?"

Jean knew she could make more money if she stayed out overnight. She knew she could fish a quarter more of the time if she didn't leave from home every morning and go back home again every evening. She knew all she needed to do was haul extra groceries to the boat, putter off, spend two or three days out there filling the live tanks, and she couldn't bring herself to do it. What if she made a mistake with her lights? What if something went wrong? What if a freighter ran over her, or a barge of chips on the way to the pulp mill or any of a zillion possible alternatives? What about sudden storms, what about freak waves, what about tripping and falling down the stairs, what about slipping in fish shit and going over the side, what about feeling like a goddamn fool if your anchorline broke and you just drifted silently onto the beach because the supposed skipper was snoring in her sleeping bag and didn't notice? What if it was true the sky is falling?

Anything Jean had ever tried to force had turned to shit. As long as there was a knot in her gut at the thought of it, she wasn't even going to try to make herself plan anything. That knot might cluck like a hen at times, but it was instinct, it was what Einarr had told her was the difference between the quick and the dead.

She made her first overnighter after school on a Friday, with Mark and Sally. When they came back on Sunday night Jean had all the proof she needed that her caution was costing her money. Lots of money. And she wasn't sure what she was going to do about it.

"Damn shame." Eve put the pot roast in the middle of the table and took her seat. "They've closed clamming again. Whole pile'a people gonna be back on pogey, and a whole pile more gonna be ess oh ell because they don't qualify for pogey."

"There goes the part-time job," Mark rolled his eyes. "Back to child labour around the house and a mingey occasional allowance."

"Yeah, but before you start feeling sorry for yourself think about Joe," Sally agreed. "His whole family is going to be ess oh ell." Mark looked up, caught Sally's eye and nodded. They both flicked glances over at Jean. She saw the look and pretended she hadn't. For all they knew she was totally absorbed in filling her plate with pot roast and vegetables.

"Damn shame." Eve got in on the gentle pressuring, too. "I understand the guy's a good worker when he can find a job, which I take it isn't too often, what with the recession and the fact nobody around here trusts the Veets as far as they can throw 'em."

"Oh shut the hell up," Jean laughed. "I don't need a brick to fall on my head."

He told her to call him Sam. He was waiting at the front gate with a small pack on his back and a nervous smile on his face. He bobbed his head and almost pulled his knit cap off his head. "Good morning," he managed.

"Hi," Jean smiled. She couldn't think of another thing to say and neither could he so they walked in silence along the street, down the hill and across the wharf.

It probably wasn't true that everyone in town happened to be looking out windows or doors and saw them head off together on the *Old Woman*. Probably only two or three people actually saw them leave, but by the time they came back four days later the whole town was well aware of the fact the Veet was deckhanding for Einarr's daughter. And they'd stayed out together.

"People's talking," Bill warned her.

"People always do seem to find a way to do that," she agreed.

"There's some who wonder if you know what you're doing."

"That puts them in good company. Been years since I knew for a fact I knew what I was doing. How about you?"

She grinned, rolled a cigarette and handed the makings to Bill, who nodded thanks and began to roll his own. He watched her carefully, then grinned.

"You'll do, kid," he decided. "I don't know that I approve of you bein' out there with him, but I'd probably worry no matter who it was."

"I know. It's been like that all my life," she winked. "It is hell being an international sex symbol."

"Still," Bill placed it flat out where it could be seen, "there's more than a few figure there's something wrong about hiring a Viet Cong when you coulda hired a local."

"He's not Viet Cong," Jean corrected, anger strengthening her voice. "If he'd been Viet Cong he might not have had to leave! If he's anything, he's Viet Minh. The ones supposed to be on *our* side. Even though," she added, still angry, "we were *supposed* to be neutral in that one!"

"Nobody's neutral in anything," Bill observed, nodding.

"No," she agreed, "and in *this* one it'll be fuckin' war if there's any trouble for those people. They've been good friends to us. And everyone's entitled to kick a boot at the can."

"People are talking," he insisted stubbornly.

"Yeah," Jean smiled suddenly, "and if bullshit was music those people would be a whole brass band!"

They had been out a day and a half when Sam came into the wheelhouse and stared at the chart Jean was studying. She half turned and saw him watching, so moved slightly, allowing him a better view. He moved closer, and she watched his eyes, saw him check the compass, then look at the map again. Jean reached for the parallel rulers, held them out questioningly. Sam took them and stepped closer to the map. All she did was tap their present position. Sam nodded, and Jean moved from the chair, watching as he very carefully followed their course from the dock to where they had stopped for the night, from there to where they were. He nodded and something inside her relaxed.

"You've run a boat before," she guessed.

"One day," he promised, "I will get another."

"What happened?"

He shrugged, exhaled heavily, wearily. "Oh, you know. Licence cost money, moorage cost money, insurance cost money, gas cost money, everything cost money. Then Fisheries close Howe Sound. What they call tough tittie," he grinned suddenly. "My son calls it shithouse luck. He tells me if it isn't a kick in the teeth . . ."

"It's a kick in the teeth, right?" she guessed.

Sam shrugged again, then examined the map, finally pointed. "Maybe a good cod hole," he hinted. "Water very deep here. You ever try?"

"Not there but if you think we might have some luck . . . go for it."

The water was deep but for all they caught it might well have been totally empty. Several hours of skunking, and they moved on. A fine rain drizzled down on them, gradually turning itself into a decent storm. The rain dimpled the surface of the sea, flattened the foam, the waves heaved sullenly and the *Old Woman* rode it easily, trolling lines still set, stabilizer poles extended.

They had planned to be out three days but Jean didn't like the look of the sky. The weather report wasn't bad, she had no reason to worry, but as the afternoon faded the uneasiness grew. "We could be home by midnight," she said quietly. Sam looked up at her, blinked several times, then looked at the cold grey water and nodded wordlessly.

"Bring in the lines," she smiled with relief.

"Good stuff," he agreed.

They didn't get back to dock until two-thirty, and by then the sea was pitching a fit. As they slid past the breakwater, Jean drew a deep sobbing breath. "Jesus," she confessed, "I'm glad you thought we should come home, too."

"I got over being brave a long time ago," he answered. "It's a good boat and it would ride out the storm but why take chances."

"She," Jean corrected, "a boat is 'she'." Sam looked at her, his face blank, then he nodded, and she knew he had filed it away to check it out with Joe. She was also quite sure he would never again call the *Old Woman* an it.

Nine-thirty in the morning Jean was back on the *Old Woman*, off-loading the cod, yawning occasionally and wishing she'd taken the time for one more cup of Eve's killer coffee. The Mickey Mouse crackled, she almost turned it off, then Bill's voice, distorted and scratchy, caught her attention. "*Lazy Daze* calling *Old Woman*, you there, Spunk?"

"Hey, *Lazy Daze*," she said into the hand-hold mike. "What's your excuse?"

"*Lazy Daze* calling *Old Woman*," Bill repeated.

"*Old Woman* here," Jean spoke more firmly.

"Need you, kid," Bill blurted.

"Where!" and she was signalling the packer to get his pulley bucket to hell and gone out of her way, reaching for a pencil, marking down the position Bill was reciting, repeatedly.

The packer pulled his gear out of her way, she wrestled the hatch lid shut, the packer cast off her lines, and she was fired up and moving from the wharf, past the breakwater, ignoring every rule of speed, blowing her horn to warn anyone near her that she was on the move.

She was lucky. The storm had sent most of the boats back to the wharf, the ones not tied up safe at home were still snugged in tight in protected coves, she had the channel to herself, and she took advantage. The *Old Woman* had never been intended for speed, but she did her best. The engine Sally kept fine-tuned purred like an enormous cat.

"*Old Woman* calling *Lazy Daze*," Jean managed. "On our way. Hang on, Uncle Bill."

"Need you, Spunk," he repeated,

Oh dear God, please don't let it be anything unbearable. Please don't let me have to go to Auntie Alice and start the conversation with I'm sorry. Uncle Bill *can't* be hurt, he *can't* be in trouble, not real trouble, please God, I'm not ready for this. Uncle Bill is the one told Einarr to back off, leave the kid alone, give her a chance to make a mistake or two before you start expecting her to be totally perfect, Chrissakes. Uncle Bill is the one said For the Love'a God, Einarr, you act like you never had a young day in your life! You want me to believe you were born *old*? Aunt Alice is the one who would come into the house smiling, and quietly take over so Gran could get off her feet for a few hours every day, and it was Aunt Alice who said

Listen, I want to ask a favour, and don't say no before you give me a chance, can Jeannie please spend more time at our place because it seems like I just don't see enough of her. And it was Aunt Alice sat down with Einarr and talked for a good hour, calming him down and keeping him from reaching for the three-oh-three when he found out Jean had been hanging out with Tommy Pritchard. Nobody knew *what* Aunt Alice had said that time, but it had worked and put off for a few years the bucketload of grief Jean herself had kicked over when she rushed headlong into what Einarr told her was the second worst mistake in the history of the world.

She painted a hundred horrible pictures in her mind before she got to him. He wasn't racked up on the beach, he wasn't in pieces on a reef, he wasn't sitting ass-to-the-stars on a rock, he was tied up, as safe as anyone could be, in Fiddler Cove, hugged up safe behind the wind-sculpted rocky outcropping everyone called the Fiddlehead.

She cut her engine, drifted in beside him, grabbed a rope and jumped from her deck to his. She had the two boats secured more quickly than she would have thought possible, and then she went looking for Bill Fergus.

He was on the floor of the wheelhouse, the Mickey Mouse on the floor beside him, his face grey, his lips a heart-stopping bluish colour.

"Somethin's wrong," he admitted. She knew right away what it was. He was talking out of only one side of his mouth. "My arm." He looked at it, flopped useless across his lap. "Somethin's wrong."

She didn't try to move him. She just ran for the sleeping bags, got one under him, one over him. The *Lazy Daze* was fifteen years younger than the *Old Woman* and her engine power showed it. "You put your head back on this pillow," she said gently, "and I'll get us to hell and gone back home."

Even towing the *Old Woman*, the *Lazy Daze* made the trip back in less than a third of the time it had taken to get to Fiddler Cove. The paramedics were waiting on the dock and had Bill in the back of the ambulance before Jean had both boats secured.

"Come on, Mom," Sally yelled, waving. Einarr's old bazoo was waiting, doors open, exhaust pluming. Jean raced for the car and jumped in. Her bum no sooner touched the seat than Sally was gunning the motor. Jean pulled the door shut and locked it, her heart pounding.

"Heard you on the Mouse." Sally drove easily, the steering wheel seeming to come out of the ends of her fingers, as much a part of her body as her wrists or hands. "Boy, those medics work fast, huh?"

She didn't get to see Bill at the hospital. She didn't even get to see his doctor. But she did get to sit on a bench in the hallway and hold Aunt Alice's hand.

"I told him," Alice said quietly, "I told him he was getting too old for it but would he listen?"

"Probably not," Jean sighed. "Obviously not."

"I told him Listen, I said, listen, I just buried my brother, you think I want to bury you, too? Know what he said? He said I'm not gettin' buried and you know it, woman, I'm bein' cremated so stop fussing me. And finally I said to him Listen, I said, I've had enough for one lifetime, I'm entitled to some peace, it's been your way from the start and I'm tired of it. I want some of it my way, I said. Well, by God, I'm going to get it my way from now on."

"He's going to be all right," Jean insisted.

"No, he isn't going to be all right, not at all. He'll live, but that's not all right. Damn stubborn old fool! I asked him, I said what's the damn use of buyin' that big fifth-wheel gas guzzler if the most we're ever gonna do in it is go down to Madeira Park once in a blue moon? I said Listen, you, I want to see the desert! I've lived all my life with mushrooms and mildew and I want to see some cactus that don't grow in a pot on the windasill. And he said Sure, of course, we'll put 'er on the drawing board." She began to sob. "My whole damn life has wound up on *his* drawing board. Well, no more!" Later, when she was calm again, she took Jean's hand and patted it. "You know," she confessed, "when your mother walked out on Einarr, I never even asked myself why. He was my brother, and that's all I cared about. And when Einarr died, I was still so *mad* at Evvie that I hardly showed my face. And now, I can't for the life of me remember why it all seemed so important. Don't you waste any of your life hangin' on to old angers and hurts, Jeannie. Take it from one who knows. It's not worth it."

"I'm not," Jean said softly. "I'm not angry about all that old stuff and I'm not even hurt about it. I just don't see why everyone — even you — seems to think I should care about someone I don't know! I mean the kids can leap and pole vault into the middle of Dear Sweet Gramma just like in the storybooks, but . . . she's nothing and nobody to me."

"She's your mother!"

"So? What's that? As far as I'm concerned she's someone who walked in out of the rain less than six months ago. I don't dislike her,

I don't particularly give a poop one way or the other, I just wish I didn't feel so damn *obligated* is all. How many people knock at your front door and the next thing you know they've moved right in on you? And I don't know," she laughed easily, "why in hell I just kind of moved into a corner like Little Miss Muffet and let myself be painted into it. It would take dynamite to shift her now! She's in there like weevils in your rice."

"Your kids adore her."

"Yeah, and isn't that kind of funny when you think of it? They'd seen more of their grade four teacher than they saw or knew of her and she just showed up and said I'm your Gran and it was *pow*. I mean for all they know she might be no relation at all!"

"Oh, she's a relation all right. Same old Evvie. Well, not exactly the same, but none of us are. I wonder why she never said anything about . . . you know . . ."

"Going bald?" Jean said it as levelly as she could and saw Alice's face relax as soon as the word was said. "Well, who knows the why of anything? Now I myself," she grinned faintly, "haven't bothered shaving my legs since oh, I bet about the time Tom and I split up. And you're the first person I've admitted that to, so what does that mean?"

"Nothing at all."

"Right. Same with Eve's head, I guess."

"Don't you ever call her Mom?"

"No." And something in her tone stopped the next question before it was asked.

Jean stayed with Alice until Sally came back with Mark, then he stayed while Sally drove Jean home. "Mr. Nguyen finished unloading the cod," Sally said. "And don't have a fit, he didn't take your tagged baby! He said," Sally giggled, "that the old bugger is getting so big and so fat down there that he's probably worth a fortune, but he figures you're saving him for a rainy day, when you really need some money."

"Poor Alice." Jean ignored the chatter about the cod. "She's just about sick herself."

"Yeah? Taken a look at your own face in the past couple of hours? You should go to bed before you wind up in one next to Uncle Bill."

Eve had thick stew and dumplings waiting and Jean ate everything on her plate, then took a second helping. She wanted to talk, and didn't know what to say.

"Alice okay?" Eve finally asked.

"She's really upset," Jean answered. "She talked about you."

"Yeah? That musta curled your hair," Eve sounded hurt, and bitter.

"Nope." Jean mopped up gravy with a crust of bread. "No, she didn't say anything the least bit mean. Just kind of wondered why you'd never said anything to anyone. About your hair, I mean. Said she'd never had any idea at all why you hoofed off down the road, so she stayed mad for years. I don't think she's mad any more."

Eve glared. "Well, maybe after all these years of being hard-nosed by the whole damn bunch, maybe *I'm* mad."

"Fine 'en. Be like that," Jean shrugged. "Have it your own way. Cut off your nose to spite your face. It's no skin off my ass one way or the other. I just told you what she said. And only because you asked about her."

"Proddy, aren't you?"

"Goddamn right I am! That's why I'm goin' to bed. It'd be easier to be Secretary General of the United Fuckin' Nations than to try to keep a family from each other's scrawny throats!"

She slept until her bladder wakened her, got up, peed, went back to bed and slept until morning, then drove herself to the hospital to see Bill. There was no sign of Alice in the corridor or in Bill's room but he was sitting up in bed with a clear drip running into his good arm.

"Helluva thing," he said wearily, "one arm won't do anything, so they tie the other to a board and shove a needle in 'er. I said to them put 'er in the bad one, but they didn't even answer."

"How'd you like it if some lab technician stepped on the *Lazy Daze* and started telling you how to troll for salmon?"

"So why ain't you out makin' some money?"

"Because by the time I got my lazy eyes open the *Old Woman* was gone. Sam's out with the kids. I guess if they get stopped by Fisheries without the permit holder on board, I'll be the one catches the blast." She shrugged. "Oh well, what the hell, maybe they got sick of waiting."

"Just as well. I mean when the skipper's too damn lazy to get outta bed someone has to take over!" he tried to smile but only half his face worked. He shook his head. "Do I talk funny?" he asked, and she knew he was frightened.

"No more funny than you ever did. You never did make much

sense," she teased. "It'll get better." She patted his good hand. "I think probably you've been real lucky."

"Spare me such good luck." He looked out the window and his eyes filled with tears. "Alice is real upset."

"Alice has a lot of reason to be upset," Jean lectured. "You might think you're made of stainless steel, but you're not."

"I guess I coulda brought 'er out there," he admitted.

"If you don't take her to the desert," Jean warned, "you're gonna find out you have to take cooking classes, because she'll go on her own."

"Yeah," he nodded. "I know. Proper thing, too. So," and he turned his still-teary blue eyes to her, "you gonna buy the *Lazy Daze* off me?"

"Oh, sure," Jean laughed, "with what? I could wait until next winter and write you a cheque on a snowbank."

"You could gimme a hundred dollars down and the rest on the never-never," he countered.

"You can't afford to just..."

"Don't you tell me what I can afford and what I can't afford, Jeannie-bean. My old lady is on my case. May you never know what the hell that means! She's decided. And when she's decided..." he pretended to be defeated and unwilling but Jean knew something inside him was pleased as punch. "Just don't get in her way." He closed his eyes and pretended to go to sleep.

"You don't fool me, you old fart," she laughed. "You're not asleep!"

"I am so," he said. "I'm asleep and I'm dreamin'. We're crawlin' across the desert, dyin'a thirst, with bleached bones all around us, buzzards circling in the sky and snakes ready to bite. Can hardly wait."

"She means it, Uncle Bill. She doesn't want you dead. Is that so much to ask?"

"And comin' toward us is the twenty mule team stuffed with Borax an' old Ronny RayGun is singin' 'Get Along Mule'. Helluva prospect. There's places down there it hasn't rained since Christ climbed the hill."

Jean sat by the bed and watched Bill Fergus fall asleep. Even stuck to the business end of an IV tube, even chalk-white and weak, he looked like a mountain of a man. A mountain of a man who had gone through life with the world knowing he was unable to father a child. And even though nobody thought Bill himself was at fault, they had reminded each other it was his fault, there was no ready vocabulary to word it any other way. And the whole world knew Alice was fertile. After all, hadn't she got herself knocked up, and hadn't she had the baby and put it out for adoption, and didn't all that happen before she was even sixteen, and didn't everyone know that she'd have been a fool to marry and keep the little girl, but even so, isn't it a caution how things work out, you make a mistake, you try to clean up your mess, you put the kid for adoption, then you never get another one. Almost said something about giving away, some even said throwing away, something you might want yourself later on, and never again get. Isn't it just too damn funny to make you laugh, the ones who want kids, the ones who would be the best parents, the ones who could do the most for some kids never get them and the ones who can breed as easy as rats have a dozen and neglect them all. Well, and doesn't that just go to show you. He worships Einarr's girl, they said, you can tell he'd give his right arm for some of his own. Best place for the kids to go at Hallowe'en, they said, he practically stuffs their pillaslips all by himself. Every kid knew whether it was books of tickets to be sold or boxes of chocolate-covered almonds, bottle drive or garage clean-up, go to Bill Fergus's place, he's a soft touch.

Brucie was sleeping on the rug in the kitchen when Jean came down to make coffee. The dog lifted her head, wagged what was left of her tail, and amiably got to her feet and moved to the back door so Jean could kick her outside. "G'wan, ya mutt," Jean said affectionately, scratching behind Brucie's ears and under the burgundy collar. "G'wan, ya ugly reject. Got a head as big as any cow's and no more brain in it than in one of the fleas living off you. Go lie down in the middle of the road so the oil delivery truck can flatten you. G'wan with you." Brucie licked Jean's hand and went out into the back yard. She sniffed a while then found a place to squat and pee. "Kill it all," Jean muttered, "lilac bushes, daffodils, the whole thing dead of dog pee."

She closed the screen door but left the wooden door half open. She could smell Brucie in the house, and wanted that stink aired out. She couldn't get used to the smell of dog. Especially Brucie, who seemed to be part some kind of breed that was intended to float forever, held up by the oil in her skin and fur. Brucie after a rainstorm was such a powerful stench Jean had suggested they contact the Department of National Defence, have the reek put in canisters and dropped from high-flying U-2s over enemy territory. "But I guess the international regulations against chemical and germ warfare would nix that idea."

She sat with her coffee watching the eastern sky change colour. Fisheries regulations could be a total pain in the butt, and yet they did ensure you got to see the faces of your family once in a while. Maybe that's what they were really all about, anyway; they sure weren't doing much for the fish they were supposedly designed to protect.

Dawn looked different out there. Light and colour were different. Clearer, sharper, the edges more quickly defined, and a new day didn't sneak up on you the way it did on land. Out there a new day just *bang*, or maybe *pop*, and she liked the slower, kinder shore dawn. But coffee never tasted as good sitting at a table as it did standing on deck.

Imagine timing your kid's wedding to the closure days. Oh, excuse me sweetheart, but could you get married a few days later so we can attend the wedding and not lose money? Oh, sure Mom, be glad to, what's a few days here or there when you're getting married?

Actually, it had been easier than that. They just figured it out for themselves and announced the date, then laughed and said not to worry, it was shutdown.

Well, it was, but that didn't mean things were going to be easy. God. Couldn't they elope? She'd offered. "Listen, I'll buy you a brand new aluminum ladder and put ribbons on the rungs if you'll just use it to elope. I'll buy the gas if you'll just run off to Seattle, or something."

"Oh, *Momma*," Patsy laughed. "Oh, you're so *funny*."

"Maybe plane tickets to Hawaii, and you get married on the beach over there?"

But no, it had to be here. "After *all*, Grandma and Grandpa got married at City Hall here, and you and Daddy, and. . ."

"Patsy, that isn't exactly a sterling record."

"Oh, *Mom*, you're just *teasing*."

Jean gave in and grinned. Jean grinned a lot. She shrugged more often in two months than she'd shrugged in her life. After all, Patsy was doing the planning, Eve was agreeing, and there was no shortage of people to pitch in and lend a hand. All Jean had to do was pour money into the idea. And the startling thing was, even Jean had to agree it was *not* going to be a huge wedding. What did people do if their kid decided to outdo Scarlett O'Hara? All they were doing was going to City Hall, getting married and coming back to the house for a party.

"Just friends and family," Patsy said happily. "Close friends and family."

You never know how many close friends you have until it's time to marry off one of the next generation. People you didn't think of as friends were there at the top of the list.

Like Tommy. Well, the list included family, and there was no getting around it, he was Patsy's family.

"A *motel? Momma!*"

"Well, a hotel room, then."

"*Momma!*" and the look, as if a hundred orphans had been put through a meat grinder.

"Jesus, Patsy, cut me some slack here, will you? We're jammed in here like sardines in a can!"

"Mark can sleep in the basement."

"*You* sleep in the goddamn basement, you're the one getting married!"

"All *right* then, I *will*."

"There's no reason he can't stay at the hotel."

"How is he supposed to afford a hotel room?"

"For God's sake, he can afford anything else he decides he wants! He can take trips off to Disneyland to ride on itty bitty trains with the rest of the kids, he can afford a hotel room for one night to see his oldest get married. He is *not* staying here!"

It was Mark came to sit beside her on the back steps and hand her a cup of coffee and put it all in perspective. "Mom, listen, and please, listen good. All she wants to do is grease the way for him. If he doesn't have any excuse to *not* show up, maybe he'll show up. If he has any excuse at all...like...I can't afford the hotel room..." He put his arm around her shoulders and squeezed gently. "I know it's a bitch. You think I like it? Fuck, I wind up in the basement with the toads and spiders! But it'll ruin it for Patsy if he squirms out from under this."

"Maybe I'll just sleep on the boat."

"Sure, you do that. Give the whole goddamn town something else to talk about," and he gave her a look that told her she was breaking his heart. "I don't have enough reasons to fight my way home from the bus stop. There's Gran and her boyfriends, and Gran and her wig, and Gran and her naked head, and there's you and Joe's dad fucking up a storm out on the boat, and there's Joe and Sally and for all I know Joe and Gran and now . . ."

"Oh, do shut up." She pushed him but he was expecting it and tightened his grip on her shoulder, so even though he did wind up pushed to a leaning position, she had to go with him and wound up with her head on his shoulder.

"Come on, old lady," he whispered, "come on, you know how it is, give 'em an inch they take a mile, give 'em a mile they take ten."

"I positively refuse. Totally, utterly, irrevocably refuse."

Tommy walked into the kitchen wearing only his jeans, his bare chest furred with grey hair, his bare feet padding noisily on the floor. "Hey, doll," he grinned, "you got any more of that coffee?" and he sat down, obviously expecting her to get up and pour for him. She pointed at the coffee maker and pressed her backside more firmly to the chair. It took a beat or two but then Tommy nodded, got up, went over and got his own coffee.

"Nice place you've got here." He looked around approvingly. "I always did like this place."

She didn't answer but Tommy didn't seem to care. He took his coffee to the table, sat across from her, smiling. "So you're pretty well set for life, eh Jeannie? House, car, boat, money in the bank. Not bad, all things considered." He sipped his coffee noisily. She would dearly have loved to put her hand against the bottom of the mug and push, gently, firmly and steadily until the mug wound up in his throat, leaving him looking like a snake who had swallowed a duck egg.

"Too bad about Einarr." He seemed to remember, belatedly, how Jean had wound up so set for life. "But he had a good life. Worked at what he enjoyed doing, which is more than most people get to do." He lowered his mug, the smile pasted determinedly on his lips. "So I guess we'll be grandparents before this time next year." He waited. Jean got up, went to the sink, dumped the last half inch of cold coffee down the drain and poured herself a fresh mug. "How do you feel about that? Bein' a grandma, I mean."

"I wish they'd waited," she said quietly. "But they didn't. At least she finished her course and got herself a job."

"Yeah," he nodded, "keep her busy while he's in camp."

"Give her some chance of feeding her kid if she winds up holding the bag," Jean corrected coldly.

The silence held and stretched. She carried her coffee down the hallway, out the front door to the porch, and sat on the top step, looking out at the wooded hills. But Tommy Pritchard was never one to take a hint if he didn't want to take it, he came to sit next to her, his coffee mug freshened and topped.

"What did you get them for a wedding present?" he asked.

"A waterbed and three sets of sheets and pillowslips," she answered. He nodded.

"I didn't have any idea at all," he confessed. Jean stiffened. She might have known. Another slide-past, with Tommy never quite managing to do the right thing. "Then Cheryl saved my ass," he grinned. "Phoned Simpsons and put in an order for a washer, told 'em to deliver it today. I just go blank on things, y'know. It's like there's so many choices I just jam up, and I'm still hoppin' from foot ta foot tryin' to decide and the whole thing's past history, so why make the decision?"

"Washer's a good idea," she managed.

"Gonna feel real odd being a grampa. I guess Sally'll be next. That'll be hard to take. Can't quite believe she's not still nine years old."

"Sally won't be getting married in a hurry," Jean corrected. "She's signed on for the mechanics course when it starts in September. Says when she's got that aced she wants to take marine diesel; got an apprenticeship lined up over at the boat shop."

"Now that's kind of a weird thing for a girl to do!" He looked totally disapproving. "I mean, my God, can you imagine what her *nails* are going to look like?"

"Like yours, probably."

Silence descended, and stretched, then Tommy gave it the old college try yet one more time.

"Been sorta thinkin' of takin' a job right around here." He dropped it with a thump in the middle of her life.

Jean felt as if the rest of the world was pulling away, leaving a huge distance between her and what she had begun to think of as her life. It was like the time she had the Killer Cold and her ears were plugged, so plugged all she could hear was a constant murmur.

"With whom?" Her voice seemed to be coming from the wrong end of a very faulty telephone.

"Oh, haven't gone that far with it," he smiled, but not at her. "There's always work for a good truck driver, Jeannie, you know that." He pulled a package of tailor-mades from where it was rammed down the front of his jeans. He took a cigarette, held the package out to her. She almost refused and went in for her rollings, but there are limits to how shirty even the owliest of us can be. She took a cigarette, nodded thanks and accepted a light from the paper match. "Gettin' rough in the city." He carefully put the dead match back in the packet, sideways, behind the last few unused ones. "Rent's an arm and a leg and goin' up all the time. Daycare's outta sight. Cheryl was workin' but she didn't get home until five and her kids're outta school at three, and for just those two hours, with two kids, well, she was workin' more for the fun of it than for the money; you figure clothes, shoes, gas, gotta get your hair done, all that stuff, well, I guess you know about that."

"A bit." Except the getting the hair done, and I don't think I've ever been able to pull that one off more than once a year, she thought. But she didn't say it, after all, it was Patsy's wedding day, and murder would be in very poor taste at such a time.

"Her ex, he doesn't pay child support," Tommy said very quietly. If he complained about that she'd kill him, wedding day or no wedding day, grandparents to be or not to be. "And so there we are and summer holidays coming and where do the kids go to play or to swim? Don't dare let 'em go to the playground alone, there's teenagers with Ninja sticks for God's sake, and they'll mug a little kid as fast as a big one, put lumps on a five-year-old just to take his bubblegum money." Why was he telling her all this? Why did he think she'd give a shit about someone else's kids' bubblegum money when nobody but her had cared about her own kids and whether or not they even *had* bubblegum money? "So we was talkin' yesterday, on the drive up. All them beaches. Highway lined with For Sale signs, nice places, green yards and sheds for bikes and stuff like that. That walk we took last night, after supper, with the kids? Well, that was nice."

"Tommy, in all the time I've known you I've never known you to just sit down and talk like this without a reason. What are you leading up to?"

"Ah, Jean, Jesus, it's been *years*, you know? Loosen up on it a bit, will you? All that time we spent together wasn't all bad. Damn if it was! It don't do you nor anybody else any good to just remember the tough times. So just because you went your way and I went my way, that don't mean we gotta fight all the time, okay?"

"What are you leading up to?"

"Well, someone said the guy that drives the fish down to the city was thinkin' of puttin' on another truck."

"Jesus loves us," she breathed.

"And I thought that, well, like, you know him. And you sure as hell know *me*! And you know if it's got wheels I can drive it."

"I don't think so." She stubbed out her cigarette and put the butt in the cuff of her jeans.

"What would it cost you?"

"It's only a seasonal job," she warned, "and probably only part-time even then. You're not going to live on those kind of wages."

"Yeah, but, well, they were talking about how you're gonna be takin' out Bill's boat and that Chinaman's gonna be takin' out yours and I thought well, I know I never deckhanded but I can learn. And you *know* I'm a good worker. . ."

"Go fuck yourself, Tommy. Head into the house, go up the stairs, turn right, go into the bathroom and shove the toilet brush right up your yingy," she smiled gently. "I've got all I can do to sit on these steps and be polite. You think I'm going to wind up living on a boat with you for a week at a time? I'd rather eat ground glass sandwiches and wash 'em down with Drano over ice."

"God, you hold a mad for a long time."

"Yeah," she nodded, "I do."

She would gladly have rammed her coffee mug up his nose and left him with one nostril significantly larger than the other, but before she could take aim and let fly, a brand new crew-cab pickup truck with a camper sitting where the bed ought to be drew up in front of the house and parked. Both doors opened. From the passenger side slid a huge block of beef with a glittering metal hook where his left arm ought to be, and from the driver's side came a woman just about twice the size of your average white mouse. She was dressed in levis and a maroon cowboy shirt with white piping and her tiny feet were stuffed into cowboy boots Jean knew had cost about as much as a couple of months' worth of groceries. She didn't need to be told who they were, all she had to do was look at the little woman's face; Terry Dugan without whiskers was smiling at her. "You must be Patsy's mother!" Alpha Dugan said, smiling widely. The voice told Jean why Terry had never seemed to be the least bit amazed, surprised or even impressed by the many and various versions of Evvie's life he had doubtless been clued in on since hooking up with Patsy. Alpha Dugan had obviously spent more than a few hours of her own life sitting under the fluorescents quaffing her thirst and smoking unfiltered cigarettes.

"And you've got to be Terry's parents." Jean stood up, making no

move to introduce Tommy. She headed down the steps toward the
gate to help the Dugans with their stuff and Tommy headed into the
house to put on a shirt and cover his ugly feet.

"Well," Alpha laughed again, "this is one of them times when I'm
glad I only spawned a boy and not a girl! It's the bride's parents get
stuck with the whole nine yards, and yes, I coulda come up here a
week ago to give a hand but I said to myself, I said Alpha, just thank
the good lord he give you an excuse to butt out, and then for
Chrissakes butt out, you're no good at all at that kind of thing. And
by the way, this ain't Terry's father, and his name ain't Dugan."

"Oh, I think we've got 'er under control," Jean laughed and meant
it, "but if you suddenly notice your truck and camper is missing, don't
call the cops, it'll just be me racing away with the last of my sanity."

"Helluva thing, isn't it? I told Terry, I said the pair of you make
my ass ache, month after month of not seein' no more of you than
you could help and now all of a sudden it's orange blossoms and the
rest of us supposed to do 'er all with a big grin on our faces. They
ain't worth it, Jeannie, but I guess I'm not tellin' you anythin' you
don't know, you got more of 'em to contend with than I do. Bert,
don't stand there lookin' like you don't know what the fuck to do next,
make yourself useful for a change, there's a coupla cases of booze
needs taken out of the camper and there's God knows enough
goddamn sliced up turkey'n'ham to keep you busy humpin' and
packin' for a good half hour. This here," she added, heading for the
front steps, "is my present better half, his name's Bert and the answer
is yes, he is, every bit as good as he looks like he'd be."

"Well, that which just scooted into the house is my ex, Tommy,
and the answer is yes, he's as useless as he appears."

"Oh, I heard," Alpha nodded, sliding her arm through Jean's and
linking hands as if they'd grown up attached at the hip. "Tits on a
boar, I was told."

"Or flippers on a louse, right!"

They walked into the kitchen, Alpha took one look at Eve and
burst out laughing, and Eve moved, wiping her hands on a dish
towel. They met somewhere between the sink and the fridge, and
gave each other spontaneous and heartfelt hugs.

"My God," Eve rasped, "I shoulda put two'n'two together but
didn't. I knew I'd seen that face before! It was the 'Dugan' threw me
off! How in hell *are* you?"

"You know me, there isn't a cat in the country can land on its feet any better'n I can. I haven't seen you in a coon's age! You're lookin' good. By God if you're not. Well," she laughed, "I can relax! Thought I might have to put on a show and pretend to be someone I was never intended to be, but at least I know there's a good time to be had by some, at least, or you'd'a been on your way out before now. Who would I have to fuck around here to get a good stiff drink?"

"You can fuck anyone you want," Eve brayed, "except for my grandson, we're saving him for society. Drinks are in the fridge, ice cubes where you'd expect 'em to be, just make yourself at home and don't expect to be treated like company." She turned as Bert came in, blushing and grinning. "Lord God, but you've done yourself proud this time," she laughed. "This one almost looks like a keeper!"

"He'll do," Alpha nodded firmly. "I bet if you just put that on the counter and go back for the rest someone'll know where it ought to go until it's needed," she suggested.

"I'll go with you." Tommy leaped for the breach.

Alpha looked him up and looked him down, then nodded dismissively. "You do that," she suggested. "Put yourself to use." She moved to the fridge, hauled out a bottle of rye, grabbed a big glass, filled it more than halfway, left the glass on the counter, took the rye back to the fridge and talked the whole time. "I thought if we spent the night on the other side and caught the first ferry over we'd get ahead of the traffic. I hate bein' part of a big jeezly snake roarin' around them curves, with some city fucker in a sports car doin' his damndest to kill himself and take you with him, so that's what we did, and it was nice, considerin' what it was. We got a propane barbecue stuffed in there and we just did ourselves a couple'a big steaks and washed 'em down with some of the Australian beer, then called her a night and still had lotsa time this mornin' to have a proper breakfast before it was time to get onto that ferry. But as for missin' the traffic, forget 'er. More goddamn freight trucks than hell would hold and people left over from the last sailin' last night, so they were in no mood to be pleasant. One'a these days," she threatened, "I'm gonna win the 6/49 and spend 'er all on plane rides and hotel rooms. Maybe get me a chauffeur or somethin'. You can't let Bert drive for too long," she warned, "he gets to wool gatherin' and the next thing you know you're hearin' the sound of the last trumpet. He says he spent too many years ridin' around on a bulldozer to be able to sit for long on a padded seat with the truck never presenting him with no challenges. Personally," she winked, "I think it just goes to prove that some people are good at one thing and nothing else, and he's good enough at that so's I don't mind doin' the drivin'."

"You braggin' again?" Terry Dugan walked in the kitchen in his sock feet, with the rest of him covered by new jeans and a bright red tee shirt. "I thought I heard your dulcet tones." He hugged his mother, gave her half a dozen smooches on the cheek, then just stood, holding her close, his chin resting on top of her head. Jean watched them, then turned away, almost embarrassed by what she was seeing. "How you doin', darlin'?" he asked softly.

"I'm doin' fine." Alpha's voice softened, the bantering please like me and please please please let me amuse and entertain you tone gone. "I had a couple of bad nights, but then I had a long talk with myself. And I still think you're outta your goddamn mind, Terry, but . . . it's your mind, your life, your future and your stupid decision. God knows I made enough of my own mistakes, I got no room to nag you about not makin' yours."

"It's not a mistake, Momma. You'll see. It'll be fine."

"Sure, sweetheart. You're my darlin'." She looked up at him and smiled. "My God, you're never gonna be what nobody would call tall. I kinda hoped you'd turn out more like your dad, he was tall. Well, compared to some. But," and she kissed him where the red tee shirt stretched across his chest, "even if you are still shorter than he was, you're twice the man he'd'a ever hoped to be."

"His dad was *not* tall," Eve said firmly. "He was a good lookin' runty little bugger."

"He wasn't runty!"

"Well, damn but he was! Tall for God's sake is someone like Bill Fergus!"

"Bill Fergus isn't tall." Alpha drank thirstily. "He's a goddamn mountain!"

"No, he ain't. A mountain is somebody like Tiny Rasmussen."

"Tiny Rasmussen *is* tall," Alpha agreed. She grinned wickedly, and winked at Eve. "But tall ain't all he is. 'Sides which," she continued as Eve chortled and nearly choked, "when you're built as close to the ground as I am damn near anybody looks tall. Oh well, at least I have reason to suspect mine is nice. That's what I tried for, anyway. Nice."

Jean had her hair done at eleven, was home at twelve-thirty and into her gear by one. At two they were back in town, at City Hall, and Patsy and Terry were standing side by side, looking almost old enough and mature enough to start kindergarten.

She'd seen it so many times on TV and at the movies that she felt as if she'd been rehearsing for this most of her life. And then it was done, and part of her would never be the same again.

"Weird, huh?" Mark whispered.

"That's the word I'd use, all right," she agreed.

"Almost feels like I'm supposed to think of her different, like she isn't my sister any more." His voice shook. "It feels real strange."

"Oh, she's your sister," Jean assured him. "And the fairy tales say that you aren't losing her, you're getting a brother."

"Yeah. Fairy tales, for sure."

She took his hand and squeezed, he grinned at her, and she realized he was taller than she was. His hand was bigger than hers, bigger even than his father's hand. Mark was actually taller and heavier than the groom! And still a kid, a kid who right now looked like a little boy in spite of his white shirt, his tie, his new-specially-for-the-occasion suit. "You're probably," she whispered, "the hand-somest man in the place."

"Hey," he winked, "it runs in the family. My mom's the best lookin' woman in town!"

Then there was all the crock about the pictures. And Patsy wasn't doing this one by halves; if photos were going to be taken, photos would be well and truly taken. Everyone had to be included in the group picture, the bride and groom, the best man and bridesmaid, the various siblings, parents and blendeds.

Sally, masquerading as the bridesmaid, qualified for her Academy Award, and didn't even have a bird when Cheryl and her kids were crammed into the picture with Tommy. When one of the anklebiters called Eve "Grandma," Sally grit her teeth, but held her peace amazingly well. "Shit," she whispered to Jean, "if we could round up the Nguyens and shove 'em in the back row we'd be almost complete here."

"You behave." Jean felt giddy. "Because if you don't I'll bite your ear."

"Ear or rear?" Sally smiled but her hand moved and she pinched Jean's thigh. Hard. "You don't fool me, Momma," she said, "if you were a drinking woman I'd say you were winding up for a five-day toot."

"Drinking woman or not I feel just about ready for a five-day toot! All we need is BoBo the fuckin' clown to show up!"

"If he does, Patsy'll have him put in the front row for all the world to see and marvel. If you hear a lot of noise, don't get freaked, it's just the Russian Cossack dancers doing their kick-while-sitting routine. I won't be surprised if when we step out the door we see all the Toyota guys in red jackets busy jumping in the air."

And then it was back to the house and the Nguyens had been busy while the photography crap was happening. There was just about enough food to crack the joists under the flooring. Jean found herself almost praying it would be enough.

"Well, we won't starve," Alpha decided, "although some of us might have to take 'er easy," and she laughed happily. She poured three drinks and handed the small one to Jean, the one that matched her own to Eve. "Here's to you," she said quietly, "and I want you both to know, if I'd been gonna pick a family for my kid to marry into, this is the one I'd'a picked," then she looked at Jean and spoke directly to her. "You done a good job, woman."

"You didn't do half bad yourself," Jean answered, and meant it.

Bill Fergus sat in a comfortable lawn chair and smiled, a glass of ginger ale almost hidden in his huge paw. His dead arm lay in a narrow foam rubber padded sling-support that not only hung around his neck but strapped around his chest. His smile was crooked, but it was firmly in place, his speech was slurred at the edges, but he was still rattling off jokes, one after the other. Alice made sure he had everything he needed, then she kissed his cheek and left him with his cronies. She headed for the kitchen to help with the food, looking more than a bit like someone who was heading into the cage with no whip or chair.

A dozen people already in the kitchen worked so hard at pretending there was nothing going on that they almost convinced themselves. "Is there anything I can do?" Alice asked, and you might have thought she'd been smiling at and speaking to Eve every day for the past thirty years.

"I think we've got it under control," Eve answered, as if she had been smiling at and speaking to Alice every one of those many days. "But if you see anything we've overlooked, for God's sake jump into the gap. I," she reached for her glass, and sighed deeply, "am just about wore to the bone."

"You've all done a wonderful job. The flowers look lovely, the food is just great, you must have been going from dawn to dark all week."

"Never would have got it together without Tran. I keep tellin' her she ought to start a catering business. You'd'a thought she grew up doin' this every day of her life!"

"...all the dukes, counts, viscounts, discounts, and no-accounts was gathered around the square table chewin'...." Tommy's voice came to them, and Jean winced.

"Oh, God, 'David and the Diamond-Studded Jock'," she mourned. "How come I used to think that was so *funny*?"

"Cause you were stupid," Eve answered easily. "In my day I thought it was funny, too. Guess that means I was stupid, as well."

"Maybe we were all stupid," Alice agreed. "Maybe we still are for that matter. Probably about the time Tommy finishes that one Bill will give forth with his 'Little Ball of Twine'. Which I personally find to be about the most ignorant and gross thing I've ever heard. But he comes out with it every time. I don't suppose the stroke wiped *that* part of his mind clean."

"How is he?"

"Oh..." She made herself smile and Jean could have screamed. "He's going to be fine. He's lost some vocabulary, and the doctor has warned me that almost invariably there's a personality change; says the snarly ones turn out to be sweethearts, so maybe there'll be some good in it, after all."

"Uncle Bill? Snarly?" Jean laughed.

Alice looked her squarely in the eye, no hint of joke in her voice. "Sweetheart, you don't know the half of it."

"Hey, little girl." Tommy came into the kitchen grinning widely. "Want some candy?"

"Muck off Fister," Jean said clearly, "my mother warned me not to talk to strange people, and *you* are as strange as they come." Tommy laughed and went to the fridge, hauled out half a dozen cold ones, and headed back outside, still grinning and chortling. Silence grabbed the kitchen in both hands and held it until Tommy was gone.

"Ah, you know what they say," Alpha sighed, "I had one, too, but the wheels fell off."

Three hours into the party she couldn't stand it any more. She went up to her bedroom, stripped off her new clothes, got rid of the pantyhose and shoesies, and hauled on clean jeans, a light cotton tee shirt, cotton socks and sneakers. She went back down to the kitchen and went out the back door. "Come on, ferret." She snapped her fingers and Brucie came over to her eagerly. Jean walked to the back gate, unsnapped it, went through, and closed it behind her. With Brucie walking beside her, nudging her hand and licking her fingers, Jean went down the alley to where the footpath cut through the brush and down the steep bank. She slithered down the bank, getting red clay smeared on her Nikes, then walked the littered tide line, smelling the reek of diesel and oil, the stink of fish holds, the pong of working boats. She could hear the music blaring back up at the house and knew they would be dancing in the living room, on the porch, in the front yard.

She sat on a sun-dried log and stared out at the boats tied up to the docks, the breakwater stained with cormorant and seagull shit, the crows raging constantly from the trees along the shore. A couple of kids came thundering down the beach, smeared with mud and wet to the knees. They shrilled at her, laughing, and she recognized them as Cheryl's kids. "Your mom is going to have a fit when she sees you," she scolded. "You should have changed into your play clothes." They looked at each other, looked at her, then nodded and started up the footpath. They skidded and slithered, climbed and clambered and by the time they got to the top they were a worse mess than they had been when they started home to change. She shook her head. Oh well, the clothes would wash. The kids would wash. One way or another everything seemed to come out in the wash.

"Come on, Brucie, let's us find some quiet place where we can have our nervous breakdown in peace."

She was going to go to the *Old Woman* and hide out there but she saw Tom and Cheryl walking along the dock. He was pointing at Einarr's boat and talking a mile a minute. Cheryl kept nodding, smiling, nodding. Tommy pointed at the *Lazy Daze*, his jaw still moving. Cheryl nodded and smiled. Jean turned up the hill, went back to the house and the party that had spread to the Nguyens' yard, too. People who hadn't been on the invitation list were sipping beer and eating potato salad. What the hell, there's a good party going on, grab a two-four pack and let's crash it. There were more beer cases stacked in the back room than there had been before the first one was opened.

Most of the food was gone but she found enough ham for a sandwich and enough potato salad to fill the corners. Someone had carefully scraped the leftovers into the compost bucket. She took it outside, dumped it into Brucie's dish. "Here," she invited, "put on another five pounds. Maybe you'll have a heart attack and drop dead, save me a fortune on dog food and vet bills." Brucie wiggled happily and started in on her scraps.

"Hey, Mom," Sally called, "they're leaving."

Jean got up, set her plate aside and went into the house for the hugs, the kisses, the tears and the goodbye waves. When Patsy and Terry finally drove off for their two-week honeymoon at various campsites along the coast, Jean went out in the back yard to find Brucie had eaten all her scraps, then cleaned Jean's plate, too.

She almost worried about the food and the crowd and nobody around to do the loaves and fishes routine, but before she could get all her frets together someone appeared with a washtub, someone else dumped an entire bag of briquets into it, and Mark came from the basement with a garbage bag hanging from his hand. He opened the bag, Tommy handed him a jackknife totally inadequate for the job, Mark laughed and said something, so Tommy put his toy in his pocket and someone Jean didn't know provided the proper knife.

She watched as her kid expertly slit the fish up the spine. Where do they learn all these things? One minute you can dress them up but you can't take them past the borders of your own yard, the next minute you could drop them down almost anywhere at all and they'd come through with ease.

Sally showed up with the sticks and cross-pegs, inserted them and set them around the washtub. She was kneeling on the grass, out of her bridesmaid gear and back in jeans and a near-new tee shirt that boasted Another Voice For The Stein, and she was laughing. Her plain little mug was turned up, toward Mark, and he was chortling, listening to her. They say only the boys get curly hair, the girls get straight, and it must go for faces, too. Sally looked so much like Einarr it was to make you laugh, and whatever else you would say about her, you would never call her pretty or lovely or beautiful, but all her life people had told Jean one day Sally would be a very handsome woman, and that day had arrived. She made the pretty girls look like people you'd seen everywhere all your life, and only Sally was the one who had just ridden into town full of mystery and fun.

"Helluva lookin' woman," Alpha said. "You ever take time to notice the body on her? Jesus Christ, they ought to pass laws against it. Put 'er in jail under the Combines Commission regulations, you know the one that says nobody's supposed to set 'er up so's he can hog the whole market to hisself?"

"I was just thinking the same thing. Funny how you don't notice it creeping up on them until one day *wham* and there it is."

"So what'n hell are we now, you suppose? If a sister-in-law is the sister of the person you're married to and a mother-in-law is the mother of the person you're married to, what are the mothers-in-law to each other? Do I call you my son's mother-in-law or something?"

"Co-defendant, probably. Or co-accused."

"Co-accursed, more to the point," and she smiled, then floated off on an almost visible sea of fumes to find the hunk with the glittering hook and the quiet smile.

"Now there," Alice laughed softly, "goes a woman whose exploits are legendary."

A woman in a light green outfit said something to the older man standing beside her. He looked over at Sally, still fussing with the barbecue sticks. "Hey," he called, "you mean what it says on that tee shirt?"

"Sure do," Sally answered easily.

"What about our jobs?" he asked.

Sally sat back on her heels and stared at him a long time, then smiled. "Oh, I don't know," she answered softly, "You look like someone with sense enough to know you can't cut down every tree tomorrow and still expect your grandchildren to have trees."

"I think you're wrong," he said quietly. And Sally smiled.

"That's okay. It means we share a common opinion. I think you're wrong, too," and the man laughed softly, then nodded. Sally turned her attention back to the barbecue.

"That charcoal you're usin' used to be a tree." He wasn't going to let it go that easily.

"That's right," Sally agreed. "And I'm not saying we have to stop logging. I just think we can do it a better way, is all. We don't have to slice it down quicker'n it can grow just so some lard-arsed son of a bitch can drive a brand new Jag every year." She smiled up at the guy and something in his shoulders relaxed. "I'd like to know who figured it out," she said softly, "because if you fight with me and I fight with you and we both fight with the Indians and they have to fight with us all, we'll be so busy fighting with each other we won't notice they've taken everything out from under us. We're cutting more trees than ever before and yet I bet you're on pogey right now. So what are *you* getting out of the massacre?"

"We need jobs," he insisted.

"Yeah. We do. So how come half the IWA is out of work and the companies are making record profits?"

"We gonna spend this whole party yappin' away about this?" Mark protested. "I get sick of it, so help me God I do."

"Oh shut up," Sally laughed.

"Me? Shut up? Hey, I'm the one doin' all the work here, *you're* the one doin' all the talking."

As fast as the fish cooked, it was eaten, and as fast as it was eaten, more fish was cooked. They used up all the paper plates and started in on the real ones. Jean filled the sink and washed plates for half an hour, and when she left the sink Cheryl moved to take her place. Jean supposed there were some who would find that inordinately funny. "Thanks, Cheryl," she smiled, "I really appreciate it."

"The kids are just about falling on their faces," Cheryl worried. "Do you suppose I should lock them in the garage, or something? Get them out of people's way?"

"If they get out of line someone else'll do it for you. Relax, everyone here's had kids and knows how awful they are and if they don't know, it's time they found out."

At midnight, the party hadn't even begun to wind down. Mark was dancing, that had to mean he'd been into the beer. Sally was yawning and looking decidedly wilted, and Jean felt as if her feet were numb to the knees.

"I guess it's not polite to turn off the electricity and holler at them to fuck off, eh?" Sally mourned.

"No. And politeness says we're supposed to stay here until the last dog is hung. But I, myself, being nobody to pay attention to shit like that, am heading down to the boat, and I'm going to sleep there."

"Yeah? Gimme five," Sally headed upstairs at a dead run. Jean sighed. She had halfway hoped to be alone but obviously not yet. "Come on, Brucie." She snapped her fingers. "And if you shit on the deck I'll feed you to the crabs."

Brucie didn't shit on deck and didn't get fed to the crabs, and Jean was glad Sally had joined her on the *Lazy Daze*. They sat in the bunk with a sleeping bag unzipped and spread open over them, smoked cigarettes, and even managed to talk like two human beings instead of Mom'n'Kid.

"You're kidding me, aren't you?" Sally said quietly. "He actually wants you to give him a job recommendation?"

"And a job, as it turns out," Jean nodded. "Thinks he can learn to be a deckhand."

"Oh, he probably could learn," Sally sighed. "But would he? And having learned, would he bother to show up for work? And if he showed up, would he work? The variations are endless."

"Now, now, don't you start," Jean teased.

"I'm amazed you didn't just kill him and get it over with."

"Couldn't do that." Jean was astounded to feel tears dribbling down her face. "Patsy would never forgive me for ruining her big day."

"And isn't that a fright!" Sally's face was wet, too. "I mean if your big day is the day you as good as give up on any ambition you might ever have had . . . and don't bother to tell me it doesn't have to be that way! I look at the magazines, too, you know. What they print as statistics are really people's lives. People's dreams. And what I see is that if you keep on thinking and hoping and trying, you wind up in the divorce statistics; if you don't want to wind up divorced, why you trade your brain for marriage and just settle for whatever it is they say is security."

"I wish you didn't believe that." Jean took Sally's hand in hers, lifted it to her lips and kissed softly. "But at the same time, I'm glad you do, although I wish you didn't *have* to believe it. And I wish I could say you were just bitter, and disillusioned, and that someday you'd meet that guy on the white horse and . . ." She waved her arm.

"Yeah. I wish so, too. But until I hear the Choir of St. Martin in the Fields coming from the sky, I think I'll hang on to my cynicism. Imagine the nerve of the bugger! Wants a job!"

"Don't you jump him about it. You've jumped him so many times he doesn't even listen when you do. He expects you to jump him. He's like a deranged movie director, and he's cast you as his conscience."

"Me? He doesn't pay any attention to anything I say."

"Right, and he never paid any attention to his conscience, either. I don't know, it seems to me that people don't change after they're twenty-five. They just become more of whatever it was they were in the first place. But what you can overlook at twenty-four, you can't overlook at forty-four and, my God, by the time the face sags and the dentist slides in the China clippers, we've each of us become like a bad joke of who we used to be."

"And he worries about my fingernails," Sally laughed, and there was no trace of bitterness in the laugh. "Maybe I'll start worrying about *your* fingernails. Are you sure you always remember to anoint your hands with Oil of Olay before hauling fish over the side?"

"Always." Jean slapped the thin mattress for emphasis. "And I never, *ever*, go out in the teeming rain and howling wind without first putting on my lanolin-enriched hormones-added ten-dollars-an-ounce glorified lard."

"And it's time for the old beauty sleep, right?"

"You know it."

When they went back up to the house the morning sun was warm, and the tourists were getting ready to take their rented tupperware sailboats out for a cruise. A half dozen of the recently arrived French-Canadians were sitting on benches outside the coffee shop talking together and paying no attention at all to a group of grubby kids playing on the dock.

"Why do you suppose they came out here?" Sally asked quietly. "They don't speak the language and don't seem to want to learn, they've got almost no education worth talking about, and the only jobs they've got any chance of getting are the ones nobody else wants, and those jobs don't pay enough to keep the roaches in the cupboards eating balanced meals."

"Yeah," Jean nodded, "I guess they got here by picking other people's crops and moving on to the next one. When they got here..." She shrugged. "Well, at least they don't freeze in the wintertime. I guess if you've got bugger-all and no hope of having more than bugger-all, even a chance to pick brush seems like a step up the ladder. All I'm sure of is that I really don't know what in hell is going on or where all those jobs we used to have are going."

Alpha's truck and camper were still parked beside the garage, the blinds pulled over the little windows. The house was quiet, and that had to mean the kids were sound asleep. Jean and Sally moved almost on tiptoe, not wanting any company but their own. The reality of the whole thing was starting to sink in and it felt downright weird. Patsy and her italics had moved on, not quite out of their lives, but no longer really part of them.

Jean made coffee and sat sipping it, deliberately ignoring the clutter in the house. Someone had made a stalwart effort to clean up, the dishes were washed, rinsed and put away, the counters wiped clean in the kitchen, but the living room, hallway and bathroom looked like hell. Paper napkins, paper cups, overflowing ashtrays, and every windowsill decorated with beer cans placed side by side from one end to the other. The house smelled of cigarette smoke, stale beer and a sour fruity smell from the powder-and-water drinks mixed for the kids.

Quiet as they had tried to be, someone was moving around upstairs. Whoever it was did not choose to come into the kitchen to join them for coffee. Perhaps whoever it was didn't know there was coffee. Maybe they'd been so quiet their presence wasn't even suspected. Maybe someone else wanted to be alone for a while.

Her head felt jammed, her eyes gritty, and she couldn't stop yawning. She would have liked nothing better than to sleep another six hours but she knew she wasn't going to be able to do that. She was awake. Not fully, and not happily, but too awake to snuggle under blankets and ignore the mess.

She heard the vacuum cleaner start up in the hallway. The sound drove through her left eye into her head. She took her coffee outside and sat on the back steps with it, looking out toward the alley, and beyond it, the bay and harbour. Sometime, either during or between yawns, Sally seemed to have dropped into the cracks in the floor.

Tommy came out in creased suit pants, still no shirt, no socks, no shoes. She wondered why it was he felt it was okay to wander around half naked in someone else's house. He sat next to her, lit a cigarette, drank coffee eagerly, and smiled as he looked up and down the beach. "Sure is nice," he said. Jean didn't answer. He looked over at her, and winked. "Cat got your tongue?"

"Guess so."

"Tired?"

"Yeah."

"You bombed out early. Looked for you, couldn't find you."

"Yeah?"

"Kinda surprised to find your mom so . . . installed."

"Yeah."

"You make it up with her?"

"I don't know I'd call it that. The kids are nuts about her. She's here when I have to be at work. Although they're old enough they don't need a babysitter and can more than take care of themselves. It's just . . . convenient. Good for everybody, I guess."

"Feels kinda weird, Patsy married, and all." He stared at the bleached wood between his bare feet. He took a deep breath, almost a sigh, and dove in. "I was wonderin' if we could talk about that garnishee you took out against me."

"No," she said, almost idly. "We can't. Unless you want to suggest we get the amount increased."

"Jeannie, you're killin' me," he said quietly. "You don't need that money. Those kids make more every month on their part-time jobs than is bein' screwed outta my paycheque! *They* don't need that money! I already told you how it is for me; I'm bleedin' here."

"You've been off the hook for Patsy for years," she said, yawning, "and now you're off the hook for Sally, too. There's only Mark, now, and that's just about finished. And the back payments, well, they'll just continue until they're caught up with. You shouldn't have got behind in the first place."

"You've always been just about as hard as an oyster shell," he sighed.

She knew he was going to start in again. She knew he was convinced if he could just get her at the right time, just say the right thing, she'd relent. Well, why wouldn't he think that? For years it had been true. All he had to do was wait long enough and she'd cave in and give him his way in things. If he was a superb pain in the ass, maybe she was the one had trained him to be that.

She got up, went to the sink, emptied out the last of her coffee and got a black garbage bag. She went from room to room picking up napkins, emptying ashtrays, clearing up everything except the beer cans. When they were all the mess left, she got a different garbage bag and started picking up the cans. Tommy sat on the steps the whole time, staring at his feet, staring off over the fence to the vacant lot where a striped cat and her litter of feral kittens were involved in bird-stalking lessons. The birds seemed fully aware of what was happening, and quite unconcerned.

She had the downstairs bathroom tidied and cleaned and was on her way to the living room for a quiet cup of coffee when she caught the tail end of a conversation between her son and his father. They were just the other side of the screen door. Tommy was still sitting on the top step, Mark was standing with his shoulders pressed against the big support post of the porch roof, one knee bent, and the foot of that leg propped on the post. He was fully dressed in clean, near-new jeans, tee shirt and his best Nike high-tops, his hair still party-combed. He looked totally adult, and could have passed for one of the leisured money set.

"Why you cheap shit," he grinned widely, his voice soft, almost gentle. "What we're talkin' here is *my* fuckin' job! Boy, what a grouch you turned out to be. First you have to be hauled into court like a criminal before you pay child support and now you want her to give you *my* fuckin' job. Listen, if there's something else I should know in all this . . . like maybe you really *did* find me on the garbage dump and I'm no relation to you . . . maybe this is the time to tell me, eh? Because I gotta say, fella, it gives me pause for thought sometimes."

"Never found you on no garbage dump." Tommy was forcing a smile, too. "And I have no doubt in the world I'm your dad. Your mother didn't play those kind of games. Ever."

"Well, it's a puzzle, then," and still the wide grin, the companionable tone. "I mean, seriously speaking, all jokin' aside, I got me a dog in the back yard there that I do more for than my dad has done for me. And she ain't even a whole helluva lot, as dogs go. No flaming hoops, no holding a flag in her mouth while walkin' a tightrope. Just a potlicker of a dog. But I never once tried to take her pot away and lick it myself, you know?"

Jean eavesdropped shamelessly. It isn't true, she thought, that they never talk to each other. It isn't true they don't communicate their feelings. They do. But in such a weird fuckin' way we never recognized what was happening. No wonder Sally never got anywhere! No wonder I never got anywhere! We made the big mistake of saying what we meant, of describing how we felt. And they can't understand that language any more than we understand theirs. They aren't even *looking* at each other!

"I guess maybe when I was seventeen I knew it all, too." Tommy sipped his coffee. "I guess maybe somewhere along the way I forgot most of what it was I knew when my nose was still wet."

"Well, I'm still seventeen, so I still know it all. I'm smart. I still know it all, old man, so listen up and I won't even charge for the lesson. That garnishee stays in place. Because that's my money. It's not hers. It's child support and I'm the cheeeee-ild. And maybe those little rugrats are nice kids, I don't know, but they're no nicer'n I was. Sure as hell they're no nicer'n Sally; you could start now and walk for a week and you wouldn't find any little kid any nicer'n Sally was, and you know it. And if their dad don't care if they starve, why should I? He don't care if they starve no more'n you gave a shit if I starved. He's leavin' it all up to Cheryl the way you left it all up to Mom. Know what I mean? But nobody's leavin' it up to me, nobody's depending on me, and I don't feel any obligation to Cheryl or her kids. Or you, either, I guess. Nobody taught me how to care about that. The only person other'n myself who ever made sure I wasn't skin and bones dead in a ditch was my mom. And smart as I am, when it comes to why I should give a shit about you or Cheryl's kids, I haven't figured it out for myself. So it's my money, and if I have a part-time job, well, that's up to me, I guess. Got nothing at all to do with you or them or anybody else I know. But you gotta stop turning the screws on Mom, okay? Because maybe she can handle it, but I can't." He finally looked at his father, the smile still firmly nailed in place. "And I wouldn't want anything to interfere with our father-and-son relationship, know what I mean? Don't try to take my job away from me. If anyone's goin' out deckhanding this summer, it's me."

"And what about when you go back to school?" Tommy asked.

"Oh, somethin'll work out," Mark laughed a harsh, short laugh. "The sad-assed, bleary-eyed, incompetent and desperate are lined up six deep for the chance to fuck the dog and get paid for it."

He came off the post, opened the screen door, stepped into the hallway and nearly bumped into his mother. Jean opened her mouth to say something. Mark shook his head, his eyes bright with unshed tears. His mouth quivered, just the way it had when he was a year old and had been stung by a bee. "Butt out, Momma, please," he asked.

"Me?" She decided to give his kind of communication a try, she wanted him to hear and understand fully. "I'm just some old broad wandering around looking for a place to sit and drink my coffee, that's all, sweetheart." And then, because she wanted him to learn how to communicate her way, too, "I love you, Mark. You're probably the nicest young man I've ever known."

He nodded, then brushed past her, and she pretended she didn't hear him sniff, pretended she didn't see him brush flooding tears from his eyes.

"You've got you some nice kids." Alpha spoke quietly and slid her arm around Jean's waist. "Sometimes, so help me God, you look at them and you wonder how they'll ever make it. I think we done too good a job bringin' them up. I vowed on my soul, if I had one, that my kid would never know the kind of BS I grew up thinkin' was normal life. And to keep him from knowin' it, I turned myself inside out, or as close to it as I could get and not make a mess on the floor.

And one day I looked at him and thought Jesus aitch, the rate I'm goin' with him he'll never be tough."

"Terry?" Jean laughed. "Terry's as tough inside as they make them."

"Jesus aitch I hope so," Alpha sighed, "but we babied 'em. Protected them from all the things that made us tough as old boots, and in protectin' them made them soft."

"Only on the outside," Jean insisted. "Inside, they're as tough as old boots themselves."

Jean stood, accepting what Alpha was giving her, and in the accepting giving something back. She looked through the screen at Tommy, sitting on the top step, sipping his coffee. He knew she was there, knew Alpha was there, and didn't care. For once, blessedly, he didn't turn and grin and try for the trophy, he didn't come up with a joke or try to charm anyone. He just sat and she knew everything his son had said to him, everything his son had left unsaid but understood was echoing. And she knew she wouldn't change places with him for all the money in the world. He looked fine from behind. You could still see the hunk he had been, you would still call him a hunk if you met him for the first time without knowing anyone else's opinion. She supposed even a hunk could feel puzzled, even a hunk could feel baffled, even a hunk could recognize the taste of ashes in his mouth. She almost felt sorry for him.

There had been more opportunities than enough to patch the holes, and it wasn't just Tom Pritchard had said piss on it. It wasn't just Tom Pritchard had made choices knowing doors were being closed and locked. They'd both started out with a big number one, and it wasn't anybody's fault that when she'd tried for a five he'd decided to continue to enjoy his three, it wasn't anyone's fault that by the time he decided to try for five she'd gone on to eight and a half because five hadn't seemed like fun to her any more than three had. And now he was trying to get past five and it wasn't anyone's fault she'd thrown all the numbers away and wasn't interested in the slightest. And what was wrong with trying to clean up his act with and for Cheryl's kids? Jesus, if he'd chosen to repeat the way he'd been with his own, the world would be accusing him of not learning his lesson. He'd learned it. And it wasn't his fault nobody much gave a shit. He was what he was and at one time in her life what he was had been what she wanted. Whose fault was it she no longer wanted any of it? Not hers. And not his. And why did the word "fault" have to enter into any of it? Some things just are. No fault, no blame, just how it is.

She wished she could get it clear in her head, wished she could explain, at least to herself, what it was she thought she meant, but it wouldn't come quite in focus. She only knew Tom Pritchard had been an asshole for several years. That didn't mean he was going to deliberately remain that way the rest of his life. It wasn't his fault he couldn't change overnight.

Sally decided she might make less money working at the Marine Engines than she'd make deckhanding, but she'd be better off, in the long run. Jean found it hard to get used to the idea of people she still thought of as children even bothering to try to think of the long run. Mark made it clear he fully expected to go out with her on the *Lazy Daze* for the summer. He also made it clear that while he didn't expect man's wages, he did expect to do a man's job. That led to being treated like a man and not a kid. And, somehow, that meant he was fully prepared to act like an adult. Eve seemed content to contribute her share to the cost of things, even though Jean had suggested Eve was certainly doing more than enough work to pay her keep.

"No," Eve said sternly, "I've always paid my share."

"But the amount of work you do around here . . ."

"I'd have to clean up if I lived on my own. It's not worth discussing."

Patsy phoned at least once a day, and seemed so settled into her routine Jean was astounded. Patsy, who hated any kind of housework, kept her rented place spotless, Patsy who had waited years before she even began to think of tomorrow had everything planned for the next twenty years. Terry Dugan came home from camp every weekend and seemed to look forward to Sunday Dinner With The Rellies before leaving on the eight o'clock ferry to drive back to work. And if he didn't look forward to it, he put on such a good act someone ought to have nominated him for an Academy Award. He started calling Jean "Mom," Eve "Gran," and Mark "bro," but he still called Sally by her name, as if he knew all too well how quickly she would kick the shit out of the first hint of familiarity.

And life slid from one blistering hot day to another, the days grouped at the whim of Fisheries, so many days open, so many days closed, and either they were working like mad bastards or sitting numb with fatigue, resting up for the reopening, so they could work like mad bastards again. "Funny how things work out," she mused, sitting on deck and drinking a half-cool beer straight from the can. "You see movies and read books and you'd think a fisher's life was one exciting thing after another. And it's just as boring as any other damn job!"

"I guess that's why they call it work," Mark agreed. He was wearing an old pair of cut-off jeans, and the fine hairs on his legs gleamed as if he were made of gold. His feet were covered with the tattiest pair of canvas sneakers Jean had seen in years, his skin was deeply tanned, his hair sunbleached, and there was almost no sign of her little boy left. He gulped his own beer, turned his head aside, and belched freely. "How's your back?" he asked.

"Don't ask. I'm too old and worn out for this kind of life. For any kind of life. I don't know why I wasn't smart enough to have chosen to be born into the Bronfman family, or something."

"Ah, you wouldn't get along with that bunch anyway. They're from back east, and you know what humourless bastards that makes 'em." He reached for her makings and rolled himself a cigarette, the first one he had dared light up in front of her, another gesture of independence. "You ever slow down and take a look around and ask yourself what it's all about?" he asked.

"Oh, once or twice," she grinned. "It's like you're walking down the road minding your own business, and suddenly you realize there's something more going on than you ever knew. I don't know what it is," she admitted, "and I don't know why it is or how it'll turn out, but that doesn't stop it from being."

"I get scared sometimes."

"Yeah, me, too. Whatever it is we're up against, it's something big."

Mark nodded, then rubbed his leg, and squinted against the light sparkling off the water. "I'm not much interested in going back to school," he said quietly. "But the way I figure it, I wouldn't be doing much fishing in the winter, anyway. So I might's well go to school. I'm not like Joe, eh, he's heading off to UBC and he's got it all pretty well planned. And he'll do 'er. There's no way he won't do 'er. I talked to him about it all, and he told me if I didn't go back and get twelve he'd clean my clock for me, and he probably would. If he could." He finished his beer and yawned. "I heard this guy on TV the other night talking about how everything is changing. Said we'd all have to be prepared to take job retraining at least ten times in our lives. Enough to give a guy nightmares. But then I thought well, look at you."

"Yeah," she agreed, "look at me and take warning, boy!"

They laughed softly, companionably. And when the bells on the poles started ding ding dinging they put their beer cans in the yellow plastic milk crate on deck and got ready to bring in their lines.

It was meaner than cod fishing. There was more work after you brought the salmon over the side than there had been getting them to the boat. No taking out the hook and dropping the fish down into the live tank. You had to bap the poor bugger on the head, then later sit cleaning fish and emptying buckets of guts over the side.

There was crushed ice to spread on the fish, there was blood and slippery slime to wash off deck, it was one damn thing after another and then, if you were lucky, it was time to bring the lines in, again, and start from scratch, again, removing hooks, smashing in heads, slicing open bellies, hauling out guts, rinsing out blood, and praying, all the time, you were making payments and maybe even making wages.

Sally waited until they had slept, bathed and eaten before she threw her wrench into the works. "I'd rather you didn't drive the old car for a while," she said quietly. "She's sick. And it's something more than just a case of measles."

"Oh my God."

"Yeah. And I don't want any of those dozey buggers in town turned loose on her. They don't have any more feeling for what it is they're doing than you'd expect from a trained ape. I'll fix her up."

"What are we talking here? Five hundred dollars?"

"I think what we're talking here is you should buy yourself a good used car and drive it, and leave Miranda for special occasions, is what I think."

"Miranda? And what kind of special occasions?"

"Me," Sally grinned, "when I get the grease and oil from under my fingernails and put on my war paint and pull on the clean clothes and drive into town for pizza."

"You want me to give you the car."

"Right."

"Oh, yeah," Mark groaned, "and ain't life great when you're the last one in line!"

"Oh, shut up. You couldn't keep her running for a month. Get a pickup truck, it's about your speed."

"So I should buy a used car *and* put money into Miranda for you."

"I'll put the money into Miranda. But yeah, you should buy a used car. There's one in town for thirty-five hundred. I've checked it out. It's about your speed," she grinned. "You know, the little old lady from Pasadena . . ."

"Go granny, go granny, go go go!" Mark shrieked.

"Any other bad news?"

"Yeah," Sally nodded cheerfully. "The plumbing in this house is shot to hell. And if you don't get a new septic tank we're going to have a basement full of shit."

The backhoe operator leaned on the big rubber tires of his machine and smiled widely as if he was giving her the best news in the world. "You need a tank, cement's better because then you don't have to worry someone might drive over it and crack it. Fibreglass is lighter, but all it takes is one oil truck and you need a new tank. So you need that, and you need a distribution box. Then you need a hundred and fifty feet of drain pipe. And about fourteen yards of gravel, inch and a half or less in size. "

"How much are we talking here?"

"Oh fifteen hundred for material." He made it sound like something you just picked off the lilac bush once the flowers had faded. "And I need someone on the busy end of a shovel and rake, to spread the drain tile." He looked at Mark. Mark looked at Jean.

"He's got a job," Jean sighed, "so we'll have to hire someone."

"Okay," the backhoe guy nodded, "I can find someone." He started listing all the other stuff she was going to need and Jean had a mental image of dollar bills hiking off down the street, their little feet stuffed into basketball sneakers.

"Wait a minute," she made herself smile, "I think I'll go get a pencil and a piece of paper. A long piece of paper."

The plumber shone his flashlight along the pipes and sighed. He swung the broom at spider webs and sighed. He looked at the ceiling and sighed. "Oh, it's going to be fun," he sighed. "Looks like ten different people with ten different ideas did ten different jobs on this, and not one of them did a good job."

"How much?"

"Oh, it's hard to say until I start hauling stuff outta here. You got galvanized in some places, and that's gotta go. Poison the whole family. You got copper in some places, you got plastic in others. You got pipes added onto other pipes and pipes cutting into other pipes and from here it almost looks as if you got pipes that don't go anywhere, but I can't figure out how that could be. Say three thousand."

"Total?" she asked.

"Oh, total. Well, I can't say total. Sometimes you get in there and it all goes slick as you'd want. Other times, well, you're lyin' on your back for longer than you'd believe possible fighting with something that's got no brain. So I can't say total, but I figure three's the very top for material. Can't see it going any higher than that. Unless there's something goes wrong," and she knew something would go wrong, knew from his tone something always went wrong and you were lucky if everything didn't go wrong.

She had never thought for a minute about the walls, or what it would do to them if the plumbing needed replaced. She had expected a degree of mess because of the upstairs bathroom. She hadn't stopped to think about the vents that went up through the walls, through the attic, and even through the roof.

"Got 'er made," she mourned, remembering Tommy's envious comment and looking at the mess of gyproc dust on the floor. "No doubt about it, got 'er made. House, car, boat . . . everything a person could want. House is fallin' apart, car's ready to blow up in my face and the boat could sink and drown us all in a minute."

She also had a deep hole into which was lowered a huge concrete rectangle which so effectively filled the space the left-over dirt had to be spread, as evenly as possible, over the side yard. Leading away from the hole were trenches, into which went drain rock over which was placed a layer of biodegradable unbleached paper, to protect the new drainpipes from the sharp edges of the gravel, which turned out not to be rounded gravel but jagged-edged bits of broken rock. The guy with the backhoe dumped gravel into the trench and the one with the rake and shovel spread it over and around the drain pipe. Then the backhoe operator pushed dirt back into the trench and the guy with the shovel and rake took a swipe or two at the mess and that was the levelling off done and finished.

"We'll be forever getting it properly spread," Jean sighed.

"Yeah, and no use trying to do it until it starts to rain because right now the damn stuff is so dry it's as hard as rock."

"Rain. I can't even start to think about this place in the rain."

And with all the hammering and slamming, cutting and disconnecting of pipes, shutting off of water, changing of water pressure and general rumbling of equipment, other things started to vibrate. The vibration shook loose years of rust which came out of the faucets in large flakes. The plumber looked at the flakes and shook his head. The backhoe operator stood listening, nodding, then got back on his machine and another trench was dug, from the house to the main valve connection to the water system.

"Let me guess," Jean rolled her eyes.

"Right," the plumber sighed. "But one thing about it, once you put in that plastic piping you got no worries for the next sixty or eighty years. That stuff'll still be in the ground, still doin' its job, when you and I are long gone."

"At this rate you and I ought to be long gone within a day or two."

Of course it didn't end with plumbers and backhoe operators. The wall in the bathroom had to be cut to allow the plumber access to the pipes. That cut exposed dark, damp stains. "Bad news," the plumber told her. "And there's a hunk of floor gone punky, too."

So the carpenter arrived and dollar bills grew wings, flew out the window, and headed off down the road, migrating happily.

"Rat piss," Jean mourned. "It wasn't leakage, it was rat piss. The whole goddamn bathroom is rotting because of rat piss."

Sally brought home the rat poison. Jean stared at the package and then started to laugh. "I can't believe it. You no longer get rat poison! It comes in what they call a 'cafeteria pack' and it's bacon-and-cheese flavoured!"

"Why not?" Mark shrugged. "We got very particular rats."

"I only hope it's true they'll go outside looking for water to drink and die somewhere other than in the walls and between the floors. Otherwise, this place is going to reek of dead rat!"

"We ought to get a cat," Eve said stubbornly.

"We can't afford to *feed* a cat!"

She decided she wasn't going to think about any of it, she wasn't even going to take an active part in it, she was just going to take the *Lazy Daze* out and catch as many fish as she could so she could sell them and hand the money over as fast as she got it. "They passed a law," she explained to Eve, "up in heaven, years ago. And that law says I'm never, not ever, allowed to get ahead."

"Yeah," Eve agreed, "and if you *do* manage to get a head, the next thing you know the hair falls out of it and you go broke buyin' wigs."

Autumn tried to sneak up on them and when that didn't work she threw a tantrum, sent wind that drove the rain almost sideways and filled the eavestroughs with leaves and bits of evergreen tips. The back yard, where the drain field had been laid, turned to a bog but the new septic tank worked like a dream. It was nice to sit in a tub of hot water and not cringe when someone emptied the dishwater in the kitchen. Nice not to have to leap out of the tub as the greasy water from the sink spewed from the overflow, forced out the plug and sent bits of spaghetti and stuff you didn't even want to think about back out of the jerry-rigged interconnected pipes.

The new car ran well. Even the heater worked, and you could just open the door, not have to give it a solid shove with your shoulder. The walls were fixed, the carpenter was paid, Sally had Miranda purring like a mother cat with a box of kittens, and Mark had decided grade twelve wouldn't kill him after all. "If Sal could get through it, I'll get through it," he said, winking at Jean so she would know it was supposed to be a joke. "She's so stupid it'd make your teeth ache, and I'm the genius in the family, so it shouldn't be hard at all."

"It won't be," Sally said easily. "After all, now that they've put you in the special needs program you'll get A's just for having your shoes on the right feet."

Patsy was busy with her pregnancy. She phoned every morning to let Eve know whether or not she had morning sickness, then phoned again after supper to tell Eve about her day at work. Eve fussed and worried because, after all, you just don't know what to believe, they say those computer screens don't cause any problems, but you expect them to say that, if they admitted anything they might have to pay compensation or something. "But don't you get Patsy worried about it," she warned, "because she's having a hard enough time as it is."

Patsy's hard time was because Terry didn't want to quit his job and sign on for a retraining program at the college. "You knew the kind of work I did before we got married," he argued angrily, "and if you didn't want to marry a logger you shoulda said so and called the whole thing off!"

"You'll wind up *dead*!" Patsy sobbed. "It's dangerous work. It's *awful* work!"

"You want to know what *awful* work is?" he yelled. "It's any kind of work you don't want to do!"

"Now, now," Eve soothed, "it's just her nerves. Because of the baby, and all."

"Yeah? What about *my* nerves?" Terry asked, his voice flat. "Or aren't I supposed to have any? Is that something else I'm not allowed to have, like feelings?"

"If you had *feelings*," Patsy wailed, "you'd think about other people once in a while."

"Shut up," Jean said. They all stared at her. "If you want to fight, do it in your own house."

"Well, and isn't that *nice*," Patsy sobbed. "My own *mother*!"

"She wasn't *fighting*." Eve leaped to the barricades, sword in hand, ready to fight to the death to protect her Patsy-baby.

"Really?" Jean looked at Eve. "Maybe you'd like to show me what a fight *is*, then?"

"Shut up," Sally yawned. "If you want to fight go out in an alley and do it there."

"I sure hope *my* kid doesn't talk to *me* the way you talk to *Mom*," Patsy sniffed, her lip quivering. "It's just *awful* how people in this family *treat* each other."

"Set us the example, Patsy," Sally challenged. "Let's see you talk to Terry in a reasonable, mature and constructive fashion. Then we'll all have seen how it's done, and maybe we'll be so knocked on our asses, we'll try it too."

"Oh *stuff* it," Patsy replied. "I don't *know* when it is you think *you* got so smart. Maybe you fell on your *head* and shook something *loose*."

The CBC radio was talking about clouds with occasional showers turning to rain in the late afternoon. The morning wind clawed at the corners of the roof and tried to pull the downspouts off the house. In the bush behind the vacant lot two alder trees parted company with the ground, they swayed too far and didn't manage to sway back, the rootball rose, mud flew and the trees crashed to their sides.

Mark and Jean put on heavy sweaters and rain slickers, and walked through the mess to the wharf to check the moorings and make sure the *Lazy Daze* was secure.

"Better throw an extra couple'a Scotchmen over, just in case," Mark shouted over the noise of the wind and the pounding waves. "Just because she's secure doesn't mean all these others are."

Even the seals had decided to cuddle in behind the breakwater. They bobbed there, only their heads showing. Brucie barked challenge, one of the seals answered, and before Jean knew what was happening, Brucie was in the water, chest-deep, growling and raging. "Brucie!" Jean yelled, "you get the hell outta there!"

"Brucie! Come back!" Mark jumped from the *Lazy Daze* deck to the dock and raced along it, his gumboots slipping. Brucie edged deeper into the water, still yapping stupidly. And then the seal came up out of the water and grabbed, dragging Brucie under, pulling her away from shore. Mark pounded back down the dock, raced down the beach, kicked off his boots and headed into the cold waves, yelling and slapping his hands on the water. Jean shrieked and grabbed the dip net, ran to the back of the boat and tried to scoop the dog, but no matter how far she stretched, there was still a good six feet of empty space between the metal rim of the net and the wildly thrashing dog.

Mark screeched with fear and anger, grabbed Brucie's back legs and yarded. The seal decided everybody had been taught a lesson in humility and she turned gracefully, slipped under the waves and swam back to chortle with the others.

Brucie's shoulder was ripped open and pouring blood, her face was cut, one of her ears looked as if it needed a tube of Krazy Glue and she was shaking with terror. "And you can damn well *walk* home, you stupid mutt!" Mark shouted, wet to the chest and already blue with cold. "Why in *hell* you won't come when you're called is a goddamn mystery!"

"A bigger one is why every dog who ever lived near the beach is too stupid to know better than to bark back at the seals." Jean snapped her fingers. The bleeding dog ran along the wharf, jumped to the deck and moved to her, whining. "I bet there's three or four mutts a year do the same dumb thing and wind up supper for the whole pack of water-wolves." She pushed Brucie aside before the dog could wipe blood all over her clothes. "Piss off, fool," she laughed. "And don't think you're going to the vet, either, you can damn well heal yourself, you got yourself into it, I didn't, and I'm not spending fifty dollars to get you stitched up. Ninety percent of the world is born, suffers, lives and dies without medical treatment, you don't have to think some goddamn *dog* is going to do better."

It didn't cost fifty dollars, it cost a hundred and fifty and Brucie came home so shaved they called her the Giant Chihuahua. The storm blew for five days and two seiners vanished in the chuck. They found three of the seven men, but the other four were taken by the selkies, those supernaturals who are neither seal nor people but can choose to be either or both and who lust for human sexual partners.

Not even Sally seemed to understand why Jean decided to go to night school. Even before the season closed, she was down to the college, and registered for upgrading.

"But *why*? I don't understand why a person would go to school when she doesn't need to," Mark shook his head dolefully. "Next thing I know it'll be Let's sit down and do our homework together. I can barely," he shook his head, "manage to do it by my*self*, I'll never get finished if I have to wait for *you* to catch up."

"Gee, thanks, guy."

"Upgrading? Why?" Sally asked.

"Because I have to learn all over again how to study, how to take notes, how to remember important stuff. . . and everything has changed since I was in school. Except maybe the date of the Battle of Hastings."

"The who?"

"See? We had to know that kind of stuff. But we didn't have to know a tenth of what they taught you! So if I take upgrading, and get my brain back in shape a bit, then I can go on to something else."

"Why? Is this like cake decorating classes or something? A thing you do instead of Good Works For The Poor?"

"You think I'm going to be able to catch fish for a living all my life? Sally, my nose is pushing closer every day to fifty. There was a time I thought fifty was ancient! I'm not sure I was wrong, either. Some days my back hurts so much I can hardly make myself move. One of these days I won't be *able* to make myself move. There are times when I finally get into that bunk and I think I'll never get out of it. Other times when I don't think I'll ever be warm again. And one day I just simply will not be able to DO what needs done. Then what will I do?"

"You're in great shape!" Sally argued stubbornly. "There isn't another mom your age who can even hope to look as good! Anyway, Grandpa managed to . . ."

"Einarr didn't have four pregnancies and three babies," Jean laughed. " We used to say every baby cost the mother a tooth. But it costs more than that. Just *having* them changes how your hips fit into your pelvis, I'm sure of it. And whatever it looks like on the outside, only I know how it feels on the inside."

"So what you going to do?"

"I don't know. I have no idea at all what it is people do any more. That's why I'm going to school. To find out."

She was a hit in class. The English teacher asked each of them to introduce themselves, say why they were in the class, tell what kind of work they did and how they felt about it. As soon as Jean said she fished for salmon the attitude changed. "You'd think I just got elected to the head of the Women's Liberation Movement," she groused. "All of a sudden I'm some kind of symbol. What I can't believe is that some of the guys act as if I'm personally responsible for whatever is stuck in their throat."

But not all of them. Some of them acted as if a non-traditional job was proof of some kind of ravenous sexual appetite. They seemed both disillusioned and disappointed when they found out she wasn't prepared to leap into the Smithrite between classes and whip off a quickie. And the women seemed even more surprised. "God, they act like I've betrayed them," Jean mourned. "One woman seems convinced I've somehow been part of the reason we need a juvenile court system. Keeps talking about how mothers working outside the home have ruined our traditional family values. Then she looks at me as if I'm supposed to pour lighter fluid on my head and strike a match, to atone."

When the English teacher assigned a composition "on any topic that interests you," Jean researched until she was sick of the smell of books, and wrote an essay on women working outside the home throughout history. "How in hell anyone got the idea it's something that only started a couple of years ago is a puzzle," she groused over supper. "What the hell do they think Charles Dickens was writing about? Who do they think ran the big machines during the Industrial Revolution?" The kids stared at her, then looked at each other, then at Eve who was busy deliberately ignoring the whole thing, concentrating on her meat loaf.

"You sure use a lot of garlic," Eve said quietly. "I don't know I've ever had meat loaf with this much garlic in it."

They were learning why people have for years said there's no room in any one kitchen for two cooks. Eve's food was good, and it was plain. Jean's food was good and pungent with herbs and spices. For the most part they both liked each other's cooking, as long as it wasn't something supposed to be familiar, like meat loaf or pot roast. Meat loaf is supposed to taste a certain way and while Eve's did, Jean's didn't. Dumplings don't often have little green flecks in them, unless Jean cooked them, with lots of chopped parsley, basil and dill. When Eve did the potatoes she mashed them. When Jean did potatoes she mashed them, then added finely chopped onion, two eggs, a big dollop of margarine and a hint of coffee cream, then whipped the whole thing into fluffy mounds, sprinkled pepper, mixed it again, and topped it with paprika. Eve stared and asked what it was supposed to be. The kids ate everything and waited for an argument which never came.

"I cut back." Jean looked up. "Only used half of what I usually use."

"I use a can of tomato soup."

"Oh. I never do. Makes it too salty."

"My meat loaf is salty?"

"No, and I don't know how you manage that if you use tomato soup. Yours is never salty, but if I use the stuff, it is. Funny, huh?"

"You don't use enough bread."

"I don't use any bread. I use crackers."

"There you are. I bet it's salted crackers," and Eve smiled, nodding her head as another mystery of the universe was solved.

We're almost at the point where we're ready to have one of those goddamn television conversations about yellow wax on the hallway floor or how many flushes you can get out of a plastic bottle of blue weirdness left upside down in the toilet tank. By this time next week we ought to have the laundry sorted into two piles and we can compare if Brand X or Brand Y got the whites whiter and the colours brighter. About the time we have that conversation I think I'll go slit my throat; and who knows, maybe I'll use those sword-edged blades, the ones guaranteed to cut closer, shave smoother, and never *ever* give you a rash under your chin.

Russ Hanson was an inch or so taller than Jean, probably thirty to fifty pounds heavier, and maybe a year older. He had close-cropped dark hair going white at the temples, a nose half the size you would expect it to be, and a little gap between his front teeth. He also had a rosewood cane. When he walked he didn't quite limp, but did move stiffly. "Logging accident," he explained at coffee break the first night. He waved his cane slightly, and grinned, embarrassed. "Got hit across the smalla my back and kind of crunched a few things."

"You were lucky," someone said.

Russ nodded, and stood against the wall, his back flat against the gyproc. "Gets tired sitting," he admitted. "Of course, it gets tired standing, too."

"Wasn't the accident did that," Jean said firmly. "I never had a logging accident and *my* back can't decide what it wants, either."

He grinned and nodded. "You seen that bumper sticker? If I'd'a known I was gonna live this long I'd'a taken better care of myself."

"Yeah. You see the other one? Any day above ground is a good one."

The college was nonsmoking. There wasn't a room in the place where an addict could grab a puff and not set off a smoke alarm. Jean took her habit outside and stood under the overhang of the roof, shivering, puffing and cursing. Russ came out, already pulling his smokes from his pocket. He saw her, grinned, and came over to join her.

"Some cold." He stepped around a puddle.

"Oh, well," she shrugged. "We could reform and stay inside where it's warm and dry. But you watch, before long they'll all be out here, even the nonsmokers. I don't know if it's that they like to stand around and call us names for being smokers, or if it's just that we're more interesting than they are and they know it as well as we do. Besides, nonsmokers don't tell jokes, they only like to hear them, and we're the ones tell them, so. . . you watch, it might take a class or two, but they'll all be out here."

"What are you taking?" he asked, cupping his hands around his match to protect it from the wind as he lit his cigarette.

"Upgrading my English. Which, as you may have noticed, can stand some upgrading. You?"

"Compensation is supposed to be retraining me. So I'm taking this math course that's supposed to pave the way for me to get into something else. Nobody seems to have decided what, yet," he grinned. "Can't do anything heavy, so even mechanic work is out. Can't take any amount of jiggling or shaking, so there goes any hope of a driving job. And somehow I can't quite see me in cooking school." He smiled, but his eyes were dark and worried. "It's kind of a bugger," he admitted, "I been workin' in the bush since I was seventeen. But I'm not gonna be working there any more."

"That's a tough one."

"Yeah. So why you upgrading?"

"I figure I'd better start now, because I'm getting too old to do what I'm doing."

She liked it that he didn't try to say she wasn't old, liked it that he didn't say she looked no more than thirty. He just nodded, and asked her what it was she was doing that made her feel she was too old to do it. She told him, and he just gave her a long hard look, and nodded. "Damn hard work," he agreed.

It isn't easy finding someplace to go when you finally break down and agree to go out. Agree to go out on what would be called a date if you were both twenty years younger.

There were, of course, the pubs. You could sit there in the stench of old beer listening to stale music pounding from a jukebox and shout at each other across a small round table covered with a terrycloth bib. Every now and again, just to provide some extra entertainment, a couple of toothless bozos might leap to their feet screeching insult and take ineffectual roundhouse swings at each other. Maybe you'd all get so excited by the breeze resulting from the missed haymakers, you'd wander over to watch a couple of totally inept drunks try to pretend they were playing pool. If things got boring you could always watch aging floozies trying to compete with their underage counterparts, and every now and again someone cursed with a particular form of wit would take out his/her false teeth and drop them in someone else's beer, that was always good for five minutes of either hysteria or hilarity, it was often hard to tell which.

Or you might go to a hard bar where the same kind of thing went on except the men were dressed in polyester pants and what were still called sports coats instead of in jeans and tee shirts, and the women were dolled up in tasteful numbers from page fifteen of the Mammoth Sale catalogue.

There was, of course, the movie house. But if you're both too old to call it a date, chances are you're both too old to sit and watch a Kung Fu movie or yet another myopic revisionist Viet Nam movie, complete with flamethrowers and recognizable villains, all of whom, of course, were Asian.

They talked often about what there was to do, where there was to go, and finally Jean suggested Russ might want to come out on the boat. "If the weather's okay," she amended.

"I'd like that," he agreed.

The kids went, too. Not because Jean felt she needed protection, not because the kids felt she needed protection, but because she had done such a good job of making it seem like no big deal, it never occurred to them to stay home and she couldn't think of a way to suggest it without feeling self-conscious.

They didn't put out lines or do any fishing, they just cruised the coast for a couple of hours and Russ unpacked an array of expensive camera gear that caught Mark's interest immediately. While Jean sat on her stool in the wheelhouse and watched, amused, Russ set up his tripod, screwed on his camera, and took pictures while explaining to Mark and Sally what he was doing and why.

When he changed film, he let them take turns, and they shot a roll, too. "Now we can fight over who took the good ones," Sally laughed.

"There won't *be* any good ones," Mark predicted. "Yours won't be properly focussed and mine will be overexposed. You'll see."

They unpacked their picnic lunch and sat on the hatch cover, their heavy jackets zipped to the throat, watching the seals and otters in the kelp beds. The thin winter sunlight held little warmth and the breeze was starting to pick up and bite at their earlobes. "Jesus, Mom," Mark said, "are we havin' a good time, or what!"

She took them home and as they tied the *Lazy Daze* to her posts the whole thing hit Jean's funny bone and she started to laugh. Sally joined her immediately, pointing at Mark and handing him a wad of toilet paper for his dripping nose. He took it, grinning, and hugged himself, pretending to shiver uncontrollably.

"Sure is hard to make the move on your mother," Russ said quietly. "I mean I've heard of women who'll freeze you out, but . . ."

"Yeah." Mark wiped his nose, wiped again. "Just think what she'll do to you if she ever gets really turned on, eh fella?"

Eve was wearing her quietest wig and had supper on the go when they arrived. She was so busy being Red Riding Hood's grandma they hardly saw her and only knew she was still alive by the good smells coming from the kitchen. Then Patsy and Terry arrived, and things got quite weird for a while.

"My daughter Patsy and her husband Terry," Jean said, "and this is Russ Hanson."

"How ya doin' fellow?" Terry did not smile, but stuck out his hand almost eagerly.

"Fine as silk, yourself?"

"Never better."

"How's the job?"

"Oh, we'll be outta there before long. If snow season holds off we might even finish 'er up before we come home and put our sock feet on the TV cushion."

"Then maybe he'll get work around home and not have to go to camp," Patsy said hopefully.

Russ smiled and nodded as if there was every chance in the world this would happen, then he and Terry just sat, quiet as pictures on the wall, while Patsy talked of painting the baby's room, finding the absolutely most perfect little rocking cradle, and how she thought maybe she'd get the print-out of the scan framed and hang it on the wall.

"If you knew what you were looking for, or knew what it might look like if you found it," she laughed, "I bet you could tell if it was a boy or a girl. But we didn't ask, because, well, that's almost like cheating. After all, life has to hold *some* surprises in store for a person."

"I doubt there'll be any shortage of surprises," Jean smiled. "Seems to me like my whole life's been one big surprise after another."

"Are you a logger?" Patsy asked Russ.

He smiled slowly, and shook his head. "Used to be," he confessed. "I'm back in school now." Terry looked at the floor, pressed his huge fingers against his beer can, collapsing the middle slightly.

"School?" Patsy smiled. "What kind of school?"

"I think they think they're going to teach me to be an accountant," Russ winked, "because I think we've pretty well decided there's no way I would be any good in hairdressing school. Now all I have to do is learn how to count up past fifteen, and you never know, I might wind up with my own income tax evasion office."

"Didn't you like logging?" She leaned back in the chair, looking like someone's idea of the madonna-in-waiting. Terry peered into the hole in the top of his beer can, and Russ shook his head.

"I heard tell," he confided with a wide smile, "there was this woman taking the upgrading course. And I heard tell she owned her own boat. And I figured well, she's got brains *and* money . . . so I quit m'job and signed on because you can't hustle someone unless you manage to find a way to get close to them."

Patsy laughed happily and Terry relaxed. He shot a look of such open gratitude at Russ that Jean wondered how Patsy didn't see it and recognize it for what it was. She wondered if loggers always tried to hide from the wives how dangerous their work was or if it was just something they did when the wives were young, still foolish and obviously pregnant.

Supper was another of Eve's masterpieces. Jean would have used more garlic and more spices, but if you don't do it yourself you accept with good grace what others come up with, and certainly nobody seemed to hesitate. Eve fussed over Patsy, giving her the choicest portions of everything, then nagging at her to eat. Patsy was having no trouble packing it all away, and supper was relaxed and easy. Mark and Sally actually volunteered to do the dishes, and then Terry was glancing at his watch and almost leaping off his chair. "Jesus!" he laughed. "Been having such a good time I let it get away from me. I gotta head out or I'll miss the ferry."

"I'm coming," Patsy said, but her heart wasn't in it.

"I can drive you home later," Jean offered, and Patsy smiled widely. She walked Terry to his pickup, they hugged each other gently, kissing often, then he patted her rump and got into the pickup.

"See you Friday," he called.

"You take care," she answered, waving.

As it turned out, Jean didn't drive Patsy home, after all. Eve decided it made no sense for Patsy to go back to an apartment where there wasn't even a cat waiting for her. "She can bunk in with me," she said firmly. "As close to her time as she is she shouldn't be alone." Jean almost asked how it had happened she'd gone through three pregnancies and a miscarriage without so much as seeing Eve's face, but it seemed unimportant, and worse, it seemed foolish and childish to bring that one up out of the cobwebby cellar and wave it around again.

Patsy, Eve, Sally and Mark went into the kitchen to play cards, leaving Jean in the living room with Russ and the TV. They chatted quietly, then Eve brought in a pot of tea and what was left of the chocolate cake, put the tray on the small table and left, wordless.

"Nice family," Russ laughed.

"Oh, they're all on their best behaviour," she warned. "There's times around here it sounds like the Bay of Pigs invasion."

"Yeah," he nodded. "I remember the sound." He sipped his tea, and for a moment his face was glum. "But then they grow up and head off on their own and you're left with nothing but this funny feeling that maybe you shoulda done more. Mind you, I don't have the slightest idea what more I coulda done, all things considered, but . . ." he smiled, "but there they are, one of 'em is selling real estate in Vancouver and driving a goddamn BMW around, as if to the manner born, and the other's out in Coquitlam, commuting back and forth to the Stock Exchange. Now, *she* won't drive anything as obvious as a BMW, says conspicuous consumption is as close to a sin as you can get, but I notice she's already bought her own house and filled it with furniture, so I guess we're looking at two hundred thou worth of consumption, and it might not be exactly conspicuous, but I don't much see the difference."

"And your wife?" she probed.

"My ex," he corrected gently. He looked at Jean, and smiled. "She and I split up about eight months after I got my back buggered." He looked into his teacup and Jean flashed on Terry staring into his beer can. "I was mad, at first. Wanted to pay her back. It's a helluva thing when the person who knows you better'n anybody else in your life ever did lets you know it ain't good enough, makes you feel like *you're* not good enough. But you get a lot of time to think things through when you're lyin' on your back. She was there for me at the time of the accident, she was there all through the first surgery, she even stuck 'er out through the recuperation and physio and all. It was when I had m'feet back under me she said she was leavin'. When they said I had to have another operation, she said she'd hang in for that one, too, but I said no, just pack and go, it's what you want to do. Sold the house, all that kinda stuff." He hesitated, then took a deep breath and dove into the deep water. "I got over bein' mad when I realized that the only thing I'd ever really given that woman was my pay-cheque. And if ever there was a woman deserved better than that, it was Lorraine. It wasn't that I was an asshole," he smiled, tilting his head to one side as if hearing memory voices, "because I don't think

I was. I just..." and again he shrugged, "I just talked about what had happened, not what I wanted to happen, or what I thought, and I never talked about what I felt or regretted or wished. Hey, I was a logger, eh? And we not only got caulks on our boots, we got 'em on our balls, too, eh."

It was nice to snuggle up to his warm body and rub her hand gently on the greying fur on his chest, nice to stroke the soft skin of his belly and that place on his inner thigh where his jeans rubbed a smooth patch on his legs. "You're as fuzzy as a bear. You've even got fur at the base of your spine."

"Yeah," he yawned, "and a dimple, too. My mom used to say it was where my tail was when they found me swinging from the branch of a tree. She didn't want the neighbours to notice so she pulled it off and it left a dimple."

Sometimes, after long pleasurable loving, she would fall asleep curled tight against him, her cheek on his chest, her hand on his belly. The sleep she got then seemed deeper, more refreshing, and when she snapped awake an hour or two later, she felt as if she could climb mountains or walk the distance from his place to hers, instead of driving.

She never stayed the night.

"Ah, come on," he teased, "live dangerously."

"I do." She kissed his earlobe. "Every time I head off to work I live just about as dangerously as anyone except a mercenary soldier."

"You know what I mean."

"Yeah. And you know what I mean, too."

"Your kids aren't babies."

"I don't think it's the kids. It's me. Staying overnight means something I'm not ready for yet." She nuzzled his neck. "You know how it is, first you stay overnight, then it's wait a half a minute and I'll make you some breakfast. From there," she warned, "it's a short step to why don't *you* make the breakfast, and once a woman starts cooking bacon at a man's stove, it somehow becomes *her* kitchen. Then she winds up cleaning *her* oven and scrubbing *her* floor, and from there, it's a short, sad slide into doing *her* windows. And I'm not ready for that. I haven't recuperated from the last time."

They never went to her bedroom, they didn't make love in her bed. She went to his place, and then she went home. Sometimes, often in fact, he came for supper, they played cards or watched TV, then he left and she followed in her car. Eve knew what was going on and so did the kids, and she knew they knew, and still, that was the way it went. "You serious about him?" Sally asked. Jean shook her head, then corrected herself. "I don't know," she admitted. "I really like him. I'm just . . . well, I don't know, maybe it's once burned, twice shy, but . . . does it bother you?"

"Me?" Sally thought about that a moment. "Why should it bother me?" she laughed. "Does my love life bother you?"

"I always kind of figured your sex life was your business and my sex life was my business," Jean said carefully. "Once you knew about things like the birds and the bees, contraception and disease, that is."

"You ever, you know, go out with guys before you and Dad split up?"

"Never," Jean said firmly.

"What about after?"

"Who had the time?" They both laughed. "Or the energy for that matter. No, I didn't. Not even once. It wasn't even a consideration."

"Boy, havin' kids sure ruins your life, eh?" Sally was still laughing, but there was something in the tone of her voice, something around the edges of her eyes that gave Jean the hint something heavy was being thrown her way.

"Ruins it?" She pulled out her cigarettes, took one, then, almost as an afterthought, offered the package to Sally, who took one, then produced her own lighter. "I don't think having kids ruined my life," Jean said softly. "It did complicate things, it'd be a lie to say anything else. And I have to admit sometimes I looked at people who didn't have kids and I wondered what in the name of God they did with all that extra time and money they must have! But I can't even play around and daydream what my life would have been if I hadn't had my pack."

"You could have just had one. Or two."

"Yeah. On the other hand I almost had four, so there you go. Who would you have me kill off here? I mean if I'd waited longer I wouldn't have Patsy, and I'm used to her, you know? And I kind of like Mark. So . . . maybe you're wondering if it's you I'd bump off?"

"Well, no, I guess I was wondering how you thought about stuff like, well, say abortion."

"Oh fuck, drop a heavy one, why don't you?" Jean groaned and

Sally smiled, leaned back in her chair and waited. "How do I feel about it? Well, I guess I feel that it's not a decision I had to make, so I don't really have any right to make judgements."

"What about other people having them?"

"How would I know what their reasons were? I go in the super-market sometimes and I see these pale little buggers with big dark circles under their eyes and the skinniest arms you can ever want to see and I wonder what in hell their opinion might be if anyone asked them. Or I read about some kid who grew up in a shit heap and got twisted so much it either hit the streets and wound up with its throat slit in a whorehouse or was the one did the slicing and chopping and I wonder about the sanctity of life. Sometimes I hear about an earthquake or something and fifteen hundred people just gone in a wink and I wonder why there's all the fuss about one or two who never happened. Or we get to waving flags and shooting bullets and I can't figure out why the ones we're paying tax dollars to kill aren't part of the sanctity of life they talk about so much. We drop a bomb and poof! When did those lives stop being sacred? So mostly I figure that it's not anything that ever impinged on *me*, so . . ." She shrugged. "But I *do* know if any of my kids felt she was stuck, or didn't want to, or couldn't, or needed or . . . the first person who steps in front of her to shout 'murderer' is going to catch my boot with his teeth." She dragged on her cigarette, watched the blue smoke rise, then fixed Sally to her chair with a hard look. "Why? You pregnant?"

"Me?" Sally looked surprised. "Hey, if I am, go to the window and watch for the three creeps on camels, okay? I don't do that stuff."

"Why not?"

"I don't know," Sally stubbed out her cigarette. "It doesn't appeal to me . . . the idea of it turns me off in fact, and I don't think I'm afraid of it."

"Don't be," Jean urged. "But don't feel you have to prove anything, either."

"Yeah, well, maybe I've got a problem," Sally looked uncomfortable. "The guys in class seem like such . . ." She shook her head, sighed deeply. "I don't know, but it's like as long as we talk about engines we're fine. Stop talking about that and the silence is about as deep and cold as that water out there. It's as if . . . I don't know, as if they all sound alike! You know, you've heard one, you've heard 'em all. Maybe they feel the same way about us, I don't know."

Something inside Jean that had tightened when Sally said maybe she had a problem, relaxed. She just nodded, and smiled. "Maybe that's the real price we'll have to pay for equality," she suggested. "Maybe when we get to know each other the Ah, Sweet Mystery Of Life won't seem to be the other half of the population. It sure seemed to me that's where it all was when I was your age. I thought the stuff I didn't have and couldn't take a swing at might become available by proxy, or something."

"Must have been fuckin' grisly," Sally laughed. "What was there around here for you to want to do?"

"Exactly," Jean yawned. "So, for lack of any other options I fell madly in love with the first half-decent guy who came down the pike. And here we are. Involved in a philosophical discussion that is so interesting we're both going to sleep in our chairs!"

"You figure life is just one big. . .kleesh?" Sally teased.

"Oh, a kleesh for sure. That's why we're so nayve and blayze, right?"

Jean had a bath, washed her hair, rubbed ginseng creme on her hands, face, neck and arms, pulled on her warm ankle-length flannel nightgown and went to bed, but she didn't fall asleep immediately. She lay watching the black winter branches of the alder tree dance in the cone of light from the corner lamp, wondering if life really was just one cliché after another. She heard Eve pad down the hallway, and moments later there was the flush of the toilet. Then Eve padded back to her room. Brucie took a tour around the back yard, on guard against hungry coons and stray cats. The buoy dinged monotonously, and somewhere out on the chuck a tugboat was yarding a string of booms down to the mill. She wondered if Russ was awake, maybe sitting in his recliner with a heating pad on his back, sipping a strong drink and watching TV. Some nights he slept in his recliner because it was the only place he could get comfortable. Some nights the only way he could get comfortable was to wash a couple of Tylenol-with-codeine down with a good solid blast of Canadian Club. Seemed a helluva price to pay for the chance to support your family.

The fourth of April Jean stood in the corridor and looked through a large glass window at her granddaughter. Paige Ellen Dugan lay tightly wrapped in a pink receiving blanket, her fists covered with little white cotton bags pinned to the sleeves of her nightgown.

"She *scratches* herself," Patsy worried. "Why would she deliberately *scratch* herself?"

"It isn't deliberate," Jean soothed. "They don't know they're doing it. They put up their hands, feel something, and their fingers move. It's not their fault they have fingernails."

"Well, she does it." Patsy's eyes welled with tears. "And you can't even tell her *not* to do it. But she scratched her face!"

"It won't leave marks," Jean promised. "You'll see, she'll be over it in a few days."

"It's not the *marks*." Patsy had given up on italics the last few months of her pregnancy, but it was starting to sound as if they were back in her life again. "But what if she *hurts* herself?"

"If it hurts she'll stop." Jean put her arm around Patsy's shoulders, gave her a light hug. "Come on, let's get you back to bed. You don't want to be worn out when Terry gets here."

"I wish he could have been here when she was born! I *told* her, I said Baby, please, just one more day, that's all, just wait for Daddy, but no, she had to come last night."

"There, see, a woman after my own heart. I admire independence," Jean teased. "After all, you'd wind up bored to tears if she was the kind of kid just sat like a pudding."

She got Patsy back to her room, helped her brush her hair, and while Patsy filed and fussed with her nails, Jean read aloud to her from a cheap pulp magazine. "Here, listen to this, you think you had a rough night? Woman gives birth to thirty-pound SuperBaby. I'm glad he's not twins, says tired mom."

"My God. You'd think they'd do a Caesarean or something," Patsy winked. "Or maybe they were afraid they wouldn't be able to lift him out on their own."

"Here's a good one: Grandmother gives birth twenty years after hysterectomy. Now there's a nightmare!" She scanned the article. "Says here the baby grew in her abdominal cavity, between her skin and her intestines."

"I don't believe that," Patsy said firmly. "They tell lies in that thing, you know."

"No!" Jean pretended to be shocked. "It could happen. What if they only took the uterus, and left the fallopian tubes? What if the fertilized egg implanted in the tube and grew out?"

"Oh, give your head a shake," Patsy laughed. "How'd the egg get into the tube, the end would be sealed shut from where they cut it off. I'm sure they don't just leave them dangling, like old electrical wires, hanging there with nowhere to go and nothing to do! And then how'd the sperm get to the egg, I ask you? You can't tell me they went blundering in there and just snip snipped out her womb and left everything else gaping! I mean they close off the end of things, you know. Even if they left her cervix in they'd still sew things shut. It's all just a story to scare up a market. Enough stories like that and every woman who ever had a hysterectomy will whip out and buy birth control pills, just to be sure she isn't growing a kid somewhere between her spleen and her liver. Honestly Mom, you're so gullible!"

"Here's some woman locked her husband's mistress in a cage for two years."

"Good. Why'd she let her out? Anybody starts messing around with Terry and I'll lock her in a crab trap and drop it over the side of your boat. Into *very* deep water."

"Yeah? What you going to do to *him*?"

"Rusty razor blade," she said promptly. She laughed, then her face changed. "Oh, hell, I'm flooding. Gimme a hand to the jane, will you?" Jean helped Patsy out of bed, walked with her to the bathroom and waited. A few minutes later Patsy came out, shaking her head. "Damn, it's a messy business."

"Oh, it's just draining stuff out, is all. I only did it for a day or so and then nothing until I started a regular period."

"Well, you'd think they'd figure out a better way to go about things. They've got all this labour-saving stuff for doing your dishes, why not put their minds to *this*?"

"Because they have to do dishes if they live alone, but they never have to do this, so why should they bother?"

"Then we'll just have to get some of us into research science."

"Good, you can go back to school in September and leave the kid with Eve."

"Don't tempt me. I might even take her to school with me, to remind me why I'm there. Computers," she yawned, climbing back into bed, "are just glorified typewriters. The work is just every bit as boring as it ever was." She lay back, yawning again. "I just might, too," she warned. "And why not? I bet I could put her in the kiddy-care thing. And if not, there's always Grandma," she giggled lightheadedly. "Well, I guess *you're* Grandma, now. But not mine."

"You go to sleep, you're getting weak minded." Jean leaned over and kissed Patsy's forehead. "You have a good sleep so you'll be wide awake and gorgeous when Terry arrives. And I'll see you tonight."

"I love you, Momma," Patsy smiled. "Would you phone Daddy for me? His line was busy each time I tried."

"Sure," Jean agreed. "I guess I can stand to talk to him long enough to tell him he's over the hill for sure, now. You go to sleep, baby. Love you lots."

"Love you." Patsy closed her eyes, still smiling, and Jean put the stupid magazine on the bedside chair. Maybe when Patsy woke up she'd want to read the story about the guy who made a hobby of eating barbed wire and bits of broken glass. For a bet he had once eaten a bicycle, little piece at a time. Probably shits Volkswagens, she thought.

On her way out of the hospital she stopped in front of the big glass-fronted nursery and stared for long minutes at what little she could see of her first grandchild. Paige Ellen Dugan. She waited, half expecting the intense surge of uncontrolled emotion she had felt each time her own newborns had been placed in her arms. She didn't feel that. She didn't feel anything even remotely resembling it. What she felt was puzzlement and more than a slight hint of something she thought she identified as fear. It didn't matter that Paige looked like nobody in particular; Patsy and Mark hadn't particularly resembled anyone else in the family, either. It didn't matter that there was as much of Alpha Dugan in the genetic pool as there was of Jean Pritchard. What mattered, what made Jean feel tentative, even frightened, was her own inability to project any vision or dream of what life would be like for this helpless mite. She'd had plans for her own kids. She'd had some idea of what their lives would be, and everything had changed so much already, she couldn't make pictures of Paige at age ten. Or age six, for that matter. She was afraid of the childhood cancer statistics, she was afraid of the growing link between pulp mill effluent and birth defects, she was suddenly terrified of the changing climate, the rising negative evidence of the dying Gulf of Georgia. She hadn't been able to do much for her children and now she was facing her grandchild. She didn't know what she was supposed to do. She didn't know what she could do. At least when her kids had been small she could put them out in the yard to play without worrying they'd get skin cancer from the sunshine. At least when her kids were small nobody was telling her to make sure they wore sunglasses when they played on the tire swing, otherwise they might go blind because we've put holes in the protective ozone layer. And what about the neutron bomb?

"Jesus," she muttered, "time to head for the shrink's office, old girl."

She dialled Tommy's number four times, got the busy signal three times and the machine the last time. "Tommy, it's Jean. You're a grandfather. A little girl, Paige Ellen, and everybody's fine. Patsy tried to phone you but your line is busy all the time. What you doing, taking book? Uh, guess that's it. How's it feel being a grandpa? I feel kind of. . .overwhelmed." I probably couldn't have said that much to him if he'd answered the phone, she realized, maybe if we just call each other's machines we'll learn how to keep our fangs out of each other's throats.

Terry arrived at the house in time for supper, passing out cigars with pink ribbons around them. "Congratulations!" Mark shouted. "Now you're a proper human being! Dad-dee!"

"You seen her?" Terry looked like a man who had just stepped off the earth and discovered he could walk on air. "My *God* but she's tiny!"

"Hey, *you* try to shit a nine-and-a-half-pound watermelon," Sally challenged.

"Not me," Terry blurted. "I don't know why Patsy's already talking about having another one. I wouldn't do it!"

They left the dishes stacked in the sink and drove in together to see Patsy and Paige. They left early to give Terry some time alone with Patsy, then drove back telling each other over and over again how beautiful the baby was and how happy Patsy seemed. "She's tired, though," Eve fussed, "I hope she can rest while she's in there. They send them home so quick these days."

The phone was ringing when they came in the house. Jean got to it first. "Hello?"

"Jeannie, it's Tommy," he sounded subdued, but hopeful. "How's Patsy?"

"Tired. A bit pale. But it's only to be expected, I suppose, the baby was nine and a half pounds."

"Yeah? Who's she look like?"

"I think the discussion is still open on that. To me she might just as easily be the neighbour's kid. Doesn't look like any of mine did."

"Listen, I'd like to come up and see her, and, well, you know, it's the same old problem, right, they won't give you a hotel room without making you pay a whole buncha money."

"Sure," she said wearily, "why not, nobody else is sleeping on the floor in the living room these days."

"You're great, Jeannie."

"Yeah, only these days they're calling it 'enabling behaviour'."

"See you tomorrow afternoon." He preferred to pay no attention to her last comment. Which told her more clearly than anything else, he had understood it completely.

Alpha Dugan roared up, honking her horn and waving madly out the driver's window. She parked her pickup and hurried to the house with a big brown bag under one arm and a two-four under the other, her little bitty cowboy boots tippy-tapping happily. "Not one word about being over the hill," she warned. "This kid isn't changing my life one little bit!"

"You'll change your mind when you see her," Eve laughed.

"You look and sound like you *lost* your friggin' mind." Alpha put her bag on the table, put the two-four on the floor and cracked it open immediately, hauling out several cans of beer. She pulled the tab, handed the beer to Eve, opened another for Jean and one for herself, and grinned. "So now we got a nine-pound excuse to get blasted, right?"

"When did we ever need an excuse?" Eve laughed.

"That kid of mine behave himself properly about it?"

"Did just fine. Cigars with pink ribbons, big bunch of flowers, got her a gold chain for her neck and another for her wrist. Looks like he can't believe even the first part of it, but he's holding up just fine."

"He'd better," Alpha said softly. "I didn't raise him to be a gomer. Well," she sighed deeply, "I don't know how any of *you* feel about it but I kinda feel like. . ." she sighed again, "like I don't know what the hell is going on any more. I never really planned on havin' a kid, and now. . ."

"Right," Jean laughed softly. "Well, at least this time there's a bit of money for things like new carriages and strollers and stuff. I think each of my kids was born into hand-me-downs and secondhand stuff."

"Jesus, ain't it the truth."

Tommy arrived in the early afternoon, parked his new car, walked up, opened the recently constructed gate and started along the path toward the front door, and Brucie very quietly walked up to him and bit him on the leg.

Brucie had never bitten anyone before in her life. Brucie hadn't even growled at anyone. But then Brucie hadn't growled at Tommy, either, she just came around the side of the house from the back yard, walked across the green patch of front lawn and buried her teeth in his upper leg. Nobody knew a thing about it until Tommy's shrieks of pain and terror jarred them from their peace. Eve frowned, put down her book and went to the front window. "My good God," she said quietly, "Brucie's going to kill him."

"Who?" Jean asked, but she rushed for the door.

"Get this mutt *off* me!" Tommy shrieked.

"Brucie, you stop that!" Jean yelled.

Brucie unlocked her jaws and walked away, head down, tail stub flat against her backside, the same ah, shucks posture she assumed when caught digging a hole or knocking the lid off the garbage can. Brucie wasn't fond of the new front fence and gate, maybe she had taken umbrage at the thought of someone actually using the damn things. Maybe she knew they had been put there in the hope they would influence her not to go lie in the middle of the road and fall asleep, where any traffic that might mistakenly wind up on this section of broken pavement might run into her corpulent body. Maybe she thought the fence had been put there in case Tommy drove down the road.

Tommy headed for the bathroom, came out minus his shoes and jeans and stood in his jockey shorts and sock feet displaying the rapidly swelling bite on his front thigh. The four deep puncture wounds outlined a large bruised area, and blood puckered at the jagged edges of the holes, then dribbled down his leg.

"I'll clean it and bandage it," Eve offered, "but then I think you should find a doctor and get a shot of some kind."

"Shot?" Tommy raged. "I'll tell you who should get a shot! That damn mutt should get a shot right in the head, is what."

"Oh, don't carry on so," Eve said easily. "Good God, man, you been livin' in the city too long, you're startin' to sound like one of 'em."

"That dog is vicious."

"Nah, she's not," Eve laughed, "nothing of the kind. The last time you came here you had kids with you. This time you come alone. So she's lettin' you know if you want to be friends with *her* you bring kids every time you come. Brucie's nuts about kids," she finished easily.

He sat on a kitchen chair sucking his breath in little gasps and going Easy easy, careful there, watch it while Eve swabbed his leg with alcohol and put a sterile dressing on it. Jean watched and grinned when she noticed Eve putting adhesive tape down without first shaving the leg. It would hurt more coming off than it hurt when Brucie chomped.

"That dog had her shots?" he snarled.

Eve's eyes narrowed, always a danger sign. "Yeah, she has, but I'll take her in and get some more. I don't want her catchin' nothin' off you."

"Lady, *look* at my *leg*!"

"Ah, g'wan, I've had worse and called 'em love nips." Eve turned away, her little fuzzy slippers making scornful noises against the linoleum. "Good job you and I didn't meet up when I woulda been your mother-in-law," she muttered, "or my daughter mighta been a widow in a real hurry."

"The fuckin' dog bites *me* and then *you* give me static! Give the dog some static! What do you think, I put my leg in her mouth?"

"It ain't her mouth has me disgusted, it's yours. I can't *stand* a man who whines. Or a woman, neither, for that matter. God help us all if you ever get hurt!"

Tommy went to the Emergency and got his backside peppered with shots of one kind or another, then went up to see Patsy. He came back in time for supper, grinning widely and claiming Paige looked just like him.

"When you going to get married and start a family?" he asked Sally.

She stared at him for so long he started to blush. Jean waited for the balloon to go up and Sally to call in the heavy artillery. "Oh," Sally shrugged, "I don't expect I'll get married. My girlfriend and I went down and applied but they said it wasn't allowed." Tommy stared. "As for having a kid or two, well, I think we still have a lot of time," and she smiled widely, then walked out of the kitchen. Jean wanted to follow her so they could both laugh into their pillows, silencing the sound, but she was busy dropping dumpling dough into her Killer Stew.

"Is she serious?" Tommy asked in the same tone some people reserve for discussions of ghosts and insanity in the family.

"About what?"

"Her girlfriend."

"Oh, I don't think they're really serious. They might have been, but I think the edge got taken off it when the clerk at the marriage licence department shot them down." Jean might have carried it off but the look on Tommy's face fixed her, and she brayed loudly with laughter. Eve bent over the kitchen sink, chortling into the dishwater, and Tommy stood, realizing he'd been had.

"What a bunch," he finally said, "what a bloody bunch." He even forced a smile to show he, too, could recognize a good joke, even when it was pulled on him. "A person never knows if it's bullshit or gospel around here."

The smile vanished when Russ arrived for supper. Russ didn't seem too bothered to wind up sitting at the same table as Jean's ex, but Tommy didn't know what to do or how to be. Jean took a grim pleasure in it all. Maybe Tommy would think twice about bringing Cheryl and the kids up again, maybe the idea of her giving him a job would evaporate. Maybe purple cows would become commonplace. The kids seemed to take detestable pleasure in the situation, and Eve just pulled out her years of experience and acted as if nothing was the least little bit out of the ordinary.

"You, Mark and Eve ride home with your dad," Jean told Sally as they all left to troop up to see Patsy and Paige.

"You really do believe in living dangerously, don't you," Sally warned.

"I see no reason to reorganize my life just to accommodate *him*."

Tommy was waiting up when Jean came home at three in the

morning. He sat up in his sleeping bag and eyed her almost accusingly. "You always come in this late?" he asked.

"No," she confessed, "sometimes I come in a lot later."

"You know what you're doing? I mean, is he a decent guy?"

"He's fine," she assured him. "And, yes, I know what I'm doing. As much as I ever did." She went to bed hoping that between Russ and Brucie, Tommy would get the hint and next time maybe stay at Patsy's place, which he could easily have arranged this time, but then he'd have had to do his own cooking.

She couldn't keep her bitter ugly mood going, though. She tried, but it was like trying to keep a sick goldfish alive. Yes, Tommy could have stayed at Patsy's, but he would have wound up alone, while the rest of them shared excitement, relief and happiness. Yes, he could have stayed at Patsy's, but he'd have wound up watching Harvey Kirk on the late news, not watching Eve trying to deal with the marvel of being a great-grandmother.

And maybe he really did believe the old water-under-the-bridge routine. She'd been so mad at him for so long he had stopped being just a person and in her mind assumed some of the proportions of the Anti-Christ, but surely the Great Satan was more than an obviously tired truck driver with a dog bite on his leg. Surely Diabolocus had at least a widow's peak, not a bald spot.

Patsy got out of the hospital with Paige and went home for a week, while Terry took time off and played at being chief cook and bottle washer. "He's wonderful," Patsy gushed through the phone. "He can cook and everything. He gave her a bath last night and I get breakfast in bed every morning. And he's *nuts* about Paige, Mom, he got up in the middle of the night and got her and brought her to bed and after I'd fed her he took her so I could go back to sleep. And there he was, sitting in that rocking chair you gave us, holding her up against his chest, rocking and singing this little teddy bear picnic song, it was so *cute*, I wish you could have seen it."

Tommy was back in the city. He stayed three days and saw Patsy and Paige back into their own home. Then, obviously regretful he couldn't hang around longer and maybe teach the kid how to pitch a softball or kick a soccer ball, he got in his car and drove for the ferry.

Jean felt sorry for him, but not for any longer than it usually took her to sneeze.

"I don't see why Patsy doesn't move in here for a while," Eve suggested. "She can go back to the apartment when Terry's out of camp, then come back here until she gets her strength back."

"Suits me," Sally agreed.

"I could move into the basement," Mark offered. Sally stared, and Mark grinned widely. "Of course," he added, "I'd expect to be rewarded. Like maybe I get to hold the baby whenever I want to, or something."

"A crack on the head or something, you mean." Eve poked him in the ribs. "You can't just carry that baby around all the time, you'll make her bones ache. She needs to be put down once in a while."

"Oh, really? For a while there I thought they'd smeared her with Krazy Glue and stuck her to you."

"Well, after all, I'm an old woman and I probably don't have long to live, so if I don't get to see her *now*, I won't get to see her later!" Eve laughed with the rest of them.

Patsy came with Paige but Mark didn't move into the basement, he just replaced Tommy in the sleeping bag in the living room. He didn't even complain the floor was hard or the rug smelled of dust. Jean looked at him, stretched out, watching TV and eating popcorn, and wondered when it was he had grown up and become a young man. It wasn't fair, he hadn't even finished grade twelve, he still had at least two months to go!

But she was busy, too busy to worry much about losing her last chick, there was overhauling to either do or arrange to have done, there was scrubbing and painting and all the getting ready stuff, and because the *Old Woman* was, after all, her boat, and Nguyen only fished it for her, she felt obligated to make sure everything was tickety-boo there, too. She was in the last throes of her upgrading for the year, there was all the excitement of having a baby in the house five days a week, and Russ was starting to make noises about not seeing enough of her.

"If you won't move in here with me, and you won't let me move in there with you, maybe I should sign on as deckhand and at least get to go out on the boat with you!" He was angry, and she knew it. They both knew he couldn't do the deckhanding work, he'd only wind up hurting his back again, but neither of them wanted to come right out and say it. "Damn it, I feel like we're pretending to be teenagers; a drive up to the gravel pit, some quick groping and then humphump and now go home before the folks get angry!"

"I think I'll just take a rain check on this one," Jean said quietly, getting out of bed and reaching for her clothes. "Of all the things I can think of to do with my time, arguing over bullshit isn't high on my list."

So much of the work on the boat was repetitious she had plenty of time to think, more time than she wanted. She wasn't sure what it was had Russ feeling so proddy, and was less sure what was behind her own reaction. Thinking of Russ made her think of Tommy, in the early years, before disillusion and resentment had taken root and begun to grow. He'd said it hadn't all been bad, and he'd been right. For a time, for quite a long time, it had been anything *but* bad.

Einarr had been furious, of course, but Einarr had been the kind could go into a six-day temper tantrum over something the suits in Ottawa had pronounced. Somehow, Einarr having his shirt in a knot wasn't a very big deal. And Tommy Pritchard was *not* some kid from down the street, some kid she'd known since they were both being toilet trained. Tommy Pritchard didn't fit in, he didn't blend in, he didn't even try.

So off they went, over the border to Blaine, and got married. She let Tommy do the talking when they phoned Einarr and told him. Tommy just laughed while Jean leaned against the wall of the booth and waited for the receiver to explode.

And they fit. Everything about them fit. She knew bugger-nothing about sex and Tommy let her think he knew as much as there was to know. In reality, they learned together. No shame, no fear, no thou shalt or shalt not, just two healthy young people who couldn't keep their hands off each other and didn't try. Why should they? It was legal. And they joked about that together, licking and sucking, touching and stroking, hey, the government says I can do this, okay?

Someone once said if you put a dollar in a jar each time you are sexual in the first year of marriage you'll have enough money to buy your weekend beer for the next ten years. If they'd tried they'd have gone broke and bought enough beer to float the navy.

Sometimes, when she was well along in her pregnancy with Patsy, they would walk to the corner store hand in hand, Tommy laughing and teasing her that if they slowed down at the bus stop six people would come at her with tokens in their hand, wanting a ride. He wasn't being mean, he wasn't laughing *at* her, they laughed together and walked home with big ice cream cones. In the last two weeks, when her ankles swelled so badly she couldn't wear shoes comfortably, he dropped all the bus jokes, all the eighteen-wheeler jokes and instead brought basins of cold water with a shot of alcohol and some ice cubes, in a vain attempt to relieve the swelling. He made her comfortable on the sofa, with pillows to raise her feet and legs, and told her not to worry about the doctor cutting her off salt, he was probably getting too much of it too, they'd just cut it out of their diet altogether. And he didn't eat potato chips, salted peanuts or pretzels around her, he pretended he preferred apples instead.

It was different with Russ. Sometimes, after long loving with Tommy, she had felt so full of emotion she knew it leaked out of her eyes and slid down her cheeks. Sometimes what she felt was so close to gratitude she didn't know what else to call it. With Russ it was just easy, and loose-making, and pleasant. There had been years with Tommy when she would bend over backward not to argue or even bicker. With Russ she just swung her legs over the side of the bed and reached for her clothes. It seemed almost as if from the first time she saw him she had expected to spend all the days of her life with Tommy Pritchard, and with Russ all she expected was a few pleasant hours. She wondered if you only felt that lifetime expectation once, and when you lost that you never got it back again. Even now, as pissed off with Tommy as she was, she could close her eyes and picture what he'd look like when he was eighty-five. She could hardly make herself think of Russ past his next birthday.

They held off Paige's one-month-old birthday until Terry could be there. Paige was unimpressed but everyone else had a great time. Russ was over his pique and brought his camera, set up the tripod and got into the spirit of the fun. He took pictures of Paige with Patsy, Paige with Terry, Paige with Eve, Paige with Jean, Paige with Sally, Paige with Mark, then got pictures of Terry and Patsy, Jean and Patsy, Eve and Patsy, Sally and Patsy, and even set them all up so they could get the generational shot, Paige, Patsy, Jean and Eve, all perched on the couch, smiling widely. "Hey," Eve laughed, "this one is supposed to look different! Where's the blue-rinse hair? How come Grandma there is wearing jeans and sneakers instead of a tasteful frock? Why ain't Great-grandma in a wheelchair with a bib tied around her neck to catch the drool? And what's Mom doing laughing as if she's just heard a filthy joke? She's supposed to look shy, and overwhelmed and helpless, for God's sake."

"Oh *you*," Patsy laughed, "are so *funny!*" and Russ got a shot of Patsy and Eve, facing each other, foreheads touching, laughing freely while Jean flopped against the back of the sofa, giggling.

There's no good reason in the world for the phone to ring at three in the morning, and Jean was out of bed in a shot, and down the hall. "Can you come to the hospital?" Terry asked, his voice thin. "They're admitting Patsy. She's bleedin' awful bad, Jean."

"She's . . . what do you mean she's bleeding?"

"We thought it was her period starting but . . . it's pretty awful and I've got Paige here, but . . ." He swallowed noisily. "I need some help here."

"On my way, son," she said. She raced back to the bedroom to haul on jeans, socks, sneakers and a shirt, then headed for the front door.

Eve was already in the car, adjusting her wig. "I'm goin'," she said flatly. "Dressing gown or no dressing gown, slippers or no slippers, I'm goin'."

Patsy was ready for the operating room when Jean and Eve got there. Terry stood holding Paige and trying not to look as if he was ready to start screaming.

"Momma," Patsy said clearly, "you didn't brush your hair."

"No," Jean agreed, "I think I was in a bit of a rush. You okay, baby?"

"I'm scared, Momma." Her voice was soft, her words slurred. "I felt like I had to pee and then when I got out of bed it all just . . . gushed, and . . ." She was silent for several seconds. "Someone will have to clean up the rug by the bed."

They took her to the operating room. Jean held Paige, Terry went outside to smoke a cigarette and Eve sat with her hands clenched tight together, looking twice her real age, shivering, but not with the cold. Terry came back with three styrofoam cups of coffee, his pocket stuffed with little plastic creamers and paper-wrapped sugar. He sat holding the cup between his knees, his forearms on his thighs, staring at nothing at all. "Nobody ever told me about this kind of thing," he said accusingly. "I thought this shit went out with the Dark Ages."

"It happens sometimes," Jean admitted. "Not often, but it happens."

"Well, if anybody had'a told me," he wiped at his eyes, "I'd'a sure done things different, I'll tell you!"

Sally and Mark arrived with a thermos of coffee and Jean's travel bag. She smiled thanks, handed Paige to Mark, and took her little plastic zipper bag to the women's washroom. She got her hair under control, but not her hands, checked to make sure she had the right buttons in the proper buttonholes, and went back to sit on the bench and try to feel calm and confident. But the voice inside her kept warning to pray for the best and prepare for the worst.

But you never are.

She half expected Eve to just open her mouth and start screaming, but it was Terry who came apart at the seams. He gasped as if all the breath had been knocked out of him, then moaned "No," and started to sob. Jean wanted to go to him but she couldn't move. She sat shaking her head, hearing the roaring in her ears, feeling the ice move from the centre core of her to the very tips of her fingers. Mark snuggled Paige close against him, tears flowing from his eyes, down his face, dripping off his chin onto the baby's blanket. It was Sally who got up, moved to Terry and held his head against her belly. Eve just sat, her face sagging, her hands suddenly still. The doctor spoke but nobody heard a word he said.

"I'm going home," Jean said clearly. "I want to go home, now."

"I'm goin' with you," Terry sobbed, "I don't want to go back to the apartment because there's all that blood!."

Sally turned and disappeared down the hallway, running. Jean hoped she wasn't going to be sick to her stomach. She wanted to go with her and make sure she was all right but her legs wouldn't work. Then Sally came back and reached to take Jean's hand. "Come on, Momma," she said firmly, "you can't drive. Give me your keys and I'll take you home."

They drove home in Einarr's old car, Sally's car, now. Jean knew Sally had taken her keys to keep her off the road, but she didn't mind leaving her car on the hospital parking lot, she knew she was a menace behind the wheel, and sat watching the road come toward them. Behind them Mark drove Terry's pickup. The headlights of the truck shone through the back window of the old car, and when Jean turned, she could clearly see Eve and Terry sitting in the back seat, looking like people with no idea why they were still bothering to breathe. Paige squirmed, and Jean shifted her to her other arm. The baby settled again, her fist against the side of her face. "I guess we have to find out about formula," Jean said stupidly. "I hope she doesn't kick up a stink about it."

"Oh Christ," Terry groaned. "Oh Jesus Christ, I never even thought about that . . ."

And still Eve said nothing.

The lights were on in the house and when they went inside, Mrs. Nguyen had tea ready for them. She moved forward, took Paige from Jean and nodded sympathetically, saying nothing. Jean was grateful for the silence. She drank two cups of tea, then went to bed and fell into a sleep so deep that when she wakened she knew it hadn't been sleep at all, but escape. She got up, went to the bathroom, had a shower, brushed her teeth, then went back to bed and again fell asleep. When she wakened the next time it was afternoon and her head felt as if it had been hammered with rocks all night. She went downstairs and Mrs. Nguyen wordlessly put a plate of food in front of her.

"No thanks," Jean managed.

"Eat."

"I don't think I can."

"Eat."

She was afraid the food would choke her, or that she'd get it down and then heave it all back up again. But she ate. She didn't choke, the food didn't come back up, and the headache went away before she had finished her scrambled eggs. "Thank you."

"I am sorry for your trouble," Mrs. Nguyen said quietly. "And you are not to worry, we take care of everything. I phoned Joe, he's coming home to help Mark. He very sad for this. He cry very hard on phone."

"I can't cry," Jean confessed. "I know it's true but even so, I don't believe it."

"Maybe you take Brucie for a walk," Mrs. Nguyen suggested gently. "Maybe you go down to your boat and just look at pretty things, think gentle thoughts."

It didn't help. It gave her something to do, but it didn't help. When Tommy arrived he moved toward her as if to hold her and comfort her but she put her hands up and he stopped. She didn't care if his feelings were hurt. She didn't want to be touched.

Alpha and Bert arrived and checked into the hotel. Jean supposed someone should go down and start washing the floors in Patsy's apartment, but she knew it wasn't going to be her. If she had to see what Terry described compulsively, repeatedly, she would go around the bend and never find her way back again. She was so determined not to be the one who had to clean it up that she put the whole thing out of her thoughts. She had all she could deal with already, she didn't need that.

It was so much like Einarr's funeral, and nothing like it at all. Nobody managed an encouraging smile. Everyone was in shock. Tommy dragged around looking as if a hole had been driven through his belly, and Terry ignored him totally. There was nothing anyone could think of to say to Eve that wouldn't sound stupid. The baby howled with bellyache and flailed her fists each time she felt the rubber nipple or tasted the prescribed formula. "Sweetheart," Jean told her, "I know, and I sympathize, and I'd give everything I own to have it the way it was, but there's nothing I can do and you aren't making any of this any easier on yourself."

Eve finally spoke. "Take her up to my room. I can look after her once she's up there, I just can't carry her, is all. I'm wobbly and the steps are too steep."

"You sure?"

"I'm sure. I can't stay down here anyway, every time someone says something to me about God's will I've got all I can do not to plough 'em in the jaw."

Jean went down to the *Lazy Daze* and sat on the hatch cover, trying to make some sense of something, anything would do. None of it made sense.

"Hey." Sally came on deck and moved to sit next to Jean. She brought out cigarettes, lit two and passed one over. Jean took it automatically. "You gonna make it?" Sally asked, her eyes red and swollen, her voice coming husky from a throat sobbed raw.

"Yeah. And right now I feel like that's the bad news."

"You cry yet?"

"No. And it doesn't matter what I do, I might get rid of this goddamn headache for a little while, but it comes back again. I feel as if my skull is going to burst."

"That's what Alpha said," Sally agreed. "She arranged with someone to, like, you know, clean the apartment."

"God, what a rotten job."

"Yeah. I guess I shoulda gone down, but...I couldn't," Sally cleared her throat. "I would think about it and it was like a big door just slammed shut."

"Who did it?"

"I don't know," Sally admitted. "Alpha said not to worry about it, so I didn't."

"How's Mark?"

"He's probably drunk. Terry's probably drunk. Russ took them both off with him and said he was gonna get them pie-eyed. Probably for the best, they'll maybe pass out or something." She flicked her ash onto her jeans, rubbed it into the fabric. "Might be something for you to think about," she hinted.

"No thanks."

"You just gonna sit here and catch pneumonia?"

"I love you, Sally," Jean said firmly. "And maybe I'm going to drive you nuts saying that from now on. And I'm going to tell Mark, too. Because I don't know if you'll ever understand how much it means to me that I got to say it to Patsy before she died. And I'm sorry I didn't think to wake you up so you could get there in time to speak to her before they took her to the operating room. I didn't think she would die," she said sadly. "I didn't think it would be that. . .final."

"It's okay," Sally sniffed. "I know you were in a tearing hurry. And I coulda been there sooner but I didn't think it was going to be. . .I mean, I was kind of ticked off about. . .well, I might not even have *gone* but Mark kept yelling at me to hurry the hell up. . ." She wiped her eyes. "I thought it was like the time she fell down the stairs and kept insisting her arm was broken and we all wound up sitting in the Emergency for about a hundred years so they could wrap an elastic bandage around her wrist and send us all home feeling like fools for bothering them!" She sniffed several times, brought tissues from her pocket and wiped her nose. "She was always so. . .well, you know. So fuckin' *Patsy* about things!"

"Italics," Jean agreed. "She always talked in italics."

They walked up the hill, their arms around each other's waists, and Brucie came waddling down the alley to meet them, her belly full of everyone's leftovers and scraps. They went in the back gate and up the walk to the steps.

"I don't care what you do with your life," Jean said clearly, "as long as you live it happy." She felt compelled to make a joke, even a small one, even a bad one, anything was better than nothing. "So if you and that girlfriend of yours decide to run off to Tijuana, you let me know, okay. I want to give you a send-off, same as if you were getting legally married."

"Oh, we're not going around together any more, I'm playing the field again, but thanks all the same." Sally hugged her tightly. "I'll keep it in mind."

Eve was wearing her war paint and her best wig, and sat at the table with a glass of something very dark amber. Mark was burping Paige, who seemed settled for the first time in days.

"And don't you bother givin' me shit for it, either," Eve warned. "I done it to you when you were little and it didn't hurt you none, and if she starts raising hell again, I'll do the same thing."

"She put brandy on a spoon." Mark seemed decidedly blurred at the edges but far from being ready to pass out. He didn't even seem particularly drunk, and there was no danger of him dropping Paige on her head. "Just tipped the kid's head back, put her finger on her chin to get her to open her mouth, and dumped 'er in. Worked, too," he grinned.

Jean looked over at Eve who sat as defiant as a cat, waiting to catch a load of shit. "Well," she smiled, "if ever I need an excuse for being the way I am, I've got one now. It's not my fault, my own mother fed me booze when I was a baby."

"You were the world's worst baby," Eve admitted. "You screeched day and night for months."

"And you, of course," Jean laughed softly, "were the world's best mother."

"Better than you deserved," Eve grumped. "Kid like you deserves to be born an orphan. Well," she shrugged, "maybe not that bad. But close." She looked up, her face haggard, her eyes still on the verge of tears. "You gonna be okay?"

"I'll be fine, Momma," Jean assured her. "I'll make 'er."

"Jesus aitch." Alpha poured more rye into her glass, swirled it and stared at nothing at all. "Jesus aitch, but if it's not one thing, it's another," and she reached up and wiped at her eyes, her long manicured nails glistening with cosmetician-applied red lacquer. "You didn't have this one comin' to you, Jeannie, damn if you did. None of us did. We paid our dues, we even paid the goddamn GST on our dues, we didn't need to pay this."

It wasn't until she was in bed, floating in that soft dark half-state more comfortable and enjoyable than either sleeping or waking that Jean realized she had called Eve "Momma." The realization jerked her wide awake. If ever anybody had never been "Momma," it was Eve, if ever anybody should choke on the word, it was Jean herself.

But she hadn't choked. Weirdest of all, nobody else seemed to notice. Maybe they'd all had more than they could handle, their brains had turned to butterscotch pudding and drizzled out their ears onto their shoulders.

Work was the only way to get through the days following Patsy's funeral. When she wasn't working until her hair was plastered to her head with sweat, and her body ached, Jean felt so hollow and hurting she wanted to roll on the ground and chew holes in the rocks. If she could work, she could make it from the time her eyes opened until they closed; if she didn't have work, she couldn't sleep, except those times when she couldn't seem to wake up and just kept going back to bed, curling in a ball and going somewhere else where she didn't have to deal with anything.

When Paige wasn't in the care of her great-grandmother, she was next door at Nguyens, being fussed over in a different language, one she seemed to understand every bit as well as English. Eve wanted to look after Paige full time but even she knew the truth of it was she had seen her best days years before and the more Paige thrived, the less Eve could handle it. Patsy's death had hit Eve harder than it hit anyone else. And nothing anybody said or did could pull her back from the place she had been thrust. She sat for hours staring at her cup of tea, not drinking it, not stirring it, just staring, and so often nobody even bothered mentioning it any more, the tears slid down her face and off her chin. Her eyes were red-rimmed most of the time and her hands shook like those of a feeble old woman. In fact, they had to admit, Eve had become a feeble old woman. She didn't talk about Patsy, she didn't talk about being brokenhearted, she just was. And everyone around her felt totally helpless.

Jean worked. Mark worked right alongside her. Sally worked such long hours her face was seldom seen at home. And Terry Dugan went back into camp and worked his ass off, losing weight and looking like someone who has been slammed between the eyes with something very large and very heavy. "I know I'm no help to anyone," he apologized, "I just can't stand bein' anywhere we were together. Can't stand the apartment, can't stand drivin' up to your place and knowin' she isn't there. I can't even stand to look at my kid!"

"That's okay," Jean said, knowing it wasn't okay at all. "I understand," and both of them knew she didn't begin to understand anything about it. Any more than she understood why Eve did want to be where Patsy had once been, and spent hours sitting looking through the wedding album, turning the knife in her own heart.

"I got no idea what to do," Alpha confessed, swirling her ice cubes in her glass and blinking back tears. "He don't talk to me about it. Comes home on his days off and sleeps his life away. Gets up, eats, goes back to bed again. When his days off are finished he goes back to camp."

"It'll work itself out," Jean assured her, but neither of them believed it.

Sometimes at night she came wide awake knowing Something was waiting for a chance to sit on her chest and stop her breathing. Part of her knew there was nothing in the room, but a bigger part of her knew someone had jimmied the door, come into the house, made it up the stairs and was standing at the foot of her bed, waiting. The slightest sign she was awake would rouse that unseen and unknown to fury. She had to pretend she was asleep, make herself breathe regularly and evenly, fool whatever it was into feeling safe enough to just piddle-paddle off, leaving them alive. Sometimes she wakened hearing the sound of an infant wailing with agony, and yet she knew, the way she knew how to cut her own toenails, that Paige was safe, Paige was asleep, and whoever had been wailing wasn't real. She knew, and yet the horror of it, the helplessness of it turned her guts to ice and her belly to a cramping pain that not all the cream or Tums in the world could appease. She swung wildly from terror to horror and back again, and just when she was convinced she would never sleep again, she realized she already had, and it wasn't the middle of the night at all, it was morning, and time to get up and at 'em.

She made good money that summer. She no longer gave a rat's furry back end if a storm was brewing or not, she worked anyway. Mark was there and you'd have thought he'd been born on a fish boat, grew up on a fish boat and been fishing all his life. "Must take after his grandpa," the old-timers said. Publicly Jean agreed with them; privately she figured Mark was in just about the same shape she was, it was work like a bugger or get taken off to a room with rubber-lined walls. More than once she heard him sniffling and sobbing softly as he worked himself to the point where he could lie down and go to sleep. Sometimes she would just walk over to him, put her arms around him, and rest against him, holding him, giving and taking some small measure of comfort. On their closure days he lugged Paige everywhere, changing diapers, giving baths, even doing the washing and hanging her diapers and undershirts on the line.

"It's the least I can do," he said, "it's not her fault."

"Nobody's talking fault," Jean answered gently. "There's no fault in any of it. There's nothing anyone could have done any differently. The goddamn world is too full of words like fault and blame, anyway. Things just are, that's all. And a lot of the things that are, stink!"

By the time salmon season closed Jean was tanned as dark as any Salish, except in the squint lines around her eyes, and they were startlingly white. She had lost twenty-six pounds and was as solidly muscled as Sally. Out on the *Lazy Daze* she spent most of her time in a pair of cutoffs and a tank top, unless the weather was crummy and then it was jeans, shirt and drybacks.

"You not worried about the hole in the ozone layer, skin cancer, and all that new stuff?" Mark suggested.

"Fuck," she snorted contemptuously, "it wasn't *my* doing! They've just got us all bent out of shape worrying about getting cancer from sunshine because they don't want us to know we're really getting it from all the garbage, shit, crap and corruption that's wound up in the water we drink and take baths in! More crap in our food than they can identify, not an underground aquafer that isn't contaminated with some goddamn thing or other, and they want me to worry about sunshine and cigarettes? Fuck 'em all." She waved her arm in a half circle that encompassed most of the coast. "Look at it! Just *look* at it. The garden of Eden couldn't have been more beautiful. And they fucked her to death within my lifetime!"

Russ Hanson knew about losing big hunks of your life and while he understood what a kick in the teeth Jean had taken, he wasn't about to stand around and let another large chunk of his own life drift off and leave him behind.

"Snap out of it, Jeannie," he said. "You've got to start getting your life together."

"Just back off a bit, okay?" She reached for her shirt and pulled it over her shoulders.

"I've hardly seen you all summer."

"Well, Jesus, Russ, I'll go have a talk to the salmon and see if they could arrange their big run to suit you a bit better. Maybe they could just come for eight hours every day five days a week and hold off the rest of the time."

"You know what I mean! Even when you're here you're not *here*!"

"Then you won't fuckin' miss me when I go home!" and she swung her legs from the bed, stepped into her cotton underpants and reached for her jeans.

"Where in hell you *going*?"

"Home," she answered coldly. "You know, where the heart is and all that good stuff."

It got worse. It got so she didn't even want to be bothered going to his place because it always unwound the same way. Everything would be fine. For a while. And then it would start to unravel and they would both know it, but both be helpless to stop it or do anything that didn't just make it worse. She had images of balls of energy, or electricity, or magnetism, or...something. And she had her own little ball of it, with sparks zinging out like firebees from a hunk of cedar driftwood in a fire. Russ had his, just like hers, with other sparks zinging. Somehow her sparks and his sparks merged, the static focussed on other static and soon there was a third ball drifting around, growing, strengthening, and two people trying to ignore it, be careful, just don't notice the big white tiger in the corner and you'll be fine. But the big white tiger wouldn't be ignored, and soon they were into it again. And she knew if they could fight that third energy, that thing, that white tiger in the corner, they'd be fine. She knew it and was unable to even begin to think how to do what needed to be done, because the more she tried to talk about it the deeper the wedge was driven between them, and the more often the white tiger feasted.

She wished he was a jerk. She wished he was a drip. She wished he would go out and get drunk, show up outside her house shouting and raving. Then she'd have an excuse. He did none of those things. He was a nice guy, and all he wanted was what he'd been promised he would have, which would have been okay, but he wanted it from her.

"*Talk* to me," he pleaded.

"I'm talking," she answered.

"No. You're answering, you're making little jokes, you're making conversation, but you are not *talking*." He leaned across his kitchen table, his hands clasped together earnestly. "One thing I've learned is that we have to really *talk* to each other, about everything."

"You may have learned that, Russ, you may even have learned *how*, but you didn't learn it with me. And you haven't learned how to *listen*."

"I'm listening!"

"If I say things you want to hear, and say them in the way you're used to hearing them, you'll listen. But Jesus, you have to learn to listen to the silences, too, okay? Maybe I don't *want* to do group grope, did you ever think of that? Maybe I don't *want* to spew a lifetime of stuff onto the oilcloth covering this table then pick at it, pick at it, pick at it until it's all neatly arranged in chronological order and maybe even in alphabetical order for all I know! You talk to me about pain pools and how we need to do some damn thing or other until we can dive into what used to be pain and swim around in it. I don't want to swim in old shit, okay? I don't have to relive stuff to know I don't want it or need it."

"I don't know what you mean," he said, and she grinned, but not nicely.

"See? Hear the tone in your voice? Naughty naughty Jeannie, back to Go, do not collect any money at all, and consider yourself lucky you didn't get sent to Jail. . ."

"Okay." He nodded, unclasped his hands, nodded again, even got up from the table, took their coffee cups to the counter, poured out the cooled coffee and refilled the cups. When he came back to the table, he was obviously determined to try again.

"Tell me your own way, then," and he sat down, forearms resting on the oilcloth.

"That's the big problem. I don't *have* a way, and I don't particularly feel like getting into a big *telling* session. Listen, I'm tired, okay? I feel like a gerbil who lived in a little cage all her life and suddenly some well-meaning kid bought me and took me home and put me in this enormous fucking cage with a gigantic treadmill in the middle. And I was freaked out by the space around me. So I headed for a thing that looked like something more along the lines of what I was used to. It just happened to be the fuckin' treadmill, okay? And I got on and it moved and I had to shuffle to keep my balance and that made it move more and now I'm going like a mad bastard and getting nowhere. Okay?"

"You just slow down," he smiled. "That's all you do, Babe, you just slow down, and it'll slow down with you, and when you've slowed down enough it'll stop and you can jump off."

"No."

"Sure, try it."

"There's other gerbils on the treadmill. There's Eve-gerbil, and

Sally-gerbil and Mark-gerbil, and two-boats-gerbil and there's *Russ* gerbil. And *Russ* gerbil is pushing."

"You stop that," he glared. "I am *not* pushing!"

"Try to hear what I *mean*, not just what I say! And try to talk for no reason except to clear up the mess. You're talking so you'll win, you're talking so you'll get what you want, you're talking so I'll see it your way, and that's no different than arguing, it's still a power trip, you're just using nicer words is all." He opened his mouth to protest and she held up her hand. He closed his mouth and nodded, and she continued, talking rapidly, trying to get it said before the rules got changed or he stopped listening. "Russ, I'm not your ex-wife, okay? You're trying so hard to make sure that the mistakes you made last time don't happen again that you're trying to *organize*, trying to make us into who you were with her! I'm not your ex-wife, and you can't make up for stuff with me that happened with her."

"I don't know what you mean."

"I know you don't, that's part of what's got the treadmill spinning. Listen, this is not a *relationship* for me. I've told you and you don't want to hear, but I'm going to tell you again; I don't *want* bacon-and-eggs-together-every-morning-for-the-rest-of-our-lives. I don't *want* a white picket fence and me in the kitchen baking bread while you go out and wrest a living for us or poke spears into dragons or whatever in hell it is you do when you go. I thought I wanted that. Once. And what I came away from that one with is the deep and sincere conviction that stuff *doesn't work*. And if it does, it still doesn't work for *me*."

"You're running away from reality."

"No. I'm not. You are." She was tired of sitting on this goddamn chair at this goddamn table trying to make herself understood. She was tired of a whole bunch of stuff and none of it was Russ's fault. "We get along good," she said soothingly, "or at least we used to. And we're good in bed. And that's about all I've got room for." He opened his mouth to speak and she slammed her palm flat on the tabletop. "Russ, *listen*! I do not *want* some kind of big heavy interdependent relationship, I do not *want* a merging of two souls, I do not *want* whatever in hell you meant when you talked about a primary commitment. I *have* primary commitment. Jesus, do I ever! I have my kids. However old they are, they are my primary commitment."

"For God's sake your kids are grown up and as good as on their own!" he argued.

"They are still my kids, okay? And I've just had my nose rubbed in the fact that just because they've hit some magical birthday it doesn't mean you're finished with them! And anyway, how much control am I supposed to have over what I *feel*? If I *feel* they are my primary commitment who's to say they aren't, or shouldn't be, or have stopped being, or never were?"

"Well, I have kids, too, and I'm not living their lives for them. Or letting them live *my* life!"

"That's you. I'm talking me. And after them I have a house nobody but me can keep going, with pipes draining and roof not leaking and all that good stuff."

"You aren't the only person can keep the pipes draining and the roof not leaking. There are three other people in that house and one of them has a steady pension, one of them is making decent wages, and one of them . . ."

"And after that I have two boats to keep together and after that . . . what it all adds up to is that my primary commitment is to my own life. *My own life*. And then there's you, talking capital-R Relationship and primary commitment . . . Whatever you call it, to me, what it boils down to is some kind of *marriage* and I do not *want* that!"

"Well, I *do*!" he yelled.

"There," she nodded, "that's the 'it' we've been trying to talk about. That's the 'thing' we've been supposed to be dealing with! That is what I mean when I say you're trying to make *this* into what you had before and fucked up on. I am *not* your ex-wife. SHE is the one you should be telling this stuff to, *she* is the one you should be sitting at this table with, *she* is the one who might want and need to hear you say you want to be able to discuss anything at all, share everything . . . but not me."

"You won't even try," he said bitterly.

"No." She stood up and moved toward her jacket. "Why should I try for something I do not want? With my fuckin' luck I'd get it and then be stuck with it for the next forty years."

"Oh, thanks a bunch, Jean! Stuck with it? *Stuck* with it?"

"If you don't want it in the first place, and then you get it, even if it's a zillion dollars, if you didn't want it, you're stuck," and she went out the door and closed it gently behind her, praying he wouldn't decide to do something noisy like follow her down the stairs and along the walk to the front gate where her car was parked. But Russ didn't go after her and the neighbours didn't get a real live on-the-sidewalk soap opera. Jean just got in her car and drove home.

It wasn't the last time they tried to clear the air, but it was the last time Jean felt any hope at all that the talking would do any good. Russ really wanted to say something which would turn on a light bulb and make her say "My God, you're right!" She couldn't shake the conviction if he wanted to communicate he would talk and then at least allow things to continue the way they were. But he wanted something he saw as an advance and she saw as a threat. He didn't want to understand how she felt or why she felt that way, he just wanted her to stop clinging to her autonomy and see things his way.

"Can we stop this?" She was almost weeping. "Can we just put all of this in a box, then put the lid on the box and store the whole thing in the attic for six months? If things between us were so good you want *more*, then why can't we go back to when things were that good? And just wait on the 'more' until we've both calmed down a bit. Right now I don't want *more*. But damn, I do miss what we used to have."

"I miss it, too," he agreed. "But it wasn't enough."

"So rather than have something that isn't quite enough you'll shove and push and prod and pry and yammer until we wind up with something that is absolutely nothing at all?"

They stared at each other across the widening expanse of table, both of them realizing she had actually said something other than what her words translated into, either individually or collectively.

J ean knew there was absolutely no reason to take any more
business courses, computer courses or office procedure courses
to qualify herself as a prime candidate for pleasant gainful
employment. She was never going to be a prime candidate for
anything worth getting out of bed to go somewhere to do. Why would
anyone want to hire her when for the same money they could get
someone twenty-five years younger, someone who really Wanted to
do that kind of work, not someone who had decided to settle for it
because she could no longer do work which paid and held out the
promise of something remotely resembling a career, with promo-
tion and upward mobility? Why would anyone hire someone long
in the tooth and no longer believing the bee ess? Why would
someone go out of their way to hire someone who had already seen
what the Philistines and their lawyers could do to a union and the
protection it tried to ensure? Employers want to hire people who
still believe we are all working together, still believe we are all on
the same team, still believe we are sharing in the future. They want
someone who can be scammed by the twenty-second manager
courses and the manipulative little encouragement talks. They
don't want someone who knows full well the supermarket where
she had worked for years had closed simply because that way the
union workers could be ignored, the store could reopen under a
new name, with nonunion employees who got paid less and worked
fewer hours in a week, thus saving the company the cost of those
benefits the previous workers had managed to negotiate. Employers want to hire someone who does not know the Compensation

Board is nothing but a paperwork barrier erected to protect the employers and the government from being sued by people whose years of work have ruined them physically.

But she took the courses anyway, and did well at them. She even sat down and paid close attention while the life skills counsellor addressed the class and laid out for them their employment opportunities. Jean could, for example, take an accounting course and then go to the city for a month to take a special course which would teach her everything she had never wanted to know about insurance. Then if she passed that course she could take another one, only two weeks long, and if she passed that, she could write the qualifying test. And if she passed THAT she could apply for a job with an insurance company and if she got it she could make twelve hundred dollars a month. She made that on winter unemployment insurance. And during fishing season she could make that in one day. If it was a good day. If there was no storm. If the fish came. If fisheries didn't close them down. If the pollution from the pulp mill didn't extend the size of the contamination zone. If God didn't shit on her face.

Six species of previously bountiful bottom fish had already become virtually extinct because of deteriorating conditions on the West Coast and the other fifteen species, each of which had once swarmed thick on the seabed, were declining at a rate which scared the fishers and caused them to glare bitterly at the pulp mill, but that wasn't God shit, the blame belonged elsewhere for that.

Or she could take an accounting course and then go to the city for a few more number-crunching courses, come back, and spend who knows how long looking for office space to rent. Once she had that she could sink five or six thou into office furniture and another five or six thou into computers and equipment. Then she could hang a tasteful little sign in the window and sit buffing her nails until some people came in to get her to balance their books. Maybe the accountants from all the other nearly dead-in-the water offices could come over and they could all sit together smiling bravely and sipping delicate little cups of strong coffee with rum in it to ease the nagging cramps in their stomachs as the days moved closer to the next time the rent was due on their office spaces.

Or maybe they could go together on office space and just take turns going in to sit waiting for the one or two customers a week who came in with a hundred dollars' worth of work.

"A parking lot," she told Sally. "That's what we need. If we could just figure out some way to tow some of this empty space down to the city we could get rich renting it out as parking space."

"Good idea," Sally smiled and winked. "I was thinking maybe we should write to the Russian government about it; after all, the pulp mill companies are approaching Russia with these great and glorious plans to put pulp mills all over the place now that the iron curtain is down; maybe we can go into a profit-sharing deal with the Kremlin. Use your parking space idea. Rent out the steppes. All that flatland that used to be the Ukrainian grain growing region until Chernobyl made the soil glow in the dark could be used to ease the rush hour gridlock. And if we had the snow removal contract, too...fuck, it would be easy!"

"The iron curtain didn't come down," Mark said sombrely. "Watch the TV and see for yourself; it corroded away in the pollution and just crumbled. Gonna cost the next forty years of our lives just to clean up the goddamn mess those guys made."

"Those guys?" Sally pretended to frown. "Who *are* 'those guys' anyway? Are they the same guys that have dumped so much shit in the ocean here that the entire Gulf is teetering on the brink of biological disaster?"

"Same guys," Mark agreed. "Exactly the same guys."

"I think," Jean said softly, "'those guys' are...us."

"We could open a restaurant," Eve offered. She was sitting with Paige on her lap. "There's an empty space right next to the vet's office; we could bust a hole through the wall and every time they gave the old blue needle to a dog or a cat..."

"Oh, *Gran!*" Sally moaned, "you just get worse every day!" and Eve grinned happily.

But it was too close to the truth to be a joke. Eve did get worse every day. Eve was not well. The same kind of exhaustion that was dogging Jean had caught up to Eve. She spent much of her time with the baby, and yet she didn't really do any of the work that came with the baby. She was Paige's amusement, she was Paige's cuddles, she was Paige's entertainment, and thank God she was there, because all the rest of the stuff that came with Paige was wearing Jean down rapidly. Diapers to wash, hang on the line, bring in, fold, put away, then put on the kid's backside. Little undershirts, little nightgowns, little pyjamas, little romper suits, little bibs, little bits of your life chipped away minute by minute. Pick it up, change it, put it down, feed it, wipe its face clean, pick it up and change it again.

Terry Dugan came every weekend, and sat holding his daughter awkwardly, trying hard not to burst into tears. "I know it's not her fault," he confessed, "it's just . . ."

"Things will be better when she's a bit older," Eve soothed. "You'll see, once she starts to walk and talk and is . . . more interesting. Right now she's sweet and she's loving and . . . she's a lump!"

"Yeah," he nodded, even managed a smile. "Yeah, there's sure not much to *do* with her."

"Why don't you go down to the pub as soon as she's asleep," Jean suggested. "It can't be much of a weekend off for you just sitting around here waiting for a baby to wake up so she can sit and drool on you for an hour or two before she goes back to sleep again."

Alpha visited a few times, and sat watching Paige trying to learn how to get somewhere in her jolly jumper. "I don't envy you," she said bluntly. "I damn near went outta my tree when *mine* was small, and I was a lot younger and more energetic than you are. Soon's he was old enough to shove outside the door, I done 'er! And I made damn good and sure I never had another one, either."

"I'll admit to you although I might not admit it to anyone else," Jean laughed softly, "I think she's a great kid, and she's welcome here, but by Jesus if there was an alternative I'd be upstairs packing her stuff."

"No!" Mark flared. "She lives here!"

"She might live here, Mark," Sally said sternly, "but that doesn't mean if there was an alternative I wouldn't be upstairs helping with the packing."

"For Christ's sake, she's *family*!" Mark shouted, startling Paige and making her face pucker into a pout.

"Son," Alpha sighed, "she's my family, too, but I want you to know that while I'm ready to give money, money and more money, and I'm even ready to give encouragement and maybe a birthday party now and again, I am *not* about to dive into twenty more years of living someone else's life insteada my own."

"You're kidding!" He stared at her as if she were an exotic creature newly escaped from a zoo.

"I'm not kidding. And neither is your mother. Nor your sister."

"If I wanted a kid," Sally said in a very thin, strained voice, "I could have one of my own, okay? I haven't done that. And I probably won't do it. And if I do, it likely won't be for a long long time. There's other stuff I want to do first."

"And I've done 'er. I don't regret having done it but I had hoped it was over and done." Jean tried to turn it into a joke and knew she failed totally.

"Well, I want her." Mark was angry, and he didn't care that his anger showed.

"I would bet," Sally almost wept, "that *Dad* wanted us, too. When we were little and teeny and cuddly and didn't know how to say the word No. And I bet he thought you were just about the best thing since sliced bread; his son, his heir, his immortality and all that good shit! But where *were* you after that part of it wore out, fella? The same place the rest of us were, nowhere. And where was he? Gone. Gee Oh Ehn Ee."

"Patsy was our *sister*, Sally!"

"Right. But she wasn't *me*. And I'm not *her*. And *she* chose to have a baby, I didn't!"

"She didn't choose to *die*, God damn it!"

"And I didn't choose to throw my life down the tube, either! Paige is a nice little kid; fuck, Mark, they *all* are! That's how mother nature guarantees they'll survive, she makes them round, cute, fat and cuddly! But they don't stay that way. Hell," she moved quickly, put her arms around him and hugged tight, "look at you!"

"It's not Paige's fault," he sobbed. "It's not her fault at all. And everybody ought to be entitled to be loved and wanted, damn it."

"Ought to be," Sally agreed, weeping herself, "but what's ought, anyway, if not another way to say nothing?"

"Listen, you two," Eve tried pouring oil on troubled waters. "Terry will meet someone else, he'll get over his loss, he'll get married again, and then Paige will go to live with him and his new wife, it'll work out fine."

"Don't count on 'er," Alpha warned. "Number one, what happened to Patsy has scared the shit out of that boy. Scared him so bad he got himself a vasectomy for Chrissakes! Number two, this coast is cluttered with guys who never tried it the first time let alone the second time. They might have sad eyes like a spaniel dog, and they might sidle up to every woman as comes into the beer parlour and beg 'er to take 'em home outta the cold for a few days, but as soon as it's time to go back to camp they're gone like any other good intention." She looked over at Eve and winked. "Met a few of 'em myself," she confessed.

"By the dozen," Eve agreed. "By the gross, peck, bushel and Imperial gallon, by God."

"And number three," Alpha continued relentlessly, "why would any woman want to tangle herself up with a guy who comes with a kid attached? Either she's got kids of her own and doesn't need any more of 'em, or she wants kids of her own and isn't going to hook up with some guy as got hisself fixed, *or* she don't want kids at all."

"What a fuck of a lousy deal you got, baby." Mark moved to hunker in front of Paige, who still hadn't made up her mind whether she was going to howl or not. "But don't you worry, my pretty one, Uncle Mark wants you. Uncle Mark loves you. Uncle Mark's gonna *keep* you."

"Uncle Mark has rocks in his head," Sally said pleasantly.

Paige looked at Sally and smiled widely, bounced in her jolly jumper several times, then grabbed a double handful of Mark's hair and pulled.

"This glass is just about empty." Alpha reached for the bottle she had brought with her. "So yours must be getting down, too. Push 'er over for a refill, Eve, because it's a cold dark world and the only way to make your way through 'er is to go half lit."

Russ Hanson didn't just fold his tent and vanish. He hung in and followed the old try, try, try again we have been taught to believe is the foundation for success.

"My God," Eve sighed, "even an engorged wood tick has sense enough to drop off when it's had its fill."

"Maybe he hasn't had his fill," Sally offered.

"Some people not only won't take no for an answer," Mark said quietly, "they don't believe you mean it."

"What's to not believe?" Eve snapped. "What part of 'No' isn't easily understandable?"

"The part where you don't get what you think you want," Mark answered with a smile that only a few months ago would have been called cheeky. But he was too big to be cheeky now, he was tall enough, heavy enough, strong enough and old enough for cheeky to have become charming and for his opinions to be taken seriously. "Even if Mom got herself another boyfriend Russ wouldn't believe what it meant. He'd convince himself it was just some crazy stunt she was pulling and that she'd get over it. He'll be like an old dog looking for a new home until he finds someone else to go out with. Because," he winked at Eve, "*he* is not going to be the one to get dumped, okay? Until *he* does the dumping there isn't going to be any! What you women don't understand," he risked Sally's anger and ignored her oink oink Mark-o, oink oink, "is we learn something you don't seem to catch on to very easily. Winning might not be everything, but coming second sucks. There *has* to be a winner. And it isn't supposed to be the other guy! And the one who does the dumping *wins*...so he'll just dig in his claws and hang on until he can win, and if he can't win, at least make it look like he did. Let him find someone else, then he can make it look as if he dumped her, and when that's in place, you won't see him for the big cloud of dust. All your experience," he teased, "I'm amazed you didn't clue in to that yourself."

"God damn it," Eve laughed, "I'm sure glad I'm over the hill. I gotta tell you, son, life is a lot better on this side of that hill than it was all those years I was strugglin' my way *up* the damn thing! If you've got that baby to sleep then come play a coupla hands of Stuke with me, make yourself useful."

"You owe me ten dollars already," he warned her. "I'll skin you if you aren't careful."

"You think so? You're about to find out that what I've been doing is not losin' at Stuke but suckin' you in to where you think you can beat me. I was skinnin' cats before you even knew they did more than drink milk."

And Russ did hang in, just as Mark said, although his visits became shorter and the time between them stretched longer. Then Jean saw him with someone else, in the pizza parlour. She looked up from her Number Seven Feta Cheese Pizza and there he was, with his hand on someone else's waist, smiling and moving toward a table. She didn't know if what she felt was sorrow, regret or relief. But whatever it was, it didn't interfere with her appetite.

She sat on the back porch feeding pizza crust to Brucie and watching the western sky changing colour over the long low blue-black outline of the island, and she wondered about Russ, and what it was had made her feel so twitchy and threatened.

She had read, and believed, that most of the difficulties in any relationship come about because of control, or the lack of it. She had read, and believed, that those who feel they have little or no control over their lives and the things which affect their lives have the most need to grab onto and hang onto any kind of control they manage to get.

So which of them was a control junkie? Russ? Or herself? What *had* the upset been about, anyway? So he'd nagged for more visible and deeper involvement. Why had that made her angry? Sally had nagged for three years for a pet lizard and Jean hadn't once threatened to disown the kid or take her down to the welfare and drop her off to be a foster kid. She had just laughed each time and said No way, Sally, no exotic mini-dragons on *my* floor. No way, kid, and no Christly snakes, either. Of *course*, darling, just as soon as you've finished school, got a job and have your own place; but not in *my* place. And if you bring it home I will either take it right back again and throw it at them or I'll give it the old flush into the plumbing system. But there had been none of that with Russ. It was something far more threatening than a newt, a salamander, a chameleon, an iguana or even a monitor lizard.

And why? Probably some feminist rhetorician could talk for several days about how Jean's life had been too formed and shaped by domineering males, but if you looked at Einarr and then looked at the average male voter you didn't come away with the impression Einarr had been a rigid or battering dictator. Hell, at least half the year he was hardly ashore! Tommy, well, he *was* a horse of a different garage and anybody who had the idea there was any way they could get him to do something he wasn't eager to do was in for a quick dose of disillusion. But Russ wasn't Tommy. Besides which, from what Jean could see, Cheryl had found the key that made Tommy run, and she knew how to turn it.

Maybe she'd just had enough encroachment when Brucie was dumped in her life. From the ditch to the porch, from the porch to the mud room, from there to the kitchen, bit by bit, inch by inch, tail wagging the whole time, until now you were apt to find the big fool anywhere on the ground floor she had chosen to flop and there was some evidence to suggest she often followed Eve up to her room and did the old snore routine on the oval rug beside Eve's bed. Maybe Jean was afraid Russ would creep into and over her life until they wound up epoxied to each other, referred to by others as Russ'n'Jean. She didn't expect rainbows across the sky or the sound of angels singing, she didn't expect pink clouds and the scent of roses in wintertime, and for all but the last little bit, it had been good.

"Jesus, Brucie, what do you think about it, anyway? I mean there you are and God knows you're ugly and when it rains you get wet and start to stink even worse than usual and here you are, shoving against me in what you probably think is a demonstration of love and I think is a big flea-infested shove toward the edge of the porch. Shift over, damn it, I don't like you *that* well. You've got a big cold wet nose, Brucie, and his nose was small, warm and dry, so it wasn't that. He didn't have bad breath and that's more than can be said about you. Death-breath, that's what you are. Run an ad in the paper. All those found guilty of dealing drugs will be subjected to Brucie's death-breath. That'll clean up the streets. And you know what? I don't know *why* I told 'im to take a hike but I'm not sorry I did. I'm just puzzled about the *why* part, is all. And part of that puzzle is why I'm sitting out here with the cold creeping up from my ankles, chewing over something as stupid as *this*. Go to your kennel, will you? G'wan now, Brucie, go home, I'm going in the house. No, damn it, you are *not* sleeping inside! I mean it, now, off you go or I'll put you on a chain. No! If I could just learn how to get *you* to listen, maybe someone else would learn how, too. That'd be a big change, believe me. I said *kennel*, Brucie! Kennel, not the rug in the kitchen. Bugger off, mutt."

She brushed her teeth, took her vitamin pills, got undressed and pulled on the old tee shirt she used for pyjamas, then went back downstairs to make sure Brucie had a bowl of water and something to chew on during the night. Brucie didn't care much for dog biscuits. Brucie preferred rock-hard stale bread crusts. Probably Eve or Sally would soon start buying sourdough french loaves and leaving them out to get properly solid. "Just shut up, okay. Not a friggin' word."

She was busy, too busy to get tied in knots over any kind of emotional stuff, too busy to write episodes of All My Horrible Kids or As The World Blows Apart. She was even too busy to give two hoots in hell that Tommy was still trying to wangle a job out of her.

"Talk to me about an engorged tick!" she raged, not caring any more, no longer trying to keep from her kids the news there was a strong streak of assholiness in the genetic pool from which they had been fished, and not all the contribution came from the paternal side. Maybe when they had been younger she had smoothed things out, covered things over, calmed things down and made things up, maybe she had even downright lied about the way things really were, but no more. "Does he think I'm going to go around singing 'Auld Lang Syne' and pretending old acquaintances are *not* going to be forgotten? I'd love the chance to forget! His name, his address, his face, his existence, just give me the fuckin' *chance* to forget! I have told him and told him and then just for a change I told him and he still thinks he can weasel me into turning over the keys to the boat. Why stop there, why not the keys to the car? The keys to the house? My God, give the man the keys to the Kingdom of God so he can *go* there and leave me alone!"

"You've done better," Mark told her quietly. "That didn't even hit three-point-two on the downgraded Richter. You're losing it, Mom."

"I never *had* it!"

"Well, that, too, but we tried to keep the news from you. Want me to talk to him?"

"No, I'm not trying to off-load the problem onto your shoulders," she laughed softly, her rage evaporating. "I just thought I'd dump some of my frustration there."

She wasn't taking Tommy out on the damn boat and that was the end of that. But she still had to get down to the damn wharf and shovel the damn snow off the damn deck before the damn boat wound up sinking under the damn chuck! When she went out the back door, Brucie was sitting with big hopeful eyes, wagging what was left of her never-properly-docked tail.

"Forget it," Jean snapped. "You're staying here. You are *not* coming with me. There isn't anything in the world dirtier than a dog on a boat. *No*, Brucie. Sit. Stay. You are *not* welcome!" She crossed the back yard and made sure the gate was closed securely behind her, then cut down the alley, taking the short way, even if it was the slippier way. The last of the snow all coast dwellers try to convince everyone else they never get was slushing around in ugly stained heaps, leaking gallons of water which collected in minor lakes before drizzling downhill to the sea. Where the alley intersected with the roadway there was a particularly mammoth mess but Jean was wearing her knee-high gumboots so made it through with only slightly damp feet, and she wouldn't have got damp at all if it hadn't been for the damn federal government Fisheries truck coming down-hill as if it were high noon in mid-August and spraying slushwater cavalierly. "May your balls fall off!" she yelled, but the back-easter driving the truck either didn't hear or didn't understand or had never had balls so was in no danger of losing any.

The federal Fisheries truck was parked by the time she made her soggy way to the bottom of the hill. To satisfy herself and get some of the vengeance she was starting to feel she dearly needed she wrote in the dirt smeared across the back end OTTAWA IS THE EM-

PLOYER OF ASSHOLES. That didn't seem strong enough so she wrote ASSHOLE in the smeared mud on the driver's door, with an arrow pointing up to the driver's window. With any luck it would be dark before he came twitter-patting back in from wherever it was he'd gone to make the lives of working people miserable. He was probably going out there to take some more samples and close some more fishing grounds. Of course, even if he found one hundred percent arsenic out there it would be a while before the news filtered through the bloat. They'd taken samples last winter, known the results were bad before springtime but somehow didn't get around to telling anyone until the beginning of December, just in time to ruin what was left of the Spirit of Goodwill at Christmas, but at least the market had absorbed all those tons of contaminated fish caught in the time the Feds were busily doing five times the square root of bugger-nothing-at-all.

Then they enlarged the closed area by five times its size. "They'll probably decide to either shut it down tight or give it away with the rest of the country they've handed over because of free trade, the fuckers. Doesn't matter *who* you vote for, you wind up voting for a fuckin' politician!" Brucie gallumphed up foolishly, fat body bent almost double, stub tail wagging so hard her arse end was vibrating, lips pulled back in what looked like a vicious snarl but was really some kind of canine smile.

"I told you to stay home," Jean told her. "I was pretty goddamn specific about it as I remember. One word from me and you do anything you want, just like everyone else in the world. Nobody listens! My whole life, it seems, nobody has believed what I say. Unless I have myself the most time-consuming, energy-wasting, high-volume fit! Then they think I have PMS and it'll go away in a few days. And you, supposed to be my best friend, you agree with them. Listen, Brucie, you're just a reminder to me, a reminder that if it can get worse, it will. There's days, so help me God, if it wasn't for dirty rotten stinking shithouse luck I wouldn't have any luck at all. The day you came into my life was just such a day. Go get yourself run over or something."

She shovelled off the wheelhouse roof, then came back down and started in on the deck. She ought to be getting good at this. It was the fourth time she'd done it. Mark got stuck with the porches, steps, garage roof and front walk, and Sally had taken it upon herself to make sure the once-in-a-blue-moon passage of the road grader didn't bury them under what had been shoved off the road. And anyway, Sally wasn't on seasonal shutdown, she had a full-time job and it was dark when she headed off to work, dark when she got home from work, and how do you shovel snow or anything else in the dark?

Jean finished the deck then decided she was sick and tired of sliding around on the dock as if she'd taken up raising geese. She wasn't Elizabeth Sweetheart Manley and she'd had it with skating in a mad mix of slush and seagull shit.

The Fisheries vessel was heading for the harbour as if it had a tail and someone had lit fire to it. Pity they couldn't move as fast and as aggressively when the yanks stopped, boarded and impounded boats fishing in what were still Canadian waters but might not be for much longer if the ones busy kissing the eagle's ass continued to whimper and tremble and let the great Satan extend its boundaries bit by bloody bit, totally ignoring all the international rules while at the same time blethering and bellyaching about how rah-rah gung-ho they were about preserving freedom. The back-easter probably wanted to check and see if she had a permit to shovel snow on a government wharf. Probably put a tax on it. She'd give them their seven percent Gee Ess Tee, all right, seven percent of the damn snow, right down the back of the old bureaucratic neck. What is fourteen inches long and hangs just in front of an asshole? Mulroney's chin.

Well, Fred Brown had shown them. Fred had been the garbage collector for more years than anyone wanted to remember and then got word from the pencil pushers he was going to have to pay Goods and Services Tax on the five dollars per customer per month he charged to take garbage down to the dump. So he stopped collecting garbage and started selling potatoes, which are exempt from Goods and Services Tax. For five dollars a month Fred would sell you one unwrapped potato. If while he was at the house you wanted him to be a good neighbour and, since he was going there with his own trash, take yours along, too, free gratis and for no reason except this is after all a country of loving people, why Fred would be glad to do it; and I hope you enjoy your potato, neighbour. Sooner or later they'd catch on, of course, but until they did it was at least good for a snicker and there weren't enough of those going the rounds these days.

She heard the roar of the Fisheries engine. She turned her back on the fool. Bad as a pimple-faced sixteen-year-old with a hot car, rev rev rev, pedal to the metal, give 'er till she quivers, if you don't go as fast as you can you're in danger of losing your testicles. Then she heard the incredible sound, like the slamming of the largest and heaviest door in the world. And then the flagpole on the Fisheries vessel snapped and the last thing she saw was the red-and-white nylon maple syrup advertisement coming down, the stylized leaf heading for her face. She had time for just one timeless utterance, *"Fuck around why don't you?"* and then they turned out the lights.

She fought her way up out of grey slush to a pallid light that still managed to hurt her eyes. Her mouth tasted like someone had crawled in there and died. A few days ago. She managed to look around the room and the realization hit her that she wasn't even in her own hospital.

"Where am I?" she asked.

"In the hospital," the faceless one told her.

"I know that. Which hospital?"

They'd air-evacuated her to the city. "I want to go home," she said clearly. They made yes-yes noises and rest-now noises and slid a needle into her upper arm. That was good for another six hours of nothing at all.

When she crawled out of the hole again she asked them for one of those magical shots in the arm. Her entire left leg hurt so badly she couldn't believe a person could feel like that and not go insane.

"You're very lucky," they told her.

"I don't feel very lucky," she replied. "I hurt and I need to pee and if I don't get a cup of coffee I might kill someone."

They told her she didn't really need a pee, it was just the catheter made it feel as if she did. "Take it out," she suggested, "and let me pee."

"Later, dear," she was promised. But they did bring a basin of water, a tiny sliver of soap like the kind they used to hand out in orphanages and jails in old novels, and some mouthwash. "Do I have a toothbrush around here?"

"Later, dear," the faceless one said.

But they did bring her a cup of coffee. It was instant, it was lukewarm and it was in a styrofoam cup but all things considered it was the best thing had happened in a couple of days. She drank it and went to sleep. When she wakened they were putting a food tray in front of her. She looked at it and smiled. "Didn't they tell you?"

she said sweetly, "it's my leg, not my teeth," but she got the liquid diet all the same. And didn't graduate to mushed-up baby food for another two days.

"I want to go home," she said.

"We're making arrangements, Mom," Sally assured her. "In the meantime, here's your toothbrush, hairbrush, toothpaste and something to read. I didn't bother with the slippers for obvious reasons, and I didn't bother with the lace-trimmed nightie because Mark is wearing it," and she winked.

"I want to go home."

"I heard you, Mom."

"Did you? Then why aren't we going home?"

"We will."

The nurse came in and slid in the needle. A few minutes later Sally's face began to go all funny and the distance between them seemed to increase until Sally was staring down at her from the far away end of a long, dimly lit tunnel. And then Sally went away.

Jean wakened knowing she had been moved and someone had done something to her. She managed to lift her head two or three inches off the pillow. Someone had put a metal frame over her bed and from it hung several light chains and a canvas sling. In that sling was her leg; or what they wanted her to believe was still her leg. It was encased in a urine-yellow fibreglass cast out of which came several rubber tubes, each of which ran to a bottle strapped to the side of the bed, in which was blood-streaked nausea-inducing drainage fluid.

"Oh shit," she sighed.

"Hang in there, kiddo." Alpha Dugan's gravel-voice was as soft as she could make it sound.

"How'd you get here?"

"Well, I guess I coulda come the same way you did but I figured I'd pass on the air evac and just drive the pickup down, the way I usually do. Figured if what I'd heard about you and your leg was true, the cost of a ticket on that taxpayer-supported Lear jet was just a bit high."

"I got a ride on the Lear, huh? How'd that happen? There's usually some dipshit cabinet minister takin' a little trip on it."

"Musta timed your trip right."

"Where's Sally? Sally was here."

"Yeah, I sent her back to the hotel to get some sleep. She was startin' to look like she was in training to be cottage cheese. Mark stayed home to look after Paige although we managed to make Evie think he was stayin' home because he was too upset to travel. Then we convinced her she had to look after him while he was lookin' after Paige. Otherwise she'd'a been here, too, and we figured that would be just about enough to make you find a way to slit your own throat."

"I can't handle her at the best of times, thanks."

"Figured. She's in a helluva flap, though, I have to tell you."

"Oh, fuck her helluva flap. She can't seem to get it through her head that it just isn't possible to make up lost time. She wants to be my momsie-poo, Alpha, and I don't remember *havin'* one so I don't know how to *be* to one. I wish she'd never come knocking at the damn door, I really do. She makes me feel as if *I've* done something wrong."

"Easy on, old girl, it could be worse. And prob'ly will be before long."

"I want to go home."

"Don't we all. You'll get there. And a lot quicker if you just close your baby blues and get some sleep so you can start healin' yourself."

The next time Jean fought her way up out of the fog a man in a suit was smiling down at her and offering her a ballpoint pen. "We would appreciate your signature right here, please," he smiled.

"What am I signing?"

"Oh, it's routine," he smiled.

"What is it?"

"Some forms we need to process," he smiled.

"Who are you?"

"Right here." He pointed. And of course smiled.

"Who do you work for?"

"Basically, I suppose, I work for you," he smiled.

"Mom, don't touch that," Sally said loudly, coming in the door with a big brown bag in her hands. "Who are you?" she demanded, "and what are you trying to get her to sign?" and before the smiling man could move, Sally had the papers. The smiley-face dental display expert reached for them and Sally gave him a shove they call a hip check on Hockey Night in Canada. "You bastards," she said pleasantly, flipping through the pages, "you cocksucking dog fuckers, if you don't get your ass out of this room and down the hall and stay to hell and gone away from my mother, I am personally going to take from you whatever vestiges of masculinity were left after they asked you to hand in your gonads so you could qualify to be a bureaucratic ball-less wonder!"

"Miss!" he blurted.

"You sure did miss, you bastard. *Out!*" and then Sally kicked up such a totally impolite and loud-mouthed stink the nurse gave the joker the boot.

"What's going on?" Jean asked.

"He was trying to get you to sign a *release!*" Sally was outraged. "He wanted you to let them off the hook. I'm getting a lawyer."

All hell bust loose for a few minutes and while the nurses contacted security and security contacted their superiors, Sally and Jean ate the take-out Chinese food Sally had brought. "I figured," Sally smiled, "they'd be feeding you mystery meat and throw-out food. So . . . I even got you a thermos of hot green tea."

"You," Jean managed the grimace which was passing for a smile these days, "have saved my life."

Of course nobody had been able to get Smiley's name so each and every department of the federal government denied he was in any way associated with them. The various insurance companies denied he was in any way associated with them, either. And Jean knew full well he wasn't in any way associated with her.

"That does it!" Sally roared. "The woman isn't *safe* here! Make out the papers, I'm taking her home!"

"Get a lawyer," Alpha said clearly.

"Four days since that sucker was here and nobody has any idea who he was or how he got into her room or even how he knew where she was! I like the idea of a lawyer."

They didn't need a lawyer. Two weeks after the Fisheries Department vessel ran full-tilt boogie into the *Lazy Daze*, through her and into the dock, knocking the flagpole off the federal vessel and sending it crashing down on top of Jean Pritchard, with some of the shards and splinters piercing her leg and hip, ten days after the operation to remove bone shards and reconnect severed tendons and ligaments, she was installed in a rented motor home, lying on a comfortable bed, watching out the window and drinking cappuccino. "Damn the expense," said Mark, who had flown down to help with her transfer. "After all, we're going to sue!"

"Who you calling 'we', white man, said Tonto," Jean grumbled. "It's *my* goddamn leg, my hip, my smashed foot, and Uncle Bill's boat. Where do *you* fit in?"

"Oh. I fit in from start to finish." He spoke softly but she knew he meant every syllable. "My job is gone. By the time all the ditzing and putzing and farting around is done it's going to be too late to go salmon fishing this year. So I need my wages. And since this year I was going to be the skipper and *you* were going to be the deck-hand...which is how we're going to tell them it was decided, what with you being no younger than you are and me being the man in the family har har...it's going to cost them a friggin' fortune. And then there's the boat. Uncle Bill will take them to the cleaners on that. And last but not least...your leg."

"Last but not least? This leg is going to seem bloody well gold plated by the time I'm through!"

"Why not?" Sally called back. "After all, we can prove it's lined with sterling silver where the bone used to be! Why not gold plated, too."

"Well, let's make jokes, at least." Jean sipped her cappuccino. "Because I have to tell you, if I can't laugh I'm going to cry. The bugger hurts!"

Small wonder. What wasn't broken was cracked, what wasn't cracked was crushed and what wasn't crushed was so bruised and swollen she wanted it amputated so the hurt would stop. But they made the trip home as easy for her as they could, even if she didn't exactly get "home." She at least got to the hospital close enough to home people could come to visit her.

"Here." Eve handed her a small casserole, still warm. "Shepherd's pie. When you were a kid you loved shepherd's pie," and her faded eyes filled with tears, she wiped at them with a hand so wrinkled and old looking it hurt to see it. "I had these little oval dishes, white on the inside, green on the outside, and I'd make oh, say a dozen or so of them full of shepherd's pie and put the extras in the freezer. Then I'd whip 'em out and put 'em in the oven to warm up for your lunch. You were just a pig for shepherd's pie!"

"I still am," Jean admitted. She tasted it and grinned, "Hey, this is just about as good as it gets."

Eve dabbed at her tears with a tissue from the little blue box on the chipped enamel bedside table, and sat, her old hands shaking, nodding her head and sniffling. It took so little to make her happy these days. Jean resolved to at least try to take things a bit easier on her.

She had more time than she wanted to pick all the old scabs, look at the scar tissue growing beneath them, think about ancient wounds and ponder what, if anything, was the meaning of life. Even when she was being helped out of bed and into a wheelchair, her mind would split without warning from what she was doing and wander off down paths she thought she had forgotten. Issues she had thought were resolved suddenly presented themselves, things she had thought unimportant were standing on the end of her nose demanding she deal with what she had thought she could ignore or forget. And things she had thought were overwhelmingly important suddenly didn't seem to matter at all.

She knew she wasn't dying, she knew she was going to mend, go home and continue to heal. She also knew if what had smashed her on the hip had, instead, bonked her on the head they would have had to dig a hole next to Einarr and put her in it. She wondered if Uncle Bill would have shown up with the catawumpus. Probably. He had said often enough that he took it to the funerals of all his friends because he knew it was one way to ensure their spirits didn't stay around to haunt him; at the first wail the wraiths turned and sped off as fast as they could, preferring even the flames of hell to the screech of his pipes.

If you measured it, she had missed extermination by only eighteen inches. That's close enough, thank you. Too close to ignore, close enough to push your nose right into all the stuff you tried to deal with by not dealing at all. Close enough to give you a glimpse of how much cat muck you'd pushed into the shadows in those times when you were busy coping with the need to survive on a day-to-day level. Scab-picking is time consuming, maybe that's why it seems only those with a degree of wealth can ever manage to find the hours required to indulge themselves in it. What if, and what if instead, and what if otherwise, and how do I feel about it, and what am I going to do about what I feel, and how do I find my healing process, and ya-ta-ta-*tat*, and none of it means frig-all when you need to work *this* many hours at *this* much per hour simply to make the rent.

She'd made the rent. She'd bought the groceries. She'd bought the jeans, the tee shirts, the underwear, the jackets, the increasingly expensive sneakers, the gumboots, the sweaters, she'd even bought the patch kits for the bike tires. To do all that had taken so much time and energy she hadn't been able to sit down and think about how she *felt* about any of it.

But she'd done it. And now that all she had was time to think about how she *felt*, she found that what she felt was mostly fatigue.

Sally had put a thing on the fridge door one time, held in place with a magnet made to look like a big orange-with-black-dots lady-bug. Attributed to Gertrude Stein. Something about It's not easy being a genius, you have to sit around and think all the time. Bugger thinking. Seems as if you can either think or you can do, and if all you do is think you wind up doing nothing, and if you do nothing what you start to think about yourself isn't pleasant. Sit thinking long enough and you might wind up realizing you're wasting everybody's time.

"Son of a gun!" Uncle Bill blurted. "You look like hell, girl."

"I feel like hell, Uncle Bill," she admitted. He sat on the edge of the bed and put his good arm around her and she could cry, then. "Oh, it's just so *awful*," she sobbed. "It hurts and it's all cut up and it'll be scarred and ugly and every day they make me do these exercises and that *hurts*. And Eve looks a thousand years old and both Mark and Sally look like they've been scared half to death and the *Lazy Daze* is wrecked."

"She sure the hell is," he agreed. "That big fucker of a Fisheries boat sliced into her as clean as a wire through cheese. Bang, and that's all she wrote. She filled with water and went down, took 'em the better part of a week to haul her back up again. By then what wasn't smashed was soaked with sea water and stuffed with mud." Then he winked. "And by God you wouldn't believe the quality of the stuff in that boat, either! 'Course it's all ruined, now. So water-soaked and blistered you can't even tell that was real mahogany boards and not just veneer plywood!"

"You crook."

"Gotta add on the Gee Ess Tee, too. That's another seven percent. After all, they made me pay tax on all that new stuff. . . and I got the goddamn re-seats to prove it." They both laughed like fools, and Jean wiped away her tears.

"What are you up to?"

"Well, there's more people owe me favours on this coast than you could shake a stick at, and everyone who got new gear of any kind is bringin' me the re-seats so we can prove, if we have to, just how spunky-do wonderful the stuff on that boat *was*. I bet there isn't another one on the coast worth what we can prove she was worth."

The Fisheries guy said something went wrong with the gas feed and he couldn't slow down the engine. "Then why didn't the fool take 'er up on the beach?" Uncle Bill asked the obvious question. "Why try to berth her at the dock if you've got no friggin' control over your speed? Wasn't no damn gas feed problem at all. The sucker was drunk."

"They say not," Eve countered, "they say he passed his blood sample."

"Federals got no blood to test. They got ink and duplicating fluid, but no blood. And if it wasn't booze, he was on drugs. Besides which, you don't think they'd admit he was crocked up, do you? Nobody's yet admitted one of the prime ministers was a wife beater, why would they admit they've got lurching drunks at the wheel? Whose lab did the blood test? Well ho ho, huh, a federal lab." Uncle Bill had his beliefs firmly entrenched. "Nobody, not even a fed is stupid enough to have 'er open full bore and decide he can slide 'er up to the dock and tie 'er up. You'd'a thought he'd'a known he wasn't in his bathtub at home when he didn't see no little yellow rubber ducky!"

It didn't much matter why, it was done. And life would never be anything close to the same.

Russ came to see her. He brought her a paperback copy of Jack Hodgins' *The Invention of the World*, which she had read when it first came out and enjoyed so much she knew she would enjoy it all over again. He also brought an azalea covered with blooms and a box of chocolates. "I hope you're feeling better," he smiled.

"I'm better than I was." She knew he was going to try to kiss her so she turned her face slightly and felt his lips brush her cheek. "But I hope this isn't as better as it's going to get."

"They're having a huge investigation."

"Yes," she nodded. "I read about it. Someone came up to ask me some questions. Actually, three someones. One guy asked questions, the other two were there with tape recorders, as witnesses. One of them," she shook her head, "was supposed to be working with my lawyer, and was taping the whole thing on *my* behalf. Everyone," she laughed softly, "is going to make a pile of money out of this!"

"Let's hope you're one of them." He pulled the chair closer to the bed and sat down, crossing one leg over the other. "How you feeling? Really."

"Kind of low," she admitted. "Not enough energy yet to be able to feel really involved with what's going on. I sleep a lot. When I'm not sleeping I'm sort of drifting in the ozone because of the painkillers. Then there's the physio, that takes it out of me. Funny how your body's impulse is the very one that cripples you; all I want to do is lie curled in a ball with my thumb in my mouth. What they want me to do involves standing up, balancing on crutches, moving around, soaking the leg in the swirl-pool and moving it as much as I can. But I think I've convinced them I should be allowed to go home. I'm sure they'd keep me here for however long the insurance was willing to pay for the bed!"

"You'll do better at home," he agreed. "I know I did. And there's this thing I want you to think about, want you to *know*: don't try to stifle your anger. You're going to be mad. Real mad. And I guess we got taught to keep being mad to ourselves. Which is a better thing to do than just spew it on other people. But there's something else you can do with mad. You use it for energy. You call on it when you feel like you can't do one more thing, you're just worn to the nub, you'll die if you have to move that swollen aching bastard one more time. That's when you just get so bloody mad you almost worry your eyeballs will pop out of your head! And with that rage you move the bastard!" He took her hand in his and stroked. "I don't think they *know* about mad or they'd teach you first crack off the reel. I think you have to have been hurt real bad to find out about mad. When I was so wore out all I wanted to do was suck my thumb, I'd remember the accident and how goddamn stupid and unnecessary it was, and it was like I could *see* energy coming at me from everywhere. Maybe," he smiled, "maybe if we give ourselves permission to be mad we become like mad-magnets, and all the little mads everyone else has, the mads they can't use or do anything about, feel there's a place to go, and they come too, because I could damn near see red and gold streaks of mad comin' at me from every corner. And I gave it a place to go to, and I used it and it helped more than anything else did."

"Thank you." She squeezed his hand. "I'll remember that."

"Atta girl." He released her hand and leaned back in his chair. "Saw you at the pizza parlour," he put it out in the open, airing the slight distance between them. "But it didn't seem the time to come over to talk."

"No," she agreed.

"Do we need to talk about it?"

"No," she shook her head and meant it. "No, it's not a problem for me."

"Good," he smiled. "It's not serious," he admitted, "it's not a huge thing, and it's not exclusive. We're not 'going steady' or anything heavy like that. I'm not ready. And anyway, she's got two kids just going into their teens, so . . ."

"Full plate," she laughed. "You're lucky she has time to answer the phone!"

"Yeah," he grinned, then reached for his back pocket, brought out his wallet. "I've got a job," he laughed softly, "the retraining program must have done some good, eh?" and he handed her a business card.

She looked at it and then started to chortle, forgetting the pain in her leg. "You're kidding!"

"I am not kidding," he shook his head, still laughing. "If you ever decide to put your house up for sale you'd better not list it with anyone else! I'll queer the deal for you if you do."

"Real estate?"

"Hey, lady, I know damn near everyone on the coast! Even loggers have to have a house to live in! And anyway, you know as well as I do that there's been the most enormous Monopoly game goin' on out here ever since the first fools arrived, people buyin' and sellin' and tradin' and swappin' back and forth as if they knew what they were doing. I might as well get in on it and shave my percentage anywhere I can!" Then he looked almost embarrassed. "Keeps a body busy, though. Sometimes I hardly have the time or energy to even phone someone, let alone pull 'er together to visit. And most of the time it's easier to watch an hour's TV, have a bath and go to bed than it is to, oh, you know, go to a movie or something," and Jean knew he wasn't apologizing or kissing her foot, he was just trying to do something brand new for him.

"Yeah," she smiled, and reached out to squeeze his fingers. "Yeah, I know. You go out to work for a living and it takes so much out of you the first thing you know you're not living any more!"

"Take you dancin' when that leg starts to work?"

"Sure. But you're not going to wait until then to drop by the house for some of Eve's meat loaf, are you?"

"I'll take you up on that. What do you figure to do about work?"

"Oh," she shrugged, "I think maybe I'll just win the 6/49 and leave the work to those who are stupid enough to still believe there's a future in it."

Russ grinned, then winked at her. "You got your ticket?" he teased.

"I'll get it first thing I get out of here," she promised. Then, she couldn't help it, she yawned. He laughed softly, reached over, turned on the radio, found a station with moldie oldies and sat quietly, watching as Jean lost the fight to stay awake.

The next day on his lunch hour, Russ went to the hospital with fish and chips and two thick vanilla milkshakes. "I know about the kind of swill they serve," he told her. Then he handed her a lottery ticket. "Here, you can't win if you don't have a ticket."

"Is this the winner?"

"You betcha," he said. But it wasn't.

She tried not to worry about money. She tried to believe she Had It Made Now. She lectured herself repeatedly on how one of the quickest ways to wind up on a pension was to get hurt by someone working for the government. But she couldn't believe it. No way the Fisheries were going to set her up so she could see the great cathedrals of Europe. Be lucky if she could afford to go see the Little Brown Church in the Vale. Anyway, money alone isn't what it's all about; nobody ever seems to get enough compensation, insurance, settlement, pension, whatever, to allow them to *enjoy* the leisure time forced on them. Money aside, what was she going to *do*?

Alpha came to visit. Her brick shithouse wasn't in evidence. She drove up by herself, parked the pickup in front of the house and gave the Nguyen kids ten bucks to divide amongst themselves if they would wash the dried mud off and clean all the windows. She stomped into the house in her high-heeled cowgirl boots with a two-four of beer under one arm and a brown bag with three bottles of scotch in it under the other.

"Evie," she declared, "you're gonna wear yourself down to a nub fussing over my granddaughter."

"I enjoy her," Eve insisted.

"I never said a thing about enjoyin' or not enjoyin'. Seems to me what I said was you're gonna wear yourself down to a nub. You're most of the way there already."

"She's a dear little thing."

"Yeah, but she's not tough enough. We all been so busy babying that baby we ain't give her no room to grow some hide. If we're not careful she'll turn into one of them godawful little Prissy-Missys who traipse around in those stupid-lookin' nylon dresses made out of rows of ruffles and petticoats, with those patent leather strap-across-the-top shoes on her feet. You know the ones, they look like they belong on a doll sittin' on someone's mantlepiece or somewhere useless like that. Here, Chrissakes, open the fridge door so's I can tuck the beer into bed for a while, and then get some jam jars or something so's this scotch can come outta the bottle it's been trapped in for the past eight years. You'n'me's gonna have ourselves one of those Remember the Good Old Days times . . ."

"Alpha, I got to tell you, the good old days didn't seem good at the time and they don't seem a whole helluva lot better in retrospect, either."

"Fine, we'll bury 'em then. Did you ever think, way back when, that it would all wind up like this?"

"No." Eve drank deeply, directly from the bottle. "No, I never did. I kind of thought that as time went on I'd manage to . . . well, I don't know what, but something!"

"It's the gettin' stupid bothers me. I used to think I knew this stuff, and that what I knew was important. You know, to thine own self be true and all that good shit, and now . . . I guess I forgot it or something. Stuff that used to be so important is now . . . nothin' much of anythin'."

"You, too, huh?"

"Damn right. Some days I can't for the life of me figure out anything at all. Seems like the more I try the less I manage. All this stuff they told me I'd understand when I got older, and here I am, and I'm older and I don't understand any of it. The good news is," she winked, "at the rate my mind is giving out I'll soon forget what in hell it was I been worrying about."

They arrived for visiting hours with a small meat-and-potato pie, still warm and wrapped in a clean tea towel. They were both pretty well packed, but neither of them noisy or obnoxious. Alpha sat on one side of the bed, Eve on the other, and they played three-handed crib with Jean until the nurses' aide came in to remind them, for the third time, that visiting hours were over and she hated to be a party pooper but she really did have to ask them to go.

"Right," Alpha agreed. "I can take a hint."

"Right," Eve got to her feet and smiled widely. "Now all we got to do is make 'er down the hill and we're home free."

"Well, we're home. But even that ain't free," and off they went, as close to a matched pair as Jean had seen in a long time.

"Don't you worry none," Alpha called over her shoulder, "I'm stayin' for a while to help Evie look after the kid."

"Great," Jean smiled. She hoped nobody was putting a lot of store in any of it because it looked as if the party had barely started and would be another for the annals once it got into full swing. "Oh well," she sighed, "at least nobody expects *me* to do anything about it."

When she wakened in the middle of the night and rang the bell for a bedpan she realized that in all likelihood nobody had ever expected her to do anything about almost anything she might care to name. Certainly nobody except herself had ever expected her to do anything about Eve or Eve's carryings-on.

Sally came in on her lunch break the next day to update Jean on the festivities. "They didn't come home when they left here," she laughed. "They went down to the pub and started in at the pool table. Alpha figured she was the better player of the two so now Gran's ahead two games to one and Alpha's got her mind set on outlasting her. Says if she has to stay parked by the side of the road for the rest of her life she's going to come out ahead. And Gran said the only way Alpha would get a head would be to go to the produce section of the supermarket and buy some cabbage."

"Jesus."

"He'll probably be in the pub tonight for round two along with everyone else in town. Mark figures the pub ought to give them their beer free of charge just for the advertising and publicity."

"What about Paige?"

"I don't think they're going to let her in there, Momma, the Mounties check every now and again and they take a very dim view of such goin's-on. Stop worrying, it's all under control."

"Yeah. It's stuff like that makes me worry. Any time Alpha and Eve are loose on the world together and the sensible one in the family is saying everything is under control . . . well, we're all in trouble."

"No sweat. At least we don't have to worry about either of them ruining their reputations. Neither of them has any left."

And that was a true thing. So why was it mildly amusing to think of Alpha, no bigger'n a minute, with a voice verging on baritone because of all the cigarette smoke and hard liquor that had rubbed the walls of her throat, and not the least friggin' bit funny to think of Eve in exactly the same situation? Neither of them was going to come home pregnant. Any more. And hadn't *that* always been the big threat, the rationalization for forcing so many women into a mould of propriety and good behaviour?

Finally the day came when they let Jean out of her cage. She went home and started trying to learn how to move around on crutches without spearing the baby or being sent ass over appetite by the dog.

"Will someone *please* put Brucie outside?" she yelled repeatedly. "She's doing it again."

"C'mon, dog, for cryin' out loud!" Alpha opened the front door and snapped her fingers. Brucie tried to pretend nothing had happened and nobody was giving her an order, but Alpha stamped her foot and the dog decided she'd better at least pretend to obey. She tried to crawl under the table. "Out, damn it!" Alpha insisted. Brucie moved from the table to a chair and even got partway under it before the chair tipped on its side. Alpha shook her head in disgust and said something bitter about shotguns up the ying-yang.

"Get your hairy ass *out*!" She grabbed the tipping chair, lifted it just far enough to get some swing to it and slammed the legs against Brucie's butt. The dog yelped with surprise, toenails clawed and scraped at the lino, and then Brucie was streaking for the open door, but not fast enough to avoid the teeny tiny cowboy boot. "Take a damn tellin', will ya!" Alpha carefully replaced the chair, then gave both Sally and Mark a long hard look. "You want to keep that mutt?" she said pleasantly. "Or you want me to make discreet arrangements? One bust leg is enough for anyone."

"Yes, Alpha," they agreed.

"It ain't the damn dog should get its arse kicked, believe me." Alpha looked over at Eve and shook her head. "And you're the worst of the bunch."

"Well, I feel sorry for her sittin' out on the porch."

"Then go sit on the bloody porch with her! She's gonna send Jeannie arse over teapot with her carryin' on."

Brucie was convinced the crutches were attacking her person. For a dog the size of a chesterfield she could hide in the smallest of places and wait for the chance to streak out, grab a crutch and try to demolish it so Jean would be at least half free. However many times she was put outside she found her way back in again.

"Jesus God!" Jean shrieked, grabbing for the wall, dropping both crutches and clinging to the pattern of the wallpaper. "Someone grab that mutt!"

"Come on, Brucie, you aren't appreciated." Sally put the dog outside where she lay on the porch licking her lips and glorying in the taste of the varnish on the gnawed crutch.

"Why is that dog in the house? I thought we all had an understanding about that? I thought you could keep the dog if it stayed outside. Doesn't anyone ever *listen*?"

"We did have an understanding," Mark agreed, "we just didn't clear it with Brucie, is all. And why get so bent out of shape over a chewed-up wooden crutch? Why not just get some aluminum ones?"

"Now I have to get a special kind of crutch so the damn dog doesn't. . . I can't believe you said that."

"Hey, whatever's easiest, right? Anything's easier than trying to teach Brucie to *do* something!"

"Just pray to God she doesn't decide Paige is trying to do something vile to your arm," Jean groused. "You lug that kid around twenty-two hours out of twenty-four and if Brucie decides you're in trouble, she's apt to eat the baby. Why not, she eats everything else! *Look* what she's done to the rocker bar on my chair!"

"Oh, that wasn't Brucie," Sally contradicted, "that has to have been a rat or something. Why would Brucie chew the rocking chair?"

"Because she chews everything else. Why would she chew my crutches?"

"She thinks they're attacking you."

"No. Because they are there. Like the rocking chair."

"*Put* the damn mutt outside!" Alpha suggested. "And *chain* her to the porch rail."

"*Chain* her?" They stared, horrified.

"The dog's psychological comfort is more important than your mother's safety?"

The brick shithouse showed up unannounced. He did not come bearing long-stemmed roses, he did not come weighed down by a mountain of chocolates or staggering under the weight of little bottles of imported perfume. He just arrived at the front door with a shy smile on his face.

"Alpha here?" he asked quietly.

"Uh, yeah, she is. Come on in." Mark stepped aside, opening the door. Metal hook gleaming, the hunk stepped into the hallway, kicked off his shoes and padded sock-foot toward the sound of laughter in the kitchen, where Alpha was playing poker-for-pennies with Eve, Sally and Jean.

"Hi, darlin'," Alpha smiled as if only an hour had passed since she had last seen him.

"Hello your own self," he answered.

"Pull up a chair," she invited. "If you need a beer, you can imagine where it'd be kept, right?"

"Right," he nodded, but made no move toward the fridge. He just sat smiling and watching the game. Once he got up and went to the biffy and once he opened the back door so the dog could go outside, but for the rest of it he just sat, seeming totally at home. When Alpha announced she was off to bed he stood, smiling, and followed her from the house to the camper.

In the morning Alpha announced her vacation was over. "Time to start tryin' to pretend to be normal, I suppose," she said. She cuddled Paige, kissed everyone chummily and told Jean, "if you need anything at all — except the hunk, you have to find your own — just gimme a shout," and by half past eight she was gone, camper, pickup, shit brickhouse and all.

"Nice guy," Sally smiled, watching the truck drive off to catch the ferry.

"Was he in camp?" Mark asked. "Is that why she showed up by herself?"

"In the bin," Eve corrected.

"The who?"

"The what?"

"The bin. He flips out every so often and they have to haul 'im off to a padded room for a while."

"You're kidding," Sally gaped.

"Why would I kid about a thing like that? I'm tellin' ya, the man's crazy. Well, not all the time. Probably not more than one-third the time."

"Crazy how? Does he think he's Napoleon, or Jesus or someone?"

"Naw, worse'n that. He starts to thinking he's normal."

Jean missed Alpha. It had been nice to have someone on her side around the whole question of the dog and whether or not it was part owner of the house. She got very adept at putting all her weight on the crutches, lifting her bad leg out of the way and firing a kick with her good one. Brucie got even more adept at avoiding the kick.

Terry Dugan showed up less and less often and stayed for shorter periods of time, but he sent money for Paige regularly, and sent more than enough to support her and pay for someone to come in and help with the housework, even sent enough they could think of putting her in daycare when the time came she was old enough to go. She was, after all, by God, his kid, and he'd do right by her. And when she became a person, with a vocabulary, and a fellow could *do* something with her, like go fishing or kick a ball around or whatever, Terry would be back in her life, because whatever else you might say about him, he was a damn nice guy.

"Would it be all right if I invited some people for Sunday supper?" Mark asked on Wednesday evening, after Paige was in bed.

"Sure," Eve nodded. "How many?"

"Three." He sounded so casual and offhand the hair on the back of Jean's neck began to stiffen. She'd heard that tone before, usually just before he pulled the sky down around her ears.

"Three. Okay," and Eve nodded again.

"One adult." Mark began tugging at the clouds, pulling the edges of the sky loose so it could drift free. "And two kids. Boy'n a girl, seven and five."

"And I don't suppose the adult is their father," Jean guessed.

"Don't suppose so," Mark agreed, so busy examining his fingernail he had no time to look up and meet her eyes.

"I won't ask how serious this is," Jean decided, "because if it wasn't serious we wouldn't be having company for Sunday Supper."

"Find out," Eve ordered, "what the kids' favourite food is. No sense gettin' off on the wrong foot with them."

"Manicotti," Mark said promptly. "With *lots* of cheese."

"Instant coffee," Jean sighed, "instant soup, instant noodles, instant family. The progress we've made is absolutely amazing."

Sally worked at the marina and fulfilled every requirement of her apprenticeship, and Mark went to college financed by an allowance from the federals pending the hearing, the appeal, the insurance settlement and the inevitable reappeal and whatever other stalling tactic the legal profession could invent.

"It's better than Unemployment Enjoyment," he laughed, "because on pogey you're not allowed to use your time to improve your education, you have to sit by the phone waiting for a job to phone you."

"When they settle," Jean asked, "are you going to go back fishing?"

"I don't know. I'm good at that. I'm as good as Grandpa ever was. If I'd been born in Grandpa's time I could have been a highliner. But there's fuck-all left to catch out there! What there is has been contaminated with crap the names of which I can't even pronounce. It's gonna take a hundred years for the poison to leave the beaches and nobody will even guess how long for the chuck itself to get healthy. So what's to catch, and who'd want to eat it if you did, and would you feel good about calling it food if you found someone willing to buy it? I been talking to a lot of guys, talking to Joe, talking to his dad, talking to Uncle Bill, talking . . . and thinking . . . and feeling shitty about Paige and . . . maybe I'll just open me a health food store or something. But I doubt it'll be fishing. I was thinking of maybe going in for a lawyer." He seemed almost afraid to approach the idea. "I mean, all this into court and out of court and lawyers meeting with other lawyers and forms to be filled out and witnessed and rah rah rah three bags full that's going on about your leg and the *Lazy Daze*, and all of them getting Christ knows how much an hour for pushing pencils across sheets of paper, well . . . I could do that!" He looked defiant and waited for her to tell him only the upper middle class had kids who headed off to law school.

"Like if you have to send a shark into the pool to make it safe for the kids to swim, it might as well be your own tame shark?"

"Yeah. Why not?"

"I can't think of any reason why not. After all, one way or the other, there's going to be a bit of cash around here for a change."

"Yeah. And besides that," he laughed softly, "there's no way the old man can take *that* job away from me, right?"

"Oh, I'm sure he'll try. At least he's sure to hire you to sue me to try to get back what I managed to squeeze out of him with the garnishee order."

"Whatever happened to that?"

"Well, you, you dumb bastard, grew up, didn't you? So he got off the hook for his monthly payments and I haven't pushed on back payments because it keeps him away from me."

"Cheap at twice the price?"

"Yes," and they both knew she meant it.

Later, lying on the sofa with her leg propped on pillows, she wondered if Mark might have wanted to try law all along but felt he should be a man and support himself. He was at least as smart as Joe Nguyen. He'd been so excited from the get-go about Joe's plans to head off to the city and conquer the world. Would he have gone, too, if things had been just a little bit less tight? Had he been living his dreams through Joe? What expectations did other people have that had nearly put walls around her son's chances? How was he going to go off to law school and do all that diddly-doo when Charlene and her kids were increasingly involved in his life? And why did Jean think that was her problem? For that matter, how much did she even care?

Jean learned to walk all over again. Her gait was uneven and her balance seemed to have caught the bus and taken a round-the-world vacation trip, but she could make it from the house to the dock and back again, given enough time. Uphill was worse than downhill and she didn't seem to be able to learn not to be frightened if things got slippery underfoot, but she no longer needed help getting up and down steps. The day she came home from town with a walking cane she'd bought at Pharma-Save, they stored the crutches in the garage. "The guy said you stand straight, with your arm hanging, and measure by the bend-line in your wrist," she explained. "Then cut off any excess."

"But not on the curved end, right?"

"Probably not." She stood, they measured, and Mark took the cane out to the garage. He came back only a couple of minutes later, the rubber tip in one hand, the cane with the bottom end raw in the other. "Try this, if it's too long I'll nip off a bit more, if it's too short you can buy a new one and we'll try again." Jean tried it. The cane felt heavy, it felt awkward, and she felt both dumb and clumsy, but it was the right length and she supposed sooner or later she'd get used to it. She wanted to say thank you but all she could do was nod and pretend to be pleased.

They knew her well enough not to make any claims about the cane being progress of some sort. They knew just needing it made her feel diminished.

She even started back to night school. But she switched from office procedures, administration and computers, and instead went in on Thursday nights to learn how to play the guitar.

"Why?" Sally laughed. "You've got a voice like a crow."

"So what? I'm not takin' singing lessons for God's sake, I'm taking guitar lessons! I've about given up on my plan to win the 6/49, but I figure all I have to do is learn two chords and I can dye my hair orange and green and join some kind of travelling road show, then live like a bloody millionaire."

"Oh Mom." Sally picked up the guitar and picked at the strings. "What are all these little diddly-doos on the neck?"

"That's my cheat sheet. The green dot on the first fret there, and the other green one on the second fret, when pushed down together, make C chord. And the red dot? Well, it's the F chord. No it's not," she corrected hurriedly, "it's the F note and when you chord with it shoved down it's the G-7. Blue, now, that's G and gold is D. Nothing to it as long as I don't lose my diddly-doos!"

"Do you think Liona Boyd did it this way?"

"I have no idea at all how Liona Boyd did it or even *why*. I just know if I don't use the dealy-bobs I can't remember where anything is or where my fingers should go."

"I hate to be the one to wet-blanket your plans." Sally put the guitar aside and sprawled on the couch, stretching like a lazy cat. "But I do think you're going to have to look around for some other way to make our for-toon. I don't think the rock star idea has much of a chance," and she grinned.

Jean noticed a small love-bite on Sally's neck. She leaned over and poked at it with her finger. "Is this what you call working overtime?" she teased. Sally grinned again and yawned. "What's his name?" Jean reached for the guitar.

"Phyllis. And she's twenty-six, has very *very* dark skin, pitch black hair, huge dark eyes and a body to stop traffic. And she's a registered nurse with a full-time job and I met her about three and a half months ago," Sally said, and Jean laughed. Laughed until she looked over and saw that Sally wasn't laughing, joking or teasing. Jean put the guitar down and just sat, thinking overtime.

"What are you thinking about?" Sally asked. Jean looked at her daughter and was filled with so much raw love she could barely hold it inside her body. All this stuff she'd been taught, all this how to and how not to, all this yes you will and no you won't, all the you must and you mustn't, you ought and you oughtn't, thou shalt and thou shalt not.

"I was wondering. . ." She knew her smile was easy and would seem totally genuine. She'd had years of practice, years of covering up bouts of panic with lovely wide smiles. "Who took over when Secretariat was retired?"

"Jesus, I don't know. Some horse," Sally frowned. "Why?"

"I was thinking maybe I could go to the doctor and tell him I was cracking up."

"That shouldn't be hard to prove."

"Right! For that matter, we could all go, get a group rate. So I tell him I need some nerve pills. Tranquillizers. Strong ones. And I get a month's worth and save 'em, then go back and get some more, and when we've got enough, we go to wherever it is they keep whoever it was replaced Secretariat. Then we bet against the bugger and stuff all my sleepytime pills either down his throat or up his ass. . ." and she didn't finish because Sally was howling with laughter, her head back, the love-bite on her neck visible, obvious, smacking Jean right between the eyes with yet another dose of reality. She wondered if she could handle it. And knew she'd muddle through somehow. Most of what she'd been taught to believe had turned out to be either incomplete truth or total bullshit, and she'd made it past that. When she wasn't getting a kick in the teeth she was getting a kick in the teeth and she'd made it past that. Whatever it was she was up against, it was bigger than anyone had ever warned her, but she'd make it past, and if not, she'd learn to live with it.

"Jesus, you're a nut," Sally said fondly. "I wonder what normal people do with their lives?"

"What do you mean 'normal'?" Jean threw a cushion and bounced it off Sally's belly. "*I'm* normal. You," she knew she was diving into deep water, and she knew there might be rocks lurking in it, but she knew she couldn't stay in the shallows forever, "might not be normal, but I am, for God's sake."

"I'm not 'normal', Mom." Sally obviously had decided to dive into the deep water, too. "Does that bother you?"

"Listen." Jean rubbed her face, so nervous her skin itched. "One of the nice things about being crammed into a small house with too many other people is there's no closets to live in so nobody needs to leap out of them at any time. If you're happy, then that's what's important. As long as you know there's no happy ever after, and as long as you know there's nobody in the world can fill the holes in your life, you're stuck doing the backfilling yourself, and as long as you know that sooner or later you're going to wind up rolling on the ground biting hunks out of the lawn because your heart is in little bitty pieces, and if you're willing to pay those dues, then go for it."

"Fuck." Sally threw the pillow back. "I hope when I grow up I can talk in better sentences than that! And you took upgrading."

"I not only took it, I passed it." Jean tossed back the cushion and Sally caught it, then returned it. "But you might remember, I never said I was smart, and I never said they'd taught me the answers."

"Phyllis says that she doesn't give a toot what the answers are, because she refuses to listen to the question."

"Well, there you have it," Jean agreed. "So, do I get to meet this paragon of all wonderful things?"

"If you want to." Sally's smile showed Jean just how convincing her own wide brave grimace had been all these years. Convincing only if you wanted to be convinced, and not at all if you were trying to deal with the truth.

"Whenever you're ready, darling. I don't know how well I'm going to do with this," she warned. "I mean you know me, when in trouble or in doubt, run in circles, scream and shout. I don't understand bugger-nothing in life at all, but it's no more of a mystery to me that you've got tied up with Phyllis than it was a mystery to me why Patsy picked Terry Dugan!"

"Or you picked Dad," Sally dared.

"That, too."

"Or why you didn't pick Russ."

"Oh, I know why I didn't pick Russ," Jean laughed. "He's a nice guy. The world is full of nice guys. You can't step out of the house without tripping over a nice guy. But they all want you to pick 'em up, dust 'em off, take 'em home, put ice on their bruises and kiss 'em better! And if I want to do *that*...I can do it for Paige, I guess."

They laughed together, softly, but later, lying in bed with her sore leg propped on pillows, looking out the window to the bay where the boats were moored, Jean wondered if what she had said was true. Maybe if she had been able to figure out exactly what it was Russ thought he wanted she might not have had to react to what it was she knew she didn't want. Maybe she had just put Russ in the same bag in which she'd put Tommy and overlooked the fact that all they had in common with each other was an involvement with her. She just wished she could stop gnawing away at the unresolved the way Brucie gnawed at the mouldering old bones she unearthed. Jean also wished she would, just sometimes, not hide behind the kind of joke she'd made to her daughter. So what if it probably was true!

She came out of the house and the dog was lying on the porch looking up at her with huge hopeful eyes, her stub tail wagging her fat back end. Jean nudged the dog with the rubber tip of her rosewood cane. "Come on, Brucie, cut me some slack, here, will you. Move, please. Heft the bulk, and give me at least half a chance to make 'er down the steps, okay?" The dog got up, shook herself and ambled down the steps, her black hide glossy over the layers of fat swathed on her frame. "You're gonna drop dead of clogged arteries," Jean warned, moving carefully down the stairs, "or your heart will just stop pumping because it's squeezed by all that pork. You come here and eat every friggin' thing that goes within two feet of your food dish, then when you've had more than your share of the world's calories, you waddle over to Nguyens and convince them you're half dead of starvation and polish *that* food bowl with your tongue, too. You're a bloody disgrace is what you are."

The dog looked at her with a Gee-I-love-you-too-Jeannie look, then put her huge head against the gate and pushed it open, stood holding it until Jean made her way through and started down the road, step-and-fetchit-ing carefully, aware of the discomfort that could flare into pain without warning. "Old ninety-nine-clump," she muttered, "the three-legged woman strides again. Dear God please make my leg like the other one, the woman prayed and there was a clap of thunder, the Hallelujah Chorus rang from on high and her other leg crumpled into uselessness and dumped her in the dirt. Big fucking help that was she said but God preferred to misunderstand. Brucie, for *Christ's sake* don't press against me!"

Brucie moved a half step to one side and plodded faithfully, doing her level best to stay between Jean and a world that had not always proved itself to be safe or kind. Bit by bit she edged closer and closer until she was practically leaning on Jean's good leg. Without missing a step or giving any warning at all Jean lifted her cane and brought it down with a hard *swat* on Brucie's broad head. Brucie leaped aside, landed all four feet in a puddle and splashed mud on Jean's clean pants. "Bitch," Jean said companionably, gimping her way along the side of the road. Brucie stayed eighteen inches from Jean's cane, and paced, on guard, still the self-appointed protector.

"So whattya think, Brucie? You figure the price of eggs is worth the wear and tear on the chicken's hind end?"

Maybe it was because nobody had a horse of sufficiently good breeding or fast enough feet to replace Secretariat, that Jean's plan to dope it up, fix the race and retire a buhzillionaire had to be put on hold. Or maybe it was because she seemed to lack whatever kind of choosiness required to pick the winning numbers for the 6/49. Or maybe some kind of cosmic accident had arranged it so every time the devil took a shit it landed on or near her head. Any, all or none of the above might have been part of the reason, but there she was, a full year later, gimping down to the dock to watch other people get their boats ready, first for herring, then for salmon. The only difference was Paige was trudging right alongside her, one hand on Brucie's thick neck, either for balance or for company, Jean wasn't sure which.

Almost two years since Paige had been born, almost two years since Patsy had died, and the hurt had barely begun to heal. Sometimes Jean looked at Paige and didn't know if she wanted to scoop her up and smooch her or put her hand on the kid's head and push her out of the way; and that was so awful she couldn't talk about it to anyone because why should a grandmother want to put her hand on her granddaughter's head and push her aside? The last person in the world to be held responsible surely ought to be the little girl.

And on those times when Jean could separate her brain from her emotions and see Paige as a person, she had to admit the kid was a great little soul. She was, in fact, many of the things Patsy had never been, things Jean had thought she wanted Patsy to be. Paige was walking before she was one and talking by the time she was a year and a half old, she was easily pleased and no more demanding than any kid had a right to be. Any mother would have felt herself fortunate to have a kid like Paige. And maybe the only thing sticking in Jean's throat was she wasn't Paige's mother and shouldn't have to feel she ought to want to be.

"I wonder if *my* grandmother felt like this?" she said aloud. Paige looked up at her, and smiled. "I lived with my gran when I was a little girl," Jean explained.

Paige nodded. As far as she was concerned living with your grandmother was how life was. What did she know of mother, or grandmother. When all you know is all you know how can you know anything different? "Boats," she decided, pointing. "Fish."

"Yes, the boats will be going fishing soon," Jean agreed. She leaned against a pole, propping herself with her cane, keeping the weight off her bad leg. The wind was stiff, with a bite to it, and there was fresh snow on the peaks, the trees turned bluish under the thin cover. By afternoon the sun would melt that frosting and the trees would again seem green.

"I go swimmin' wif you?" Paige asked hopefully.

"You want to come swimming with me? Why would I take you swimming with me? I only take good girls swimming."

"I a good girl," Paige laughed. "Sally says I a good girl. Markie says."

"Well, why don't you go swimming with Sally, then?"

"Sally don' go swimming. You go swimming."

"Go swimming with Markie."

"Markie go fishing. Paige can't go fishing. Markie says no."

"Did Markie say no to you? I can hardly believe that. Markie never says no."

"Markie say Paige wait. Too cold. I go swimmin' wif you?"

"We'll see."

"I go," Paige laughed. "Paige hide inna back seat," she teased. "Sally says Paige hide inna back seat."

"Yeah? Why don't you hide in Sally's back seat and give me a break?"

"Sally don' go swimmin'. Sally go *work*. Paige can't go to work. Sally say Paige stay home and look after Gran."

"Boy, they've got it all figured out, huh?"

"I go swimmin' wif you."

"Yeah, I guess you go swimmin' wif me. What else? *If* you're good," she repeated the warning. "If you aren't, you'll stay home with Nana."

"I go swimmin' wif you."

"Jesus you're a nag! Anyone ever tell you there's no welcome in the world for a nag?"

"No," Paige shook her head positively. "Markie never said. Sally never said."

"Well, *Gran* says. You remember that. No welcome in the world for a nag."

"I'n not nag," Paige argued, her brows drawn together in an already fierce frown.

"You don't even know what nag is, how do you know you're not one."

"Markie never said."

"Oh, well, my God, eh?" Jean came off the post, balancing herself carefully before turning. "If Markie doesn't say it there's no use anyone else trying because you only believe Markie."

"We goin' home?"

"Might as well. C'mon, Brucie."

"Get hot choc'late?" Paige looked up, face hopeful.

"Hot chocolate? Only good girls get hot chocolate."

"I good girl. Sally says."

"Right. Okay, hot chocolate it is. Hey!" She lurched, grabbed Paige by the collar and hauled her back. "No running! If you want to come with Gran, you walk. I can't chase you, you know that."

"You gotta gimp," Paige agreed.

"Right, I gotta gimp. And that means if you want to come, you gimp along, kiddo, and make life easy for me. You can always stay home with Nana, you know."

"Nana don't get hot chocolate."

"No, Nana doesn't take you into the cafe for one overpriced cup of weak glup they want you to think is hot chocolate. No. Nana just melts Baker's semi-sweet, adds it to warm milk, sweetens it and tops it with canned whipped cream, that's all Nana does for you. It hardly compares, does it? Okay, then, you gimp with me and we'll go to the cafe and get us some of that powdered wotzit in a cup."

Paige loved the cafe. Paige loved everything about the cafe. She knelt on the oilcloth-covered bench in the booth and slurped happily, chattering a mile a minute about anything that came into her mind.

Between slurps and gulps she drew pictures in the steam on the window.

"You realize," Jean told her, "that when the others were little, I'd have made them stop that. I'd'a given them the lecture on how drawing pictures in the steam leaves ugly marks on the glass. You get away with murder, kiddo. It all seemed very important, then. Now, I don't know what's important and what isn't."

Uncle Bill came in then. He saw Jean and Paige, grinned from ear to ear and moved to the booth. He slid in beside Paige, who forgot about the steamy window immediately and put her arms around Bill's neck and squeezed.

"That's my girl," he said softly, "you give me a great big *uhrr*, I need one."

"Uhrrr," Paige obliged, squeezing and half growling. She smeared a few wet kisses on Bill's face and rumpled his hair.

"What you got in that mug?" He bent over, peering.

"Hot choc'late," she said proudly. "Gran got me hot choc'late."

"Is it good?"

"Yes."

"I think I'll have me some of that hot chocolate." He pretended to reach for her cup. Paige smiled and pushed the mug toward him, and he sipped. "Good stuff!" he agreed, then ordered coffee and a plate of french fries.

"Your wife catches you eating french fries, old man, your name's gonna be mud," Jean warned.

"Damn, Jeannie, don't you start too! I could eat a mountain of that damn healthy food and still feel like I'm starvin'! I don't think it does a body any good at all to have to adjust to a whole new way of eating. Thousands and thousands of generations of people have got accustomed to a certain kind of diet, you can't just go chargin' in and switch 'em over to something altogether different, it don't make sense. I don't think I got them enzymes or key-tones or whatever to get full nourishment out of that stuff. And anyway, I figure the less of it I put in me, the more I'm doin' for world peace."

"How do you figure that?" she grinned.

"Mao Tse Tung said the next war is gonna be fought over empty rice bowls," Bill lectured, "so the less of that damn brown grass seed I eat, the more there is for the Red Chinese, and the less likelihood there is of a war."

"Rice," Paige said scornfully. "I *hate* rice."

"Me, too, kiddo," Bill agreed. "Awful bloody stuff."

"You liked it well enough until you heard Uncle Bill bitching about it," Jean argued. "You like rice pudding."

"Not rice, though."

"Yes, you do."

"No, I don't."

"Yes, you do."

"Do not. I know."

"That's my girl. You tell her. You say 'I know what I know'."

"I know what I know," Paige parroted.

"Great," Jean laughed, "just great. Next thing, you'll be teaching her to take the caps off beer with her teeth."

"Beer's bad." Paige slurped her hot chocolate and turned her attention back to the steamy window.

"How's it going?" Bill asked.

"Oh, it's going, that's about all I'll commit myself to."

The waitress brought the coffee and fries. Bill placed a napkin on the tabletop in front of Paige and lined up four of the biggest fries. "You want vinegar or ketchup?" he asked.

"You havin' binginger?" she fished.

"No, I don't have binginger on mine. Nor ketchup, either. But some do."

"Not me," said the one who loaded both on her fries when she was with Mark.

"Hey Jeannie." Tim McDougal slid onto the bench beside her, grinning. "So how's it going?"

"Just fine," she smiled. "Yourself?"

"Great." He ordered coffee and toast, then shrugged. "Prob'ly be bankrupt this time next week, but other'n that life's great. Bill?"

"Oh, I'm fine," Bill lied. "Just got back from Arizona so I gotta get used to the chill in the air again, guess I'm gettin' soft in m'old age."

"Yeah? How was it?"

"Great!" Bill sounded convincing. "We rented a trailer down there. There's prob'ly fifty or sixty Canadians — most of 'em west-coasters — stay at the same trailer park, so it isn't like you're drownin' in yanks, eh. We flew down this time, and rented a car down there . . . last year we took the motor home but my Jesus aitch but it's a long drive!"

"I know what you mean," Tim nodded, spreading jam on his toast. He cut one of the diagonal half slices in half again and handed it wordlessly to Paige, who smiled and accepted it daintily. "Person-

ally," he offered, "except for Washington and Oregon, you can take
the whole goddamn country and push it up your nose, by me. They
got the *ugliest* roads I ever seen! Nothing to see but traffic."

"So we flew down, like I said, and rented a car. It was nice. Warm.
Sunny. That was nice. Had a pool and like that. Drove out to the
desert a few times, that's different. Don't know as I'd like to live there,
mind you, it's as bare as the shell on a hard-boiled egg. Wife liked it,
though. She's out with her camera gettin' all these pictures of the
cactus in bloom. Jesus, she sees this old cow skull on the side'a the
road and nothin'll do but we have to stop so she can get out and lie
on her belly on the road to get this shot of the cow skull and the desert
and then these big painted hoodoo rocks in the background! I was
expectin' Tom Mix to come ridin' up on Tony, eh! I told her if you
see that twenty mule team with its loada Borax you better get up offa
the road or you'll get run over for sure. Nice to be home," he
admitted, pushing the last few of his fries to Paige, who was finished
the soft centre of her jammed toast. She put the crust of toast on her
napkin and started in on the last fries.

"You're gonna be rounder than you are tall," Jean warned.

"How's she makin' out?" Tim asked.

"Oh, she's fine. I'm about worn to a nub, but she's doing just fine."

"Helluva thing," he sighed. "Just when you think your job's almost
over you find out you were wrong again, eh? Seems to me I spent
my whole goddamn life being Wrong Again. I hear your boy decided
he wasn't gonna be Ironside, after all, nor Perry Mason, neither.
Heard he was goin' fishin' again. That true?"

"That's true," she sighed.

"He still hangin' around with that Charlene?"

"That's right."

"Well, no sense sayin' anything, Jeannie," Tim warned, "you know
as well as I do how much good that would do. Hear tell he's linin' up
a new boat."

"Yep." Bill held up his cup for a refill. "All the BS is just about
wound up and it looks like all we gotta do is sign on the dotted line
and the *Lazy Daze Two*'ll be tied up alongside all the other goddamn
fools who're waitin' impatiently for the chance to go tits-up bankrupt."

"How'd you make out yourself, personal, Jeannie? You gonna be
okay?"

"Oh, hell," she laughed, "I'm gonna be just fine. You'll go broke payin' the taxes it's gonna take to keep me in the style to which I damn intend to become fully accustomed, but as far as financial goes, I'm fine. Me'n'Donny Trump, you know how it is."

"That bad, huh?"

"Just about. All I gotta do is keep breathin' in and out and they'll give me this allowance keeps me just about balanced on the poverty line for the resta my life. Damn nice of 'em, I think."

"Well, I gotta warn you," Tim smiled and shook his head, "if you're expectin' your settlement to come outta *my* taxes, you're apt to wind up as thin as a rail because not even the feds has figured out how to get blood outta a rock."

"Like to smother the whole damn lot," Bill smiled angelically. "You about finished turning the top of this table into a disaster zone, Babba?"

"I goin' swimmin' wif Gran," Paige smiled. "Gonna gimp home and go swimmin'."

"Out of the mouths of babes," Jean laughed. She reached for her cane.

Tim stood and let her slide from the booth, then took his seat again, moving closer to the window, leaving room for someone to possibly join him. Bill lifted Paige from the smeared window and put her feet on the floor.

"You take care of your Gran, now, you hear?"

"Goin' swimmin'," Paige headed for the door.

It wasn't what people said so much as the way they said it. There was more hidden in Tim's question than a casually listening tourist might hear. He still hangin' around with that Charlene said it all. Hangin' around with wasn't like being tied up with or involved with, hangin' around with was about half a step up from screwin' around with and a mile below shacked up with, which came close to being married to.

And Mark was hangin' around with Charlene. That Charlene. No need for a last name. That said it all. That Charlene.

Funny, it seemed so ordinary at first. Supper at the house, meet the family, two nice enough kids, a bit quieter than you'd expect but that's a welcome relief after the way some people's kids behave. The first tiny hint — not even a hint, really, just a bit of a jarring note — came the first time anyone saw Charlene in shorts. You just don't somehow expect to see a goddamn tattoo on a woman's upper leg. And if you do, well, it's maybe a little ladybug or a butterfly or something. But on Charlene's inner thigh it was an arrow, pointing up, and the words Men At Work.

Jean tried to pay it no attention. After all, some people have very tacky senses of humour. They must, or who makes up, tells, or repeats those gacky jokes?

"Sense of humour?" Sally stared. "Mom, you've got to be kidding."

"Well, I don't know," Jean tried to blow it off. "Who's to say what turns other people's cranks, eh."

Then Mark started spending the night. Jean knew full well he wasn't sleeping on the couch, fully dressed, defending his virtue. But what do you say? You can't very well sit your grown son down at the table, give him a cup of tea and start explaining the difference between a one- or two-night stand and a more or less regular sleepover.

More than once Jean gimped down to the beach, found a dry rock and sat on it, watching the mirage that made things look as if the sea was calm and still and Savary Island was rising and falling. She liked letting her mind go to sleep, or turn off, or whatever it did, she liked the illusion of land moving, hills and trees not fixed, but responding to the tug of the moon. Sometimes she would indulge herself with the daydream that one day, Savary would pull loose, tuck up her skirts and tiptoe off, for a day of shopping, perhaps, or a visit and a cup of tea with her sister Quadra. Whatever it was she did inside her head to allow herself to go along with what her eyes thought they saw allowed her, also, to pick at her own scabs and calluses more thoroughly than she would ever be able to do at home.

She knew it wasn't true that the whole world was trying hard not to smirk and say things like What's bred in the bone will come out in the flesh. Entire areas of the earth's surface were home to people who had no interest at all in where Jean Pritchard's son dipped his diddlybob. There was every chance, for example, the population of Scandinavia had better things to do with their time than stand around on street corners talking about it. And probably massive sections of Africa had other things to occupy their attentions. But something in her cringed. Some part of her that had grown thin-skinned and self-conscious when she was a kid, when everyone in her world knew Eve had skipped off and was busy dancing the polka in beds not her own, had started to squirm and shout again. No matter how often she told herself she was being silly, no matter how often she lectured herself or how many articles she read on how to improve your self-image, all she had to do was walk past a cluster of undeniably vacant-headed teen-aged girls popping bubblegum and chattering like squirrels, and she felt self-conscious; and let even one of the zipperheads snicker or giggle, and Jean knew, the way she knew day follows night follows day, the little twist was laughing at her. While her mind rebelled and called on all the bright ideas from the articles, her body did what it had done since she was less than seven years old; her shoulders stiffened, her belly felt as if it was falling out of her body and would wind up on the street, and the corners of her eyes tightened. Her rational mind told her people had better things to do with their time than to point at her and laugh, but the rational mind cannot control the reflexes, and some part of her knew, some part of her Knew Full Well, and had Known for almost all her life, that there was something unacceptable about her. And now there was yet another reason for her to cringe.

Christ Jesus, other people and other people's kids were up to at least as much! One of the supposedly most respectable families in town spent much of their time pretending their son and daughter were merely sharing accommodation, much more economical that way, you know, what with rent going sky-high and all. The kids were so busy saving money they not only shared a rented house, they shared the bedroom, and even the bed. Shared, too, parenting duties of the two kids who had appeared as if by magic, and so much for all the hoo-haw about that, too, the kids seemed fine, no more idiotic than anyone else's kids. And what about the elementary school principal who didn't want women teaching nontraditional subjects like math or science so chose only male teachers, except, of course, for the Introduction to Home Skills course. The guy moved through life like Napoleon in a grey polyester suit, dropping Bible quotations into every conversation, attending some strict hierarchical congregation, and pole-vaulting in and out of other people's beds, rutting energetically in the back seats of cars, getting more grunt than most of the working bulls at the artificial insemination farm. For that matter what about the junior high school teacher who had the somewhat regrettable habit of making obscene phone calls?

So why would she be so convinced people were fixated on Mark's affair with Charlene? And yet she was. And she knew it was stupid. Knowing it was stupid didn't seem to connect anywhere with feeling or doing. She could hear it, she could even recognize and identify the voices doing it. Yes, my dear, and isn't it just too much like his grandmother? Really, some families just repeat the same mistakes, generation after generation.

Better get off the rock and head into the clinic, see if you can get a referral to go see the local shrink. You could limp and hobble into his very tasteful office, sit yourself in his nice two-hundred-dollar chair, look across the top of his nine-hundred-dollar desk to where he sits in his six-hundred-dollar chair and you could say Doctor, I hear voices.

You should have heard them a few years ago, old girl. You wouldn't have had to go out there and work your hands into what they are today, big appendages with enlarged veins and knobby knuckles, your history written there for all the world to see. Maybe your wrists wouldn't ache at night with the warning signs of Carpal Tunnel Syndrome from all those years of feeding prices into the cash register. Maybe you wouldn't have had to pay twenty-two dollars each for a set of wrist supports so you could manage, on bad days, to actually open and close doors and give mind-boggling displays of strength and courage by actually picking your coffee mug up and drinking from it without having your fingers and hands go dead and spill the whole shiterooni on the lino.

You could have waltzed into Welfare and told them you heard voices. They'd have put you on a goddamn disability pension, enough for you to at least raise the kids while sitting in a chair watching television. And who's to say you *don't* hear voices? They might be able to prove you do not have a bad back which keeps you from working, but how in hell could they prove you didn't hear voices? Maybe go in, anyway. Get the insurance pension doubled. Excuse me, gentlemen, but ever since the flagpole came down on my noggin I've had this slight inconvenience. I hear voices. I didn't mention it earlier because we were all so concerned about whether or not I'd ever walk again, but now I'm walkin' and the voices are still talkin' and I want double my money every month because I can't enjoy the tee-vee for all this conversation in my gourd, here.

If they didn't leap up, chequebook in hand, ready to shell out, she could start talking about how the Reverend Sun Myung Moon had gone from sending converts out with flowers at airports to openly promoting the idea of one world without borders, one family united. United, of course, with a Big Daddy in charge of all action and thought. A Big Daddy chosen by God to be the One True Father on Earth. Funded not by the grace flowing on him from heaven, but by the money coming to him from sources which tried their very God damnedest not to be identified, sources which included old men who had thought Tojo was a fine man, sources who in their youth had travelled to Italy to listen to Mussolini and learn from him, sources who had spent years in Sugama prison for class A war crimes, for which they had never stood trial, because they eventually agreed to go to work for the American CIA.

A few verbal paragraphs like that and even the arsletarts would be convinced she heard voices. There was, however, as much chance of being put in a rubber room as of having the pension increased. Some people were just too swift and too good at putting other people in rubber rooms. Probably best not to mention that, either.

You're only allowed to hear voices if all the voices tell you is that Little Bo Peep has finally found her sheep, everything is fine, dear, there there, now now, let me pat you on the head.

If she could have ignored what she thought people might be saying, if she could have just responded and reacted without the unexpressed pressure, she might have grabbed Mark by the front of the shirt, shoved him into a chair and said Listen, bucko, right now it's your woodie doing the thinking for you, and a woodie doesn't have a brain. That woman is not, repeat not, going to be good for you. But Mark would get angry, and why not, who wouldn't. If he got angry he'd probably move out. Then the whole friggin' town really would be talking a mile a minute.

So you just sit and you wait. Not for long — the ceiling will come down on your head, no problem there. The ceiling always comes down on your head. Maybe they make them so they'll do just that.

Mark eased himself into the situation. At first he would sleep over and arrive home first thing in the morning to shower and change before heading back in to class. Then he went to class from Charlene's place and showed up back home for supper. After a while he went back to Charlene's place and showed up a day or two later. And eventually he moved his stuff into a rented house, then helped Charlene move her stuff from the little auto court unit she'd been renting.

The voices in Jean's head did more than whisper about that, they became a chorus, so loud a chorus other people heard them, too.

"Mom, can't you *say* something to him?" Sally demanded.

"Oh, great, Sally. And what do you suggest I say?"

"Well, *something!*"

"You think that'll do it? He walks in the door and I go up and stand nose to nose then yell 'Something, Markie, Something!'. You figure he'll smarten up?"

"Mom!"

"Do I do it before or after I go nose to nose with *you*? Something, Sally, Something!"

"That's *my* business!" Sally yelled.

"Sure it is," Jean agreed, wishing she felt as mild as she sounded, "and I guess this other is Mark's business."

"But the goddamn woman has a tattoo, for Christ's sake."

"She may have a tattoo, darling, but I doubt very much she got it for the sake of Jesus Christ."

Sally's affair with Phyllis lasted less than a year, and the only way Jean had even a hint it was over was that Sally abruptly took her holidays and went off by herself for a couple of weeks. She came back quiet, but must have done her crying in a motel by herself, because she did none of it at home. She just continued her life as it had been before she got involved, and said nothing much, even when indirectly asked.

"I haven't seen Phyllis for a while," Jean dared.

"No," Sally nodded. "Nor have I."

"I'm sorry. I mean... well, I'm sorry."

"It's okay." Sally didn't even try to smile. "She's moved."

"Before or after you split up?"

"After. Probably because of, but who'd admit to a thing like that, eh?"

"You okay about it?"

"Well, I'll have to be, won't I?" and Sally did smile. "It's not as if I'm going to change anything just because I don't like it particularly well. I guess things have a way of being how they are, you know."

And they did have a way of being how they are. One of the ways they were was that Mark was living full time with that Charlene and coming over by himself to pick Paige up and take her over for visits. But even Mark had more sense than to suggest Paige sleep over. There were some fights he wasn't yet ready to dig himself in and bring down on his head.

"I miss her," he admitted. "I wish I had enough money to build the Taj Mahal and move all my favourite people into it so I wouldn't have to get white-line fever driving back and forth trying to stay in touch."

"I doubt if we could all live together without ripping each other's throats out," Jean laughed.

"Yeah." Mark picked at the cuticle of his thumb. "Listen, Mom, I'm sorry you and Charlene don't hit it off. I mean...I wish it was different. I wish you could get to know her better or...I mean..."

"It's okay, Markie," Jean lied. "There's no law says we all have to get along like farts in a mitt, okay?"

"Did Grandpa get along with my dad?"

"Your grandfather detested your dad."

"That bad, huh?"

"Worse. Einarr had all he could do not to go for the throat." She shrugged and laughed softly. "As it turned out, of course, he was absolutely right, but at the time all it did was add gas to the blaze."

"That why you haven't said anything?"

"You got 'er. I've *thought* it, and come within an inch of saying it but...it's your life, Mark-oh. I think you're throwin' years of it down the tube here, but I'm not going to say that because I don't want anything coming in the way of you'n me, so I just keep telling myself that if I don't take a side, or make a side, you won't have to choose a side. Because right now, what with hormones and gonads and all that other stuff, my side would lose."

"Maybe it's like chickens," he said suddenly, laughing as if he were ten years old again, with another elephant joke to tell her. "You know how the old hen hatches the eggs and she'n the rooster watch out for the chicks and then all of a sudden the rooster is picking on some of them? Turns out what he's doing is making life so unpleasant for the little roosters that as soon as they can they peel off on their own, take a hen or two with 'em, maybe, and start a whole other flock. If they didn't do that, there'd be one huge flocka chickens, probably some-place in Peru or Unbangistan or somewhere, but because they *did* do that, fuck, there's flocks of chickens all over the place. And maybe that's what this is. Lions kick out young male lions, don't they?"

"Is that as far as you got in philosophy?" she teased. "Jesus, I can hardly wait to find out how far you've got in sociology!"

"So why don't you like her?" he demanded, changing her mood totally.

"I don't know. She's never even so much as looked at me crossways, and yet I know she and I don't think highly of each other. She doesn't like me one bit more than I like her, and I bet she couldn't say why, either. Some people just *don't* like each other, is all."

"She thinks you judge everything she does and every word she says."

"Maybe I do. I'd be the last one to know, wouldn't I? You know what they say, even your best friends won't tell you. So maybe I do and I don't know I do, but if I do it isn't what I want to do. It just *is*, I guess."

"So tell me," he persisted.

"Okay. I can tell you this much. I think you're her goddamn meal ticket. I look at her and all I see is fluff. She's as tall as I am and as strong as I ever was, and she's one helluva lot younger'n I am, and she sits on her ass on welfare instead of going out and getting a job. That pisses me off."

"She's got two kids!" he defended.

"I had three."

"It's not the same."

"It's the same, it's just that she's different than I was. And don't bother telling me about how kids need to have their mother at home with them. Her kids are in school all goddamn day, just like any other kids. She could go to work and not deprive them of a thing. I don't notice peanut butter or chocolate chip cookies pouring out of the window because she's been so busy baking she's got noplace left to store them! The kids probably put themselves off to school in the morning! She could work. She just doesn't bother doing it. And that pisses me off. I don't mind payin' taxes for people that need a hand. I don't mind that one little bit. And when the kids are still at home I figure a woman is entitled to be there with them if that's what she wants, and, for sure, I'd rather have my taxes spent on that than on bombs'n'bullets and steak dinners for the fat-asses in government. But once the kids get into school, there by God isn't any reason in the world she can't get up off her ass and go find a job and feed herself. If she needs help feedin' the kids, fine, I'll pay taxes for the kids. But she can at least feed herself."

"She's on the list for job training."

"So what's keeping her from doing something until her name comes up on the list? Ever look at the Help Wanted section of the paper? I mean, if all else fails you can do babysitting or daycare. Okay, look, I'm not trying to cut you down, but how many goddamn years does a person have to sit on her ass before she realizes that sitting on her ass is nothing but sitting on her ass? I don't expect her to jump up, run out and take Adam Zimmerman's job away from him. But...how many years has she been on welfare? So that sticks in my throat because I see her using you as her meal ticket."

"I don't mind."

"I know." Jean turned away, swallowed several times. "That sticks in my fuckin' throat, too, Mark. Want to know what I think? I think that when it was up to *her*, she was perfectly happy sitting on her tattooed ass in an auto court, with auto court furniture and auto court rugs and auto court curtains. And I think real soon you're going to be working like a mad bastard to come up with the money for a trip to the city to get a whole raft of Ikea furniture, and you'll be paying some gomer from Carpet City to come up and measure the place for new wall-to-wall or that fuckin' awful shag shit. And it'll be drapes for the living room and curtains for the kitchen and it'll be another coat of paint for this and Christ, let's give the deep-six to the fridge and get a new one. And when it ends, which it'll do, just as sure as there's shit in a seagull, she'll pack all that good stuff in a moving van and you'll be left with nothing but the goddamn paid-in-full receipts."

"It's not going to end," he laughed. "Why would it end?"

"And that," Jean said softly, "is the worst scenario I've had."

She tried to talk herself out of it. She had long debates, even arguments with herself about the scarcity of jobs and the paucity of wages. She reminded herself that if you want any assistance at all, the government insists that you prove you are totally without other resources. For all Jean knew, Charlene didn't have a job because if she got one she would no longer be unemployed and only the unemployed could qualify for job retraining. For all Jean knew, Charlene was really chomping at the bit and yearning for the chance to make five dollars an hour doing an honest day's work.

But Jean doubted it. She tried not to doubt it but she doubted it. All she had to do was look at the woman and she knew her own neck began to glow scarlet. Mark deserved more. He deserved at least a taste of whatever it was had been promised him. But maybe he thought he had it. And maybe thinking you have it is at least as good as having it and certainly better than having it and not knowing.

No wonder Charlene didn't like Jean! You don't have to open your mouth and say anything when you feel that way. It comes off you in waves and is broadcast at top volume by the stiffness of your smile. And of course Charlene was right when she thought Jean judged her and found her lacking.

Well, by Christ, she was lacking. Lacking any get-up-and-go, any gumption, any ambition, and what was she doing but a somewhat sanitized version of prostitution? Because it didn't have to be Mark;

there were probably one hundred fifty other candidates, any of whom would have done just as well. Mark just happened to be the one jumped up and volunteered. Dumb bugger. With or without the marriage certificate, he would wind up on the dirty end of the stick.

And Sally. Well, you wear yourself out just as bad worrying over things you don't have the vocabulary to put a name to as you wear yourself out worrying over the easily identifiable. Every time Jean tried to think about Sally, and about Sally and Phyllis, or Sally and Whomsoever, her mind came to a dead halt, then skittered off in the first direction to present itself.

It wasn't a case of Oh my, whatever is it they *do* with each other? Jean's mind could figure that one out with no trouble at all. Anything your little heart desires, kiddo. It wasn't even the old cringe reflex about what people might think or say. It was looking at your kid and knowing there probably wasn't a tougher row to hoe than the one she'd chosen. It gets to a person after a while, knowing the rest of the world is busy going tsk tsk tsk and that everything you do is added to or subtracted from that one facet of your life. Oh yes, I'm sure she's very generous, very hard working, pays her taxes in full and on time, helps little old ladies across the street, is a soft touch for suffering stray dogs and cats, contributes liberally to charity and recycles her compost, *but*, my dear . . . That kind of hard-nosing and cold-shouldering can wear on the soul as surely as water wears holes in rocks. But you can't tell a person to stop loving, there is never enough love in this world. Jean would have preferred to grab the backbiters and over-the-fence gossipers, given them a good shaking to jar their brains into gear, and made them lay off where her kid was concerned. She knew all the shaking in the world wouldn't do any good. She just wished she, herself, Sally's mother for crying out loud, didn't feel deep down inside that her daughter had merely found a way to give the flying finger to the face of the world. So there, fossil!

Oh, God, darling, why don't you just grab a big roll of gauze and bind your feet until they bleed? Society doesn't approve of *that* any more, either!

But the trip to Ikea didn't happen. The trip was to the real estate company because, after all, it doesn't make any sense to put any time or effort into a rental place, all you're doing is giving the landlord money and then free labour.

"So I can easy get a mortgage." Mark had all the papers on the table, all the arguments neat and tidy in his mind. "But what I might need some help with is the down payment, or second mortgage." Jean just nodded, but said nothing. She didn't trust her tone of voice, yet. "And I'm not asking you to give it to me. I'll pay it back. It might be that all I need is a co-jo at the bank, I don't know for sure."

"I've got the money," Eve said suddenly. "But there's a condition." Mark half turned, as surprised as any of them. "I'll give you the down payment *if* you, me, your mom and your sister all go to the lawyer's office and get a paper that's like an iron-clad contract."

"Sure," he said immediately.

"And that contract," Eve reached out and stroked Mark's cheek gently, "will be signed by Charlene and it will say that the house is yours and she has no claim on it."

Mark's face paled. He blinked rapidly, then his chest muscles heaved as he dragged in a deep breath. "Ah, Gran," he sighed.

"I know." She stepped closer, put her arms around him and pulled him against her scrawny body. "I know, darlin'. But look at the history of this fuckin' family. Einarr and me came apart like a cheap paira shoes in the rain and I headed off down the pike with one cardboard suitcase. Anything else I got in life I got for myself, the hard way. And you know as well as anyone the kind of goddamn hoo-rah *you're* comin' out of! I figure your mom paid through the nose and is probably still payin'. And it don't last. It just don't ever last. And when it comes apart there is always a go-round about money. And however nice she is, or however whatever it is she is, Charlene don't have piss-all and on her own she'll never have piss-all and I am not of a mind to give her half ownership of a house she hasn't put one thin dime into payin' for and that's where she's at by me. I figure she's gettin' more than her share as it is; she's getting a place she'd never be able to afford to so much as look at let alone rent on her own, and she's gonna have her kids fed and clothed and taken care of in a way she'd never be able to do herself."

"And me," Jean agreed. "I see nothing at all wrong with a . . . a . . . a paper."

"A prenuptial agreement," Sally nodded. "All the best people are doin' it these days anyway. Even Donnie Trump had to do 'er." She poked Mark sharply in the ribs. "If she doesn't intend to take you to the cleaners, fella, she won't mind one little bit signing a paper saying she doesn't intend to take you to the cleaners."

"What about..." He struggled, up against both the rock and the hard place. Three of the four people he loved best in the world were telling him something he did not want to hear or even think about, ever. "What about whither thou goest and half'n'half and..."

"Tell you what, old man." Sally poked him again. "Whither thou goest I will go and you'll pack your gear and I'll pack mine. Whither thou lodgest I will lodge and you'll carry your sleeping bag, I'll carry mine."

"Ah, Jesus, Sally..." He looked across the table and something passed between them. Jean had seen that look so many times and still didn't fully understand it.

"Hey, guy, come on," Sally spoke softly. "Give me a break on this one, okay? Slide *you* out of it. Maybe put *me* in it. What if Phyllis and I had come up with this bright idea? What would you have thought? There I am and there she is and she doesn't have a pot to piss on or a window to chuck it out of and never has and never will. And I'm living in la-la land and you know it but I don't... would *you* say Sure Sal, tell you what, I'll mortgage the next fifteen years of *my* life so's you can play housie with good old wotzername?"

"Is this what all that damn liberation stuff does? Do I have to spend half my fuckin' life hearing you say oink oink Mark and then you turn around and you go oink louder'n I ever did?"

"I'm all for liberation, and I'm all for equality." Sally's face pinkened, but not with embarrassment. "And I'm all for the kind of responsibility goes with it, too. And none of it has bugger-nothing to do with who's gonna open the fuckin' door or give up a seat on the bus! It doesn't even have a lot to do with who's gonna do the friggin' dishes, and you *know* that, Mark! About the only thing that makes me madder than having some friggin' man think he should get ten bucks an hour more than I get because he pees standin' up and I sit down to do it, is having some goddamn slit sit back and want the best of both worlds without doing anything at all for herself or her kids. I mean Jesus Christ in heaven!"

"Don't it count that she makes me happy?"

"All *that* does is make me feel sad that you're so willing to settle for piss-all!"

"Whoa, there, hang on, now, let's not get ourselves into a fight about it," Jean stepped in before fingers sank into the soft flesh of throats. "Let's not say anything any of us are going to regret."

"Oh, we've prob'ly already done that," Eve sighed.

In the end he said he'd talk to Charlene about it and get right back to them. A month later he said they could go to the lawyer and get the papers drawn up. Jean knew it had been a terrible month for him. She could just about imagine what Charlene had found to say about it. The same angry things Jean herself might have found to say when hit between the eyes with other people's judgements.

With the papers signed, it wasn't just Eve who put money into Mark's house. Jean put in some. Sally emptied her savings account. It brought the mortgage payment down to about half what Mark would have been paying for rent.

"I really appreciate this," he said, and meant it. Charlene didn't say much to anyone. Jean could hardly blame her.

And when the house was theirs, papers signed and title registration finished, they took their trip to the city, but not to Ikea, after all, they went to Furniture Warehouse, chose their stuff and made arrangements to have it shipped up in three weeks.

Those three weeks were hectic. Walls just absolutely had to be painted. Carpets could not survive without getting the guys with the pressure steam cleaners busy on them. The bathroom, of course, was impossible the way it was, and had to be redecorated because if you don't do it before you move in it's hell to do after you're there.

"Why would a person buy a place if it needed so much done to it?" Sally groused. "Jesus, Mark, this is about one baby step away from insane!"

"In which case you must feel you're right at home," he answered. It was almost like when they were young and some of Jean's hopes and dreams were only mildly tattered, still salvageable, still able to lift their groggy little heads once in a while.

"Dipper," Sally muttered, "why would I feel right at home in your house? Or did you sign away the next fifteen years of your life just to provide me with a roof? Probably leaks, anyway. Probably got bats living in the ventilation space."

"Stop mumbling and just, for a change of pace, in case the TV cameras are catching this for the folks at home, do some work, okay?"

Jean tried hard not to lie in bed mumbling to herself about how on her own Charlene had been perfectly willing to live in an auto court where the toilet burped and the taps dripped, but as soon as someone else was paying the tab the bathroom had to look like page sixteen in the Workie Dream Home Standards. She tried not to mutter to her pillow about how it had been just fine with Charlene that her kids shared a bedroom and slept on geriatric beds and suddenly each had to have its own room with brand new stuff. She tried not to taste the bitterness festering inside her and knew that part of it was directed at herself because maybe she'd been the biggest fool in the world not to off-load Tommy and find herself one like Mark, willing to pick up all the tabs and smile while doing it. She could tell herself she'd rather face the price tag on the furniture than the price tag on the meal ticket, but she wasn't sure how sane a choice she had made.

But then it was done and the freight company arrived with the new furniture.

"Come on," Eve commanded. "Don't bother getting tied in knots about what you think or what you feel. Start cookin'! I don't like that little twist he's got himself tangled up with but she *did* sign that paper. And that couldn't'a been easy. And by damn if she knows that much about how to be, this family's gonna show that we got an idea or two about it, too."

"Ah, Mom," Jean protested.

"Don't give me none of that. You just start in on that chili you're so damn proud of, for whatever reason it is you think you've got to be proud of it. Anyone as will put macaroni in her chili is about apt to do almost any disgusting thing the mind of man can come up with. We're going to have supper ready and all set to serve by the time the moving in and putting away is finished. And don't bother limpin'! If you can hi-de-hoe around this rock heap with that cane goin' tippy-tappy over the rough ground, you can tip-tap your way around the kitchen."

Brucie whined, put her mud-encrusted paw on Jean's knee, then nudged with her broad head and whined again. "Oh shut up," Jean said pleasantly. She patted the dog, and rumpled her floppy ears. "Jesus, Brucie, what do you think? What does it all look like to you, anyway? Where's the rainbow and the silver lining? Where's the white knight on the big palomino horse? Couldn't we at least have the Mormon Tabernacle Choir singing some hymn of praise? Or even a her of praise?"

The guy on the horse didn't show, nor did the choir. But by the time the furniture was moved in and put in place, the gas stove in the kitchen was working overtime. When the boxes of clothes were unpacked and everyone's stuff hung in the closets or folded and put away in the drawers, the smells from the kitchen had spread through the house. Mark was so happy Jean could almost overlook the things about Charlene which had her uneasy. But then it was time to sit down and eat, and that's when the fridge was opened and the cans of beer brought out and snapped open; immediately the two kids did this thing that told Jean more than any words would have done. Their eyes slid sideways, each of them looking to the other, exchanging glances and becoming very very quiet. Obviously they'd seen too many cans of beer opened, and knew all too well what might follow, and obviously the whole thing scared them. They folded their hands in their laps and sat, heads down, waiting for someone to put something on their plates and give them something to do for a while.

"So," Jean plunked herself next to Connie, then hung her cane over the back of her chair. "What do you like that we have here tonight? Anything?"

"Yes, ma'am," Connie answered, her voice so soft it was almost a whisper.

"Ma'am? *Ma'am?* My heavens!" Jean fished in her pocket, brought out a quarter and put it by Connie's plate. "Here, this is yours. I thought everyone in the world had forgotten that word." She looked past Connie to Bobby. "Do you know that word, too?"

"Yes, ma'am," he nodded.

"Well, then, you better have a quarter, too. Things are lookin' up, the world isn't in such sad shape as I thought, there's two kids know how to be decent and polite. I hope," she raised her voice slightly, "botha *my* kids take a few lessons from these two. Mine could do with some politeness lessons." Of course she had to find some money for Paige, too, and she didn't have a third quarter. Sally found one and kept rebellion from spreading, distracted Paige by giving her a slice of breast meat. Jean picked up Connie's plate. "So what do you like? Chili? Potato salad? Maybe some turkey."

"Yes, please."

"Turkey. White meat or dark?" and when she had Connie's plate ready, Connie passed Bobby's plate. "And you, sir. What do we have that might tickle your fancy?" She made sure not to put too much on their plates, she had an idea they would feel obligated to munch down every scrap and she remembered all too well how easy it was to get a bellyache with someone giving you the gears about the world being full of starving children and how lucky *you* were to have any food at all. As if a seven-year-old was to blame for any of that damn mess, as if a nine-year-old could put a halt to what the politicians were allowing and even causing to happen. "Don't you fill yourselves up on this old stuff," she warned, "because Eve, there, might be as old as Methuselah, and she might look like a sack of wrinkles walking around in little-old-lady shoes, but she can still make a dessert that just screams to be eaten, and if you've filled up on dead bird, you might miss out on dessert."

She tried not to see how much beer Charlene packed away, tried not to notice how easily it slid down her throat. But she saw, and she noticed because there had been too many beer slide down too many throats for too many years in her life. Einarr had been able to pack away beer from the time he got home until the time he headed off again, and then, fool that she was, she'd turned around and married a man who could drink the stuff in his sleep. There's something about the way a dedicated boozehound snaps the cap that tells you this has been done before, often. Something about the way they pick up the can and find the tab without even looking, the hand holding the beer doing a thing similar to reading Braille. The thumb lifts and strokes around the rim of the can, finds the little nub that holds the tab in place, while the other hand reaches over and, still not even looking, pulls, and the can rises, as if by magic, to the mouth, while the hand holding the tab moves to drop it in the ashtray. If the time spent attaining that manual dexterity, that hand-eye co-ordination, had been aimed in a different direction an enormous segment of the population could have been employed as brain surgeons.

"Appreciate everything you did today." Charlene smiled, and anyone in the world would have thought it a pleasant and sincere smile. Maybe it was. Maybe it was only Jean thought the smile was as false as the tone of voice. And maybe Jean only thought that because she had all the makings of a pizmire.

"I've moved a time or two myself," Jean answered, "and I really do think it ranks right up there with thumbscrews and the Iron Maiden."

"Tell me about it. I don't know what's worse, finding a box to pack stuff in or finding a place to put that stuff once you get where you're going. Just about the time I'd have found a place for all the stuff it would be time to pack it up again. One year we moved four times. That's when I said to myself Self, this is starting to get boring."

"The part I hated," Sally said suddenly, "was the smells. Every new place we moved into smelled like someone *else's* home, not ours. It wouldn't smell like *us* until we'd been there a month or two. So you had all that time walking around with your own stuff out where you could see it but it was out where you could see it in a place your nose told you belonged to other people. I kept expecting to see these strange-smelling people sitting on *my* chair."

"Noises," Connie said, her voice still so soft and low it was next best thing to a whisper. "I don't like the different noises," and Bobby nodded.

"The bathroom," Eve contributed. "You have to be in a place for a while before you know for sure where the bathroom is."

"Bobby got lost one time," Connie agreed. "He was still sleepin' and he got out of bed to go pee, but he went where the bathroom had been in the *old* place and he wound up falling down the stairs."

"I bet he peed then!" Sally grinned at Bobby. "Did you?" He nodded, and even smiled.

They made it through the family dinner, they made it through the coffee and cake, they even made it through the do-the-dishes-and-tidy-up-afterward. And then with wide smiles all round, they prepared to go back home.

Jean grabbed Mark and gave him a tight squeeze. "You take care, now," she managed.

"Hey," he squeezed back, "don't worry yourself, okay? It's all going to work out fine. You'll see."

Paige didn't want to go home with them. She dug in her heels and got all ready to raise hell. Mark didn't say anything, he just looked as if his guts were being put through a food blender.

"Uh, Mrs. Pritchard, I, uh," Charlene stammered, her face as red as any beet in anyone's garden, "I mean, well, she's no trouble at all, you know, and, well, I don't want to butt in or anything but, like, it's fine by me if she wants to stay over for a couple of days. I mean, you know, like from her point of view here's this new place and there's all this stuff going on and kids to play with and we know she thinks the sun rises and sets in Mark's ear and well, anyway..." She was miserable by now, obviously wishing she hadn't opened her mouth, probably feeling all she'd managed to do was get both feet rammed in up to the ankle. "I guess what I'm trying to say is that any time it's okay with you that she stay here, it's fine by me, too."

You stand there and you know you're eyeball to eyeball with the only chance anyone is going to get to either make 'er or break 'er. What has been said isn't exactly what has been meant. Every word of it might be sincere as hell but underneath there is something else coming down and all it's going to take is one eyelash quivering at the wrong time and that's it there she goes ker-thundering-boom with nothing but little bits and pieces raining down on everyone's life for a time close enough to eternity for it not to matter that it's a bit less than that.

"You must be just about dead on your feet after all this packing and moving and shifting and unloading," Jean hedged, making sure she didn't add And all that beer drinking because whose business was that and anyway Charlene was nowhere near half packed. So far, anyway.

"Well, yeah, it's been rough but they'll all be in bed inside of an hour and I won't be five minutes behind them. It would be kind of nice if she felt she was part of what was going on in Mark's life. I don't want her to start to feel as if she's been left out or to feel that Connie and Bobby are swiping something that's hers."

"Don' wanna *go!*" Paige wailed wrapping her arms around Mark's leg and snottering on his jeans. "Wanna *stay!*"

Sally and Eve looked at Jean. Jean looked at Charlene, then looked at Mark. And she knew he knew they were all eyeball to eyeball with something bigger than any or all of them. What harm could come to Paige, anyway? It wasn't as if whatever it was Jean objected to was contagious. And if it was, Paige was probably already infected because her maternal great-grandmother and her paternal grand-mother had both done at least as much and probably, if the truth be known, more in their lives than Charlene. Was that what was stuck in Jean's throat? Was she choking on how similar Charlene's choices had been to Eve's?

"You could maybe drop her off at the house when you come out to check the boat?" It was as much a question as a suggestion.

"Sure," he said, so quickly she knew he would have agreed to almost anything, so quickly she knew only twenty-three or twenty-four years had kept him from wrapping his arms around *her* leg and snottering all over *her* jeans. "Sure, whatever you say."

"Paige, you listen . . . you listen *good*, okay? Stop that whining or I'll just throw you in the closest Smithrite and leave you there!" Paige stopped whining and stared. "You can stay with Markie and Char-lene . . . but when Markie brings you home, you do *not* cry. Okay? When Markie has to go back out on the boat you come back to Gran's, and *no whining*." Paige's eyes slid to Charlene and Jean stomped on that one before it was even given a chance to take a breath. "Auntie

Charlene will *not* look after you when Markie is on the boat. She's got work of her own to do. You only stay here when Markie is home. Period, Paige, Period!"

"Wanna *stay*," Paige insisted, her face sulky, her mouth pouting.

"You fix your face, little lady, or you'll be in the car so fast you'll catch cold from the breeze of your own passing. Don't pull that Tyranny of the Weak shit on me!" Jean gave Paige time to fix her face and stop looking like something you'd prefer to step on. "Uncle Mark will look after you, and when he goes on the boat, you come home. And if you want to ever come back for a visit, you won't whine when you *get* home, understand? Because if you whine you won't get to come back for another visit sometime."

"Jesus," Sally said clearly, "we gotta *do* something, you know. That kid is so damn spoiled she makes me want to warm her backside just for the satisfaction of hearing her shriek with surprise."

"She *is* getting kind of sulky," Mark agreed.

"Yeah," Charlene blurted, "I told you she was a pain in the ass a lot of the time," and then her face reddened.

"A *lot* of the time," Jean agreed. Charlene looked up and they both laughed softly. No huge breakthroughs had been made. Each knew they would never be close friends, each knew that at the bottom of things they really didn't like each other, but each knew, now, there were some areas of agreement. "To you from failing hands," Jean quoted, but Charlene only half understood.

"Yeah," she nodded, "well, it won't be *my* problem. Captain Crunch can take care of 'er."

It was so quiet in the house Jean couldn't sleep. She lay on her left side, then rolled onto her right side, she tried lying on her belly but she couldn't get her foot comfortable that way so she rolled on her back and that was even worse. Finally, she got out of bed and went down to the living room, sat in the big chair looking out the window, and when all that did was piss her off, she went back up to her room and pulled on her underwear, her jeans, some thick cotton socks and a turtleneck, then padded back downstairs with her sneakers in her hand.

She hauled on her sneaks, tied the laces and got her jean jacket, then went out the front door and along the walk. She heard Brucie's nails clicking behind her, so swung her cane, warning the dog not to bump into her and send her sideways. Brucie moved alongside and pushed her nose into the palm of Jean's free hand. "Bugger off, mutt," Jean said pleasantly.

She walked along the side of the road to the intersection, then turned left and walked down the hill to where the road ended and the dock began. Her cane thumped hollowly on the weathered cedar decking, her sneaker soles squeaked on the damp.

She stood beside the *Old Woman* and watched the waves slap slap slapping against the new paint job. Well, you didn't have to go on board to know the last big cod on the coast was in the live tank, his fins moving gently, keeping him balanced and in place while he slept. She'd thought often of turning him loose. Rejected the thought each time because it would be the fastest way in the world to guarantee the end of him. He wouldn't last long out there with sewage and corruption and dioxins and furans and the good lord in his mercy knew what-all dripping, dribbling and even flooding into the Strait and an entire fleet of crazed coasties out with bait, line and hooks vying for the chance to catch him and cook him in black bean sauce. "Maybe find another big one of the other gender," she mused, "put 'em in there and start our own hopeful breeding program. Who knows, it might be the salvation of the fishing industry."

Brucie sneezed, then sneezed again. Jean took the hint and moved on, gimping along the dock to the *Lazy Daze Two*. She could still sit on a yellow plastic milk crate and slice open bellies, haul out guts, dump 'em over the side and clean the deck, for God's sake. Just because the goddamn doctor and the goddamn physiotherapist and the goddamn soft-palmed Townie bunch of them were yammering on about how she might slip and fall and hurt herself didn't mean she was guaranteed to slip and fall and hurt herself. She hadn't slipped, fallen and hurt herself before, not in that sense, anyway. If there was something wrong with her goddamn leg they couldn't put the blame for that on her.

Of course there was Paige. Well, Jesus, if Jean was going to slip and fall and hurt herself, better the kid not be around to see it; after all, she might slip and fall on the kid and hurt both of them! Eve couldn't do five times the square root of diddly-squat except maybe some cooking, and Sally was busy most of the time, but what in hell was Charlene doing but sitting on her ass and anyway, isn't there enough money we can find some for one of those companion house-keeper people? If push came to shove she'd take Paige out, too, maybe she'd slip and fall and hurt *her*self but probably not. Certainly not without Markie's say so!

"No reason we can't find someone to be what they call caregiver," she said, and Brucie wiggled herself because there wasn't enough tail to wag. "Maybe pay the Nguyens, she'd be just next door that way. Tran thinks the damn sun rises and shines on the kid, probably spoil her even more rotten than she already is. Be better than giving Charlene an excuse to not at least take the job retraining when it gets offered. Not that she'll do squat-all with it once she's taken it."

They'd talk of course. They'd gather over cups of oily crap coffee in the local greasy spoon and say things like Well, I suppose maybe they need the money, or Well, you know how it is, she never stayed home with her own kids you can't expect her to stay home with someone else's. Uncle Bill might say Oh I don't know, she hasn't done so bad considering what she had as an example, and then they could have another bite at Eve's ass and keep themselves occupied for another cup of crap coffee. And the bullshit would fly and the brass band play on, and so what, for God's sake, it didn't *really* hurt, not any more than anything else in life was apt to hurt.

It all hurt. The whole fuckin' lot of it hurt. Some less than others but maybe none of us were ever intended not to hurt at least some. "Brucie, you bitch, if you push at me I'm going to shove you over the edge into the chuck for the seals to eat, and I mean it, too. I'm sick and tired of nobody listening. Break a precedent and pay attention here."

Brucie backed off and Jean stood a while longer, then gimped her way back down the pier and along the beach. She found a butt-high rock encrusted with the shells of dead barnacles and half sat, half leaned against it. The moon came out from behind the clouds and for a while the whole shoreline was over-lit.

"How come everything gets made to look like a bloody disease, Brucie? How come we're all dysfunctional, we're all co-dependent, we're all busy working overtime at enabling behaviour, we're alcohol addicts or work addicts or relationship addicts or sex addicts or gambling addicts or shopping addicts or eating addicts or starving addicts or fitness addicts or whatever? Hell, for all I know you're a bone addict or a hole-digging addict or something! Can't we just *be*? I mean does everything have to be a disease? We're actually giving respect to these dinkheads who are telling us we eat too much to escape the pain of life, or drink too much to escape the pain or . . . pay attention to them to escape the fucking pain. Maybe we could all save a bundle if we stopped worrying about all that and just accepted the fact that life *is* pain of one goddamn kind or another. Don't shove against me or I'll whack you, I mean it! Back off, damn it! I don't know. I just don't know. And I never have. And if the truth ever be known I probably never will know! But I guess whatever it is, it beats going to the beach with a big spoon and a ball-peen hammer and using the spoon to scoop sand and the hammer to pound the sand up your ass. I wouldn't'a picked Charlene, I have to tell you. Of all the people on the face of God's suffering green earth I would not have picked her. But then I prob'ly wouldn't have picked any better than any other time I picked. I mean God, look at Tommy. For that matter look at *you*! Well, I'm not to blame for that, I didn't pick you, that was your own damn poor choice. I think I'll just ninety-nine clump 'er back up the hill and catch me some sleep." She heaved herself off the rock and gimped back along the beach. "I might just stop all this nonsense with physiotherapy and take tap dancin' lessons, instead. Or," she swung the cane and the dog dodged expertly out of the way, "I might just turn myself into a goddamn teapot and sit in the middle of the table wearing a blue crocheted cozy. Maybe I'll come up with a better idea but right now it looks to me as if I'll just go gut fish for a while because I have to tell you, the noise from that fuckin' brass band of bullshit is giving me a headache. And I think the worst part is realizing I'm the one playin' the trombone."

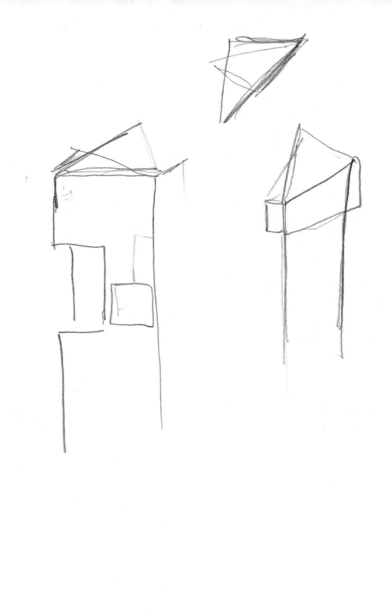

brick

NewCastle
- used
→ Steel Industrial
- McCalls
across
John McAdam

Student Driven